I0613206

Chief of Thieves

Chief of Thieves

A Novel

Steven W. Kohlhagen

SUNSTONE
PRESS

SANTA FE

© 2015 by Steven W. Kohlhagen
All Rights Reserved.

No part of this book may be reproduced in any form or by any electronic or
mechanical means including information storage and retrieval systems
without permission in writing from the publisher, except by a reviewer
who may quote brief passages in a review.

Sunstone books may be purchased for educational, business, or sales promotional use.
For information please write: Special Markets Department, Sunstone Press,
P.O. Box 2321, Santa Fe, New Mexico 87504-2321.
Cover illustration › Veronica Zhu
Book design › Vicki Ahl
Body typeface › Pertetua
Printed on acid-free paper
∞
eBook 978-1-61139-352-1

Library of Congress Cataloging-in-Publication Data

Kohlhagen, Steven W.
  Chief of thieves : a novel / by Steven W. Kohlhagen.
     pages ; cm
  ISBN 978-1-63293-046-0 (hardcover : acid-free paper) -- ISBN 978-1-63293-045-3
(softcover : acid-free paper)
  1. Ranch life--United States--19th century--Fiction. 2. United States--History--19th
century--Fiction. I. Title.
  PS3611.O3676C48 2015
  813'.6--dc23

                                    2014044959

WWW.SUNSTONEPRESS.COM
SUNSTONE PRESS / POST OFFICE BOX 2321 / SANTA FE, NM 87504-2321 /USA
(505) 988-4418 / ORDERS ONLY (800) 243-5644 / FAX (505) 988-1025

To the Descendants of

Kappen-Itzick (1795–1875)
and Thunder Bull (1856–1920)

Preface

This novel, *Chief of Thieves,* is the sequel to my earlier novel, *Where They Bury You.* The first novel is an 1861–1863 historical fiction account of an actual murder in the New Mexico Territory on August 18, 1863 during Kit Carson's Navajo War.

That original novel tells the story of a group of con artists who arrived in Santa Fe in early 1861. Those con artists include historical figures: Augustyn P. Damours who became the aide de camp to General Edward S. Canby, the commander of the Union Army in the West; and Joseph Cummings who became both a major in the Union Army and the U.S. Marshal in Santa Fe. Also involved in the cons is the fictional Lily Smoot, a Santa Fe poker dealing ex-prostitute. The con artists' activities were interrupted when the Civil War came to New Mexico and Arizona in the midst of the ongoing Apache and Navajo wars. Red Cloud, a fictional Ute Chief, and Cochise, an actual Chiricahua Apache chief, befriend Lily in those confrontations.

Kit Carson confirmed in his Army records that on August 18, 1863, during the Navajo campaign "…(I heard of) the death of the brave and lamented Major Joseph Cummings who fell shot thro' the abdomen by a concealed Indian." Cummings' Military Records report that, on his death, he had the equivalent of seven hundred thousand to a million of today's dollars in his saddlebags.

From my research, I concluded that Kit Carson must have been mistaken. Carson, the U.S. Army, the Franciscan Church, and the Department of New Mexico were all duped by Damours, Cummings, and the rest of the con artists, who stole three to four million of today's dollars from them in that two year period.

Where They Bury You is the story of how the cons were likely carried out, what I believe could really have happened to Cummings that day in 1863, and how Lily and Damours came to be present at the Pah Gosah hot springs in south central Colorado Territory on September 1, 1863 in the opening scene of *Chief of Thieves.*

Acknowledgements

I would like to thank Don Hodgson, Lindy Schroeder, and, especially Carol Eckhardt for their aid in teaching me the history of the Kelly's and Chugwater Valley's early settlement. For the curious, Chugwater later became a town. It still exists, and Carol happily opens its museum to visitors.

Thanks also to the librarians of the Cheyenne Public Library and the University of Wyoming's Library for their invaluable help in developing a picture for me of the genesis of both Cheyenne and Laramie, Wyoming.

A sincere thank you to Chris O'Rourke for his painstaking research into 1860s and 1870s Western firearms, to Larry White for his detailed fact checking and helpful editing, and to Jim Smith for his editorial suggestions and aid.

And a heartfelt thank you to Donnie Shahan of Chromo, Colorado for spending time with me so that I could make an attempt to understand the chore of open range cattle ranching in 19th Century Wyoming. He vociferously claimed that he had no personal experience in 19th Century ranching, but he left me unconvinced.

But mostly: Galen, thank you oh so very much for being patient with my research and my writing, and understanding about my life in the fantasy world that are my characters.

CAST OF CHARACTERS

(In Order of Appearance)

HISTORICAL

Lieutenant Augustyn P. "Auggy" Damours: Aide de Camp to General Edward R. S. Canby. Previously, a New Mexico Territory con artist.

Lieutenant George Armstrong Custer: Just demoted Aide de Camp to General George McClellan.

Gus Smoot: Auggy Damours' fictitious alias, post his (historically accurate) disappearance.

Joseph Cummings: Major, U.S. Army and U.S. Marshal, Santa Fe. Murdered August 18, 1863 under mysterious circumstances during Kit Carson's Navajo War.

John Wesley Iliff: Pioneer cattle rancher in the South Platte River area northeast of Denver City, Colorado Territory.

Holon and Matilda Godfrey: Ranch owners, South Platte River; believed by many to be the parents of the first baby born to permanent settlers in the Colorado Territory.

Black Kettle: Southern Cheyenne chief, Member of Cheyenne Council of Forty-four.

Lame White Man: Cheyenne chief.

Black Moccasin: Cheyenne chief.

White Bull: Cheyenne chief, Son of Black Moccasin.

Black Coyote: Cheyenne chief.

Antelope: Cheyenne girl. Daughter of Black Moccasin.

Thunder Bull: Cheyenne boy.

Elbridge Gerry: Possibly the first permanent white settler in Weld County, Colorado, north, northeast of Denver City.

Medicine Woman: Wife of Black Kettle.

Colonel John M. Chivington: Commander of the Colorado Volunteers.

White Antelope: Cheyenne chief.

Philip Sheridan: Major General, U.S. Army.

George Crook: Brigadier General, U.S. Army.

Damel Wile: Hotel owner, Emmitsburg, Maryland.

Frederick Benteen: Captain, Seventh Cavalry

Charles Clay: Owned trading post at foot of Chimney Rock, Chugwater Valley. Cousin of Kentucky's Henry Clay. Married to Fingernail Woman, Lakota.

Hi and Elizabeth Kelly: Initial ranchers in the Chugwater Valley. Owners of the first home in what was later to be called Chugwater, Wyoming.

Little Beaver: Osage chief and scout for Seventh Cavalry.

Spring Grass: Antelope's cousin, two years younger.

Grand Duke Alexei Alexandrovich: The Grand Duke of Russia, son of Alexander II.

General Edward R. S. Canby: Commander of various Reconstruction Assignments after Civil War.

Captain Jack: Chief of the Modocs.

Crazy Horse: Chief of the Oglala Lakota Sioux.

Sitting Bull: Chief of the Hunkpapa Lakota Sioux.

Marcus Reno: Major, Seventh Cavalry.

FICTIONAL

Lily Smoot: Former prostitute, former poker dealer, former con artist.

Red Cloud: Ute chief. Kidnapped as a young Chiricahua Apache boy by the Navajos, who lost him in a battle with the Utes. Friend of Lily Smoot. He left the Navajo War the day Joseph Cummings was killed to find his people in the Chiricahua Mountains.

Joe Lincoln: Ranch hand. Escaped slave from South Carolina plantation.

Li'l Jack Madson: Ranch hand.

Johnson, the Man in Black: Bounty hunter.

Danny Pinckney: Cousin of the former Governor of South Carolina and Charleston plantation owner, William Aiken.

Nick O'Reilly: Twelve year old Irish immigrant; orphaned, and adopted by the Smoots.

Elly Burgess: Young girl hired by the Smoots at Fort Boise.

Ben Childress: Rancher on the Owyhee River, Oregon.

Dennis Martinez: Major, Seventh Cavalry.

Lizzie, Mary: Two sixteen year old girls "hired" by the Smoots in Laramie, Wyoming.

Readers will find the glossary on page 377 useful.

Prologue

Washington, DC
The War Department
17th and Pennsylvania Avenue
November 5, 1862

Lieutenant Augustyn P. "Auggy" Damours burst out of the War Department door onto the steps leading down to 17th Street. Temporarily blinded by the bright Washington Autumn sun, he slammed into George Armstrong Custer who was trotting up the stairs.

"Captain Custer. I'm sorry, sir," Damours said as they grabbed each other's arms to keep from falling down the stairs into the street. Damours, four years senior to Custer's twenty-two, was the taller, and, he thought, the handsomer. Each had long curly hair and a flowing moustache, although Custer's was blond and Damours' jet black.

"It's okay, Auggy. I'm fine." He caught his breath and adjusted his tunic. "I'm headed up to see General Canby. Is he up there?"

"Yes, he's in, Captain," Damours said.

In fact, Damours had just left him, claiming illness and saying that he was going up to see a New York doctor. He had glimpsed a telegraph to Canby informing him that U.S. Marshal Joseph Cummings was headed to DC to arrest him for a series of thefts and embezzlements in the New Mexico Territory. Damours wanted to get as far away from Washington as fast as he could.

"By the way, Auggy, I guess Canby didn't tell you. It's Lieutenant Custer now. Lincoln just removed McClellan from command of the Army. That demotes his aide de camp down to first lieutenant. Canby is to give me my new orders. Odd that the general didn't tell you."

"To tell you the truth," Auggy lied, "I was in a rush and didn't even give him a chance, George. I'm sorry to hear this."

"Don't waste your time thinking about me, Auggy. I'm asking Canby to send me back to the cavalry where I belong. You can have this aide de camp desk job nonsense all to yourself."

"Good luck with the old man, George. I hope you get the cavalry command. The country will certainly be the better for it."

The two shook hands.

"See you when you get back, Auggy."

"Certainly," Damours lied.

Custer headed up the stairs into the War Department and Damours headed toward Pennsylvania Avenue and into the unknown. At least that's the last I'll ever have to deal with Custer, Damours thought, as he turned left on to Pennsylvania, trotted by several Rebel prisoners under armed escort at 20th, and disappeared.

He realized he hadn't asked Custer who Lincoln had named to replace McClellan. Then realized he didn't care.

The War, and the Army, were both over for him now. He was a deserter.

PART I
COLORADO

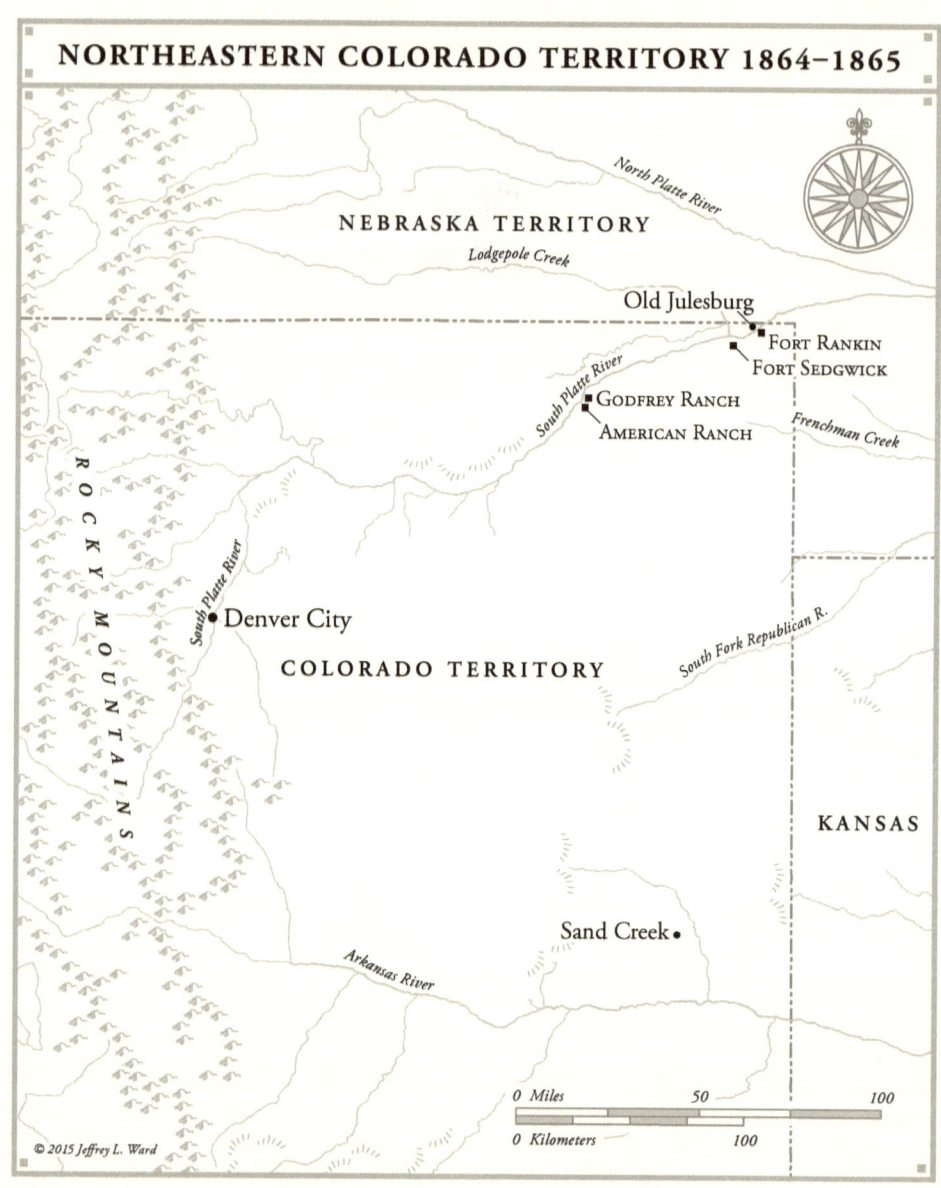

NORTHEASTERN COLORADO TERRITORY 1864–1865

North Platte River

NEBRASKA TERRITORY

Lodgepole Creek

Old Julesburg

FORT RANKIN
FORT SEDGWICK

South Platte River

GODFREY RANCH

AMERICAN RANCH

Frenchman Creek

R O C K Y   M O U N T A I N S

South Platte River

● Denver City

COLORADO TERRITORY

South Fork Republican R.

KANSAS

Sand Creek ●

Arkansas River

© 2015 Jeffrey L. Ward

0 Miles 50 100

0 Kilometers 100

1

September 1, 1863

Lily Smoot, twenty-three years old, disengaged her thighs from Damours' and lay back against a rock at the edge of the Pah Gosah hot springs in south central Colorado Territory.

"That was very, very nice, Auggy," she said. "I desperately needed that."

Damours smiled over at her, still out of breath, looking at her breasts bobbing in the bubbles and the steam, her long, jet black hair splayed behind her and out from her shoulders. They had just traveled almost three hundred miles northeast in two weeks from Pueblo Colorado, New Mexico Territory to this spot the Utes considered to be sacred. They were carrying almost forty thousand dollars they had stolen, first from the U.S. Army, Territory of New Mexico, and the Catholic Church, and then taken off the dead body of the man who had helped them steal it and then had stolen it away from them, U.S. Marshal Joseph Cummings. Cummings, their now dead former partner, had met with an unfortunate accident deep in an arroyo in Navajo country while he and the Army were trying to round up the Navajo.

Lily's face darkened as she saw a group of eight Indians riding toward them from the northeast. They had appeared on the bank of the San Juan River a couple of hundred yards away. She looked over at their own hobbled horses and mules, all now on alert and stirring, kicking up dust.

"Auggy," she said. "Toss me my rifle and grab your pistol and rifle. Then look over your shoulder."

"Those our Utes?" he asked.

"I don't think so. They look Navajo to me."

"Where are our Utes?"

"Hunting. And giving us a little privacy."

"The privacy part isn't working," he said.

The Indians approached with their hands out in front of them. All their weapons were still on their backs or across their chests. Damours shot his Remington revolver into the air and signaled they were friends, but the Navajo kept coming.

Lily fired her Sharps carbine between their heads and that stopped them. Maybe fifty yards away now.

Damours again signaled they were friends while Lily reloaded her single shot rifle. The Indians seemed more impressed with Lily's prowess with the rifle than with Damours' efforts at sign language.

Finally, the lead Indian shouted to them in Spanish. "We are Dine. Navajo. You have nothing to fear from us. We are merely heading back to our homes to the southwest."

The Utes who had escorted them here had warned them that the Navajo in these parts disputed the Ute claim to the hot springs, and had warned them that they should be leery of any contact.

Damours frowned. The Navajos would want to take their horses and mules, and would be curious about what was in their bags. They were unlikely to want to capture the two of them, but certainly might kill them if they got in the way.

It didn't occur to him that they were already in the way.

All Navajo eyes were on the couple's horses and mules, shuffling nervously behind them.

"Your homeland is that way," Damours said, pointing to the south, away from the horses. "We have just arrived from there."

Half the Indians now started riding closer, while the other half separated and headed north around their hot springs pool. No Navajo seemed inclined to take Damours' suggested directions.

Wordlessly, Lily shot the lead oncoming Indian off his pony. Damours fired his Remington into first one set of the oncoming warriors, then the other, while Lily reloaded.

The Navajo now had their bows and rifles out. An arrow clipped Damours side and one barely missed Lily's head, going through her hair. Damours took several more shots, hitting one, and Lily shot another off his pony.

The lead Navajo leapt off his pony and waved a club toward Lily as she reloaded. Damours shot at him and missed. The Navajo swung at Lily, but she hit his arm with her rifle barrel, fired and missed. Struggling, she grabbed his hair and pulled him into the steaming water.

Damours turned and took one shot at the Navajos, wounding one. He then leaped toward Lily. He reached the two struggling figures, pulled the trigger, but the revolver merely clicked. As the Indian grabbed for Lily's hair with one hand and pulled a knife out from under the water, Damours clubbed him on the head once, then again, with the butt of his pistol.

The Indian dropped the knife and went under. Damours and Lily both worked to hold him there until he quit moving. As Damours turned around, an arrow slammed into the rock behind Lily, and they saw two Navajos working to steal their horses, while a third aimed his Sharps at them.

Suddenly the sound of shots rang out from the hill to the southwest. The Ute escort party was racing toward them. The remaining four Navajo took off, each choosing his own point of the compass. The Utes took out after them, shooting rifles and arrows as if they were after a scattering herd of antelope.

That night, smoking by the campfire, after Lily and the Utes had bandaged Damours' wound, the Utes related exaggerated stories of the chases and the four skirmishes. To hear them tell it the Navajos had each run like rabbits through the surrounding hills and forests, but the braver, swifter Utes had succeeded in bringing them all to earth.

The Ute chief Red Cloud had obtained permission from Kit Carson to let these Utes travel from the Navajo roundup to their old summer home, their Red Garden and Manitou Springs, before returning to the Cimarron reservation. Red Cloud hadn't told Carson that Damours and Lily would be with them, or that he, himself, would not be returning to the reservation. Red Cloud had headed south from the roundup toward the Chiricahua Mountains.

"How far to your Red Garden?" Damours asked after the speeches and celebrations had ended.

"We can ride there in seven days," said one of the Utes, and they all nodded in agreement. "It will take more than ten days with you and her and your heavy bags."

"What is at the Red Garden?" Damours asked.

"There are many sacred Red Rock formations there. The bears used to be there in the summer. In the days before the white man came and killed them and chased them far away. The Red Garden was our summer home. We followed the bear through the seasons. Taos was our winter home."

There was a long silence. All knew that the bear, holy symbol and base of the Ute culture, had been largely driven away by the white man. That the Utes had been defeated along with the Jicarilla Apaches and now lived on a reservation in the New Mexico Territory. For these ten warriors, permission to take these two whites to their summer home was a welcome opportunity. Sharing their sacred Pah Gosah hot springs had been the height of hospitality.

"From there, will you take us to Denver City?" Damours asked.

"No. We do not travel north of the Red Garden. That is Cheyenne territory. We will ride back to Taos. The Cheyenne will want to kill us. They will want our ponies. You must hire white mine guards in Colorado City. It is only a three day ride. The Cheyenne will not attack armed miners."

"Are the Cheyenne at war with the white settlers?"

"We hear possibly so. The Cheyenne still raid our people. They will want her," he pointed to Lily. "They will want your horses. They will be curious about what is in your bags. You will want to hire many guards for that short trip, Lucky White Man."

"What did he call you, Auggy?" Lily asked.

Damours frowned. "Nothing."

"Auggy Damours," she said. "What did he call you?"

Damours glared at the Ute, who merely smiled back.

"Lily, these Utes have told me that Red Cloud wanted you as his wife."

Her eyes widened.

"When he realized that this was not something you would want, he decided he would not take you against your will. All the Utes know about it. Ever since, the Utes have called me Lucky White Man behind Red Cloud's back."

She looked thoughtfully into the fire, thinking back on her friend Red Cloud.

"And what do they call me, Auggy?"

"I can't tell you that, Lil. Red Cloud took that secret with him to the Chiricahua Mountains two weeks ago."

That night the two lay together by the hot springs looking up at the star filled sky.

"Auggy," Lily said, "How's your rib?"

"It's nothing Lil, I'll be fine. It's a minor scratch. Coulda been worse."

"I was just thinking about something. I just realized that both times we faced off with Cummings, and now again today against the Navajo, your old fear of fighting didn't freeze you up."

Damours didn't answer. After a while he just leaned over and kissed her hair.

"What's changed, Auggy?"

"I hadn't noticed, so I haven't thought about it. I guess the only thing that's changed is that I'm pretty much set up for life now. Financially and being with who I want to spend my life with. I'm not looking for the next con or trying to figure out what to do or looking for the next girl."

"So you're not afraid of being shot any more?" She propped up on her elbow and looked down on him. "Don't you now have more to lose?"

"I said I hadn't thought about it much. I just don't freeze up now is all. There might not be any explanation. Sometimes you think too much, Lil."

She lay back down and looked up at the sky, chewing on that thought. After a while, she decided to broach an inevitable subject.

"Oh great Lame White Man…" she said, and he cut her off.

"It's Lucky White Man, Lil and you know it."

He didn't join in her laughter.

"Okay, I'll call you Lucky for short, then." Getting no response, she moved on. "With your full black beard and long hair, I don't think anybody will recognize you as the former Lieutenant Auggy Damours, at least not as long as you don't talk to them up close. But with the Army and the Marshal Service still looking for you, we're going to have to change your name, honey."

"Lucky?"

"No, I was just kidding about that. What did Red Cloud call you?"

"I thought you knew. Chief of Thieves."

She laughed.

"How about if I become Auggy Jones?"

"No, Auggy. You're gonna have to change your whole name. There are wanted posters for you all over the west. Anybody could just gun you down for the reward."

"Who do you want me to be then, Lil?"

"I need to know something first."

"Sure, Lil."

"Are we gonna be together forever now?"

"Of course, Lil."

She rolled over on top of him. "Then, as of now we're a married couple. Gus and Lily Smoot."

2

May 16, 1864

Black Kettle had held his position as one of the four Old Chiefs of the Cheyenne Council of Forty-four Chiefs for ten years. Since the 1854 Sun Dance. He had been a great warrior and now, at sixty-one, was recognized as one of the great Southern Cheyenne chiefs. He had called for this Council of the Southern Cheyenne and Arapaho chiefs at the Smokey Hill River camps today. He and the other peace chiefs wanted to discuss their intention to seek peace with the white soldiers and to stop the attacks by their young warriors on the white settlers in Kansas and the Colorado Territory.

Two months earlier, Black Kettle and the peace chiefs had rejected the Lakota war pipes that had been sent as an invitation to join the Sioux and Northern Cheyenne in a war against the whites. Some of the chiefs and the Dog Soldiers, the most aggressive of the Cheyenne soldier societies, opposed Black Kettle. They wanted to join their Northern Cheyenne brothers and the Sioux to drive the settlers off the plains.

Nearly two thousand Cheyenne and Arapaho had come to these camps along the river. More than three hundred and fifty lodges were scattered in circles along the banks of the river. The Cheyenne tipis glistening bright white on the prairie. Colorful animals and hieroglyphs decorated the lodges all throughout the camps.

Dozens of wolves, scouts, were scattered in the surrounding hills and arroyos watching for any approaching white soldiers. Among the Southern Cheyenne chiefs in attendance who were arguing for war were Lame White Man, Black Coyote, Black Moccasin and his son White Bull.

After all the chiefs had assembled, they smoked the pipe in Black Kettle's lodge. They circulated the pipe around the gathering to each chief. Each receiving the pipe in his chosen manner, smoking four puffs, and then passing the pipe onward to his left on the fourth attempt.

All had smoked and there was now silence in the lodge.

Finally one of the younger chiefs spoke out in favor of peace.

Then another, laying out the history of previous attempts to fight the increasingly larger numbers of settlements, wagon trains, soldiers, and forts.

Black Moccasin was the first to speak for war. "We meet the white soldiers in peace. Then other whites break that peace. Sometimes soldiers. Sometimes settlers. Our young men hunt where the whites tell us. And then are attacked there by other whites. We are not all the people. The Northern Cheyenne are with the Sioux. They are at war with the whites. They have been chased off their lands. They have sent us the war pipes to join them. We must fight together. Or we must be at peace together. If we stay separate, the whites will defeat all the people one at a time."

After a long silence, Lame White Man also spoke for war. "The people are many. The people numbered four hundred and fifty lodges at the Sun Dance. We should join our Northern Cheyenne and Arapaho brothers. Now. We are many and there are too few soldiers in all the prairies to defeat us. The whites chase away the buffalo and the antelope. It is the same for those of the people who are at peace as it is for those who are at war. Our village they burned was at peace. More than three hundred of our people lost everything. Their lodges. Their belongings. Their ponies. Then the white soldiers tried to take away the weapons of the Dog Soldiers. How will our warriors hunt and provide food for their families without weapons?"

"Since I was a little boy," said White Bull, "still with my baby name, I have trained for the hunt. Now the white man is killing and chasing away the buffalo and the antelope. All my life I have trained for raiding, counting coup, and killing our enemies. We are the best warriors on the prairies. Now the white man wants us to grow crops. To sit in our lodges. To do the jobs of our women. Better let us smoke together. Put on our paint and our best medicines. Then dress up in our finest beaded deerskin leggings and shirts. Perform the sacred arrows ceremony.

And then all of us go out behind the two man arrows to fight the whites. We will all someday die of something. Better to die on the prairie as warriors than die in our lodges like women and children and thus lose our path."

When the chiefs favoring war were finished, after a respectful silence Starving Bear spoke. "It is true Lame White Man. We are the best warriors on the prairies. All the other tribes fear us. We are the best horsemen. The Utes fear us. The Crows. The Osage. The Apaches. All fear us."

He paused for all to agree. "I met the Great White Father in Washington. Father Lincoln. He gave me this medal. He gave me these papers. They say we are at peace with the Great Father Lincoln. I have seen the white people. They are many. Their medicine is very strong. The number of whites in any one of their villages is more than the number of all the people. And there are many villages. I have been there. Their soldiers in Washington are more than the numbers of all the people. Their other soldiers are everywhere. You have not seen the force of the whites. If they decide to destroy the people they can do so. The only way for us to protect the people is to follow the path of peace. My band and I are on that path."

Most of the other chiefs then spoke for peace.

When all but Black Kettle had spoken, a great silence settled over the lodge.

"All that you each say is known to us," Black Kettle said. "I look to my left and I look to my right and I see that all the chiefs speak the truth. Both sides speak the truth. We have said all these things and heard all these things for many years. As have our fathers and previous councils. The whites keep coming. They do not stop coming. Starving Bear has seen their strength. Some whites stay here. Some go to the west. They never stop coming. Our people and our game are becoming fewer."

He sat in silence for a brief time.

"Yesterday I rode alone across the prairies. Everywhere there was rolling buffalo grass. To each of the four directions. All the way to the edges of the sky. There were antelope. There were hawks and eagles. I saw no buffalo. This was a sign to me from Maheo. All was quiet. All was beautiful. All was peaceful. It was if I was alone in the world. As if I were the first of the people. Or maybe the last.

"Then, last night I slept alone on the prairie. At a site where I found an immense buffalo skull. There was nothing else on the prairie. Just this one naked buffalo skull. I camped under the beauty of the sky and the stars. I enjoyed the stars like I did as a young boy seeing them for the first time with my father. As if I was alone in the world. I blew songs softly into my eagle wing bone flute until both I and my pony were asleep.

"I woke to the snorting and stamping of a large buffalo bull. My flute calmed us both. The bull and me. Let us smoke together, I said. He lowered himself on to his knees. Only then did I see that his head was the same size as the naked skull next to me. I smoked, first to the sky, then to grandmother earth, then to each of the four directions. The last smoke circled his head and he blew it to the sky.

"He was looking past me to the southeast, where the sun would eventually rise on what was to become today. I turned to where he was looking. I saw a village. A village of tipis and white men's log cabins. All together in a circle intermingled. There were dogs and ponies. There were eagles and hawks flying. There were antelope and other deer all around the prairies near the village. Smoke came out of the darkened smoke holes of the white, painted Cheyenne lodges. And smoke came out of the blackened chimney tops of the white men's cabins. The smoke rose the same from both the people's lodges and the white man's cabins. It was the same for both. The smoke does not see any difference between the people and the whites.

"But there were no buffalo. There were no buffalo anywhere on the vast prairies."

He paused, looked at the rising smoke heading up and out of the lodge. "When the sun rose and I awoke, the buffalo skull was still there. But the buffalo was gone. And there was no sign it had ever been there. The only sign of buffalo on the whole prairie was the great buffalo skull."

Black Kettle sat in silence. Gathered his thoughts. Then proceeded.

"Lame White Man is right. The people number four hundred fifty lodges. More than six hundred warriors. Maybe four times that are the total of all the people. The soldiers at Fort Larned told us that more than ten times the number of all the people died in just one battle of their war. In one battle. Forty times the number of all our warriors died in just one battle.

"If the whites want to eliminate the people, they can. But most whites want peace. Most of the people also want peace. Some whites come and lie to us. Some whites steal from us. Some whites destroy our lodges and our villages. And some of our young men raid the whites. Some of our young men have killed settlers and attacked their wagon trains.

"Attacking the white settlers always brings the white soldiers. Our young men are few. They must both hunt to feed their families and fight our enemies. The white soldiers are many. They only fight their enemies. They do not need to hunt. The Great White Father Lincoln says he wants peace. Many of his soldiers also. But we know that some of the white soldiers attack the people. The fighting and killing will only stop if somebody stops first. Great Medicine foresaw that the day would come when the buffalo would be gone. When the white man would come here. We must learn to live with the whites, even in a time of no buffalo.

"The people will only survive if the killing stops. We must be the first to stop. Even if some whites lie to us or kill some of the people. Our responsibility is to *all* the people. Not just to the young warriors who have been taught their whole lives to hunt and to fight. Who have sat their whole lifetimes by our fires and heard us old men talk of old wars and old ways. If our present path could lead to the end of the people, we must try a different path. That is the responsibility of the Council."

That evening, around hundreds of campfires, the Southern Cheyenne and Arapaho families feasted and talked about the coming peace. Even those who had spoken for war shared in the optimism. All knew that if Black Kettle's peace really could come with the white settlers and soldiers, then life could return to hunting buffalo across the prairies, raiding the Utes and Pawnees for ponies, and roaming the prairies.

Antelope, the seventeen year old daughter of Black Moccasin, entered her family's lodge.

"Can Thunder Bull join us?" she asked. The seven year old Thunder Bull had attached himself to her since he was four. Most days when the boys were done playing at hunting and riding, for as long as anyone could remember, he had always joined Antelope in the camps for the day's and evening's work.

"Yes, but why tonight?" Black Moccasin asked.

"His father wants him to learn about the Council meeting from you."

"Then after he will go back to his lodge?"

"Yes, I will, grandfather." Thunder Bull said.

The two stepped to their right, respectfully walking behind those sitting around the fire. They settled in front of Antelope's bed on the edges of the rye grass mats, leaning back against her rolled up buffalo robes, sitting to Black Moccasin's left.

Dinner was passed to everyone around the fire.

"They say we are now at peace with the white soldiers, father," Antelope said.

"Yes," Black Moccasin said. "We have decided for peace with the whites here today."

"I heard some of the warriors say the Dog Soldiers do not agree, grandfather," Thunder Bull said.

There was silence as food was passed and Black Moccasin decided what to say in response.

He smiled across at the young boy. "What did you do today, Thunder Bull?"

"I hunted rabbits."

"Did you kill any?"

"Yes, one. My mother said she would save it for me to eat when I return to my lodge tonight."

"This is a fine night to share our food with a young warrior, Thunder Bull." He then turned to his daughter. "Thank you for your generosity, Antelope."

The two nodded respectfully.

"It is as if the people were a small meadow in the middle of a giant forest. If the forest decides to grow over the meadow, it can do so by merely growing. Destroying the meadow. The meadow has no power to stop the forest. The meadow must learn to flourish with the rabbits and deer and bears and small creeks that flow through it. It must learn to live with the forest all around it."

All ate in silence alone with their thoughts.

"Will the warriors be allowed to hunt and raid the other tribes if we are peace with the whites?" Antelope asked.

"The white soldiers promise the people can use some of our lands away from the settlers for hunting," Black Moccasin replied.

"And if there are no buffalo in those lands, what will the warriors do?" Thunder Bull said.

Black Moccasin nodded at his wife and sons, then at Thunder Bull. "All the people see the problem. But only young boys dare to ask. This, Thunder Bull, is what I meant when I said the Council was responsible to all the people. The Council believes that if we war against the whites, we will lose. The people may even be destroyed.

"We are the greatest horsemen and warriors on the prairies. But we are small in number. Some young men will not like this. Some will see only the old path. The path they have been trained for. The path of hunting and raiding. They will choose to die fighting, as young warriors, rather than later, as old men in their lodges.

"And by fighting, they will cause the whites to kill more of the people. Some bad whites may kill some of the people even if we stop raiding. But we have decided we must stop fighting in hopes of placing the people on a new path.

"A path that does not lead to the meadow being taken over and destroyed by the forest."

The next day began like any other for the Cheyenne village. The boys and young men bathed in the river at dawn and the women threw out the dead water from the day before and gathered live water for the village. The women then prepared the morning's meal for the clans and all ate.

But suddenly the wolves raced into camp announcing a line of white soldiers approaching on horseback.

The Criers went through the camps calling out, "Soldiers are coming. Soldiers are coming. Young men prepare to meet the white soldiers."

The young men ran into their tipis and quickly began painting their faces. Putting on their finest clothing. They sent their sisters and younger brothers for their war ponies. Each gathered his best medicine and prepared in his own way for battle.

With the village swarming around them, preparing to meet the soldiers, Black Kettle and Starving Bear joined two of the wolves.

"Many soldiers are coming. They have cannons." They both pointed to the west.

"How many soldiers?" Black Kettle said.

"Many. But less than a hundred."

"How many cannons?"

"Two."

"Are they charging the village or walking?"

"Walking. They have not seen the village."

Black Kettle and Starving Bear rode their ponies around the camps to remind the chiefs that they were at peace with the whites. They reminded those who had spoken for war and were now on their war ponies, dressed for war.

"Tell your young men not to attack," Starving Bear said to each. "Tell the women not to break down the lodges."

Each of the chiefs moved among the warriors, telling them that there might be no fight.

Starving Bear, Black Kettle, and Lame White Man led their six hundred mounted warriors to the ridges to the west of the village where the wolves said they would be able to first see the white soldiers approaching.

Starving Bear and several dozen warriors rode up to the highest hill overlooking the oncoming cavalry.

When the cavalry spotted Starving Bear and his warriors, they formed a battle line and brought their howitzers into position.

Starving Bear rode alone down to the cavalry, signaling that he came in peace. He carried the papers and wore the medal from President Lincoln. As he approached the soldiers, he held out the paper and showed the medal.

He stopped in front of the soldiers and held his hand up in the universal peace sign of the plains.

But the lieutenant in charge of the cavalry yelled "Fire."

The soldiers began firing at the Indians on the hill and at Starving Bear. Starving Bear fell in the first fusillade. As the Indians on the hill streamed down, firing arrows at the soldiers, the soldiers continued firing.

Six hundred whooping warriors now descended the hills, firing arrows and Sharps carbines. The surprised soldiers were surrounded and in danger of being massacred.

"Stop them, Lame White Man," Black Kettle said as the two raced down. "Follow me. We must stop them before it is too late."

Black Kettle drove his pony between the beleaguered soldiers and the enraged Cheyenne. Back and forth he rode between the two.

"Stop," he said to the Cheyenne warriors as he rode, his back to the soldiers. "Stop fighting. We are at peace with the white soldiers."

Back and forth he and the other chiefs rode, driving the reluctant warriors away from the soldiers, until the shooting had stopped.

"Lame White Man. Black Moccasin. We are not at war."

"They have broken your peace," Lame White Man said. "They have killed Starving Bear."

"The peace is only in the heads of the Cheyenne chiefs," Black Moccasin said. "The white man does not know of this peace. Our young warriors do not yet see your peace."

"We must go down to the soldiers and tell them," Black Kettle said.

The other chiefs looked at the soldiers and the bodies of Starving Bear and their warriors.

"You go," Lame White Man said. "It is the chiefs' peace. You represent all of us. Let us see if the white soldiers respect your peace. If not, then they will show you that it is a good day to die, Black Kettle."

Black Kettle turned his pony down the hill and rode toward the soldiers with his right hand held high. There were four dead soldiers and two dead Cheyenne in addition to Starving Bear.

He stopped at the body of Starving Bear.

The lieutenant came out on horseback.

"I am Black Kettle of the Cheyenne. We are at peace with the white man."

"Many Indians are killing the white settlers and fighting the soldiers," the lieutenant said.

"But we are at peace and wish to stay at peace." He pointed to the body of the dead chief. "Starving Bear came to tell you this. He bears a medal and a message from The Great Father Lincoln that shows he is a peace chief."

The lieutenant motioned for a soldier.

"See what the Indian is carrying," he said.

The soldier dismounted and looked at the medal and took the piece of paper, then handed both up to the lieutenant and remounted.

The lieutenant looked at both, then up at the hundreds of warriors that threatened his troops.

"I am not authorized to make peace with you. I have been sent to make war on the Cheyenne that keep raiding the white settlers. The governors have asked us for protection from the Cheyenne."

"Then who is the peace chief for the whites? Father Lincoln has said we are at peace. And we say we are at peace." He pointed to the letter.

The lieutenant shrugged. "You must meet with the governor and agree to peace."

"As we have done before. As we did with the soldiers last year at Medicine Lodge."

The lieutenant shrugged again, looking up at the angry warriors on the hills.

"It is up to you now," Black Kettle said. "We are at peace. Many of my young men will want revenge for what you have done here today." He pointed to the three dead Cheyenne.

The lieutenant looked back at his soldiers, then back at the Cheyenne warriors all around and above him.

"My young warriors think this is a good day to die," Black Kettle said. "Many do not believe in the chiefs' peace. I believe if we kill all your soldiers here now some of my warriors will die here. But many, many more Cheyenne will die when more soldiers come. But my young men are right. It *is* a good day to die."

Black Kettle urged his pony back, away from the lieutenant, and sat impassively.

The lieutenant sat on his horse a long while. He turned it around to ride back to his troops. He then turned back and lied, "I will tell the governors and the soldiers at the fort that you seek peace."

He rode back to the soldiers and organized them for the ride west with their casualties.

Black Kettle rode up to the waiting Cheyenne.

They watched in silence as the soldiers left.

"This was a very brave thing you did here today, Black Kettle," Lame White Man said.

"You saved many of the peoples' lives," Black Moccasin said. "Today and in future days."

"Maybe," Black Kettle said. "We will see."

3

May 31, 1864

"You sure I can't convince you two to stay?" the old rancher said, peering up from under his filthy brown cowboy hat at Lily on her horse. "Good help is impossible to come by and keep out here, and you four still have a lot to learn about the cattle business."

Lily and Gus had spent six months at the foot of the Rockies just west of Denver City, working for this old cattle rancher. Lily had convinced Damours that it was the best, if not the only, way to learn the ranching business in preparation for their ranch in the Washington Territory, her dream ranch that Auggy had promised her.

"I agree we've got more to learn from you," Lily said. "But, it's either now or wait a year. Nobody's gonna hire in to take us over the Oregon Trail in the winter."

"True enough, but you'n Gus and those two boys there aren't going to get very far if the Cheyenne keep attacking small groups of settlers between here'n Fort Laramie. You're going to need more than those two to get you there, girl. Plus, that bear you got mounted on the back of your wagon is a bad idea with hostiles around. They're gonna want to take a look. Maybe even want it for themselves."

Gus had shot a huge grizzly outside Colorado City back in September while they waited for an escort to Denver City. A small group of Cheyenne heading south had agreed to skin it for them in exchange for all but the hide. Gus had paid a trader to cure it and they had worked to mount it on a contrived buckboard on the back of their wagon. And there it sat, permanently standing, front legs and paws raised, a ferocious growl on its face, always looking back at where they'd come from.

Lily looked over her shoulder at the bear, which, in a moment of whimsy, she'd named Auggy the bear. "Tell you the truth," she said. "So far it's been nothing but a curiosity for everybody. Indians, ranchers, city folk, and cowboys alike. They all do as you and your misses and your cowhands did that first day, come running over to take a look at ol' Auggy the bear and wanna ask about him. Don't worry about us. Auggy the bear is Gus's and my good luck medicine. All the Indians tell us so."

"Okay, have it your way, Lily. You're good workers and fast learners. We'll miss you is all. Take real care between here and the Oregon Trail. The Cheyenne are mad and they aren't like your Utes. They don't worship bears. Some may not have much of a sense of humor about settlers traveling through their land and may want to test your good luck medicine."

"Thanks for all your help." She tipped her hat. "We'll send you word from Washington Territory. Thanks also to your wife for her hospitality." She turned back to Gus and the two hired hands and headed their small group northwest toward the South Platte River and Fort Laramie, looking to hook up with a wagon train headed west to the Washington Territory.

Lily, Gus, one covered wagon, two apprentice cowboys, one a former slave from South Carolina and the other a mere boy fresh in from Missouri, and Auggy, their giant black grizzly bear, guarding their backside.

And the forty thousand dollars they'd taken from Cummings, now hidden in Auggy the bear's hind legs and torso.

4

June 6, 1864

Joe Lincoln, the escaped slave from a South Carolina rice plantation, was racing back toward Lily and Gus as fast as he could.

"Trouble?" the other one, "L'l Jack" Madson said.

Lincoln brought his horse to an abrupt stop in front of the wagon. "Indians. Ridin' hard this way. Looks like they stole a herd of horses."

"Anybody chasin' 'em?" Gus asked.

"Not that I could see. There look to be fifty or so herding the horses at full speed."

"How much time do we have?" Lily asked.

"Three, four minutes, Miss Lily." Lincoln looked around. "The horses will probably head straight to the South Platte. Over there." He pointed up ahead to the left. "If we're over by that ravine on the other side of that hill, there's a chance they won't see us."

"Unless they all stop at the river, then start lookin' around," Lily said as they directed the wagon toward the ravine.

They hid the wagon the best they could and took up positions. Lincoln and Li'l Jack behind brush on either side of the crest of the hill, Lily and Gus behind the wagon below them. They could hear the galloping herd and the whooping of the Indians.

They waited.

The stolen herd headed straight to the river, a handful of Indians on each flank, with maybe two or three dozen racing behind.

"Cheyenne?" Li'l Jack asked.

"Looks like it," Lincoln replied.

"See any guns?"

"Nope, just bows across their chests and quivers on their backs."

The four watched motionlessly while the horses, Indian ponies and the stolen herd alike, spread their forelegs and stuck their heads and drank deeply from the roiling river. Some of the Cheyenne leaned down to cup water for themselves. Some dismounted to drink.

A few began looking around, some on foot, some on horseback.

"No shooting unless necessary," Gus said.

"Until I say," Lily said.

The Indians were in no hurry and didn't seem to have much of a plan. Lincoln had chosen their hiding place well. If the Indians were going to spend the night here, the travelers would be at risk of being discovered. If they were going to move on but spotted the small party, the Indians would have to choose between moving on with the horses or risking a fire fight. A fight could risk losing the captured herd. They would have no way to know the small party was completely alone.

Three of the Indians headed their way. Probably planning on taking a look at things from the top of the hill, Lily thought.

"Easy," Gus said.

The Indians got to within fifty yards and the lead pony stopped. Maybe smelling their horses, maybe his rider had seen the wagon tracks and pulled him up.

He said something to the other two, and they fanned off to each side, now alert.

Nobody moved or made a sound.

"Show yourselves," Lily said, getting up on one knee and aiming her rifle at the lead Indian.

Lincoln and Li'l Jack slid into the open, Henry's repeaters aimed straight, while Gus edged his horse where he and his Sharps carbine were in the open at the edge of the hill.

The lead Indian gave the signal that they came in peace.

Gus hand signaled that they came in peace as well. But he also signaled he wasn't so sure about the bluecoats behind them. He motioned over to the horizon to the south. Aimed his rifle at the middle Indian.

The three Indians continued fanning out in an odd attempt to surround the four. This attracted the attention of their comrades. About a dozen trotted over to see what was happening. The lead Indian talked to one who rode up and appeared to be in charge. The new leader looked down at Lily and Gus from his horse, then back at the captured herd and his remaining warriors.

Lily moved her rifle to cover the new leader. Gus stayed on the first Indian.

Decision time. The lead Indian said something to the leader who then raced back to the captured herd and the rest of the warriors.

"You think they've even seen the two us up here?" Lincoln asked.

"No," Li'l Jack replied.

The Indians rounded up the herd and took them across the river. Ten then rode back to the confrontation. It looked like thirty had stayed with the stolen horses.

Twenty against four, except Lily was pretty sure they thought it was two and that they would be very surprised if they pushed the issue and found out otherwise.

The leader rode forward, signaling that he came in peace. Asked if they were alone. Gus signaled "no" and, again, motioned toward the fictitious bluecoats behind them.

"How many?" the Indian signaled.

"A hundred. Maybe more."

The Indian stared at them impassively.

"Are you Cheyenne?"

He nodded. Trying to decide what to do.

Finally, he backed his pony to his twenty warriors. Curiosity appeared to get the better of him. He sent ten out to the left and ten out to the right, and shouted a command as he spurred his pony to his right to get a better sighting at Lily and Gus.

Lily, unwilling to take casualties before deciding what to do, shot the leader off his pony. Gus wounded two in rapid succession from the safety of the back of the wagon. Lincoln took down one on his right, while Li'l Jack shot another one on the Indians' now-depleted right flank. Two slightly wounded Indians rode back to the herd at the river.

The loss of their leader and four warriors, the sudden appearance of the two on top of the hill, and the unexpected vision of what looked like an enraged bear in the battle combined to send the remaining warriors galloping back toward the river.

The four settlers stood up. "Everybody okay?" Gus asked, receiving three silent nods in return.

One of the fallen Cheyenne looked to be dead, but two, including the leader, were only wounded and were now trying to get back up on their ponies.

Lincoln and Lily rode over to them at a trot, guns drawn.

The two Indians stood, holding their ponies with one hand while gripping their bullet wounds with the other, blood seeping through their fingers. Neither blinked at the white woman above them, the large black man coming toward them, or the specter of the huge black bear behind them.

They seemed to be waiting for the end.

"The bluecoats will have heard the gunfire. You should take the herd as quickly as you can," Lily signaled, pointing to the north.

"Shoot them, Miss Lily," Lincoln said.

"No, Lincoln." Lily reined in her horse as it skittered around the two Indians. "It's better this way."

"Maybe not. They may want our wagon and our horses."

"They had their chance."

"And they may want you." He motioned to the leader staring at Lily.

"Help them up on to their ponies, Lincoln," she said.

About thirty Indians on one side, and Gus and Li'l Jack on the other, were staring at the foursome.

Lincoln leaned down to the warrior and lifted him as he flinched, neatly mounting his pony with his good arm. The lead Indian stared up at the black man who was nearly twice his size as he lifted him back on his pony.

"Your bear is good medicine," the lead Cheyenne said to Lily, and then stared back at Lincoln.

"So everybody tells us," she said.

And she and Lincoln rode back to Gus and Li'l Jack, never giving a backward glance at the Cheyenne.

The four were sitting in front of the fire. They had watched the Cheyenne disappear over the horizon with the stolen horses, and then gone ten miles in the opposite direction before stopping for the night.

"You still like our chances of getting to the Washington Territory, Gus?" Li'l Jack asked.

Gus shrugged, looked at Lily. "We'll be fine once we get to Fort Laramie."

"They warned us in Denver City," Lincoln said. "The Cheyenne are increasingly angry at the soldiers and settlers joining together to kill them. Not much of a surprise there. They told us we might be in over our heads."

Lily listened to the three men worry at the problem. All four were deadly with a rifle. They had bought the most modern rifles and pistols and felt they had enough ammunition to hold off any band of Cheyenne in the Colorado Territory. At least until the traders started selling the newest guns to the Indians. These Cheyenne only had knives, clubs, and bows and arrows. Curious. It probably meant they were part of a larger war party and had just been sent on ahead with the stolen herd.

Next time, they might not be so lucky.

The three men liked to talk about their fights, what they'd learned, how to do better. It seemed to increase their confidence, so she was fine with letting them. They were a good team and they all knew it.

This Indian business was frustrating, though. General Carleton had Carson rounding up the Navajo down in the New Mexico Territory. Everybody got that. The Navajo had spent a century raiding and killing New Mexicans, whites, and all the other tribes, wouldn't stop, and now had no friends anywhere. The Cheyenne and Sioux up here on the plains lived a life hunting buffalo and deer. And now the whites were bringing them new game in cattle and horses. Probably best to leave them be, as long as they were only fighting with each other and stealing occasional livestock from the newly arriving ranchers. There was plenty for everyone.

But attacking two people and a lone wagon made no sense. The Indians and the white settlers might be able to find a way to live together out here. But not if the Indians were going to kill settlers without provocation. But of course there *had* been provocation. Maybe the whites were leaving them no choice by chasing them off their lands and killing the buffalo and the deer.

The Washington Territory would be better.

If, of course, they could get there.

She noticed that the men had stopped talking about today's adventure.

"Hey Joe, how'd you escape slavery?" Li'l Jack asked.

"I already told you that old story," Lincoln replied.

"No you didn't. You keep telling me I already know, but I don't."

Lincoln looked over at Lily. Uncomfortable. Then shrugged. "A year ago I was working the rice fields at Governor Aiken's plantation near Charleston. There were seven hundred or so of us. Most worked the rice fields. The rest were at the big houses they had on the island and in Charleston. It was the biggest rice plantation I ever did hear of."

"Were you born in Africa?" Madson asked.

"No. My Mama and my Grandpa, my Daddy's Dad were, though. We all grew up listening to stories of Africa when we were kids working in the house. After I was sold to Governor Aiken, I never saw my Mama and Daddy again. It's getting harder to remember the stories now."

Lincoln shuddered as he looked out over the black plains. "Last summer, there were rumors that a whole army of Massachusetts Negroes were attacking Battery Wagner near Charleston over on the ocean, maybe forty miles to the north. One night, as black as tonight, about a dozen of us big boys snuck out of our cabins in ones and twos. Big George killed two of the dogs on the way to the water toward Edisto Island where we knew there were some boats that the Gullahs over there used for fishing."

"What's a Gullah?" Lily asked.

"That's what we called the slaves over there on Edisto, Miss Lily."

"We've discussed this a thousand times Lincoln. You work for us. You call me Miss Lily ever again, and you can find a new employer."

"Yes, ma'am. Sorry. The slaves over on Edisto had developed their own language, partly African, partly French and English. They called it Gullah. Anyway, I got a small boat. I think about six of us did. The rest I think were trying to cross the river holding on to logs. Hopefully not trying to cross on gators." Lincoln laughed to himself.

"By then, we could hear Governor Aiken's dogs, and the answering Gullah dogs aways from the boats baying back at the noise. I never saw any of them other boys again. I have no idea what happened to them. Anyway, I traveled north by night in that small boat, and stayed hidden during the day. Nobody was going to be mistaking me for a white boy or a free Negro out in a boat around the plantations."

"What were you going to tell the soldiers?" Gus said.

"I had no idea. I had escaped twice before. First time they caught me, they dragged me back, then beat me for days and left me in the dungeon alone. Second time was with my wife and they made me watch them whip her till she died. I wasn't going back alive any more. If the Negro soldiers wouldn't take me, maybe I'd try taking my boat to Africa."

Lily tried to imagine it in the ensuing silence. She'd felt helpless that first year whoring in Nevada, but quickly got where she felt comfortable that it wasn't going to be anything like slavery. Nobody'd ever beat her. She shuddered at the thought.

"When I saw Battery Wagner up ahead, I knew I had to approach the right army. I was more likely to be treated better by Yankees. I came across three Negroes in blue uniforms, but wasn't sure about the next step. I decided to just sit and let them find me in the light of their campfire. Sure enough an officer spied me sitting all alone, and, thinking I was one of his men who was lost, he walked up. When he saw my chains, he asked who I was."

Lincoln paused as if he needed to get it exactly right. "Colonel Shaw had lost some men the week before. They removed my chains and gave me a uniform and a gun. Asked if I'd be willing to kill Rebels. My eagerness seemed to amuse them."

"Did you kill any Rebels?" Madson asked.

"Hard to say. They bombed the fort for eight hours. I'd never seen anything like all the explosions and the noise and Rebels dying in the fort. At dusk, they let us Massachusetts Negroes lead the charge. For me, it was all new. Confusion and noise and killing and screaming boys for over three hours. People dying on both sides. It seemed like half of us Negroes were killed or wounded. Maybe a little less than half. Colonel Shaw was killed at the walls. Somebody said over a thousand, near two thousand, Yankees were killed in all that night. I mighta killed some of those Rebels in all the confusion at the wall. Maybe not."

"How'd you get here?" Madson asked.

"Well, Li'l Jack, that's a story for another day."

"May as well tell him, Joe," Gus said. "We got nothing else to do and he'll never let up until you do."

"Not much to it, really. I saved a wounded officer's life, then helped him back from the fort. He took some papers and some money off a dead Negro soldier who was about my size. Name of Joe Lincoln. From Massachusetts, I'd guess. Handed them to me. Told me that I would be in trouble if I got caught with no papers and the Rebels found out I was an escaped slave. He wrote me some orders and told me to take trains as far west as I could and try to hook up with a Buffalo Soldier unit. It's a shame I can't even remember his name."

Once again, he looked off into the distance, then into the fire. "I couldn't find the Buffalo Soldiers, but hooked up doing some ranching west of Denver City. Then ran into Lily and Gus." He gestured over at Lily. "And here we are."

"Killing Indians instead of Rebels," Madson said.

"Yeah, but only in self-defense," Lincoln said. "Not the same thing. Until today, no Indian gave me any cause. It's not nearly as scary shooting a few dozen men armed with bows and arrows as it is storming a fort with thousands of people shooting at you."

Again, he looked off into the black prairie night.

"And killin' 'em's not nearly as satisfying."

Lily and Gus lay near the dying embers of their fire, staring up into the black Colorado summer sky. Lincoln and Li'l Jack always moved well away from their bosses at night. None of them felt a need to have anyone awake to watch point, but all four slept with their revolvers close at hand.

"I wonder how long the Indian problems are going to continue out here." Lily said.

"Certainly until we get to Washington Territory," Gus said. "The southwestern and plains Indians are, understandably, not being gracious about losing their homes and their sources of food. Hopefully it's already sorted out in the northwest."

"That's what they told me in Virginia City and Santa Fe."

"All the fighting seems so pointless," he said. "The majority of whites and Indians just want to find a way to live in peace. There's always a few, on both sides, that bring on the violence."

"The Indians raiding like they always have. Then the settlers calling in the soldiers. It doesn't seem like the Indians ever did anything to deserve what's happening to them, though."

"And you never did anything to deserve it if one of them kills you, Lil."

"Okay, Gus, time to do something we both deserve," she said as she slid her hands inside his belt buckle and pulled the belt off.

5

June 8, 1864

At noon two days later, they pulled up to a small building that looked to be a stage station.

Two men stepped out on the porch, one older in a white cowboy hat and flowing white moustache. The other was middle aged with a black beard and a fire red forehead. No hat.

The two looked at the party as the three on horseback dismounted. Gus had learned by now to place the wagon so that Auggy the bear was only visible from behind. He liked the drama that a delayed sighting of the bear always created.

"You folks must be mighty brave or mighty stupid," the older man said, staring curiously at Lincoln.

"Why's that old fella?" Gus said good naturedly from the wagon.

"The Cheyenne aren't taking kindly to settlers moving through here these days. Two months ago they attacked a ranch over that hill there, and then got into a pitched battle with the cavalry sent after them. Killed four soldiers."

"And just about every stage has been attacked over the past few weeks," black beard said. "Attacking ranches, too. Stealing horses."

"Who started it?" Lily asked.

"They say us. We say them." He shrugged. "Doesn't much matter until we start talking to each other again."

"We had a run-in ourselves two days ago just south of here," Lily said, pointing back from where they'd come. "About forty Cheyenne were running a herd of stolen horses westward."

"They attack you?" The old guy again.

"Hard to say," Lily said. "Like you say, maybe they started it. Maybe we did. About twenty of them tried to surround us. I thought they wanted whatever was in our wagon. But maybe you're right. Maybe they just didn't like us traveling through."

"Did you start with more than the four of you, then? Or did you stare them down?"

"They lost interest when we shot five of them off their ponies." She looked around. "You gonna invite us in? This looks like the closest thing to hospitality we've seen since we left Denver City. And now you tell us we aren't even welcome."

"There's water for your horses and for you out back. Nothing in the building that represents hospitality for a lady, though." The old man pointed to the outhouses over to the side. "If it's hospitality you're lookin' for, the closest thing in these parts is going to be the American Ranche about fifty miles down the Platte. Where you headed if I may ask?"

"My husband and I and our two cowhands, are headed to Fort Laramie hoping to hook up with a wagon train on its way to the Washington Territory. We aim to start a ranch out there."

The two men looked up at Gus, then at Lincoln. Shrugged.

"Well young lady, I don't like your chances to make it to Julesburg, let alone to Fort Laramie. Nobody's getting through in either direction. The Governor's working on getting the Army out here, but that's going to take a while still."

"I hear the Army's got its hands full with the Rebels," Lincoln said. "I don't think we should be counting on them for much any time soon."

6

June 15, 1864

"Name's Iliff, John Iliff," the short man said to Lily as he took off his black cowboy hat and stepped out on the American Ranche's front porch. "And this is Holon Godfrey. We were told you wanted to meet with us, ma'am."

Iliff was in his mid-thirties, short, stocky, with a full head of hair and full brown beard. He was dressed like he just came in from church. Godfrey was tall and thin, in his early sixties. Hair still brown, but his unkempt beard was already grey and flew all over the place in the wind. If his eyes weren't so serious and his countenance so weather-beaten, he'd look almost comical.

Gus stepped onto the porch from the sitting room.

"Yes, we do," she said. "This is my husband, Gus Smoot. I'm Lily." She looked at Iliff. "I must say, Mr. Iliff, I expected someone who looked a little more, well, I guess a little more rancher-like."

"Call me John, Mrs. Smoot."

"And I'm Holon, ma'am."

"I don't know how people around here describe me," Iliff said. "I've only been cattle ranching for three years. Before that I came out from Ohio in fifty-nine and ran a mining supply store in Denver City. I may not look the part, but it's in my blood. My dad was a cattle rancher and tried to keep me home ranching in Ohio before I headed out here."

"I'm glad I'm more pleasing to your eye, ma'am," Godfrey said, winking at Iliff.

"We're told you two can help us," Lily said.

"Be happy to if we can," Iliff said.

"We're headed to the Washington Territory, planning to start our own cattle ranch out there. We ran into a little Cheyenne, shall we say curiosity, on the way up from Denver City, and folks hereabouts are telling us there's more waiting for us downriver. We figure to be okay once we get to Fort Laramie and find a wagon train. What's your opinion?"

"How many in your party?"

"One wagon. Gus and me and two hired hands. All four of us are excellent with rifles and we have the best Colt revolvers available as well."

"That your wagon with the bear out back?" Godfrey said.

"Yes. Why?"

"It's just a hoot is all. Probably won't hurt against the Indians. Everything for them is an omen of one kind or another. They won't much like comin' up behind a wagon of whites and then seeing that bear."

"Well, for one thing we're not all whites," Lincoln said as he came out on to the porch. He shook hands with Iliff and Godfrey.

"My opinion," Iliff said, "is that you're not likely to make it to Fort Laramie."

"Can you afford to lend us some men for the trip?" Gus asked.

The two shook their heads. "We need everybody here to protect our own families," Iliff replied.

"How long till it'll be safe?" Lily asked.

"Hard to say. Probably not until the governor gets us some regular cavalry. In the meantime I hear he's going to send communications to each of the tribes offering them safety if they'll live in designated areas."

"If they agree, will that make it safe?"

"No, because they won't all agree."

"Could you use four cowhands in the meantime?" Lily said.

"You a cowhand, Lily?"

"I'm probably as good on a horse and with my Sharps as any you've got. I'm a little weak in the calf wrestling and branding department, but I've got my redeeming virtues. And the four of us still have a lot to learn before we get started in Washington."

Iliff looked amused. "Well, Mrs. Smoot, you'll be the prettiest cowhand I'll ever have the chance to hire. If the Cheyenne move on, I could use the help of four good hands until you head north, and if they don't, we definitely could use four more good guns, right Godfrey?"

"Probably more," Godfrey said, looking out toward the South Platte.

As they said their goodbyes on the porch, Iliff remembered something.

"Hey Godfrey," he said.

"Yes?"

"Did you meet that guy came through here last winter? The one looking for a deserter?"

"You mean that mean sunovabitch with the long black bearskin coat? Black hat, black horse?"

"Yeah, him," Iliff said. "Didn't he say he was looking for a woman who might know the whereabouts of his deserter?"

"Yes he did now that I think back on it."

"Am I crazy or wasn't the woman he was looking for named Smoot?"

"Now that you mention it."

They both looked more carefully at Gus and Lily. As did Lincoln.

"I have no knowledge of the matter," Lily said. "Could be another Smoot. She have a first name?"

"I don't recollect it if he mentioned it," Godfrey said.

Iliff shook his head in agreement.

"What was the name of the deserter?" Lincoln asked.

"It was a funny sounding name," Iliff said. "Foreign like."

"What did this man in black say he'd done," Lily asked.

"Said he stole a lot of the Army's money," Godfrey said. "Then deserted in Washington DC."

"Was this man with the Army?" Lily asked. "Did you get his name?"

"Said his name was Johnson," Godfrey said. "He was mean as the bear he'd skinned for that coat he wore. Dressed only in black with a heavy black beard. I doubt he was in the Army. He treated everybody poorly. Man, woman, and child alike. He sure wasn't lookin' to make any friends."

"He have a wanted poster for this deserter?" Gus asked.

"Sure did," Godfrey said. "Young man had a droopy moustache and looked just like that famous actor back east. Booth."

"You're right, Holon," Iliff said. "I hadn't noticed it at the time, but he looked just like John Wilkes Booth." He turned and looked at Gus. "Any of us'd recognize him in an instant if he ever came through these parts."

That night, Lily kissed Gus softly, then rolled off him, pulled her nightgown down over her legs, and curled up against his side.

"You seem distracted, honey," she said.

"Just thinkin'."

"That's supposed to be my job."

They both smiled into the darkness.

"You worried about this man in black looking for you?" she asked.

"No. We'll see him coming before he can recognize me. Any one of us can shoot him as a trespasser before he ever identifies me."

"Maybe so. But this makes it even more important for you to stay away from soldiers, Gus."

"I'm not going to worry about it, Lil."

"You gonna be able to do this, Gus? Be a rancher?"

"I don't mind it. I miss the poker, though. And, I truly miss the excitement of always looking for the next mark. I still find myself sizing everybody up for my next con." He leaned over and kissed her. "You okay calling me Gus yet?"

"Sure. It's natural now in public. In private, it still sounds funny. But when I slip and almost call you Auggy, all I see is that big black looming bear, and I almost giggle." She looked over at him in the candlelight. "So, yes, Gus, you're becoming my Gus."

She snuggled closer against him.

"And you can play some poker if you want. But no more cons. That's all behind us now. There's no need for that any more."

She fell asleep, pretty sure now, but not yet certain, that she was pregnant. Their ranch and their first little cub were both coming fast.

7

August 23, 1864

Godfrey raced toward the burning American Ranche in the distance. He had left his wife, Matilda, and his family safe back at his ranch compound, and was aware that he was at risk from Cheyenne along the two mile ride. When he arrived at the American, there was no one to be seen. No guests, no Cheyenne. Just a burning hotel.

Over the past two months the skirmishing among the settlers, the Cheyenne, and various small groups of Colorado Volunteers had intensified. Stages were being attacked, cattle stolen, and settlers besieged with increasing frequency. The Indians had now gone from stealing horses and cattle to actually killing cattle. The Cheyenne had massacred the Hungate family only twenty-five miles from Denver City in June. Just days before the horse stealing band had attacked Lily and Gus near the South Platte. The family's scalped and mutilated bodies, including their two little girls, were put on public display in Denver City. Fears of a general Indian uprising were in the air.

Godfrey turned his horse toward the South Platte to warn Iliff at his ranch. He saw a small band of Cheyenne downriver but didn't think they'd seen him. As he neared Iliff's, he was surprised by a larger band off to his left. They were coming fast down the slope of the hill south of Iliff's. He fired a warning shot into the air. All the Cheyenne out here knew him. He was hard not to recognize, disheveled grey beard flying in all directions as he raced across the prairie.

The Indians returned his fire, then raced after him.

Godfrey could see the ranch house up ahead, but no people. And the Cheyenne were gaining. One arrow had stuck harmlessly, but comically, between his legs in front of him on his saddle. He continued firing, wounding one but not slowing down the rest.

After another two hundred yards, he could hear a change in the whoops of his pursuers and looked back as he fired at them. They were reining in and looking over his right shoulder. Godfrey turned just in time to see Lily and Lincoln ride by him, shooting as they charged into the Cheyenne. As he turned his horse to join them, he saw it wasn't necessary. Lily and Lincoln were pulling their horses to a stop as the Indians raced back the way they'd come. Three lay dead. One was on one knee, getting up.

Godfrey watched in disbelief as Lincoln rode over, leaned down, pulled the wounded Indian up behind him, and trotted him over to one of the Indian ponies.

"You always save people trying to kill you?" he said to Lincoln when he trotted back.

Lincoln shrugged. "Lily doesn't like killing people in cold blood."

Godfrey shook his head in disbelief. "Ma'am, I sure hope you get over that before they kill you some day."

That afternoon, Iliff, Godfrey, and the Smoots sat out on Iliff's porch.

"So," Iliff said, "Ol' Elbridge Gerry was right then."

"Elbridge who? About what?" Gus said.

"He's got a place west of here," Godfrey said, pointing vaguely toward the now-setting sun. "He rode through here two days ago like some modern-day Paul Revere warning us all that the Cheyenne were going to escalate this godforsaken war."

"The governor's shut down the stage route," Iliff said. "Nobody coming or going to or from Denver City. Less they're prepared to take on the Cheyenne by themselves."

"They bother your herds yet, Iliff?" Lily asked.

"No. Not yet, anyway. They know it's my policy to let them have a few when they're hungry. If they want to unilaterally break my peace with 'em, I'll be surprised."

"Chasin' and trying to kill Godfrey right here in your front yard doesn't count?"

"If they ever succeed in killin' this ol' coot, first I'll be surprised, then I'll decide if it's a violation," Iliff said, and both men chuckled as if this was all a game. "You ever seen the Godfrey place? Met Matilda?"

"No," Lily said.

"Well he's built himself a fortress with a tower."

"Two towers," Godfrey said. "We're in the middle of building a second tower."

"See," Iliff said. "As I was saying, he's building a fortress over there. Elbridge may've been the first permanent settler out here, but ol' Godfrey's gonna outlive all of us. If it gets really bad, I recommend you take your three boys there and join the Godfreys at the fortress."

"Four," Lily said.

"Four what?" Godfrey said.

"Four boys. Gus and I are having a baby. I'd guess by February or March."

"Well I'll be darned, Lily," Godfrey said. "I'd recommend you move in with us before then. Matilda will welcome another woman and loves to help with babies."

"In the meantime, you might give some thought to letting up on charging after and shooting at Indians on horseback," Iliff said.

"I'm thinking of mounting her up there next to Auggy the bear on the back of the wagon," Gus said. "Maybe she can shoot 'em from there during childbirth."

8

September 28, 1864

Black Kettle, his American flag proudly flying in the autumn breeze, drove his open wagon down the main street of Denver City. He had succeeded in getting the governor of Colorado and the leaders of the Colorado Territory to meet with him for a Council of Peace this day at Camp Weld.

Accompanying him in his wagon were six other Cheyenne, Arapaho, and Kiowa chiefs, as well as members of their families. Other Indians followed in wagons and on horseback. Black Kettle had brought his wife, Medicine Woman, and his family as a show of sincerity.

Four weeks earlier, the peace chiefs had written letters of acceptance of the governor's June letter offering peace to those Indians who would live in designated areas of eastern Colorado Territory. Then, two weeks later, the peace chiefs met and smoked the peace pipe with the white soldiers sent by the governor.

Only the Dog Soldiers dissented.

Members of the Colorado Volunteers, some on horseback, some on foot, flanked the column of Indians as they rode along the street. Behind them on each side were many of the curious citizens of the Colorado Territory, including Lily and Lincoln. Skepticism was running deep in the Territory, but Black Kettle's appearance right there on the main streets of Denver City with his family and fellow chiefs and giant American flag had created some sense of hope.

The governor of the Colorado Territory and Colonel John M. Chivington, a forty-three year old, heavy set, bearded, balding Methodist minister from Ohio, hosted the Peace Council. Chivington had been the hero of the 1862 Civil War Battle of Glorieta against the Texans in the New Mexico Territory. That battle had ended the Civil War in the Territories and had earned him fame and his current position as Commander of the Colorado Volunteers.

After all had circulated and smoked the pipe, the governor asked the Indians their purpose in coming and if they represented all the Cheyenne. After they had answered, Chivington, hair flaring out both sides of his head, said, "Black Kettle, you have answered some of the governor's questions here today. We know that many of your people have been at war with us. We owe a duty to the settlers to stop it."

"Yes," Black Kettle said after a long period of reflection. "As we told you, the Council of Chiefs has decided for peace. Only a very few of our braves have not stopped seeking vengeance for Starving Bear."

He paused, hoping that one of the whites would respond to this comment. None did.

"Most of the Cheyenne want to live near the buffalo and in peace now with the white man," he said. "We have agreed to your request to live where you tell us. Hand in hand with you, our father. Many of the incidents you refer to were done, not by the people, but by some of the tribes with the Sioux. We are not with the Sioux. We have rejected their war pipe."

"We have received gifts from the Great Father when we visited him in Washington," Lame White Man said. "And we see that we must live in peace with you to receive these benefits."

"But some Cheyenne *have* joined with the Sioux," the governor said. "And *have* stolen horses, killed settlers, kidnapped women and children, and killed livestock as you have admitted to us here today."

"Yes," White Antelope, ten years older than Black Kettle and also one of the Council of Forty-four Chiefs, said. "We speak only the truth here today with you. We admit that some small number of Cheyenne and some Arapaho have committed crimes against the settlers. But we join Black Kettle to seek a permanent peace with you."

He stood and reached under his shirt and pulled out a medal. "I am wearing my medal given to me in Washington by the Great White Father. I am at peace. This week we brought the soldiers the four white women and children some of our braves took last summer."

"Yet you admit some Cheyenne braves are not at peace."

"Yes," White Antelope said. "We have truthfully given you and the governor the names of our people who have been fighting. But it was the white soldiers who started the shooting."

"Only after your men stole horses from the ranchers. Only after we chased them did the shooting start."

"We have traveled here today with your soldiers under the American flag to show that we want to end this fighting between us," Black Kettle said as White Antelope and Lame White Man nodded their assent. "We are here to work with our father to stop the fighting."

"Do your military societies, including the Dog Soldiers, agree to be at peace with us?"

"No, not all of them," Black Kettle said. "Some are with us here today. Others wish to join the Sioux in their war against the whites. We are telling you all, governor. We speak the truth only. We do not control all Cheyenne. But we represent the wishes and the decision of the Cheyenne people. That's why we are here today. And the other chiefs join with me in this. We want to live where you tell us. To hunt on our prairies where you allow us. To be at peace with the whites."

"We have learned from painful experience that in the spring and summer you hunt the buffalo and the antelope and wage war," Chivington said. "Every year as winter comes the Cheyenne want peace. They do not want to fight during the great snow storms. They would rather be in their warm lodges with their squaws."

"What you say is true of all Indians," Black Kettle said.

"How do we know that next summer," the governor said, "you will not return to attacking the settlers, just as in the past you have attacked other tribes and the whites every spring and summer?"

"It is true that we always are better prepared for fighting in the summer and not so well in the winter. The Council of Chiefs has decided that the old path of the people you describe is no longer a good path for the people. We are here today to seek with you a new path. A path of living in peace with the white man."

"Black Kettle speaks the truth," White Antelope said. "I was a leader of the

Dog Soldiers against the Comanche and Kiowa. Not all of them want now to be at peace with you. But some are with us seeking the path of peace."

"We want a treaty that gives us this peace," Black Kettle said. "We have traveled here today with our families to learn what you require of us to assure this peace. We ask that you tell all your war chiefs that we are at peace. And that they not mistake us for other Indians who remain on the old path."

John Iliff, Lily, Gus, and Lincoln sat with a group of Coloradans in near proximity to the Indian women and children a hundred yards from the Council. They had come in case their testimony about both the good and the bad Cheyenne behavior could be helpful.

"There," Lily said. She pointed at an Indian on the outskirts of the Council. "There, Lincoln. That's the leader of the group that attacked us. The one we wounded and that you lifted back on his pony."

"Yes. He saw us earlier. I saw him point you out to Black Kettle before the meeting started. I didn't recognize him then, but you're right."

Lily stood up and called over to a young Indian woman between them and the Council. The young woman looked shyly at the ground, but came over, accompanied by a young Indian boy.

"What is your name," Lily asked the young woman.

"Antelope."

"And what is your friend's name?"

"Thunder Bull."

"Is your family also here?"

"Yes," Antelope said. She pointed to her father with the group of Indians.

"What is his name?"

"Black Moccasin."

"Is he a chief?"

"Yes."

"What is the name of the brave sitting two people away to his right?"

Antelope stood on her tiptoes to look. She whispered something to Thunder Bull.

"His name is Lame White Man," Thunder Bull said.

"Is he a chief?"

"Yes. He is the bravest battle chief of all the Cheyenne."

Lily looked at Gus. "Odd that his name is Lame White Man. Wasn't that the joke name I gave you back in Pah Gosah?"

"Yes," Gus said. "And it's no funnier now than it was then."

"What is your name?" Antelope asked, overcoming her shyness.

"Lily."

"Do you have any children?" Antelope asked.

Lily smiled. She reached down to take Antelope's hand and put it on her belly. "No, but I will soon."

"What will you call her?" Antelope asked.

"How do you know she will be a girl baby, Antelope?"

"I don't."

"If she is a little girl baby, I will call her Antelope. But if he is a boy baby, I don't think I will call him Thunder Bull."

Antelope laughed at this as they ran back to the other Indians.

"I do not have the authority to grant you peace," the governor said.

"What must we do then to be at peace?" Black Kettle said. "You wrote us saying if we live near Fort Lyon, we could be at peace with the whites. And we have agreed."

"You must make your peace with the military chiefs. With the Army. You must agree to stop attacking the settlers. And to stop stealing their cattle and horses."

"We agree to this," White Antelope said. "We have already pledged this to you. In writing by letter. Then to your soldiers two weeks ago. And here again today."

"You must tell all your people," the governor said. "That unless they surrender to the military and go to Fort Lyon and join Black Kettle's village there, they will be considered to be at war with the white man."

"We will do as you say," Black Kettle said. "This is our new path of the Council of Chiefs."

"If you Cheyenne and the Arapaho go with the soldiers to Fort Lyon and camp on what you call the Big Sandy River under your American flag given to you by the Great Father in Washington," and here the governor pointed to Black Kettle's American flag waving from his wagon behind them. "If you agree with the war chiefs and if you live there in peace and fly both your American flag and the large white flag of surrender we will give you today, then the soldiers will not bother the Cheyenne."

"Our people will do as you say," Black Kettle said. "Two weeks ago your soldiers visited us to discuss your request. It was like traveling through the fire for them to trust us that day. We now come to you today. To your biggest village on the prairies. We come here with our eyes closed. Trusting you. We offer our people to you in peace out of this trust. By traveling through the fire."

"And all the people who do not join us will be at war with you," White Antelope said. "We understand this. We will tell this to the Cheyenne and Arapaho people."

"We will even tell the Dog Soldiers," Black Kettle said. "We will urge all our people to live under the two flags. On our new path. In peace with the white man."

Chivington stood. He towered over the Cheyenne chiefs.

"I am not the big war chief," he said. "But I am chief of all the soldiers in the Colorado Territory. My way is to fight until all the enemy has surrendered all their arms. When you have done that with the war chief then you are not my enemy."

"This Council is adjourned," the governor said.

Having been briefed by Chivington, the Smoots, Iliff, and Lincoln had started the five day ride back to Iliff's ranch.

"I don't like it, Iliff," Lily said.

"Not much to like, Lily. Neither Chivington nor the governor would look me in the eye. They promised nothing to the Indians. There was no treaty."

"So what will happen?" Lincoln said.

"Hopefully we can go back to ranching and the Indians will stay down south with the Army at Fort Lyon. But more'n likely some Indian will make a mistake, and some soldier or other will use it as an excuse to kill the wrong Indians."

"And we'll be right back where we started," Lily said.

"We have a lot of work to do in the meantime. You four have a lot of ranching to learn, and the peace may give you that chance. That'll work fine for me. I need the help. As long as peace lasts until next spring. Then you can head north to Fort Laramie and then west to the Washington Territory."

"And if not?" Lincoln said.

"Then we're going to find out if the four of you are better shots than Godfrey's and my men.

9

October 19, 1864

"Gentlemen, here is your promised coffee," General Philip Sheridan said. He poured one cup for General George Crook and one for General Custer.

It was nightfall and the three generals looked out over the Virginia countryside where they had just achieved a stunning victory over the Confederate Army on its way to Washington, DC.

Sheridan had promised to have coffee at Cedar Creek when he led his troops from Winchester that morning.

"Congratulations General Custer," Sheridan said. "Your relentless attack on their flanks turned the tide again."

Custer nodded.

"Do we have any idea why the rebels halted their attack before we got there?"

"I'm told they were plundering our troops they had captured, sir," Custer said.

Sheridan looked out over the creek, then back over his shoulder, toward Washington.

"This should put an end to Lee's plans to threaten Washington," he said.

"And should help Lincoln with the election," Custer said.

"Can't hurt him, that's for sure," Sheridan said.

"If you're not careful, Custer," Crook said. "First with Gettysburg, and now here, you just might get yourself a reputation for aggressive and relentless cavalry attacks."

The three toasted with their cups.

10

November 7, 1864

Lily and Lincoln headed the wagon to the top of the ridge overlooking Black Kettle's village along Sand Creek. It was noon. They had covered the nearly two hundred miles from Iliff's ranch in ten days. Iliff had said that they wouldn't be needed for the next several weeks. His men and Gus and Li'l Jack could keep the weaned calves from finding their way back to their mothers back in the general herd.

Iliff had also assured them that the escort soldiers would guarantee them safe passage, and that he had enough manpower without them to protect the ranch if he was wrong about the Indians. The soldiers had agreed there was no danger for them from Black Kettle's village.

Gus had shrugged. "I'm okay with your going as long as you bring Auggy the bear back with you. We'll need him at the ranch." Lily had laughed and kissed him goodbye as she and Lincoln had headed out.

The soldiers showed them the way to the village and then broke away to finish their own trek to Fort Lyon. The two looked down at the village.

"Tell me one more time, Lily, why we came here?" Lincoln said.

"Black Kettle is at peace. I've known enough Indians to know that they have plenty to teach us about life on the prairie, and I've picked up enough of their language that I thought I'd give it a try here, too. And the soldiers said there were several half breeds in the tribe who could translate the rest for us."

"We'll know soon enough." He pointed down the ridge to the edge of the village. Four warriors were riding toward them. One was Lame White Man.

Gus and Li'l Jack were out on their rounds checking on Iliff's cattle. Soon the serious snows would be coming and they needed to bring the bulk of the herd nearer the ranch so that those that survived the winter could be found more easily in the spring.

"What's it like in the Washington Territory?" Li'l Jack asked. "Why's Lily so intent on us going there?"

"I think there's more rain. And I think she thinks the cattle ranching and the weather will both be better."

"What's wrong with here?"

Gus laughed. "What's your favorite part of here, Li'l Jack? Getting shot at by Indians? The feet of snow and bitter cold all winter? You like the more than six months of snow they get here in Colorado?"

"I was talkin' to some of Iliff's cowboys and they say that the soldiers are going to clear out the Indian problem this year. And they said now that President Lincoln has been re-elected the war'll be over soon and more soldiers and settlers'll be coming and Colorado's going to be the best place to be."

"Maybe so, but my experience, Li'l Jack, is that when a woman gets her heart set on something, you best either help her get it, or just move on."

"I hear Washington Territory has its own set of Indian problems and the Sioux are making it more and more difficult for anybody to get there."

They rode on for a mile in silence, came up a rise, and reined in their horses. There, in front of them, were a dozen Cheyenne butchering two of Iliff's cows.

Li'l Jack pulled his rifle out of its scabbard.

Gus held up his hand. "No. It's okay. They know Iliff is willing to lose a few. Long as they don't overdo it."

"But I thought he said the other day they'd already taken too many this year."

"Not that he told me. Let 'em be, I'l Jack. We don't want to be the ones restarted the war."

The two men sat, watching the Indians, some two hundred yards down the slope.

One of the Indians looked up from his work and saw them. Said something and pointed to them. All the Indians stopped their work, stood, and looked at the two men. A couple jumped on their ponies.

"I heard there's been some new attacks lately," Li'l Jack said. "All up and down the Platte."

"True enough. We'll let the Volunteers deal with that. Keep your eyes on these for now."

"I was just wonderin' if these were some of those who are refusing to stop fighting is all."

Gus lifted his rifle. "Gently, Li'l Jack. Gently. We'll find out soon enough. Killing Iliff's stock is one thing. That's forgivable. But shootin' at Lily Smoot's friends would be quite another. But let's give 'em a chance to leave us be."

Five of the Indians were now mounted and armed. The others went on stripping the cows. Neither side acted like they wanted a confrontation.

And then with some signal that Gus didn't see, the five Indians charged.

"Gently, gently," Gus said. "If it's a bluff, let em bluff. If they start shooting, we'll make them regret it."

He looked over at Li'l Jack to make sure he was steady. In fact he was smiling as he cradled his Sharps carbine. Looked like he was getting into it. Like he was hoping one of the Indians would take a shot at them.

The charging Indians cut the distance in half and then let loose a volley of arrows. There was no time to decide if they were trying to just scare them off or actually kill them. Gus opened fire.

Li'l Jack needed no further prodding and they both fired at the five charging Indians, reloaded. Fired again. Three went down and the other two whirled their ponies and headed back to their companions, now feverishly packing their ponies and heading for the woods on the other side of the valley.

Gus took off in hot pursuit, not noticing that he was now alone. He shot two of the ponies packed with meat and one of the Indians who had shot at them.

He stopped to reload again and to see the best way to proceed. The Indians were fleeing toward the woods. They were fast getting out of range, and he had no idea how many more might be where they were headed.

He sighted his rifle at the closest Indian and fired. Missed. Reloaded. Tried again. Missed.

He then turned to see how Li'l Jack was faring. Li'l Jack's horse was there, but Li'l Jack was not.

Gus trotted by the three downed Indians. All were dead. Their ponies skittered away from him and headed toward the now-disappearing Indians.

There was an arrow sticking straight up in L'l Jack's empty saddle. Gus urged his horse forward through the tall grass, afraid of what he was about to find.

Lincoln signaled to the oncoming Indians that they had come in peace.

The four Cheyenne stopped twenty yards short and looked up the hill at them. Lame White Man turned and pointed back at the village. At the American flag and white flag flying from the large lodge in the center of the village.

He turned back in silence. Then signaled that they were at peace.

"You are the black white man who shot me. Who put me back up on my pony."

"Yes, I put you back on your pony, but it was Lily who shot you, Lame White Man."

The five men all looked at Lily.

"And," Lame White Man said, "you were at the Peace Council at Camp Weld."

"Yes," Lily said. "We met Antelope and Thunder Bull and they told us your name."

"Yes. They told me of that meeting. Antelope told me you are going to have a baby."

There was a long period of silence. Lily knew better than to be rude by talking too soon.

"You know," Lame White Man said, "that Black Kettle and the people here, near Fort Lyon, are at peace with the white settlers?"

"Yes. Or we would not have come."

"Why are you here?"

"That's a very good question," Lincoln said, turning toward Lily.

Lily ignored his chuckle. "We came to learn from the people. And to have a chance to know Antelope better."

One of the other braves said something softly to Lame White Man, who looked back at the village. A large number of curious women and children were pretending not to be watching them while they were working.

Lame White Man looked at the two on the wagon, then back down at the village.

"You are welcome to follow us. I will take you to Black Kettle."

The four Indians turned their ponies to ride back down the ridge. Before Lincoln had a chance to head the wagon down the slope, Lame White Man stopped and turned back toward them.

"You brought your bear. The children will enjoy seeing it."

And he turned and led them down to the village.

"And it's good medicine," Lincoln said barely audibly to Lily.

Lily and Lincoln had left Auggy the bear and their wagon on the outskirts of the village and walked to the lodge with Lame White Man. Black Kettle was there to meet them. The two prominent flags were flapping in the breeze next to him. He had an old man and an interpreter with him.

"I am Black Kettle. This is White Antelope. Lame White Man tells me you have traveled ten days to see us," Black Kettle said.

"Yes," Lily said.

"He does not know why you came."

"We met some of your Cheyenne at Camp Weld. We were curious to know your people. To learn how to live on the plains. We brought gifts for the children from Denver City in our wagon. We would like to share them."

"We share everything among the people. Even among strangers. What you offer is not difficult for us. This is our way."

Lily looked around at all the tipis. "How many live here in this village?"

"We have one hundred and fifty lodges. There are maybe eight hundred people."

"We haven't seen many men," Lincoln said. "Shouldn't there then be more braves? I would expect more than two hundred."

"Most of our young men are out hunting. There are not many days left before the winter makes that not possible. Most of the little boys are out learning to hunt now. The little ones will be back very soon."

"The women and young girls seem to be trying to look very busy," Lily said.

The interpreter laughed and then translated for the two chiefs, who responded with slight smiles.

"They are curious," White Antelope said. "Very few of our women have seen a white woman this close. And maybe none of the young girls. They want to look at your bear. And certainly none of us have seen a lone Buffalo Soldier away from the Army and in the clothes of a white settler."

"I am not a Buffalo Soldier," Lincoln said.

Black Kettle nodded in acknowledgement, then said, "Even I have not seen a black white man in a Cheyenne village. Are you also here to learn about the people and how to live on the prairies, Lincoln?"

"I work for Lily and her husband, Gus. She wanted me to come here with her."

"In case there was a problem?"

"No," Lincoln laughed. "Lily can take care of herself."

Black Kettle looked at Lily more closely. Then back at Lincoln. "Is it true what they say? That you counted coup on Lame White Man when you could have killed him?"

"Yes."

"Why did you do this thing?"

"Because Lily told me to. I would not have spared him."

Black Kettle looked again at Lily. Said nothing.

Lily knew better than to invite herself to stay in the village, so the five stood for a very long time while Black Kettle appeared to be deciding what to do.

Finally he said, "I will bring Antelope to help you share your gifts with the children. I am told you already know her. She and White Antelope will walk you around the village."

The venerable old chief and the young teenage girl took Lily around the village with Lincoln walking behind.

They stopped in front of a group of women tanning buffalo hides.

"These women are the sisters and mother of that girl over there," Antelope said. "She has just married and they are making them their tipi."

"Where is her husband?"

"He is hunting."

"Will he help them when he returns?"

Antelope giggled. "Men do not tan hides and make tipis."

The women looked over shyly. One asked Antelope a question.

"They ask about your dress, Lily," Antelope said. "How is it made?"

"This is a calico dress. It is sewn together by people and was sold to me in a store."

"You do not make it? Do you not know the makers? What did you trade them for it?"

"No. I don't even know where they live."

"Why do strangers make things for you?" White Antelope asked.

Lily looked at Lincoln.

He smiled down at her. "You came to learn from them. Maybe you're going to wind up teaching them. Good luck getting them to understand about buying and selling things."

"People make things and sell them for money." She showed them some dollars. "Then they use the money to buy things for themselves."

She received puzzled looks in return.

"Yes," White Antelope said. "I have seen this money at the trading posts. And Starving Bear and the other chiefs tried to explain this to us after their trip to see the Great White Father. The whites believe this is better than trading goods."

One of the Indian women reached out for the offered money and then touched Lily's dress, feeling the texture.

"Can you explain to us," White Antelope said. "With all the money, why did the chiefs see so many people who were hungry? Can not those whites," and here he looked suddenly at Lincoln, "those whites with money, feed those without money?"

Lily looked around the village and then back at the women and White Antelope and the grinning Lincoln.

"No. It is too complicated."

"Too complicated? Or not possible to explain, Lily?" he said. "The people share everything with each other. And with strangers."

At this point Lily noticed almost a hundred women walking into the camp in groups, each carrying large, apparently heavy, bundles on their backs. Even little girls carried bundles. But smaller.

Relieved to change the subject, Lily turned to Antelope.

"Where have all these women been? What are they carrying?"

"Some are carrying berries. Some carry roots. Many are carrying wood for the fires. They have been out all day. These are the first to come back. There are many more still out on the prairie."

Lincoln and Lily watched as the women scattered to different lodges with their burdens.

"I'm guessing, Lily," Lincoln said, "that this won't be something you take back with us to teach Gus and your future ranch hands."

After they had given the young boys and girls all their gifts and let each of the children get as close to Auggy the bear as they dared, Antelope took them to her lodge.

They followed her, ducking through the opening and standing inside.

"I had no idea it was so comfortable," Lily said. "There is much, much more room than I had thought."

"I hope someday that I can have a house this comfortable," Lincoln said. "This well-furnished. Look at all the beds, all the blankets."

"I would like all this," Lily said.

They both looked at Antelope. She was on her hands and knees on a bed pulling various size satchels and bags from behind it against the side of the lodge.

"What are those?" Lily said.

Antelope looked up. "These are parfleches. We make them from buffalo hides. We women carry everything we have in them from camp to camp."

She was rummaging frantically through them, looking first in one, then in another.

"What are you looking for?"

"It's in here somewhere. I know it. I have a gift for you and for your bear. I know I put it in one of these big ones."

Both Lincoln and Lily laughed.

Antelope looked up. "What is funny Lily?"

"I was thinking that you look just like me and all my friends. Always rummaging around in our purses, for things we can't find."

Lincoln smiled broadly. "Same for my wife. We didn't have very much, but what we had, my Sarah could never find even after hours of rummaging through her satchels."

"Here it is," Antelope said.

She held up three eagle feathers in triumph.

"This big one is for Auggy the bear. The other two are for you, my only white friends." Her eyes were gleaming in the light of the fire. "They are very good medicine."

Iliff looked down at Li'l Jack Madson, lying on the couch at his ranch house. "It doesn't look good. The arrow through his left shoulder isn't too bad. But the one through his gut might finish him off."

He proceeded to remove the arrows and clean and bandage the four wounds best he could.

"He's a good kid," Gus said. "I'd hate to see him cut short before he reached twenty, though."

"If he's lucky, that second arrow missed his vitals. Let's hope so, or his ranching and Indian fighting days will be over."

He finished up and then cleaned up the mess.

"You say the Indians were butchering two of my cattle?"

"Yes."

"We don't shoot them for that on my ranch."

"I know, Iliff. We were just observing and they attacked us. Started shooting without provocation. We knew your policy. It was self-defense."

"You kill any?"

"Yes. Three."

"We all knew that some of the Indians wouldn't follow Black Kettle. There was no way this was all going to suddenly stop. The only good news is that they'll stop attacking in the winter. And, thankfully, that's soon."

"And the bad news?" Gus said.

"If that fool Chivington feels compelled to respond to the current skirmishes by going in force against the peaceful Indians, things could go very badly for all of us.

"And for a long time. A very long time."

Lily watched as ten young men with painted faces, legs, and arms, wearing eagle feathers, danced around the fire. Many other young men beat their drums and shook rattles. Several blew into long wooden flutes. She looked over Thunder Bull's head at Antelope.

"Are there dances every night?" she asked.

"No. Today was a very successful hunt. The men are dancing to ask Maheo that the hunting season will last a little longer. Before the big snows come."

"Are the other men coming back tonight from the hunt?" Lincoln asked Black Kettle. They were sitting directly across the fire from Antelope and Lily.

"No. The hunters return to the village in the afternoons when they have been successful. They bring the meat and the hides for the women. The others stay on the hunt."

"Will these men go back to hunt tomorrow?"

"Yes. We depend on these last hunts for the coming winter."

Lily looked across the fire at Lincoln and Black Kettle talking, then up at the sky and the thousands of stars visible even over the light of the fires. Then at the dancing men.

She gazed into the fire. Took Antelope's hand in hers. What is it about us that we can't find a way to live with these people? Why couldn't Cochise and his

Apaches be left alone to live in their mountains in peace? And now why can't Black Kettle and his Cheyenne be left to live their lives as they want on their prairies?

Then she thought of Gus and their baby inside her. Can the ranch be possible on the plains? As individuals we mean them no harm and as individuals they mean us no harm. But in groups, the fighting never stops.

She leaned over and hugged Antelope, as Thunder Bull looked up at them, a puzzled expression on his face.

That night, in Antelope's family lodge, Lily woke up and looked at the fire in the middle of the lodge. At the Indians asleep all around her. Then she heard the plaintive music from the flutes. Most at a distance, but some close by.

She turned to Antelope and noticed she was awake.

"What is the music, Antelope?"

"Young men often play their flutes into the morning around and in the village."

"Some seem so close."

"Many wander in the prairies. You can hear them even when they are far away. But some play near the lodge of a girl they like. A girl they might someday marry."

"How long do the men play for the girls before they get married?"

"For most, many years. The girl's family wants to be very sure."

Lily listened. Fascinated. Thought back to the music and the candlelight at the Santa Fe fandango the night she and Auggy had fallen in love.

She looked back at Antelope and then into the fire. Put her hand on her stomach to feel for the baby, and then lay back on the bed.

"What are you thinking Lily?"

"Nothing, Antelope. It is all just so beautiful. Thank you for sharing it with Lincoln and me."

The fire crackled and the smoke rose to the smoke hole.

Lily sat up.

"What about you, Antelope? Is there a man playing a flute for you out there tonight?"

"No." Antelope turned her back to Lily.

"But you are seventeen. Where is your boyfriend? Where is your future husband?"

"I was married for several months," she said. "But last year my husband was killed in a raid on the Pawnee."

Lily put her arm around Antelope and listened to the crackling of the fire for a very long time before she could fall asleep.

11

November 29, 1864

Three weeks later, Black Kettle and his wife were sleeping peacefully in their lodge. The young men were still out hunting in the snow. All the women and children, and the remaining sixty men who were now too old to hunt, remained in the village.

It was just before dawn. Colonel John M. Chivington, at the head of his seven hundred Colorado and New Mexico Volunteers, looked down at Black Kettle's sleeping village on Sand Creek. He had sent half his forces to the other side of the village with orders to charge when they heard his gunfire from this side.

It was below freezing and a light snow was falling. The Volunteers had marched the two hundred miles from Denver City to Fort Lyon, where they had eaten their fill the night before. They had then marched all night to reach Black Kettle's camp.

Many of the Volunteers were drunk from last night on this bitter cold morning.

"Colonel Chivington, where are the regular troops from the fort?" a captain asked. "I thought they were right behind us."

"I told them it wasn't necessary," Chivington lied. "We would take care of these Indians ourselves."

"Colonel, with respect," said the lieutenant accompanying the captain. "This is Black Kettle's village. Black Kettle is at peace with us, sir."

"We have been sent out to kill the Cheyenne and the Arapaho. And there, gentlemen," he pointed, "are your Cheyenne and Arapaho."

"But these are the very Indians that you, personally, sent here with a promise that the troops would not bother them. They turned in their arms at the fort."

"Not all their arms."

The two officers were becoming angry at what was now turning into a major problem.

"You aren't intending to attack these defenseless, innocent Cheyenne, are you Chivington?" the captain asked. "You can't do this."

"Is this why you refused to let anyone know our destination?" the lieutenant asked. "Why you stopped all traffic from passing us on our march?"

"Your insubordination will not be tolerated, gentlemen," Chivington said, now matching their anger with his own.

More and more of the Volunteers started edging closer at the sounds of the harsh exchange. Every man's and every horse's breath around them was crystalizing in the pre-dawn air, as the three officers glared at each other.

"There are women and children down there," the captain said. "Babies. And the men you pledged to protect under the flag you gave them. You have no idea if there are even any Indians down there who are still at war with us."

"Gentlemen," Chivington said. "You have your orders. You will attack this village. Organize your men for a general charge. Now."

"I repeat," the captain said. "you cannot do this. Your order is illegal. It violates U.S. military policy. It violates U.S. and Colorado Indian policy. And it violates all sense of human decency. Those people, asleep down there believe that you, you of all people, have pledged to protect them."

The captain's horse turned a full circle in front of a furious Chivington as more and more Volunteers gathered around them.

"For God's sake, John, you're a Methodist minister. You can't kill innocent babies and children. Get a hold of yourself."

"You get a hold of yourself, Captain. Organize your men. I am your commanding officer and I order you and your men to charge that village of Cheyenne. Now."

"No, sir," the lieutenant said. "We will not. It is illegal and savage."

"Both God and President Lincoln," the captain said, "are above you in my chain of command, John. You can go to hell."

Chivington turned to the Volunteers. "I order all companies to attack this Indian village. Now. Charge and commence firing. Kill them all."

"John," the captain said, "may you rot in hell if you do this thing."

The two officers led those of their men who would follow them away from the now-charging soldiers.

"Shame on you, John," the lieutenant said. "Shame on you."

Medicine Woman woke Black Kettle at the sound of galloping horses. They both rose. "There is a buffalo herd running through the village," she said. "Or the hunters are returning from the hunt."

Then they heard gunfire over the horses' hooves, some from a distance, but some very close.

Black Kettle left his tipi to see soldiers riding toward them and shooting through the dim pre-dawn light. He saw the seventy year old chief White Antelope running out toward the charging soldiers, hands outstretched. "No. No," he said, trying to be heard over the din.

Women and children spilled out of the lodges, trying to comprehend what was happening. Crying babies could be heard throughout the camp. A little boy ran by Black Kettle, away from the charging horses. Complete realization came to Black Kettle as he saw the boy hurled through the air against a white tipi, with blood spattering against the white skins.

Black Kettle raised his American flag and then his white flag. Surely the soldiers would see it and stop the charge. Bullets careened through the air all around him. He heard them piercing the tipis. Heard the screams of the women and children being hit inside the lodges. He saw his wife fall, her left side covered in blood.

Then he watched White Antelope stop shouting at the soldiers. Saw him calmly begin chanting his death song as they both realized what was happening to them. To their people. To everything they had tried to achieve for the Cheyenne.

"Nothing lives long," chanted White Antelope. "Only the earth and the mountains."

One soldier shot him in the groin, and then another shot him in the head at point blank range.

The seventeen year old Antelope ran terrified by Black Kettle, stumbled and fell as bullets kicked up snow and dirt around them. Black Kettle saw his wife hit by gunfire again. He scooped up the screaming Antelope and raced toward the banks of the creek in hopes of saving the girl.

Gunfire came from two sides. Thunder Bull was caught in the cross fire. The little boy saw blue coats being shot out of their saddles by blue coats on the other side. He was knocked down by a panicked riderless horse. He fell to the ground as if in a nightmare, unable to even crawl. He saw soldiers stabbing little children, shooting the women, using their rifles to beat crying babies to death. He got up and ran among the lodges, through the noise, with bullets flying and Indians dying. There were soldiers on the inside and blood on the outside of many of the lodges. Many lodges were catching fire.

He kept running, looking for his family, looking for his friends. He thought he saw Antelope bayoneted by a blue coat riding by and ducked as the soldier shot at him. He ran over to Antelope, but then saw that it was a young Arapaho girl who he remembered playing with. But now she was dead.

Everywhere was screaming and crying and fire and smoke and noise. And blood.

He reached the creek. The few who had reached it were digging into the banks of the creek to hide. There he saw Black Kettle digging a hole, with Antelope sitting next to him, just staring. Staring back at the village.

He noticed it was quieter now. He turned. The soldiers were now scalping the women. Were stabbing already dead babies over and over again. Cutting off parts of the dead Indians. He started digging a hole in the side of the creek. He could no longer bear to look at the village.

Or at the look on Black Kettle or Antelope's faces. He could no longer comprehend what he was seeing.

"The men are killing the wounded, Colonel," the sergeant said. "They are scalping the Indians. Mutilating the dead Indians. Shouldn't you stop them?"

"Are they all dead?" Chivington said.

"I think so, yes."

"How many?"

"We think maybe thirty men. It looks like we killed eight of the Cheyenne Council of forty-four, sir. Also over a hundred women and children, maybe close to a hundred and fifty." He looked into Chivington's face. "And babies, sir. Little babies."

"And the Volunteers. What are our casualties, Sergeant?"

"Near twenty-five dead, sir. Another fifty wounded."

"So much for the cowards who claimed that the Indians weren't armed," Chivington said as he sneered.

"They weren't, sir. We found no Indian guns or weapons of any kind."

"I don't understand," Chivington said frowning. "You said we had casualties."

The Sergeant didn't answer, just let Chivington figure it out for himself.

"What are those things the men are carrying on their shoulders and saddles, Sergeant?"

The sergeant looked uncomfortable. "I'm sorry sir, the men are gathering souvenirs of the battle. Those are scalps on their shoulders. They've cut off private parts from the women and men, sir. They're drying them on their saddle horns."

"What on earth? Why, for God's sake?"

"Tobacco pouches, sir. They will make tobacco pouches from the men's scrotums, and the women's breasts and private parts."

The two men looked out over what was left of Black Kettle's now very peaceful village, one very proud of himself, the other revolted and wondering at the consequences of their barbarity.

12

January 9, 1865

"A thousand Indians attacked Julesburg and Fort Rankin two days ago," Iliff said. "About forty miles from here."

"Cheyenne?" Lily asked.

"And Arapaho and Lakota Sioux. They killed fourteen soldiers and some of the townspeople in Julesburg. They've started attacking the ranches along the river."

"Will we be okay here?"

"This is in retaliation for Chivington. We could hardly expect them to ignore the massacre. I don't think many of the ranches in the valley will be safe now. The Cheyenne would leave us alone here because of the policy on my cattle. But the Arapaho and the Sioux may not know about it or respect it. Don't see why they would, frankly."

"What about your wedding, Iliff?"

"Lily, you and Gus and Lincoln are going to have to make a decision here. You're not getting any skinnier, you know, Lily."

"What're our choices then?"

"You can go with the three men taking Li'l Jack back to Denver City or you can go with the rest of us heading to Kansas City for my wedding."

"How do you plan to avoid the Indians?"

"We'll head due east away from the river and stay well south of them. Besides, they're not likely to bother a dozen fully armed men. But if we get attacked, it could be a riding challenge for a seven month pregnant woman. Even you, Lily."

"I'm done backtracking, Iliff," she said. "Don't think I don't appreciate the wedding invitation, because I do. But I'm not giving up on my ranch in the Washington Territory. What are our chances of hooking up with Godfrey at his compound on the other side of the Platte until this all blows over?"

Iliff shook his head. "We can drop the three of you and Auggy the bear off at Godfreys on the way."

"And Li'l Jack?"

"You know as well as I do that Li'l Jack will be lucky to move on to city life in Denver City. We'll see. It's just going to be the three of you headed to Fort Laramie in the spring. Assuming Lincoln stays with you and Gus."

"I'm not worried about Lincoln. It's Indians I have to worry about until the baby's born. Then we'll be four again. Don't worry about me, Iliff. You need to start worrying about what it is exactly you're bringing your new bride into."

That night, she kissed Gus gently after they had made slow love.

"It's nice not having to worry about getting you pregnant, Lil."

She punched him. "If you insist, we can save our strength for the next one."

He kissed her back. "Sounds, frankly, like we're going to need to save our energy for the Cheyenne if they come after the Godfreys."

"It'll be so nice to get out of Colorado and on to the Oregon Trail and on to Washington. I hadn't figured on all this fighting and killing. It wasn't part of the romance of my ranch for me."

"Not for the Cheyenne or the Sioux, either, Lil. And they ain't seen nothin' compared to Lily Smoot defending her baby."

Lily rolled over and hugged the future father.

She found herself thinking about Antelope and Thunder Bull. Were they dead? Everybody said Black Kettle and Medicine Woman had been killed. That it had been a massacre.

Sleep didn't come to her for hours.

13

January 14, 1865

"Here they come," Godfrey said, long white beard flying all over the place as he came racing down the stairs at the crack of dawn. "I wonder what took them so long. I must say I'm a little disappointed, though. There's maybe only a hundred or a hundred and fifty of 'em. I woulda thought they'd have a higher opinion of us than to show up with just a hundred and fifty warriors."

When Lily, Gus, and Lincoln had shown up at their door, Holon and Matilda Godfrey, their fourteen and twenty-one year old daughters, and six year old son, had welcomed them with open arms. Matilda, carrying her four month old baby girl, and the two older girls could keep the ammunition coming and the guns loaded, but not much more. Holon had thus been more than happy to welcome three good guns, even one that was seven months pregnant.

The Godfrey compound, maybe a half mile east of the river, was surrounded by a six foot high, three foot thick adobe wall with strategically placed firing holes. Inside was the Godfrey sod home, the tower, a blacksmith shop, horse stalls, the unfinished second tower, a well, and a store and sometimes restaurant. The top level of both the house and the tower also contained defensive portholes. It was more a fortress than a ranch. Godfrey was ready for the Cheyenne and the Sioux.

"Don't shoot at the sonsabitches until they get so close you can't miss," Godfrey said as Lily, Gus, and Lincoln ran to their previously assigned stations in the tower. Their rifles and ammunition were already in place.

"Sorry, Lily. I'm not going to be much of a gentleman today."

"It's okay, Holon. Me either."

They could all hear Godfrey's cackling laughter as they looked to the southwest at the Indians racing toward them out of the river bed. The Indians stayed well out of firing range on their first pass. Then they came closer. A couple of braves counted coup on a couple of Godfrey's cows just to show how close they were daring to come.

"Not yet," said Gus. "Hold your fire."

It was a spectacle like none she'd ever seen before. She'd heard about this from those who had been on attacked wagon trains, but never seen it. Lily looked almost in admiration at the circling Indians. What magnificent horsemen. They looked to be as disciplined as the settlers in the compound, coming no closer than they had to, trying to find out how many were inside without risking their lives. Finally several rushed closer, firing arrows into the compound and bullets into the roof of the house.

"Now," Godfrey said. "Shoot to kill."

All four opened fire through the portholes. Several Indians went down, and several of their ponies. Lincoln shot a Cheyenne who was trying to get back on his wounded pony. At this distance, you could see clearly that they were all decorated in war paint. Lily had to admit that if you could suppress your terror, it would be an impressive sight.

"Hee hee," said Godfrey with a loud cackle. "Maybe we'll get lucky and the bastards will decide we're too much for them."

"Doubt it," Gus said. "If revenge is what they came for, then they'll want the women and children. They'll want to kill all of us. If a massacre is what they came for, they aren't going anywhere."

And at that moment, they came swooping around again, this time stampeding all the animals outside the compound.

"Those're our horses," Lincoln said, scrambling to the eastern side of the tower.

"Let 'em go," Godfrey said. "Nobody leaves the compound. That's what they want. You'll be dead the minute you take off after your horse, Lincoln. Stand."

"Have Matilda and the girls take occasional shots, Holon," Lily said. "Maybe from the house and then scoot over here. Make them think there are more of us."

"You gonna try to outthink those Indians, Lily?" Holon said. "Here they come again. Wait, wait."

But this attack was a cover for something more threatening. The warriors raced in, concentrating their force on the north and southwest sides of the tower. Arrows rained down and bullets pinged harmlessly off the tower while the four held their fire.

Then Godfrey yelled out, laughter forgotten, "They've set fire to the prairie to the southwest. "

And then several warriors rode in firing lighted arrows into the compound and on to the thatched roof of the house. All four started firing at the closest Indians. Several fell.

Godfrey ran down to the ground, yelling for Matilda and the children to start a fire brigade from the well. If the fire reached the stables, they were all at serious risk.

"Look," Gus said. "The American Ranche."

Two miles off in the distance, the four of them could see the American on fire, flames reaching high into the mountain winter air. They kept shooting until both the Indians on horseback and those starting the prairie fire were driven back. Several didn't make it back alive.

Lincoln dashed down to help the girls with the buckets. An Indian appeared on top of the wall, looking at the fire, and Lily shot him right through his shield.

"Hope the sunovabitch enjoyed his last view of the scenery," Godfrey said. Back to his high pitched laughter. "Girl, where'd you learn to shoot like that?"

"Been practicin' shootin' at aggressive men since I was a little girl."

"I'll keep it in my mind. Try to be more reserved around you."

"Look," Lincoln said, back in the tower. "Lily, you see him?"

Lily looked in the direction he and Gus were looking. "Lame White Man," she said. "You think he knows we're in here."

"I doubt he cares," Gus said. "Black Kettle's massacre means more to him than knowing you for a day. He's here to kill settlers. Probably doesn't care much who they are, one way or the other."

"He knows, Lily," Lincoln said. "I saw him pointing at Auggy the bear earlier. He's seen that old bear looming over the wall on the wagon. He knows we're in here. I'll bet he tries to put an arrow in ol' Auggy the bear before he's done."

"And then a few in you two," Gus said. "To pay you back for setting him free."

"I don't blame him," Godfrey said. "Stupid thing you did, girl."

"We'll see," Lily said. "We'll see."

It was nightfall now. The attacks had continued all day, then stopped. The nine of them were eating dinner.

"We safe here at night?" Lincoln asked.

"Should be," Godfrey replied. "Indians aren't as reckless as whites. In general they don't like to rush in where they don't know what's waiting for them."

"We ought to keep watch anyway," Gus said.

"Absolutely," Godfrey said. "Everybody up in the tower for the night. Take turns taking watch behind the door. If we get lucky, they'll go on to easier pickings."

They didn't get lucky.

The Indians attacked the compound in force just after dawn.

"Darn," Godfrey said. "Everybody up. They're all back for more."

All morning the Indians continued their sorties around the compound, looking for a way in. Or at least a weak spot. Occasionally trying to start the fires back up, but with no success. The defenders held their fire until they couldn't miss. It became hours of feinting, followed by retreating back to the river whenever the attackers took casualties.

Auggy the bear took two direct hits. An arrow now stuck out of his head and another out of his chest.

"Godfrey," Lily said between attacks, "why not have Matilda and the kids round up all the hats in the store and hoist them up on shovels, axe handles, broomsticks around the compound? Make the Indians think we got reinforcements during the night."

When they were done, it wasn't clear if it affected the Indians, but it definitely made everybody in the compound feel better. They were fighting the invaders to a standoff and had enough food to last weeks. Ammunition was another story. Godfrey now had Matilda and his older girls molding new ammunition in the blacksmith shop.

Late that afternoon, Gus approached Godfrey and Lily. "Lincoln and I are going to try an Indian strategy, Lil. We're going to mount up here inside the compound. The next time they send only a handful with fire arrows, we're going to rush through the gate straight at them with revolvers and Sharps blazing."

"Are you crazy?" Godfrey said. "There are still over a hundred painted, angry Sioux and Cheyenne out there in that river bed with only one thing on their minds."

"And I plan on giving them a second thing to think about."

"Honey…" Lily said.

"No," Lincoln said. "Hear him out. He's right."

"The Indians like to send out a small party as a decoy," Gus said, "And when the soldiers chase them, a larger force appears to attack them. That's what we're going to do to them. Lily's hats and brooms probably have them wondering how many we are today. When Lincoln and I come out after them, with all five of you supporting us, they'll flee back to the others, and then they'll all come after the two of us."

"Then what?" Lily asked.

"Then we race back and all of you open fire. It doesn't matter if Matilda and the girls hit anything, as long as they run and shoot from different portholes. To the Indians it'll look they're being shot at by a whole company of soldiers."

"Plus," Lincoln said. "They'll think they no longer have us pinned down."

"And if they shoot you?" Lily said.

"It's more likely that you all will shoot us," Lincoln said.

"Good point," Godfrey said. "I'll have Matilda and the girls shoot into the air."

Ten minutes later six Cheyenne raced toward the compound, arrows ablaze. They were headed for the wall nearest the house.

Lame White Man watched from the river bank. He had told them to start the house roof on fire while he and his main force watched from a distance. He was surprised when the gate opened and the two left the compound and took off after his warriors. He saw the six Indians turn and race back toward the main force, followed by the black white man and his white friend who had been at the wagon that day. Maybe Lily's husband? So Lily must be in the compound. And the bear was the same black bear he had seen on their wagon. Maybe not such good medicine for them after all.

He whooped three times, raised his rifle over his head and led all the Sioux and Cheyenne after the two charging settlers, their tremolos ringing in the winter air. Time to finish this off, he thought.

The six Indians raced back toward Lame White Man, reloading their bows and shooting back at the charging defenders on the dead run. Gus and Lincoln were firing their revolvers at a full gallop. Two of the Indians went down.

When they saw the full force of the Indians charging them, Lincoln and Gus wheeled to the right, shooting back at them until they'd completed a full turn back toward the compound, and raced for home.

As they neared the compound, Lincoln said, "Look at the gun smoke. It does look like a dozen shooters are in there."

They raced through the gate and, as it slammed behind them, dismounted and joined Lily and Godfrey in firing through the portholes.

The Indians surrounded the compound and organized a full attack. But it had no more effect than the previous thirty hours of attacks. As dusk approached, after several feints failed to bring out any more settlers, Lame White Man directed his men back to the South Platte.

That night, before the camp fires, Lame White Man made the decision to seek easier prey upriver. He asked one of the Cheyenne who said he'd frequented this ranch, what the rancher's name was.

"Godfrey," he said.

"That man is wicked. His ranch is wicked," Lame White Man said. "From now on he is Old Wicked."

"Will they come back in the morning?" Lily asked.

"I didn't think they'd come back today," Godfrey replied. "If they come back in the morning, we're gonna need help."

"And it doesn't seem to be coming on its own," Lincoln said.

"How far is it to any help?" Gus asked.

"I don't think we can count on any of the ranches having any spare men," Godfrey replied.

"If there are any ranches left," Lincoln said.

"It's twenty some miles to Camp Wardwell," Godfrey said. "There should be some soldiers there might be willing to come."

"I can get there in the dark of night," Lincoln said. "If they have fresh horses for me and the soldiers, I can be back before daylight."

"We can't afford to lose you," Gus said.

"Be safer out there at night than in here tomorrow morning, Gus."

Lily looked at the two of them. "We need you for the Washington Territory, Lincoln. You be careful."

"Godfrey, you got a black horse in that stable of yours? Those Indians won't be able to see me, so I sure don't want them seeing my horse."

***

Before dawn the next morning, Lincoln knocked at the gate. "Godfrey, open up."

Lily pushed the gate open and hugged Lincoln as he led his new horse into the compound.

"Where are the soldiers?" Godfrey said.

"Back at Camp Wardwell. They were willing to give us some food and some ammunition for your muzzle loaders, Godfrey. But when I told them our situation, they declined the honor of accompanying me back. Said they had other orders."

"Orders other than protecting ranchers from the Indians?" Godfrey said.

"So they said."

"You see any Indians on the way?"

"No. The soldiers say the Indians wiped out the American Ranche. Burned it to the ground. Same with the Beaver Creek Ranch and the Junction House. No word on Iliff's place. They said they heard reports that there's about a thousand Indians headed back up to Julesburg and Fort Rankin.

"And from what I just saw out there, I'm thinkin' they're right about that. I counted seventeen dead Indians around the compound, but there isn't a live one anywhere nears here. Their fires are cold and there's no evidence they left anything behind."

"They're gone?" Gus asked.

"Sounds like they've had their fill of the Godfreys for now," Lily said.

"Either that, or they don't like being chased and shot at by an angry Negro," Lincoln said. "You all have any coffee for a road weary traveler?"

14

April 9, 1865

General Ulysses S. Grant held out his hand as he stood in the McLean home in Appomattox Court House village. He had just signed the document on the table in front of him. He was flanked by his senior officers. Among them was twenty-five year old General George Armstrong Custer, one of the heroes of Gettysburg and, arguably, the leader of the charge that had turned back the Confederate tide in that crucial battle.

"Our work here is done, General," Grant said to the elegant, proud man before him.

General Robert E. Lee, as perfectly dressed as Grant was a muddied mess, got up from his chair at the table and took the offered hand.

"The terms," Lee said, "are as gracious as we could have hoped for. Thank you, General Grant. The Civil War is over."

The formality of the occasion belied the former camaraderie of the two fellow West Pointers, both of whom had fought for the United States in the Mexican War.

They stepped together out on to the front steps. The Union troops began a spontaneous set of celebratory volleys.

"Tell the men to stop immediately," Grant said. "We are all fellow country-men again. We celebrate together or not at all."

Inside the house, Custer turned to the most senior Union General in the room.

"I'd like to have that table," he said, pointing to the table with the signed surrender document on it. "For Libby. We've been married just barely a year now and I never had time to get her a proper wedding present."

"We've all been a little busy this past year, George. Consider it a gift from all of us. Celebrating your marriage and our renewed nation."

15

April 20, 1865

Lincoln walked into Lily and Gus's room. There were tears streaming down his face. He held his cowboy hat in both his immense hands in front of him. Practically squeezing the brim off.

Lily looked up and sucked in her breath when she saw his face, heard him gasping for air.

"Lincoln," she said. Alarmed, she looked around for her baby, the one month old John Smoot. Saw him in his cradle. "Lincoln, what is it?"

The big Negro couldn't speak. Just stood there crying, trying to compose himself.

Finally, "They killed President Lincoln," he said through a sob. "Iliff says some actor in Washington shot him dead. Last week. In Washington."

Lily ran out into the parlor. "Iliff. John Iliff. Is it true? Did they kill President Lincoln?"

Iliff was holding his wife and talking softly to a couple of his cowboys. He turned to the Smoots and Lincoln.

"Yes, I'm afraid so. The famous actor, John Wilkes Booth killed him during a play one night last week."

"What about the war?" Gus said. "Is it still over or did this start it up again?"

"No, it seems President Johnson is in office. Booth and some others tried to kill some other politicians, but it doesn't seem to have started the war back up again.

"Soldiers hunted Booth down and killed him."

That night in bed, with the baby asleep between them, Gus and Lily were still trying to digest the news.

"The war over and President Lincoln dead," Gus said. "It's all so hard to believe."

"A new President for a new country," she said. "And a new start for us, too."

"Now there's a new reason it's a good thing I grew this beard. Everybody always said I looked like Booth. This would just have had people noticing me once they saw the pictures in all the papers."

"By the way, Gus, did I ever tell you that Cummings shot at Booth in Washington when he and I were there?"

"No. Why would Cummings do such a thing?"

"Cummings was looking for you. He thought he saw General Canby talking to you down on the street. He commandeered a horse and chased after who he thought was you."

"No, you never told me. He thought Booth was me?"

"Yes. He didn't find out until later, but he was chasing Booth. He actually took a shot at him right there on Pennsylvania Avenue."

"Good God. What if he'd killed him?"

"My concern was what if he'd killed you. Then the idiot would never have gotten his money from us."

"He didn't get his money anyway."

"But none of us knew that then. What if he *had* killed Booth, Gus?"

"That's what General Canby and I asked him at the time. Turns out now that it would have been a good thing."

"I'll have to tell Canby next time I see him."

She slugged him. "That, Mr. Smoot, better be never."

16

May 15, 1865

Lincoln, the Smoots, and the two-month old John had spent two months at the Iliff ranch helping to round up the cattle the Indians hadn't killed during the January bloodbath. Iliff and his new bride had needed the help, Lily and the two men still needed the extra ranch training, and everybody needed a return to something like a normal life.

The Sioux and Cheyenne had moved on up to the Dakota and Montana Territories in February, and the trail along the South Platte River was open again. Settlers who had had enough of the West were headed back east, and, with the end of the Civil War, new pioneers were heading west.

In fact, Lily had hooked up with just such a wagon train headed from Denver City to Fort Laramie, from where they planned to join a wagon train to the Oregon Trail and then the Washington Territory.

They had been three days on the trail. Lily smiled as they pulled up at the Godfreys. It was the first time they'd been back since John was born.

Holon and Matilda Godfrey came out to greet them.

"Let me see that little baby," Godfrey said.

Lily was laughing. "When did you put that up," she said, handing John over to Matilda.

"Oh, that," Godfrey said. Looking back over his shoulder at what she was looking at.

He had posted a large sign over the door post:

FORT WICKED
Kept by H. Godfrey
Grocery Store

"I'm told the Indians now call me Old Wicked, and I kinda liked it. Fits don't you think?"

Lily just laughed and hugged him as he cackled.

"Who are *they*?" Gus asked, looking at about a dozen soldiers on the other side of the compound.

"Them? Those are the Galvanized Yankees. You didn't see any at Ilichs?"

"No," Lily said. "What are Galvanized Yankees?"

"Some call 'em Galvanized Yankees. Some call 'em Whitewashed Rebs. They're captured Confederate soldiers, stationed out west now conditional on their promise to fight Indians. The Army has them stationed up in the Dakota Territory and all along the Platte. Mostly we just call them Rebs."

"How they get along with folks?" Lincoln asked, gazing into the compound.

"Fine, just fine. They're a big help to have around now that the Indians have left."

"They tame?" Lincoln was staring intently into the compound now.

"We haven't had any trouble. They all seem happy to be done with the war and have been amazed by the plains and the mountains. And the snow."

But Lincoln was no longer listening. He walked into the compound. The Rebs drew silent. They were as curious about this big Negro cowboy as he seemed to be with them.

"Afternoon Mr. Pinckney," Lincoln said.

The soldier he was addressing looked up from where he was sitting.

"Do I know you, boy?"

Lincoln took off his cowboy hat. "Yessir, I believe you do."

Pinckney stood up. The other Rebs pulled away from him.

"Ol' Tom?" Pinckney said. "I'll be darned. Good afternoon to you, Ol' Tom. We thought you were dead."

Lincoln stared wordlessly at the man who had whipped his wife to death seemingly so many centuries and so many lives ago.

Pinckney held out his hand. Smiled. "It's a different world now, Thomas. A lot's changed in the past two years."

Lincoln didn't take the offered hand. "Sure has. I'm now Mr. Lincoln to you, Danny. Joe Lincoln. I left my slave name back in South Carolina. Here, you appear to be the slave. Mind if I call you 'Young Danny' now?"

Pinckney lowered the offered hand wordlessly. Looked around at his comrades. Rubbed his palms on his thighs.

"Danny, you know this boy?" One of them asked, more to break the crushing silence than anything. "From back before the war?"

Pinckney looked up at Lincoln. "Yes, he was my distant cousin William Aiken's plantation slave south of Charleston. How'd you get out here, Thomas? Er, Mr. Lincoln?"

"Came here of my own accord Mr. Danny. Unlike you. They drag you here in chains, Mr. Danny?"

"Listen, Mr. Lincoln, I have no intention to be carrying on any unpleasantness with you. I carry no ill will or animosity toward you. The war's over. I think we should all move on, don't you?"

"Yes, sir. I think we all should. We should indeed. I'm free now to move on just as I please, while you sit here against your will." He looked at each Reb in turn. "I sure am glad to hear that Mr. Danny there doesn't have any *animosity* toward me. How 'bout the rest of you? Now that you're done killing slaves and Yankees, you harbor nothing but good will toward your former slaves?"

Lincoln looked out the gate at the Godfreys and the Smoots. Nobody said a word. He turned and looked back at Pinckney. "You be sure and give my regards to your cousin, Mr. Aiken. I sure do hope the former governor is prospering now that his help is free to come and go as they please."

He turned on his heel, walked out of the compound, through the gate under the sign, mounted his horse, and rode out onto the prairie.

John lay between Lily and Gus, sleeping in their bed.

"You excited about tomorrow, Lil?"

"Right here at Fort Wicked is the closest we've ever come to the Washington Territory. Yes, I'm very excited. Tomorrow, we get started for real." She reached down and stroked John's forehead as he gurgled in his sleep. "You think we're ready?"

"No," he said. "You and Lincoln are ready, but I'm no cowhand or rancher yet."

"You ever gonna be, honey?"

"I just don't know Lil. I'm there for your dream, but I may not be cut out as the rancher of your dreams."

"Gus, you're the man of my dreams. That's all I care about. You're the father of my dream children. We're going to be fine, honey. You'll see. There's plenty to do building and running a ranch for all of us. It's going to be perfect. We'll get ranch hands for what we don't want to do ourselves. Graciously financed by Auggy the bear."

Gus put his hand on her stomach. Kissed her. "Fit me in your dream wherever and whenever you can, Lil. I'll be the best dream partner I can be."

Lincoln sat by his horse in the cold evening air, watching the Rebs put out their campfires and prepare for the night. He was in no hurry. Four years had gone by since that horrible afternoon under the live oak on the Aiken rice plantation. Danny Pinckney was here within reach and one day more or less wasn't going to matter much.

He figured Pinckney would make a break for it tonight or tomorrow. If he didn't, then Lincoln would find him alone one day soon enough. Lincoln could always catch up with Lily and Gus on their way to Fort Laramie when his work here was done.

A couple of hours later, sure enough, he saw a lone Reb lead a horse due east out of the campsite. He seemed to be in a big hurry and wanting to keep quiet. After a couple hundred yards, he mounted his horse and trotted east.

Lincoln got on his horse and headed diagonally toward an arroyo he knew was in the Reb's path. He lifted his rope off his saddle horn. Iliff had taught him calf roping. It ought to work equally well against rebel whelps.

Lincoln arrived at the arroyo, found a long-dead cottonwood tree, and hid behind it on his horse.

He could see the Reb approaching. Couldn't make out his features. He needed to be sure.

At forty yards he was pretty sure.

At twenty he was certain.

Pinckney passed on the other side of the tree. As he rode by, Lincoln nudged his horse out from behind the tree to follow three horse lengths behind. Pinckney whirled his horse at the sound and looked at Lincoln approaching, Colt in one hand and coiled rope in the other. There was just enough moonlight for the two to see each other at that distance. Pinckney couldn't doubt the identity of his assailant. Black horse, black clothes, black rider.

Lincoln stopped his horse and waited soundlessly.

Pinckney looked right. Then left. He kicked his horse into a gallop straight out of the arroyo and headed southeast at a dead run.

Lincoln edged his horse up and out, content to follow Pinckney at a distance. He let the panicked man get four hundred yards ahead and then followed the sound through the empty prairie from that distance, content with the knowledge that his horse was stronger and faster, and that he knew the terrain and his prey did not.

After several miles, Lincoln saw that Pinckney was running straight as an arrow with no plan or any idea where he was headed. He was riding his horse for all it was worth. Lincoln knew that the horse wasn't going to be able to keep up the pace much longer.

He decided to head him off and herd him back in the direction of Fort Wicked. He urged his horse on faster, more east than south. He wanted to head Pinckney off without him seeing it coming.

Sure enough, Lincoln got ahead and east of him. The horse saw it coming before Pinckney did and skidded to the right, throwing the startled rider just as Lincoln shot over his head.

The now riderless horse nervously stood off to the side as Lincoln rode up to Pinckney, gun drawn.

Pinckney drew his pistol as he rose to his knees.

"Uhn-uh," Lincoln said waving his pistol back and forth. "In fact, Mr. Danny, drop it right there in the dirt. Or you'll be walking back to Fort Wicked without any knees."

"What do you want from me?"

"I don't get to see many folks from back home out here. I just want to talk about old times is all."

He rode over to Pinckney' horse and brought it back. He then reached over and took the rifle out of the scabbard, motioned for Pinckney to remount, pulling his horse back into position behind Pinckney.

As soon as his back was turned, Pinckney kicked his horse into a gallop and tore back toward the northwest and the Rebs' camp.

Lincoln looked up, amused. He watched as the horse got a fifty yard head start, then trotted off behind them. He followed like that for a couple of miles until he sensed they were drawing near the arroyo and the cottonwood tree where they'd started. He didn't want to use any guns this close to the wagon train and the other Rebs.

He urged his horse on as fast as it could go now, and watched Pinckney pick it up a notch, too. Pinckney, and maybe his horse, must've sensed he wasn't far from safety now.

This was familiar territory for Lincoln and his horse. This was a vintage calf roping exercise. Iliff had taught him well.

They got within twenty yards.

Ten.

Lincoln raced to just behind and to the right of Pinckney' horse's flank. His rope snaked out, snapped taut, and jerked Pinckney off the horse onto the dried prairie grass. Bounced once as the horse kept on racing forward.

Lincoln rode over. Pinckney' horse circled back, and, again, stood a few yards away, breathing hard and looking at them.

Pinckney, the breath knocked out of him, was lying in the grass, working feebly at the rope.

"I ain't got nothin' against your horse, Mr. Danny. I hate to see a good horse worn out for no good reason. I took pity on him."

Pinckney got to his knees and looked up. Just in time to see Lincoln's right arm rise over his head and lash out. The tip of the whip snaking toward his right arm.

"Was wondering, Mr. Danny if you still remember my Sarah?" Lincoln said, just before Pinckney uttered his first scream of pain.

The next morning, Lily and Gus were saying their goodbyes to all the Godfreys.

"Good luck on your ranch, Lily," Godfrey said.

"And good luck to you all. We always appreciated your hospitality," Lily said.

"We're never going to be able to repay you for helping us against the Cheyenne last January," Godfrey said. "Take care of that baby. You're always welcome here if you change your minds."

"Iliff told us the same," she said. "Anybody seen Lincoln? We never saw him again after yesterday afternoon."

"That's him behind you, just riding up to your wagon now."

Lincoln was lifting two children up onto the wagon next to Auggy the bear, two arrows still sticking out of him from the January fight. The children loved taking turns riding along with Auggy the bear.

Gus helped Lily and John up on to the front of wagon and mounted his horse. Rode over to Lincoln as Lily drove the wagon toward the train, waving back at the Godfreys.

"You okay, Lincoln?" Gus asked.

"Yes. Why do you ask?"

"We didn't see you last night."

"My last night in Colorado. I wanted to sleep out on the plains. Had me an Old Testament night in the wilderness. Everything's good, Gus. Don't start worrying about me. You've got your family to care for now."

After the wagon train had gone, one of the Reb corporals reported that Pinckney was missing.

He was assumed to be AWOL until his remains, covered by bottle flies, were accidentally found by a patrol three days later out on the prairie. He was hanging lifeless from an old cottonwood tree he was tied to. Skin hanging off his body.

He'd been whipped to death and left to rot on his knees, hands behind his back lashed to the tree.

PART II
WASHINGTON TERRITORY

WASHINGTON TERRITORY 1863–1869

BRITISH CANADA

Pacific Ocean

Seattle

Portland

Columbia River

WASHINGTON TERRITORY
(incorporated 1853)

Columbia River

Snake River

to Idaho
Territory
1863,
to Montana
Territory
1864

R O C K Y   M O U N T A I N S

DAKOTA TERRITORY
(incorporated 1861)

MONTANA TERRITORY
(incorporated 1864)

Missouri River

Yellowstone River

NEBRASKA TERRITORY
(incorporated 1854)

WYOMING TERRITORY
(incorporated 1868)

North Platte River

Mount Laramie
FORT LARAMIE
Chugwater Creek

Laramie
Cheyenne

COLORADO TERRITORY
(incorporated 1861)

to Nebraska
Territory 1861

to Idaho
Territory
1863,
to Wyoming
Territory
1868

to Wyoming
Territory
1868

Snake River

IDAHO
TERRITORY
(incorporated 1863)

Boise City, FORT BOISE

THE OREGON TRAIL

Snake River

Malheur River

Owyhee River

Salt Lake City

UTAH TERRITORY
(incorporated 1850)

to Nevada
Territory 1863

Camp Harney

Steens Mountain

OREGON
(statehood 1859)

NEVADA TERRITORY
(incorporated 1861,
statehood 1864)

Infernal Caverns

CALIFORNIA
(statehood 1850)

© 2015 Jeffrey L. Ward

200

100

200

0 Miles

0 Kilometers

17

June 15, 1865

Lily sat on her horse looking intently south, up the valley. The mountains blocking their path to the west, endless prairies as far as the eye could see behind them. They had joined a large wagon train at Fort Laramie and were into their second day on the Oregon Trail. The train was turning right, headed to the north, away from the valley and toward the mountain passes discovered by the mountain men decades before.

"What's this valley called?" Lily asked the scout riding alongside.

"Doesn't have a name I know of, ma'am. Maybe Chugwater? I've heard some call it that after Chugwater Creek way up the valley," pointing to the south and east of where they sat.

"How far to Denver City from here?"

"Denver City's about due south of here, ma'am. If you were a bird, you could fly there in a little less than two hundred miles."

"Thanks. And the name's Lily, not ma'am. Lily Smoot."

She trotted over to the wagon. Gus was driving. John swaying up and down in a Cheyenne cradleboard on his back. Lincoln was riding alongside. As in the previous train, he had taken the job of getting children up and down the back of the wagon to ride with Auggy the bear.

"This is it, Gus," she said.

"What, Lil?"

"Look all around. This is the valley Iliff told us about. The greatest ranch-land ever."

The two men looked around at the gentle hills to the base of the mountains, the trees green in the few creek beds to the south of them. A sea of ravines hidden among the hills all the way to the looming mountains in the western distance.

"Must be quite a sight when it's covered with buffalo," Lincoln said.

"It'd be an even better sight covered with our cattle," Gus said. "Why not stop here?" he teased. "I know it's not Washington, Lil, but this looks perfect."

"You trying to get rid of me, honey?" Lily said, shaking her head. "The only reason Iliff isn't already here is the Sioux and the Cheyenne. They're still killing settlers in Kansas and Colorado where they've actually agreed to leave them alone. This is the Dakota Territory and the Indians feel it's not only theirs, but that any settlers have no right to be here and are fair game."

"Iliff told us we wouldn't last a week up here," Lincoln said. "They're not even crazy about the wagon trains headed west through here, but they've agreed to give them free passage as long as nobody stays."

As if on cue, two of the scouts trotted over.

"Gus," one of them said. "Craziest thing. There's a group of Indians approached us from the west when we made the turn to the north. The scouts said they came in peace. They asked if we had a wagon with a big black bear on it."

Lily looked out to the west. Toward the magnificence of the mountains. And Mount Laramie towering over all. On a hill above the pattern of threaded ravines, about two miles away, she could just make out a small group that looked to be two of the wagon train's scouts with three Indians.

"What'd you tell them?" Gus asked.

"I said we'd go look and see."

"You got anybody who'll drive our wagon for a while?" Gus asked.

"Sure. You going out to see what they want."

"We know what they want," Lily said.

Lily and the four men rode out the two miles around ravines and up and over the small hills to the five waiting on the horizon. John was happily bobbing up and down in the carrier now on Lincoln's back.

As they approached the Indians and the two scouts, Lily noticed that there was a riderless pony with them. Rolled up blanket on its back.

They stopped twenty yards from the hill with the Indians. The two sets of scouts signaled peaceful intentions for all parties. Lily now saw a large number of Indian braves maybe a half mile to the northwest. And she could clearly see that Lame White Man was the Indian riding down the hill toward them. He stopped halfway.

"How, Lily. Lincoln," he said.

"How, Lame White Man. This is my husband Gus."

Lame White Man nodded to Gus. "I recognize Gus from that day you shot me. Also from Old Wicked's ranch in Colorado. From his charge with Lincoln. It is odd that we keep meeting."

Nobody had anything to say to that.

"Lame White Man, we were very sorry to hear about the massacre at Sand Creek."

Lame White Man did not say anything.

"Most of the white settlers were horrified to learn of the senseless attack," she said. "As you know, we know personally that your people are at peace."

"We are no longer at peace with the white man, Lily. The Dog Soldiers and many of the Southern Cheyenne have come here to join the Northern Cheyenne and the Sioux who are not at peace with the white man. Welcome to my new home. Are you planning on staying here?"

"No," Lily replied.

"That is very good. I, personally, am obligated to you and the black white man, Lincoln, for sparing my life. But my people would not feel the same way."

"Yes, we have been told we are not welcome here. We are traveling with this wagon train to the Washington Territory."

"Ah. I hear the Shoshones and the Snakes are not any happier with the white settlers than are the Cheyenne and the Lakota."

Lily shrugged. "I was very sorry to hear that Black Kettle and Medicine Woman and White Antelope were killed. It is all so sad. Were you there at the battle?" Lame White Man said nothing, so she continued. "Were Antelope and Thunder Bull also killed at Sand Creek?"

She blinked back tears.

"No. The cowards killed White Antelope as you say. They killed many other of the old chiefs. The chiefs who were at peace. And many women and children. And they mutilated many women and children."

"I am so sorry, Lame White Man."

"I was out with a hunting party and was not there. It is not true that they killed Black Kettle or his wife. Both Thunder Bull and Antelope survived. In burrows in the mud in the creek. They both are now with Black Kettle and his remaining people at the Arkansas River. There they still foolishly seek peace with the white man."

They all sat in silence with their separate thoughts for several minutes.

"Antelope asked me, if I ever saw you, to say hello. She wanted me to meet your baby girl for her. She wanted me to find out if you had called her Antelope."

Lincoln turned his horse so that Lame White Man could see the baby.

"Please tell Antelope that his name is John," Lily said. "But that if we ever have a baby girl, we will name her Antelope as she has requested."

"I will."

"Why did you ask to see us, Lame White Man?"

He stared impassively at her for a long while. "I wanted to thank you and Lincoln again for sparing my life. I also wanted to tell Lincoln, and...is it Gus?"

"Yes, I'm Gus."

"I wanted to tell you that was a very brave thing you did from Old Wicked's ranch that day. Not many settlers lived that month. Your black bear is very good medicine for you."

Nobody said anything for several minutes.

At a signal, one of the Indians rode over with the riderless pony and put its reins into Lily's hand.

"I give your baby John this pony. These blankets are for his mother for having spared my life."

"Thank you Lame White Man. That is very generous."

Lame White Man turned then to Gus. "It is strange that we keep meeting. I was told you were coming. I asked the great Sioux Medicine Man, Sitting Bull, for some guidance. Does Maheo have some design for us? He said he had seen a vision about me and a white man with a great black bear. He told me that you and I will die on the same day, Gus. In a great battle. A long time from now. In a place far from here. He could see nothing about Lily or Lincoln in this vision. Just you and me."

"Do I kill you?" Gus said "Or do you kill me?"

"I asked him that. Sitting Bull said he could not see this."

"So you and I are safe for today, then?"

Lame White Man smiled. "Yes. Although the people do not make jokes about such things."

He gazed to the northwest toward the gathered warriors. "Maheo alone knows the day I am to die. There are many things I know. I know I have trained my whole life only to fight. I know I am at war with the whites. I know I will die someday. These things I know."

He nudged his pony forward until he was in whispering distance of Gus. "And now you and I are twice blessed by Sitting Bull's vision. No man knows when he will die. Except now for you and I. Now you and I know every day we do not see each other on a great battlefield, we will not die. Now you and I will know what few men ever know. On that day we see each other again on a great battlefield we will know that it is our day to die."

Lily looked stricken. She rode toward Lincoln and her baby.

"It's all right, Lil," Gus said. "It's a long way off. I'm bound to die of something, someday, right?" He looked at Lame White Man. "If what Sitting Bull says is true, then I do not look forward to our next meeting."

"But I do, Gus. Sitting Bull told me that it will be a good day to die. It will be a great battle and that we both will show great courage during the fighting."

Gus seemed to think about that a while in silence.

Finally, Lincoln said, "We also brought *you* a gift, Lame White Man." He rode over and handed him a small bundle. "You left these behind at Fort Wicked."

And the six men, baby, and Lily rode back toward the wagon train as Lame White Man opened the bundle and took out the two arrows that he had shot into Auggy the bear at Fort Wicked.

Lame White Man turned. His eyes following the black white man and the whites rejoining their wagon train.

The wagon master was waiting for them when they returned.

"You're Lily Smoot, right?"

"Yes."

"There was a man looking for you at Fort Laramie about ten days ago."

Major John Arnold she wondered? Her friend and father figure from Santa Fe? He'd been there that day in Navajo country two years ago. Warning her yet again to mind the company she kept. Worried about her. He knew she was headed to Washington Territory to build her ranch, but, of course, didn't know about the money. Or the company she planned to keep. Or about Gus. Of course, Gus'd still be Auggy Damours to him.

"Looking for me by name?"

"Yes. He said he was looking for a deserter, and that Lily Smoot might know where he was."

Not John Arnold, then. She shuddered.

"Dressed all in black?"

"Yes. So you know him?"

"We know about him, we don't know him. Mean sunovabitch I hear. Is he with this train?"

"No. You're right about his temperament. We told him he wasn't welcome after he pistol whipped one of my cooks over a piece of buffalo he didn't like. When I sent him on his way, he said he was headed south to Colorado. Said the reward for this deserter was fifteen thousand."

"Fifteen thousand?" Lincoln asked.

"Yup. Sure seems like a lot for a mere deserter. Especially now that the war is over."

"You got a copy of the wanted poster?" Gus said.

"Nope. But I told him he was wastin' his time."

"Why's that?" Lily asked.

"Because the man on the poster was clearly John Wilkes Booth, the man that assassinated President Lincoln. The Army chased Booth down and killed him a few days after he killed Lincoln. Somebody else surely collected that bounty that day."

18

July 1, 1865

"This here's the easternmost point of what was originally the Washington Territory," the scout said to Lily.

They were crossing the Sweetwater River and turning toward South Pass, their route through the Continental Divide up ahead.

Lily sat up in her saddle and looked around full circle. The mountains were breathtakingly beautiful. Cloudless sky going on forever, snow still covering the highest peaks, crystal blue streams spilling into lakes the same color as the high blue sky.

But the ranchland they'd been traveling through for two weeks behind them was what she'd been looking for. Green and yellow grasslands all the way to the distant mountains in every direction. Endless buffalo and endless grama grass. Maybe someday it'd be endless grass and endless Smoot cattle, she thought.

"If the Washington Territory is in front of us, what's what we just came though called now?" she asked.

"A couple of years ago it became the Nebraska Territory. But now this here's the Dakota Territory. Once we get through the pass, we'll be in the Idaho Territory for a month or so. Once we get to Fort Boise you're going to have to choose whether to go on with us northwest to the current Washington Territory, stay in Idaho, or travel on to Oregon."

"How far from Fort Boise to Oregon?"

"Fifty miles or so to the border. Then depends on where you want to go in Oregon, ma'am."

They could hear shooting behind them on the other side of the river, at the rear of the train. The scout instinctually looked away from the fire fight, forward, to make sure they weren't riding into a trap.

"Halt," said the wagon master. "First ten wagons, all men hold your ground and keep weapons ready. Everybody else, grab your rifles and head back across the river toward the shooting."

They galloped to the northwest toward the sound of fighting, back across the river. One of the women in the third wagon took John so that Lily could join the race to the battle.

As they approached the fighting, they could see that the last five wagons had become separated from the main body of the train and that three were on fire. Indians were converging on the wagons. The wagons were being overwhelmed and they were too late to save everybody.

They fired their Sharps, reloading as they charged, trying desperately to drive the Indians away before it was too late. They could see the men in the remaining back wagons returning fire at their attackers. And they could see Indians racing off back toward the mountains to the north, some with goods stolen from the wagons, and, infuriatingly, some with what looked like young children held in front of them as they rode away.

Gus, Lincoln, and a handful of scouts chased after the Indians, shooting several out of their saddles and saving one little girl.

Lily, the wagon master, and several surviving women put out the fires and tended to the wounded. The toll was discouraging. Four men dead, three wounded. Two women dead, scalped. Three children dead or nearly so, one scalped. There were four dead Indians, four missing children, and one missing woman.

"Cheyenne?" Lily asked.

"No," the wagon master said. "Shoshone." He looked at one of the scouts. "How'd this happen?"

"Nobody saw it coming. They must have been waiting for us to cross the river. It was stop and go, like always, waiting for the lead wagons to cross. First we knew anything was happening the oxen on that wagon went down. Shot by arrows. Then before we knew there was an attack, there was space between that group of wagons and the rest of us. At that moment, they came from everywhere, shooting into the wagons, using fire arrows."

"Who were the trailing scouts?"

"Me and Skip. That's Skip, over there." He pointed at his dead comrade. "Whole thing was over in a few minutes."

"We were thirteen dead passengers too late," the wagon master said.

19

August 3, 1865

Gus and Lily said their goodbyes to the rest of the train at Fort Boise, Idaho Territory.

Lily rode to the front of the train.

"The man in black." Lily said to the wagon master.

"Yes? What about him?"

"He ever comes looking for me again, tell him we accompanied you to the end of the line northwest of here. All the way to the Washington Territory."

She handed him a wrapped bundle.

He opened it. Counted the money. Looked up at Lily. Whistled.

"This personal between you and the man in black, Lily?"

"No. But if he ever shows up, Lincoln or Gus will kill him and that'll make it pretty close to personal."

She shook his hand, turned her horse and rode to the back of the train as it started its final journey to the Washington Territory.

Lily and her men were heading due west to Oregon, and, more specifically, to the Owyhee Valley in southeastern Oregon. And there to build their ranch.

Lincoln and Gus whipped their oxen to a start on this, the last stage, of their journey. They waved back to the children who were running to get one last glimpse of Auggy the bear. Sitting next to Auggy on the back of the wagon and waving was twelve year old Nick O'Reilly. His family had arrived from Ireland in February, and had been heading to Oregon to start a ranch. But Nick's father and mother were both killed by the Shoshones in the July attack. His two little sisters were last seen being carried off on the attackers' ponies.

It was the O'Reilly wagon that Lincoln now drove behind the Smoots'.

Lincoln had taken Nick in immediately that afternoon of the attack, but the young boy had taken nearly a week to even be approachable. When Lily had asked him to join them on their way to Fort Boise, Nick had agreed. He told them that he wanted to fulfill his father's dream of a ranch in America. And, ironically, his dad had always wanted to go to the Owyhee Valley.

Nick was now two days away from completing his father's journey.

Two days later they were in Oregon at the banks of the Owyhee River.

And four days after that, the four of them had laid out the boundaries of their ranch along the western bank of the river.

Lily thought John Iliff would have felt this was a perfect spot. And she would have agreed with him, if only she hadn't seen that valley west of Fort Laramie two months before. Buffalo grass as far as the eye could see. Heaven for cattle.

But no good for settlers. Not yet, anyway.

20

August 10, 1865

Lincoln and Gus were working on the main house when ten whooping Paiutes on horseback charged them from out of the trees.

A couple loosed arrows in their direction and one fired his Henry rifle, missing Lincoln by two feet.

"Lily, Nick, get behind the wagons," Gus shouted.

The two men had left their rifles back in the wagons, but quickly ducked behind the partially completed wall with their Colt pistols in hand.

The Indians mounted their attack toward the wagons, and Lily and Nick opened fire. Two Indians fell from their ponies. One dead. The other raced back toward the trees on foot, only to have Lily shoot him down before he got halfway there.

"I'll cover you," Lily said to Nick. "Take the rifles to Gus and Lincoln. Go. Now."

Nick, staying low to the ground, headed toward the house, carrying three Sharps carbines while Lily kept shooting at the attackers. He reached the wall and rolled over under Auggy the bear.

Four of the Paiutes now charged Lily at the wagons and Nick shot two in the back. The other four rode left to get at Gus and Lincoln. But Gus and Lincoln lay down a withering fire with their pistols and the rifles brought by Nick.

In a matter of minutes, the remaining Indians were racing northwest away from the house.

Lily checked on John, sleeping peacefully in the wagon, and then joined the three others.

"Nobody told us there were hostile Indians here," Gus said.

"We may as well've stayed in the Dakota Territory if we're going to have to be dealing with this here, too," Lily said.

"You, okay, Nick?" Lincoln asked.

"Yes, sir."

"Very nice job of shooting, kid. Where'd you learn to shoot like that?"

"Ireland. And after that, I had a lot of practice on the prairie."

"Looks like you're going to get a chance to stay good at it."

"I wasn't good enough to save my ma and pa."

"Don't go blaming yourself for that, Nick," Lily said. "The scouts and the wagon master let all of us down and you know it. It wasn't your fault."

"Someone's coming," Nick said, looking toward the southwest where the Indians had come from.

They all reloaded their rifles and stood. Waiting.

Presently a platoon of soldiers appeared, slowed down in surprise, then galloped in.

"You weren't here a week ago," the captain said. "Who are you?"

"Smoot, sir. Gus Smoot. This is my wife Lily. And Lincoln and Nick here work with us. We've staked out a ranch. We're intending to run cattle here."

"Indians bother you any?"

"No, sir," Lily said. "Those Indians lying on the ground over there and those by the wagons just grew out of the ground after the last rainfall."

The captain reddened. "How long ago they come through, ma'am?"

"They're maybe twenty minutes ahead of you," Lincoln replied. "There were still six or so after their visit here."

"Exactly how bad is the Indian problem here, Captain?" Lily said. "My husband and I've been fighting Indians now for nearly two years all through New Mexico, Colorado, and Dakota. Nobody told us there were problems here, too."

"The whites have been fighting the Modocs south of here ever since they got out here, some sixteen, seventeen years ago. Against the Snakes here and up north? About ten years now."

"Which were these?"

"These're Snake Indians, ma'am. Paiutes specifically. Things were mostly peaceful in these parts for a while, but the Snakes started stealing livestock from the ranchers about three weeks ago. We're trying to discourage them. They stole some cattle from a ranch upriver about two weeks ago. These Paiutes that ran into you were running away from us after we attacked their camp."

"Are we safe here?" Gus asked.

The captain shrugged. "Looks like you know what you're doing." He looked around the clearing. "After this incident they'll probably steer clear of you until you have livestock worth taking. Then they'll be back. They're having trouble finding enough food now that you ranchers are driving the game further and further away. They'll want your horses and your livestock and anything else you bring in to help feed their people."

"And if we let them take what they need?" Lily said.

That brought him short. "Then most likely, ma'am, unless some renegade makes a mistake, you'll probably be left alone."

"We appreciate the information, Captain," Gus said. "And any protection we may need in the future."

The captain touched his fingers to his cap, and led the soldiers in the direction the Paiutes had headed.

Then he stopped. Turned in his saddle and looked at them again. "If you don't mind my asking," he said. "What's with the bear?"

"Oh," Lily said. "That's Auggy the bear. We killed him and have been carrying him on his hind legs like that on the back of our wagon since Colorado. He'll be on our front porch next time you ride through. The Indians seem to think he's good medicine."

"Doesn't seem to have been good medicine for Auggy. How's it worked for you?"

"So far, Captain," Lincoln said. "So good."

21

September 23, 1865

Gus picked Lily up in his arms, twirled her around, and carried her up on to the porch, past Auggy the bear, and into their first home. She kissed him to applause from Lincoln and Nick.

She grinned. Took off Gus's hat and kissed him hard.

"Not in front of the boys," Gus said.

"Nick, let's go finish the bunkhouse," Lincoln said, slapping Nick on the back as he headed out on to the porch.

"I thought we finished it the other day, Lincoln."

"Hush boy, there's always more work to do. You wanted to be a rancher. Don't count on getting to spend much time dancing or watching others dance. And grab John and close that door behind you on your way out there."

Lily lay back in the bed, looking out the window.

"You can still wear me out, Gus. Spending all day furnishing houses and building bunkhouses doesn't seem to wear you out as much as poker used to."

He rolled over to her. "You think we learned enough that we can get cattle for the ranch starting in the spring, Lil?"

"There'll always be more to learn. How hard can it be, you see some of these idiots doing it?"

"I'm worried about you keeping interested once you start having more babies, Lil."

She looked at him. "How'd you know?"

He shrugged. "Just a hunch. You've been less help in the mornings. Just like with John. Hell, I figure you're gonna want to be having enough kids around to take care of the whole ranch once we get it going."

"We'll have all the help we need. We've got the brains and Auggy the bear has the money to make this a great ranch. Guys headed out this way to be ranch hands need only one thing, and we've got plenty of that."

"Most'll just be drifters, Lil."

"Maybe. But I bet we find some who'll stay to help us build something. Not everybody wants to own their own place. Some'll want to save money for their own place, but we'll be okay with drifters too." She looked out the window down at Lincoln and Nick working over on the bunkhouse. "It's not me, honey, I'm worried about. It's you we gotta keep interested. You're sure not gonna want to take care of babies, and I'm not so sure about cattle either."

"All I care about taking care of is you and what you want me to care for. Let's build our ranch and our family. I'll be there when you need me."

Through the window she noticed Lincoln pointing out something in the sky to Nick. Watched the two of them gazing at a large bird, gliding free out over the river. She thought about Gus now being tied down by a family and some cows. And then about that bird, high in the sky, tied down only by the currents in the autumn Oregon air. And then, surprised, she found herself thinking again about John Arnold.

She'd last seen him that fateful day in Navajo country when he and Cummings were with Carson's Army. He was probably back East now that the war was over. With his wife and kids in Baltimore. Maybe managing a store somewhere back there. She smiled to herself. It was hard to think of John Arnold being happy not soldiering. And certainly she couldn't see him being happy back East.

Lily fell asleep thinking about her own John, baby John. And the fact that there was no point in dwelling on the past. And certainly not on John Arnold.

22

December 25, 1865

"Look at the baby grab that Christmas tree," Nick said.

"First Christmas for both babies," Lily said.

"They'll both remember it the same," Lincoln said.

"I don't know," Lily said. "John's nine months old now. Seems pretty alert to what's going on. He may remember."

"He might remember eating the tree decorations. I'd guess that'd be about it," Gus said.

Nick walked over and took the angel out of John's mouth.

"So far, the other ranchers have been right," Gus said. "Once winter comes, the Indians up and disappear. Like hibernating bears."

"Leaves you with nothin' to do, Gus," Lincoln said. "No Indians for you and the other volunteer ranchers to chase. You might have to help me 'n Nick build Lily her fort."

"Fort?" Nick said.

Lily told Nick about Fort Wicked.

"It saved us from hundreds of Cheyenne. I hope we don't need it here, but I'll feel better about the babies."

"How big is our fort going to be?" Nick asked.

"I was thinking about putting the adobe walls about thirty yards from the house," Lincoln said. "Then around the bunkhouse and stables. We could put towers on each corner and a large gate on the north end, toward the woods. Pretty much Oregon's Fort Wicked."

"You really think we need it?" Nick asked.

"The idea," Lincoln replied, "is to build it so we *won't* need it."

"Seems like a huge waste of time," Gus said. "The Indians have left us alone since August."

"There's not much else to do, Gus." Lincoln replied. "We won't be getting the cattle and the other hired hands until March or April at Fort Boise. It'll take us a good two months to build the fort and furnish the bunkhouse so we can be ready for the cattle."

"Worst that happens, honey," Lily said, "is that we spend the winter working on protecting the ranch and the children instead of sitting around doing nothing."

Gus didn't respond. Just shrugged and picked John up so he could see the top of the tree again.

"What are you going to call our fort?" Nick asked.

"I'll let Lincoln name it when it's finished," Lily said. "See who did the most work."

"Can we name it Fort O'Reilly?" Nick asked. "For my ma and pa. This is my first Christmas without them."

"You do the amount of work I'm expecting from you, young man," Lincoln said. "And that's exactly the name I'd been thinking about."

23

February 16, 1866

Two neighboring ranchers came charging through the gate in the snow, and pulled up at the house, snow flying in every direction from the sliding horses.

Nick and Gus came out on to the porch.

"Problem?" Gus asked.

"Indians. Snakes. They've attacked Ben Childress's place upriver, set his outbuildings on fire. Ben's cowboys are holding them off, but they need help."

At the sound of the fuss, Lincoln had come out of the bunkhouse.

"Lincoln," Gus said. "Grab us three horses. Nick, grab your rifle and revolvers. Let's go."

After they had raced along the west side of the river for four miles, ten Paiutes rounded the bend heading straight for them, apparently racing away from the ranch they had attacked.

The five men opened fire on the surprised Indians. Three dismounted, jumped into some willows, and started returning fire. One shot Nick's horse out from under him, and Nick wound up buried in snow, sliding down the river bank.

The four mounted ranchers continued firing at the Indians, now concealed in the willows along the river bank.

Just then, a dozen soldiers came galloping up to the fire fight, having been chasing the Indians from the ranch.

At the sight of the soldiers, the mounted Paiutes dashed across the river and up the eastern bank under heavy fire.

"Stay with Nick." Gus said to Lincoln. "Keep the Snakes in the willows pinned down. I'm going with the soldiers across the river."

Lincoln and Nick, along with two soldiers who had remained behind, kept a steady fire into the willows. It turned out that there had been more in there than just the three.

The shooting and sporadic returning arrow shots continued for an hour. As it was turning dark, Gus, the soldiers, and the ranchers who had chased the Indians returned from the other side of the river.

"Nick, you okay?" Gus asked.

"Sure, Gus. My horse is dead, but I'm okay."

"I think we hit a couple," Lincoln said. "But it's sure hard to tell."

The soldiers approached the willows, some on foot, some still mounted. One Indian shot a soldier's horse out from under him. Another Indian stood up, drew his bow, and Nick shot him in the leg. But not before he shot an arrow into a sergeant's chest, killing him. Gus killed the Indian from point blank range.

The close-in fighting continued until two hours after dark, when the Indians crept away across the river.

"Is that all of them?" Lincoln asked the soldier in charge.

"Yes. We had cleared all of them from the ranch. They might lob a few shots into our campfire tonight, but I think they'll move on. We've been chasing marauding bands for a month."

"They killing ranchers?" Gus asked.

"No. They're only hungry. They're taking livestock where they can get it. Sometimes they attack the stage stations to get arms."

"And you can't stop them?"

"All we can do is chase after them whenever we get a complaint. Best we can do."

Nick grabbed one of the captured Indian ponies and joined Gus and Lincoln for the freezing ride back to the ranch.

Lily was asleep by the fire.

"Good thing we aren't Paiutes," Gus said as she opened her eyes at his kiss.

"I hear bare feet or moccasins on my porch, we'll shortly have fewer Indians to worry about," she said. "I hear your thundering boots out there and I can get a few seconds more sleep before I have to get up."

"I shoulda asked," Lincoln said. "But should one of us have stayed back here with you?"

Lily snorted. "I'm a better shot than any of you. Your question should be, 'Should you have taken me with you?'"

"Let's hold off on the galloping and shooting at Indians while your six months pregnant with my baby," Gus said.

She made a face at him. "I can outride you, too. And I'm sure going to have to ride with you to pick up our herd and hire our cowboys at Fort Boise next month."

Gus ignored that and filled her in on what had happened upriver.

She shook her head. "In New Mexico we were fighting all manner of people. Texans, Mexicans, barroom brawlers, U.S. Marshals, bank robbers, card cheaters. Ever since, all it's been is Indians."

"Give it time, Lil," Lincoln said. "There's plenty of time for all manner of people out here to come looking to take what you got. Don't be impatient. They'll show up soon enough."

"Maybe so, but ever since New Mexico, all it's been is Indians. All manner of Indians. I'll feel better when you boys get that gate finished."

24

May 26, 1866

Gus and Lincoln looked up at a column of soldiers coming down the path. Lily came out on to the porch and watched as they came through the gate. The major dismounted.

"What's Fort O'Reilly?" he asked. "I thought this was the L Bar S Ranch."

"That's the name of the ranch. We named the compound after Nick's family." She gestured toward Nick, watching from the corral.

"You all had any Indian trouble?"

"Quite a bit in February, as you certainly know," Gus replied. "Several ranches raided all over the state, major. But not this ranch. Not since last fall. We know of the recent outbreaks, but nothing here. Anything we need to know?"

"Nothing unusual. They steal a few horses at one ranch, a few cattle at another. Then they disappear. Same as has been going on all along. There does seem to be an unusually large band of Paiutes attacking stations around here and into Idaho."

"And you can't follow the trail of a large band of Indians herding stolen livestock, Major?" Lily said.

Several of the soldiers looked up at her.

"We're doing our job the best we can, ma'am. We're undermanned and getting precious little help from the ranchers. It seems we're doing good enough that you're able to keep your ranch going, though."

"I think the existence of Fort O'Reilly might have helped, Major. But we do appreciate your service," Lily said. "We surely do."

He nodded in acknowledgment, but didn't look pleased.

"But there are people out here who think that a few horses here and a few cattle there should most definitely be unusual, to use your terms, major. This isn't the Arizona or Dakota Territory, sir. This is the State of Oregon."

"I read the papers, too, ma'am. We know the citizens think we're failing. We chase every savage that breaks the law. I repeat, we're doing the best we can. You ranchers know the area better than we do. We need more volunteer scouts."

"Well, sir, it may be your best, but it's not working. I'll grant you that I don't know your job, but maybe you should change your tactics."

"Like I said, I'd like to do precisely that. And I'd like to start by getting more volunteer scouts."

"The ranchers have ranches to build and run," she said. "You've got your jobs and they have theirs."

"We came here to find out if anybody has seen the Paiutes, and you haven't. Thank you for your time."

"Major," Gus said, turning his back to Lily. "I have military experience and I know the area. I'd be happy to help you."

The major looked up at Lily, then turned to Gus. "Your wife okay with you leaving here?"

"I don't think that's any of your business, major. But since you asked, yes, we've discussed it."

"What's your military experience?"

"I fought with the Union regulars and New Mexico and Colorado Volunteers in New Mexico against the Texans in sixty-two."

"And how well do you know this area?"

"Well enough to help you. We chased some of the Paiutes around the Owyhee and the Malheur when they raided in February. And I've hunted the whole area over the past year," he lied.

"When can you join up, then?"

"Now that, actually, I *will* need to discuss with Lily."

The major looked back and forth between Lily and Gus. "Sorry, but I didn't get your name."

"Smoot. Gus Smoot."

25

June 25, 1866

First days of summer, Lily thought. Not exactly like New Mexico. More like Colorado.

They had marveled all winter at the snow. Days of it. At times three or four feet, with temperatures in the teens for days at a time. And then days of rain, wondering if they'd ever again see the sun.

"You miss South Carolina any?" Lily had asked Lincoln one day as they dug hay out of the snowbanks for the livestock.

He had playfully tossed a shovel of snow at her. "Don't think anything as trivial as a little weather could make me miss South Carolina, Lily."

They had worried at how cattle would survive these winters, but had been assured by the ranchers in the area that the combination of frequent thaws, high grass, and hay distribution worked just fine. They had spent a good deal of the winter visiting their neighbors, learning the nuances of local ranching that differed from what Iliff had taught them in Colorado. It quickly became apparent that both Lincoln and Nick had an affinity for the ranching business, a business that left Gus at best disinterested.

Today, on a beautiful Oregon summer afternoon, with the temperature in the 70s, Lincoln and Lily looked out over the bulk of the herd of fifty cattle they had purchased for six hundred dollars from the cattle drive at Fort Boise. Two of the three cowboys they had hired were out looking for the strays that had run off in the previous evening's storm.

"Nick sure picked up branding quick," Lincoln said. "I think we found us a future ranch foreman."

"That's Gus's job, Lincoln."

Lincoln looked up. Too quickly.

"You having problems with Gus, Lincoln?" Lily said.

"No, ma'am." He looked her in the eye. "I don't think Gus has his heart in the working end of a ranch, Lily." He looked over at Nick feeding the horses. Gus's horse was gone. "Is he up in the house with the babies, or is he gone again?"

"Elly is with John and Antelope, Lincoln."

Antelope Thunder Smoot had been born May 6th. When they had bought the cattle and hired the cowboys at Fort Boise, Lily had hired fourteen year old Elly Burgess to watch over the children. Elly's father had been killed by the Snakes and her mother couldn't afford to raise all the children by herself. She had agreed to let Elly work for the Smoots in exchange for a year's advance pay. The mother and Lily had both agreed to the lie that the pay would be handed over to Elly if she came back home.

"Then where's Gus?" Lincoln asked. "This being his thirtieth birthday and all."

"He went on up to the Malheur River to help with the Indians," she replied. "We agreed that with his military experience, he needs to be protecting the ranch more than runnin' it."

"And there's his known love of fighting," Lincoln said.

Lily looked at Lincoln purposefully now. Freezing him with her gaze while trying to decide how to play this. She couldn't imagine building the ranch without Lincoln. Nick looked up to him like he was his father. Any cowboy who had a problem working for a colored foreman simply wasn't hired. There was nothing Lincoln wouldn't do for her and he was extremely good at all ranching activities. There were few, if any, secrets between the two of them.

"And poker," she said. "We both know there's always a poker game at the camp up at the Malheur."

"I'll grant you that, Lily. Gus is good at poker. Good idea to keep his hands clean, though."

One of the two cowboys out searching for the cattle came racing toward them as fast as he could drive his horse. He pulled up hard.

"Childress and two of his cowboys just tried to cut out ten of our cows," he said.

"Where is he now?"

"Headed this way. We shot his foreman. He's real mad."

Lily and the three cowboys sat on the porch as they watched Childress gallop up, white hair and moustache flaring in the wind.

"Where's Smoot?"

"That'd be me, Ben," Lily said.

"I want Gus."

"Tell that to the Army. They're out chasing Paiutes together."

"One of your cowboys just shot my foreman."

"Kill him?"

"No. That's a pretty impertinent response lady."

"Why'd he shoot him?"

"I have no idea. We were just minding our own business out on the range. Trying to see who's cattle we'd run across."

"Normally, you can tell by looking at one of their butts, Ben."

"You're too new here to be telling me the cattle business, Miss Smoot."

"Mrs. Smoot."

The two glared at each other.

"Your boys can tell our cattle from yours without separating ten of them out and herding 'em to your campfire." Lincoln said.

"I don't need any ranching advice from a nigger either, boy."

"You're not going to be civil, Ben," Lily said. "You can just turn around and get off my property."

Childress looked back and forth at the two of them.

"You're new here, *Miss* Smoot. You don't find a way to get along with your neighbors, it might be a short stay for all of you."

"Rustling's a hanging offense, Ben," she said. "I recommend we respect each other's property going forward. If your foreman's still alive, I wish him God speed in his recovery."

"We gonna continue to have problems with Childress?" Lily asked Lincoln at dinner.

"I don't think so. In my experience once you stand up to a bully, they've found out what they want. Unless they own you."

"And Childress found out what he wanted?"

"Sure. He would have preferred to have your cattle, but he'll settle for the information. He got it cheap enough. One wounded foreman."

As Elly cleared the table, Lily asked, "You okay on how Childress treats you, Lincoln?"

"Today's not my first day as a Negro, Lily. The day all white men treat Negroes with respect is too far in the future for me to think much about. I had a lot of practice being patient back when I didn't have any choices. I'm good at it now that I've got them."

He stood up to head to the bunkhouse. "My new job is to not be okay when people don't treat *you* right, Lily."

And he headed out into the night.

Lily sat staring into the fire for hours. Thinking about John and Antelope Thunder and the men in her life. Her, now standing up to rustlers. Gus off fighting Indians. And Lincoln building her ranch. This is going to work out just fine.

Not how I planned it, she thought as she fell asleep on the couch, but just fine.

26

October 15, 1866

"Gus back yet, Lily?" Lincoln asked.

Lily and Nick had ridden out to the open range to join Lincoln in preparing the cattle for the coming winter.

"No, I don't expect him for another week or two. He said the soldiers were going to head back to Fort Boise before the end of the month. Nobody expects the Snakes to bother the ranchers or the stage coaches in the winter."

She rode over to Lincoln to hear him better over the wind. "How does the herd look to you?"

"Pretty near perfect. They stay together mostly. Very few needed to be rounded up." He nodded to the three cowboys on the other side of the herd. "The boys say this is the easiest job they've ever had."

"They say anything about willing to take a pay cut?"

"Nope." He grinned at her. "Not yet, anyway."

She looked out over the herd and waited for Nick to catch up. "How many you figure having to break out and bring into Fort O'Reilly for the winter?"

"We all agree that most look healthy enough to last through the toughest winter. Less than ten. Maybe only five or so."

He whistled at the cowboys. Pointed to a straggler that had wandered into the edge of the woods.

"That's one of the runts over there. It got pretty close to freezing last night and she didn't look too steady on her feet."

"Have you decided how much hay we need out here?"

"We'll bring two wagon loads early next month and put them in sheds over there in the woods. Unless this is a much worse winter than the ranchers tell us they've experienced the last dozen years or so, that should last them well into February. We won't even put it out for them until December. They should do well on their own unless the weather gets too bad."

"Who comes out here to put the hay out?" Nick asked.

"That's always a job for the newest cowboys," Lincoln replied, hiding the humor in his eyes from Nick. "That's the best experience you can get. Spending a week out in the snow and ice, gathering and feeding the herd. Taking care of the sick ones."

Pulling his brown cowboy hat over his eyes to shield them from the cold wind, Nick said, "That sure makes me feel good about all the time I put in this summer." He rode toward the three cowboys, looked over his shoulder, and said, "It'll be good for Gus to get that experience. At least he won't have to worry about any of our cows shooting arrows at him."

Lincoln watched him go. Turned to Lily, the pride clear in his eyes. "That boy sure is a fast learner. He already outrides, outshoots, and out sasses all but the best."

27

December 11, 1866

Colonel George Crook, thirty-eight years old, six feet tall and thin, with greying hair and a full black beard, arrived at Fort Boise accompanied by his second in command, Major John Arnold. They had sailed from New York to San Francisco, and then traveled northeast for ten days by rail and stage. Crook had served in the Northwest District before the War, and now had been ordered back to solve the Indian problem and the general state of lawlessness that existed in Oregon and the Nevada, Idaho, and Washington Territories.

Crook was characteristically dressed almost like a civilian, with his heavy fur coat covering his uniform and his Burnside, almost pork pie hat worn at a jaunty angle.

Arnold, the same size and build as Crook, was more than a decade older and looked it. His hair and beard were nearly white, and, in sharp contrast to his commander, he was in full military uniform.

"Did you say that vigilantes have lynched over sixty men this year?" Crook asked the briefing officer.

"Yes, sir."

"What was the Army doing about it?"

"The local citizenry is, to say the least, sir, unhappy with our efforts here. If it's not Indian thievery and murders, then it's local whites taking advantage of the general lawlessness."

"You didn't answer my question," Arnold said. "How are you dealing with the white lawbreakers?"

"We don't have the manpower for that and the local sheriffs seem either unable to stop them, or to be crooked themselves."

"And the Indians?"

"We chase them whenever there's a complaint from a rancher," the officer replied.

"Sounds like the state of siege they sent us to end," Crook said. He turned to John Arnold. "Major Arnold."

"Yes, General," Arnold said, showing the respect many showed for the brevetted Civil War officers who had unhappily accepted demotions after the war.

"I was fighting Indians here before the war. There's no point in waiting around for them to start things. Starting immediately, I want you to mobilize the senior officers here and throughout the district. We are going to relentlessly take this fight to the Indians. Starting now."

"Yes, sir."

"I want you to head up a search throughout the district for every Indian who will agree to serve with us as a scout against the Snakes. And I want all the ranchers and town settlers approached to be scouts and volunteers in both wars."

"Both wars, sir?" Arnold asked.

"Yes, Major. We start attacking the Indian villages with the Army and all the volunteers now. At the same time I want to scour the district for information on lawless whites, and on law abiding settlers willing to step up and be sheriffs and marshals. And I want all Army units under orders to support those citizens who come forward."

"Starting today?" the briefing officer asked.

"Starting right now, Captain," Crook said. "I have no interest in spending one unnecessary minute in this country. Nothing here but rain, snow, and frozen rivers."

"And," Arnold said, "thieving settlers and hostile Indians."

"At least," Crook said, "we can do something about those."

28

December 26, 1866

Crook's forces had marched for days on slim rations during heavy snow-storms and through feet of snow. His Indian scouts had led him from Fort Boise along the Boise, then Snake, and now Owyhee Rivers, routing the Indians in the hostile rancherias wherever they found them.

Now at daylight, two of his Indian scouts assured him there was a large Paiute village just ahead.

"Arnold," Crook said.

"Yes, sir."

"Once we're just within sight of the village, attack."

"The men are exhausted, cold, and hungry, sir."

"Me too, Major." He slapped his hat against his thigh and knocked off the snow. "What's your point?"

Even though they outnumbered the cavalry, the Indians coming out of the village, due both to the surprise and to their inferior firepower, were routed. Thirty were killed by the charging soldiers as they tried to turn and flee back to the village. Once back in the village, the remaining Indians took up defensive positions in the rocks and trees.

As the battle wound down over the next several hours, it became clear that the Paiutes couldn't drive off the soldiers. They eventually retreated upriver, being forced to leave all their livestock behind.

"There you have it, Major," Crook said, smiling through the crusted snow and ice covering his beard and mustache, pork pie hat practically invisible under inches of snow and ice. "All problems solved. Food and firewood for your tired, hungry, and cold men."

Arnold just shook his head. Crook had said this with all his usual cheerful congeniality. As if nothing in the world could be greater than this moment. Arnold then watched as, characteristically, Crook headed up the nearby hill to be by himself. He would probably bring back a deer or mountain goat for the men.

Arnold had never seen a more complicated man. Both happy and taciturn, both demanding and loved, and a great listener who wanted nothing more than to just be left alone.

Two days later they were heading down the Owyhee. At each ranch either Crook or Arnold checked in, looking for potential volunteers or scouts, news of the whereabouts of more hostile Indians, and spreading the word that they were looking for peacekeepers among the whites.

At the Smoot ranch, Arnold peeled off and approached the large Negro loading hay onto a wagon. Crook stayed riding along the edge of the woods leading the rest of the troops downriver.

Arnold stopped at a respectful distance and touched the bill of his cap when the Negro looked up.

"You the rancher here?" Arnold asked.

"No, sir," Lincoln replied. "He's out checking on strays with one of the other cowboys."

"Then who are you?"

"Name's Lincoln, Joe Lincoln. This here's Nick O'Reilly. We work the ranch."

"This fort named after you, kid?" Arnold asked.

"No, sir. After my Mom and Dad. They were killed by Shoshones on the way out here from Ireland."

"Sorry to hear that." He tipped his cap. Looked around, taking in the fort. "We just routed a Paiute village two days upriver. I'm guessing Fort O'Reilly keeps you folks pretty secure. Do you know of any other hostiles in these parts?"

"No sir. We haven't had any Indian problems for some time. Mostly they stay in their villages in the winter."

"Any trouble with any of the settlers? We heard there were some lynchings earlier this year in the state."

Lincoln looked carefully at the officer. He didn't see any indication that he was threatening him or suggesting any trouble.

"No, sir," Lincoln said. "Not here. We hear that's mostly been a problem in some of the towns near the forts. Mostly around here on the river there are just ranchers minding their own business." He looked over at Nick, then up at Arnold. "Mostly we're hoping you all will clear up the Indian problem so we can just run our cattle in peace."

"Well, Mr. Lincoln. That's actually the plan."

As he turned his horse and started to follow back after his troops, he stopped. Turned a full circle in the snow and took a long look at Auggy the bear. Then he looked back at Lincoln. But after a pause he didn't say anything. Just rode off back toward the troops disappearing down the trail.

Lincoln hadn't seen any need to wake Lily up at the house to talk to the soldier. He'd tell her at dinner that the Army had been by and checked in on them. Too late, he realized he hadn't asked the officer his name. He wondered if it might have been the General Crook everybody was counting on.

Then he turned and returned to helping Nick get the hay onto the wagon.

29

January 7, 1867

Gus had left the ranch five days before. Lily had reluctantly agreed there was nothing more important during the winter at the ranch for him to do than rejoining the soldiers. And he had convinced her that this General Crook sounded like a big improvement over the major he had replaced.

As she kissed him goodbye under the Fort O'Reilly sign, she had said,

"Gus. Please be careful. Crook might have some soldiers with him who might recognize you. You're playing a dangerous game. We need you back here at the ranch in the spring. And John and Antelope need you forever."

"Not you?" he asked, leaning down out of the saddle and trying to run his hand up her thigh to her bottom. "You don't need me forever?"

She slapped his hand away and kissed him again. "Just be careful, Gus. We need you here."

"Thanks, mom."

He had doffed his cowboy hat toward the ranch house and headed west toward Crook's Army.

He could see Crook's camp on the east bank of the Donner and Blitzen Creek. Five minutes later he was nudging his horse into the camp. His horse, smelling the other horses and the hay, needed no encouragement.

"Identify yourself," a sentry said, rifle across his chest.

"Gus Smoot. Of the L Bar S Ranch over on the Owyhee. I'm here to volunteer as a scout for General Crook."

The soldier pointed to a Sibley tent, toward the back of the camp.

"That's him in front of his tent, there. But it'd be best if you put your horse up with the others first, and approach him on foot."

"Crook's not too friendly?"

"Oh, he's friendly enough. If you do your job. But he doesn't much like surprises. And he has a preference for calling meetings, rather than having them sprung on him."

"Would it be better if you introduced me, private?"

"Like I said, Smoot, he's friendly when you do your job. My job right now is keeping watch. He'll be more friendly with me if I stay here and stand my watch."

And the soldier turned his back on Gus and looked out toward the distant forest.

Smoot walked his horse over to the herd as he had been instructed, opened the gate, led him into the corral, and patted his nose before releasing him. Then he walked over to a tent that was clearly home to a poker game. He looked in for a while, the players taking no notice of him, and then walked over to Crook.

Crook looked up as he approached.

"General," Smoot said.

"Yes?"

"I own a ranch over on the Owyhee. Run some cattle. I wanted to volunteer my scouting services for your army."

"What are your qualifications? What did you say your name was?"

"Smoot, sir. Gus Smoot. I fought in sixty-two against the Texans in New Mexico. And some against the Navajo. I've hunted this area since we settled here, so I know it pretty well. I helped your predecessor against the Snakes."

"How'd you feel about that experience?"

"I was hoping you'd be more effective, sir."

Crook laughed at that.

"How are you with Indian languages, Smoot?"

"I seem to have an affinity for them, sir. I'm pretty fluent with Paiute."

"You fight against the Apaches?"

"No, sir. Never had the pleasure. My wife was pretty friendly with Cochise, though."

That elicited another laugh.

"I'd like to meet your wife, Smoot. I have yet to meet a lady who's friendly with Chiricahuas. And certainly not with Cochise. How do you get along with Modocs?"

"Modocs?"

"We have several Modoc scouts who have come up from California to help against the Snakes. It would be easiest if you could work together with them."

"I speak passable Modoc. I've never had a problem getting along with any Indian that was working my side of the fence, sir."

"If you fought for the Union in New Mexico, then you know my number two."

Smoot felt his stomach tighten. Lily's warning ringing in his head. "Who would that be, General?"

"Major Arnold. John Arnold. He reported to Ed Canby and Kit Carson."

"I knew *of* him, certainly. But I never gave those three any occasion to make my acquaintance. I was just a common soldier. Working to stay alive at Valverde."

Crook looked up him. Didn't say anything.

"Is Arnold here now?" Gus asked.

"No. He took half our forces east to the Owyhee a couple of days ago. Toward your ranch, actually, Smoot. You'll meet him soon enough. We'll be rejoining the two forces after we're both done attacking the Snake villages up and down the state."

Perfect, Gus thought to himself. John'll hardly be able to miss the Smoot ranch marching up and down the Owyhee. It was Lily then, not him, who was going to have to careful. Fortunate for them, actually.

She'd be much better at that than he would be.

30

January 25, 1867

Crook was putting relentless pressure on the Snakes. Led by his two Modoc scouts and Smoot, he was routing the Snakes along the Malheur River. He had ordered Arnold to take his own companies south through Idaho, into Nevada, and now back down the Owyhee. They were each relying on their scouts to alert them if they needed to re-join forces before their plan to meet back up at Fort Boise.

On this particular day, Arnold's scouts woke him at dawn. They had found tracks of a sizeable band of Paiutes headed straight toward the Owyhee. Arnold's forces broke camp and followed the scouts, skirting the three to four foot snowdrifts wherever possible. After five hours of hard riding in sub-zero temperatures, the scouts showed him the Snakes descending the steep walls toward the river, with a village directly below on the other bank.

The soldiers laid down a fusillade all the way down to the river bank. Once down, they attacked the village and chased the Indians into a narrow canyon off the river. His scouts said it was impenetrable without great losses and that the Indians were covering for their villagers' escape out the back end of the canyon.

Arnold looked at his freezing, exhausted men, stamping their feet to keep warm. Then looked back up the creek. They had routed the Indians. Destroyed their camp. And, at least so far, with no losses.

He made up his mind. They backed out of the canyon, left the destroyed camp, and headed downriver to rest and regroup.

31

January 28, 1867

After resting the troops the rest of that night and the next day, Arnold marched them further down the river for two days. From this spot, he would launch the next series of attacks on the hostile Paiutes starting the next morning.

But first, it was time to try and find Lily Smoot. He knew from one of his scouts that, by coincidence, they had camped near the Smoot Ranch. The scout had given him directions to the ranch. He could go on ahead and then rejoin the troops on their northward march the next day. The scout had called it the L Bar S Ranch. Arnold had smiled at that. If there was any doubt it was the right ranch, L Bar S cinched it. What else would she call her dream ranch in the Washington Territory?

He wasn't sure what he was expecting to happen when Lily Smoot saw him ride up after all this time. He had no idea how this would go. Or even if Lily would be there. But there was no way he was going to get this close and let the opportunity pass by.

He had been riding for four hours. "Cursed weather," he said out loud. There were two or three feet of snow whenever you left the trees, and now it was unseasonably warm, so it had turned to slush and melted snow flowing down each incline. The going was treacherous. His two horses kept slipping and sliding in the mess.

What do ranchers do in weather like this, he wondered? Sit at the hearth by the fire and listen to cowboys lie about the beautiful weather in Texas?

As he reached the clearing and saw the open gate and the sign of Fort O'Reilly under the clear blue sky, he realized this was one of the ranches he'd stopped at during the Christmas march. The one with the big Negro cowboy and the bear on the porch.

He stopped to take it in. So this was where Lily had wound up. It'd now been three and a half years since he'd lectured her about hanging out with the whores in Navajo country. More to the point, it had been three and a half years since Lily had told him he should confine himself to being her father figure and not her father. He shook his head and chuckled out loud.

And then he saw her. She was on the other side of the corral, talking to the black cowboy and what looked like two teenagers, a boy and a girl. The girl was holding a baby and scolding a two year old boy, who kept running among the horses and chasing them into the barn.

He held his breath. Even from this distance he could tell Lily Smoot had become more beautiful. Maybe something to do with being free and running her own life. Realizing her dream. What'd she be now? A little more than twenty-five?

Then the big Negro saw him. The black cowboy was squinting into the setting sun. He reacted by reaching for his rifle and signaling the teenage boy and Lily to do the same. Arnold became aware that his heavy fur coat covered his uniform. Lily and the others wouldn't know him as military. Wouldn't realize he was harmless.

Fifteen miles to their west, George Crook listened to his scouts describe a large Paiute village near Steen's Mountain.

"Smoot, what do you think?" Crook asked.

"I know that village, General. In the summer and fall, we wouldn't be able to get near it. Too well protected. But the Modocs are right. They won't be ready for us at dawn in this weather."

"How far is it?"

"A half day's ride to the west. We can be there easily by midnight," Smoot replied.

"Okay, Gus. Tell the officers to organize back here as quickly as they can. We'll march all night and attack at dawn."

Lily looked toward the woods where Lincoln was pointing. She and Nick grabbed their rifles while looking into the sunset at the stranger and his trailing packhorse.

"Elly, take the children into the house," Lily said. "Now." She pointed to the porch. "Grab your pistol on the way in."

Elly had taken to keeping her pistol in a makeshift holster she had attached to Auggy the bear's left thigh whenever she left the porch.

"Nick, get those other boys from out of the bunkhouse." She put up her left hand to block the glare. The man waved a signal of friendship. Something about that wave reached deep into her memory. To Apache Pass.

"No, wait a minute," she said.

She looked hard. The man unbuttoned his coat and took off his hat to wave. Prodded his horse toward them. If the beard hadn't been so white, she would've thought it was John Arnold.

"That's the officer I told you came by," Lincoln said. "Might be General Crook."

Lily looked carefully at the oncoming rider. "No, Lincoln, that's not Crook."

I'll be damned, she said to herself. John Arnold. How on earth…

Arnold rode slowly toward the trio. He could see them talking. Lily laughing.

He hadn't planned this. In fact, he had no idea what he was going to say. Or, in fact, what he was even doing here. Frankly, he never thought this moment would come. It had only been imagined. And in his imagination, there had been no words.

He stopped fifty feet short. Took his hat off.

Nick and Lincoln looked at Lily.

Lily looked at Arnold, an expression of wonder on her face. Arnold could now see she had not imagined this moment at all.

"Hello, Miss Smoot."

"Hello John Arnold." She turned quickly away and walked toward the barn so nobody could see her tears. "Nick, tell Elly we'll be having a guest for dinner."

Gus Smoot and the two Modoc scouts were already several miles ahead of Crook's troops. They had nearly run into a Paiute hunting party they had been following, but the noise from the flowing slush and the crackling of branches snapping under the weight of snow collections falling from branch to branch had saved them.

Gus and the two scouts separated to reduce the chance of discovery by the hunting party.

Arnold and Lily sat at the table. Alone. Neither had any idea what to say. How to start.

"John Arnold," Lily finally said. "How'd you find me? What are you doing here?"

"Uncle Sam sent me, and General Crook brought me. As I'm sure you and all the other ranchers out here know, we're here to end the war with the Snakes and try to bring some order to Oregon and the Territories."

There was nothing for her to say in response to his sarcasm, so she waited for him to continue.

"Finding you? I figured it'd never happen. But as long as I was in the Washington Territory, or what used to be the Washington Territory anyway, I thought I'd ask. A sutler at Fort Boise said there had been a Smoot party headed to Oregon about a year and a half ago. I asked one of our Modoc scouts if there was a Smoot ranch and he told me where it was."

He spread out his hands and smiled down at her. "And here I am. Actually I was here last Christmas, but didn't ask Lincoln the name of the rancher. He told me he was out looking for strays, but didn't mention his name. What..."

At that moment there was a sound of yelling as Elly came into the room, led by the little boy and carrying the baby.

The little boy jumped into Lily's arms and stared at the white bearded officer sitting across from him.

"And who is this little guy?" Arnold asked. "I'm guessing this girl here is a little young to be his mother."

"Major John Arnold, this is Elly Burgess. She works for us here at the ranch."

"Nice to meet you, Major."

"And," Lily said, "Antelope Thunder Smoot is my daughter. Six weeks old."

"She's a beauty, Lily. Is her father a Cheyenne Indian then?"

She shook her head and laughed.

"Well, I can tell it's not Lincoln."

Lily grew silent, the room suddenly warmer.

"And who is this little guy in your arms, Lily? What's your name, young man?"

One of her two feared unavoidable moments had arrived.

She looked at Arnold and said, softly, under her breath, "John."

The little boy looked up. Arnold just looked confused.

"Yes?" Arnold asked.

"No," Lily laughed, causing the little boy to shriek happily at the sound of his mother's laughter. "I'm not addressing you, John Arnold. I'm introducing you to my son, John."

It was getting dark as Smoot neared where he had agreed to meet the two Modocs. As he skirted a snow bank at the edge of a clearing in the woods, an arrow glanced off his saddle and grazed his cheek. Two others flew harmlessly by his head.

He sped off and lowered himself across his horse's neck away from the assault. He galloped toward where he hoped to find the Modocs.

But they were not there.

Smoot raced on, following their tracks through the snow. Their tracks indicated that they were traveling at a leisurely pace, so it was likely he was the only one being chased.

Leading the Paiutes back to Crook would be a bad idea. But so too would be allowing Crook to march into a trap. No longer hearing his pursuers behind him, Smoot rode up a hill to try to make out the situation in the growing gloom.

Sure enough, the two Modocs were just below him on the other side of the hill, lying in wait for whoever came around the hill, the Paiute hunting party or him. He could see the Paiutes making steady progress toward his hill, following his tracks, but in no hurry. There were four of them, armed with bows and arrows. He couldn't see any rifles. He guessed he had maybe ten minutes.

If Crook was going to surprise the village, these Paiutes would have to be stopped.

"How is your family, John? Your wife and the boys? The boys must be growing up by now." She didn't see any need to tell him that she had seen them in Baltimore when she had been back East with Cummings in November of sixty-two. It wasn't something he ever needed to know.

"They're dead, Lily. They were killed in a great fire in Emmitsburg, on the Pennsylvania, Maryland border in June eighteen sixty-three, about fifty miles from Baltimore. They had gone there after Antietam in hopes of escaping the war."

In the horror of the ensuing silence, she realized that they must have left Baltimore right after she saw them. "Why didn't you tell me when I saw you at Pueblo Colorado, John?"

"I didn't know then, Lily. I didn't know." He put his head in his hands. Then looked up. But into the distance, not at Lily. "They were staying in the main hotel in the town square when the fire hit. Around midnight. Apparently nobody missed them amongst all the residents' tragedies. About two hundred people in the town lost pretty close to everything they had. Damel Wile, the owner of the hotel, thought Beth and the boys had left during the night or the next day, so he didn't have anyone searching for them."

He paused to catch his voice.

"I had stopped hearing from her. But mail during the Navajo campaign was pretty sketchy in general. So I was concerned, but not worried. There was no reason why word of the fire should have ever reached the Territories. Once I got back to Santa Fe, I had Carson and Carleton get the Army to try to find them, but, as you might guess, it was a low priority. Then in July of sixty-four the Rebels took Hagerstown and Frederick and threatened Baltimore and Washington. Carleton gave me official leave and I took a coach and then a train back East.

"When I got to Emmitsburg, Wile's memory of that night was surprisingly clear. Beth had checked in with the boys a week earlier. They had not been seen at all the night of the fire or during the next day. There was no evidence of their bodies or any of their belongings in the rubble, so he had assumed they had fled. Until I talked to him he hadn't thought about them since the morning after. He was a shattered man."

"Is there any chance they survived, John?"

He shook his head. "No. There's no way. I talked to practically everyone in town. A few remembered the woman and the two little boys, but had no memory of ever seeing them after the fire. And I never heard from her again. She would certainly have written to me about the tragedy and where she and the boys had gone next."

Lily had no idea what to do or say.

"No, Lily. My entire family died that night in Emmitsburg. In that fire."

Smoot rode down and then brought the two Modocs back up the hill to confront the Paiutes when they tracked him to the top.

As the four tracking him reached the crest, the Modocs let loose arrows at point blank range, killing the two lead Paiutes. Smoot clubbed the fourth one from behind, but the third Paiute shot an arrow into one of the Modoc's chest just before Smoot clubbed him senseless.

The surviving Modoc scout was enraged at the sight of his dead comrade, and proceeded to mutilate, then scalp all four Snakes.

The two then led the five ponies in the dark to the spot near Steen's Mountain where they had agreed to meet up with Crook.

And there they waited.

"Well, John," Lily said. "You found me. Now what?"

"I have no idea, Lil. I enjoyed our times together back in Santa Fe. And I was worried about you, as you know. But," and here he nodded to the two sleeping children, "I don't think I'm too crazy about being a grandfather figure. I don't think I'm ready for that. And besides, you don't seem like you need any fatherly advice from me any more."

"I'm still struggling to learn the ranching business, John. I can use all the help I can get. What are your plans?"

"Don't really have any. After the war, with my family gone, it just seemed natural to stay in the Army. There was nothing for me back East. And here I am. It's the job I'm best at now. And besides, you already know more about ranching than I ever will."

"That may be. But maybe you'll get tired of the Army. Or too old for riding and shooting all day."

"And that, also, may be. But are you sure Oregon is where you want to be? All this snow? And Crook tells me that once it stops snowing, the rain is even worse. He was less than enthusiastic about coming back out here."

"It's good for the cattle, John. I wasn't looking for a nice place to just sit and do nothing. Just a place where I could have a ranch and a family."

"Why not..."

"Actually, I wanted to start my ranch in the Dakota Territory, north of

Denver City, but the soldiers told me that the Sioux and Cheyenne would make anybody's ranching career a very short one there."

"Interestingly, Lil, we're told that the railroad is going through there later this year, and that there are already plans for several railroad towns north of Denver City. The Army will be moving in to support the towns and the railroad. Somebody named Iliff is already preparing a cow camp near the site of the first major town."

"John Iliff?"

"I have no idea. One of the captains mentioned it over coffee. Frankly, we'd all prefer if the Cheyenne and Sioux were just left alone. At least until the Apaches and the Snakes stop fighting. From what I hear, I want no part of fighting the Sioux and Cheyenne."

"I suppose all the soldiers returning from the war have to have somebody to fight, John."

"I suppose." He gave her a look that matched her cynicism. "With the war over, people are now looking to move west again. And you're right, there are thousands of former officers and soldiers with no better careers in front of them."

An awkward silence settled over the room.

"So, Lil. I suppose you know that Cummings was killed the day you disappeared, right?"

She stared at him. She'd been so focused on how to deal with the potential subjects of Gus and, even riskier, Auggy the bear's name, that she hadn't expected this. Damn, she said to herself, it was such an obvious question.

"Someone in Colorado mentioned that Cummings had been killed by a Navajo," she lied. "But until now, I hadn't realized it was the day I left Pueblo Colorado."

He stared at her for a long time. She didn't turn away.

"Lil, you don't owe me anything."

It wasn't a question, so she didn't respond.

"You know I wouldn't mind if you'd killed him. He meant nothing to me, Lil."

She shrugged.

He continued. "You should probably know he had over five thousand dollars in his saddlebags."

Her eyes widened in surprise. "Really?" she said out loud. Damn, she said to herself. That was stupid.

"It only confirmed Kit's and my suspicions about him and Auggy Damours. But we just couldn't put it together. Kit wanted to send someone out looking for you, but I convinced him that you had only come by that day to say goodbye to some of the other girls and that we could always talk to you when we got back to Santa Fe."

Lily just looked at him, letting him take it wherever he was planning to go with it. He knew she wasn't stupid enough to believe that Kit Carson would think she'd ridden out all that way to say goodbye to some whores. It was obvious he'd prepared for this moment, so she wanted to see where he wanted it to go. His family dead. And now he'd come looking for her.

But he surprised her again. Changed the subject.

"And Antelope Thunder and John Smoot's father, Lily?" Arnold said. "Where is he?"

Her second unavoidable moment had arrived.

"Gus?" she said. "Things are a little slow under four feet of snow in the ranching business, so he offered to scout for General Crook in his Indian campaign."

Lincoln, who had joined them, snorted. "Truth is, Major, Gus isn't too keen on the ranching business. And what little there is to do here in the winter, me 'n the other ranch hands can handle without him."

Lily looked from Lincoln to Arnold and back to Lincoln again. She laughed. "Truth is, John Arnold, everybody on this ranch does their part. And, as you can see from Lincoln's frankness, we're all family. More like partners, really. Lincoln likes ranching and Gus prefers chasing Indians and playing poker around the campfire with soldiers. He actually did some scouting for the incompetents who called themselves an army before you and General Crook arrived."

"It's odd though, Lil. Why do the children have your last name? Why not Gus's?"

Lincoln looked up. Looked puzzled at Arnold. Then back at Lily.

"When we got married, Gus took my name. He never had liked his. Too impossibly foreign sounding."

Arnold frowned at that. Looked at Lily while he appeared to work on it. "I guess I'm surprised I haven't met him is all. Crook and I always meet with all our scouts together. And I sure would've remembered meeting one named Smoot."

"He would be new to you and Crook. Like I said, Gus helped some fighting the Snakes before you and Crook got out here. Some ranchers were chasing off the Indians when the Army wasn't doing their job. He only left here several weeks ago to offer to help Crook."

"That'd explain it, I guess. Crook sent me off to the southeast around then. I guess I'll meet Gus Smoot when we join forces in the next few weeks."

And that, she thought, is going to have to be prevented. But she had no idea how she could now keep Arnold from meeting, or, as it were, re-meeting Gus. Or, as Arnold would immediately realize, Auggy Damours.

Smoot and the Modoc scout led Crook to a view of the village from the edge of the forest two hundred yards directly to its east. It was an hour before daybreak.

"Send men around the village to cover all escape routes," Crook said. "I'll wait back here with ten men in case a second charge is needed. Shoot only the warriors. No women or children."

All moved into position as directed. There was no evidence the Paiutes had any idea they were about to be attacked. The village was dark. And completely silent.

At his signal, the two companies charged through the sage brush-covered plain toward the village. But, against his wishes, Crook's horse charged out ahead of the others, putting Crook in the lead, at danger from both the Indians coming out of their wickiups and the shooting from his own troops firing into the rancheria as they charged in behind him.

Crook and Smoot were able to rein in their overeager horses only after passing completely through to the back of the village. From there, they both managed to turn their horses around and race back into the battle. They now found themselves charging straight into their own soldiers' rifle fire.

Two warriors emerged from their wickiups, one on Crook's left and one coming straight at Smoot.

Smoot shot the one rushing at Crook, but it did not stop his charge.

"Gus," Crook said, pointing now to Smoot's right flank. "Mind yourself."

But Smoot shot again at Crook's assailant and hit him again. Both charging Indians were now loosing a steady stream of arrows at the two on horseback. Crook also shot and hit the one on his left. But he kept on coming, singing his death song.

Meanwhile, the rancheria had turned into a maelstrom. The steady explosions of rifle fire, the din from the thundering horses in the dark, the yelling of the warriors, the wave after wave of arrows, the Indians fleeing from their wickiups as bullets poured in on braves and innocents alike.

Crook's Indian finally went down after taking his sixth shot. Crook whirled and shot at Smoot's Indian.

But too late.

Gus Smoot lost control of his horse as an arrow struck his right shoulder. The Indian kept coming, shooting arrows as Smoot's horse reared. Smoot was hit in the right side by an arrow as he fell from the wounded and terrified horse.

Crook shot at the Paiute as he lunged toward the fallen scout, but missed. Smoot rolled away, came up on one knee, and fired at him almost point blank. The Indian fell back, fired one last arrow, and limped quickly back into a wickiup, pulling the sage back over the entrance.

Smoot walked toward the wickiup, pistol drawn, and reached to pull back the sage covering.

"No, Gus," Crook said. Gus fired a shot into the wickiup. "Smoot. Stop."

But Smoot pulled back the covering and took an arrow directly into his side. He catapulted backward, unconscious from the blow and previous loss of blood. The Indian sprang out of the wickiup and launched himself upon Smoot's prone body. He raised a hatchet over Smoot's head. Crook raced over on his horse and shot the Indian dead, just as he was lowering the hatchet.

Satisfied there was nothing more he could do for his possibly already dead scout, Crook raced back into the fray, where the soldiers were now mopping up the rest of the village. He supervised the capture of twenty-seven Paiutes and the rounding up of thirty-seven ponies.

"How many dead, Captain?" Crook said.

"We count sixty, sir."

"Any women and children?"

"Some, sir." When he saw the look on Crook's face, he said, "It couldn't be helped, sir. There was shooting from the wickiups. Nobody wanted to stick their heads in there in the dark to count noses. You saw what happened to Gus, sir."

"Any of them escape?"

"We think two women and two men, sir. There was a wickiup in the back there we hadn't seen, with a path leading back toward the base of Steen's Mountain."

"And our casualties?"

"Three wounded soldiers, one dead volunteer scout, and one seriously wounded volunteer scout, sir."

"Okay, let's get these prisoners and horses to Camp Smith. Send word to Major Arnold that we're proceeding back to Fort Boise. Tell him to continue taking out all the villages he can along the way, but let's wind up this winter campaign for now."

At precisely that moment, Lily Smoot looked at Major John Arnold up on his horse, setting out to rejoin his men on their march down the Owyhee.

"You accomplish what you wanted here, John?"

"With the Snakes or with you?"

She cocked her head, letting him work on the answer she suspected he wanted to give her.

"I guess both're unfinished business, Lil."

He looked around. Took in the fortress walls, the gate, the ranch house, the stables, Lincoln and Nick already up and working on feeding the livestock. Lincoln looking over, understandably curious.

"When we met six years ago," Arnold said. "I had a life and a family, and all you had was a dream."

She nodded up at him, questioningly.

"Now I think the roles may be reversed," he said.

"My dream's not fulfilled yet, John Arnold. I got a ways still to go."

He turned his horse, then turned back and looked down at her. "I hope I'll see you again, Lil. So I can see how it's going."

"I might go to the Dakota Territory, John." She had no idea where that had come from or why she had said it. "I think the ranching will be better there," trying to make it sound like a sensible thing to have said.

"Crook and I'll be fighting the Snakes out here for a while yet. If you're gone my next time through and I get to Dakota, I'll find you if I can."

"It was good seeing you, John. I am so very sorry to hear about Beth and the boys."

He touched his cap, and turned his horse. "It was good seeing you, too Lil. I'm glad I looked you up."

"You never told me *your* dream, John."

"Still workin' on it. Maybe next time."

She smiled and saluted him good bye.

He rode the twenty yards to the gate. Then stopped under the Fort O'Reilly sign and turned back. Elly and the kids had come out on to the porch and little John Smoot was waving good bye energetically.

"I like your bear," Arnold said to Lily. "Hold on to that bear, Lil. Now that I know whose it is, it'll make you easier to find the next time."

Then he turned, and rode out of sight.

32

April 12, 1867

Colonel George Armstrong Custer sat by the fire near Fort Larned, Kansas with the rest of the officers of the combined U.S. Army cavalry and infantry expeditionary force. They had just finished marching west one hundred and sixty miles from Fort Riley in a week, Custer's first week on the plains.

Since Appomattox, Custer had spent six months commanding Reconstruction units in Louisiana and Texas, and then exploring entering politics in his native Michigan and mining and railroad careers in New York City. His decision to rejoin the U.S. Cavalry had brought him here to Fort Larned.

The expeditionary force now awaited the delayed council with the Indians. Their assignment was to bring peace to the plains. Some of the Plains Indians were living in peace with the settlers, but many were still brutally laying waste to coach stations and attacking wagon trains. The expedition was here to show the warring tribes the need to negotiate final treaties or face a war they would surely lose.

The originally scheduled council with the Southern Cheyenne, Arapaho, and Apaches had been delayed for two days when an eight inch snowstorm struck the night before. Colonel Custer's first western battle turned out to be keeping the men and horses of the Seventh Cavalry alive throughout a blinding snowstorm during the bitter cold night. They had resorted to walking the men and the horses in circles all night to keep them alive.

As promised the Cheyenne Dog Soldiers arrived at the camp after dark. They were armed with Army issue Sharps carbines.

The council this night turned out to be a very short meeting. The Cheyenne came with a very simple message.

The Indians weren't coming tonight after all.

That was enough waiting. At dawn the next day, the entire force started its twenty-one mile march north toward the Indian village.

Custer pointed to the horizon to catch his major's attention.

Major Dennis Martinez, New Mexico Territory, had been with Custer during Reconstruction after the war. Before that he had served with the Union forces against the Texans in 1862. A diminutive, extraordinary horseman, Martinez was now proving himself to be indispensable to Custer. At thirty-two, he liked to joke that he'd been on a horse for thirty-three years. "My mother had to be dragged off a horse at the ranch to give birth," he often said.

"What's that smoke up ahead?" Custer asked.

"Probably burning the grass around the village."

"Why?'

"To keep us at bay. It usually works."

"What if it burns their village down?"

"If there was any risk of that, they wouldn't start the fire, General," adhering to the custom of respecting the rank that Civil War officers had lost after the war.

That night, the chiefs came to tell the officers around the Seventh Cavalry's campfire that they would have to wait yet again. They had again moved their village.

The next morning, the Seventh began its march toward the Indian village, continuing a three day sequence of marches toward non-existent and abandoned villages. At four in the morning on the fourth day, Custer called a halt to the failed exercise.

"We learned two things from this exercise," Custer said to his exhausted officers.

"First, thanks to the Indian agents, the Indians are as well armed as we are?" Martinez said.

"And second," Captain Frederick Benteen said, "you can't meet with Indians that don't want to meet with you?"

"Correct," Custer said. "We'll have to figure out something different."

"Actually three things, General," Martinez said with a grin. "The Cheyenne call you Long Hair."

The next day, April 17th, Custer led the Seventh Cavalry south, back toward the rest of the army. At midday, he saw his first buffalo.

"Captain Benteen."

"Yes, sir."

"Take over. I'm going on my first buffalo hunt."

And off he went. Riding his favorite horse and led by his two greyhounds, Custer took off after the buffalo he had seen grazing over the next hill.

"Is he crazy?" the Colonel said. "There are maybe thousands of hostile Indians within ten or fifty miles of here who'd like nothing better than to kill and eat those two dogs. The man's crazy."

Six hours later, some fifteen miles south of where Custer had left his command, Martinez spotted something on the crest of a hill to the southwest of them. About a mile off.

"You see it?" Martinez said.

"Any idea what it is?" the Colonel asked.

"Could be an Indian," Martinez replied. "Could be a careless Indian scout. Could be a dead buffalo or horse. Hard to tell from here."

As they drew closer, they realized that it was a man sitting on the edge of the hill.

When they were only a quarter of a mile away, they saw the man stand and wave his hat over his head. And they saw Custer's two greyhounds racing toward them.

Three of the soldiers rode over to Custer with a spare horse and sped back with him.

"Afternoon, General," the Colonel said.

"Afternoon, gentlemen. Have any problems in my absence?"

"Where's your horse, George?" the colonel asked.

"He didn't make it."

"Indians?"

"Nope. Buffalo hunt casualty."

They rode on in silence for a while.

"Kill any buffalo, General?" Martinez asked.

"No. I chased one for miles, though. It's great fun, actually. They're faster than you'd think. This one was huge. He finally decided we'd enough fun for one afternoon and he turned on us. They're quicker than you'd think."

He looked around for appreciation. Or questions. Getting none, he went on.

"He was about to completely overwhelm my horse. Coming at him head on. So I shot at him. Unfortunately, my horse chose that very minute to rear away from the imminent collision, and my bullet went right into his brain. He was dead instantly. And I was on the ground not more than five feet from the buffalo."

He looked around vainly for a reaction as they all rode on together.

"They're bigger than you'd think, too."

The officers laughed.

"That's why the Indians stay on their horses when they're hunting them, George," the colonel said.

"Well, I have to say, that's the first time in my life that I thought it was all over. This monster just stared at me. He didn't know it, but this was my first buffalo. And I was probably his first human on two rather than four legs."

"What'd he do?" Benteen asked.

"He just stared at me. After a while, he just wandered off. Lost interest I suppose. Once I was off my horse, he must've thought I was just a large prairie dog. No possible food source and no threat."

"And then what?"

"Then what nothing. I was lost and on foot in Indian territory with no idea where you were."

"Or where *you* were," Benteen said.

"I just generally walked in a southwesterly direction hoping our paths would cross before I became an object of fun for the savages."

"Or the buzzards," the colonel said.

On the next day's march the Seventh came upon a burned station. They found the scalped and mutilated remains of three men. Or at least three people.

They were carved up and burned beyond any recognition.

This scene was repeated several times on the way back to the rest of the force and then on back to Fort Larned.

At one particularly gruesome scene, Custer didn't rejoin the departing troops.

Martinez rode up to him as he sat staring down at the mutilated remains of what had been a young woman.

"What is it General?"

Custer looked up. "I know we're new out here, Major. But I'm wondering if we should maybe be rethinking our approach. Chasing after councils with Indians that don't want to council doesn't seem to be working. Maybe we can't get treaties without first making war."

"We've discussed that, George. But there's something else. What is it?"

"Libby's headed out here to join me. Partway necessarily by wagon train. I was just thinking of how to get her safe passage through all this."

"Tell her to wait. We'll be done here soon enough."

"That's not going to work for Libby."

33

May 17, 1867

Benteen stormed into Custer's tent.

Custer and Martinez looked up from the map they were studying.

"Yes, Captain," Custer said. "What is it?"

"Six of my men are being paraded around the camp with each of them having half their heads shaved."

"Yes?"

"Under whose orders?"

"Mine, Captain."

"What did they do, George?"

"They were asleep on watch."

"With all due respect, that's no way to treat our men. Any man, in fact. They'll never respect you, General. We need these men following our orders against savage attacks, not resenting us."

"If sentries are asleep on their watch, I fear you and I won't be around to direct them against the savages. But thank you for your feedback, Captain Benteen. Is there anything else?"

Benteen glared from one to the other, then walked out of the tent.

"You say he's been complaining to the senior officers about me?" Custer asked.

"Yes, late nights after you've retired, he's taken to calling you a petty tyrant. Says he heard that your men had enough and almost killed you in Texas after the war."

Custer looked up at that. "Is his drinking still a problem?"

"I think yes, sir."

"I can't abide an officer who drinks too much, Major."

"Yes, sir. We all know how you feel. But almost everybody out here drinks. You're probably too hard on that. You're not going to stop soldiers drinking. In or out of combat. Even your own brothers. With respect, General."

Custer looked uncomfortable. Gazed back at the map.

"Each of these circles here represents a massacre this year?" Custer asked.

"The squares are massacres. The triangles are burned out stations. The circles are evidence of torture."

"What does this map tell us, Major?"

"I think you are going to have to convince the general that we have to spend more time chasing Indians and less time talking to them."

"Chasing Indians is all we do, Major. Look at your map. All this savagery and incomprehensible terror, and we never catch an Indian when we go out after them. I've never done so much chasing and so little fighting in my life."

"Yes, sir." He looked thoughtfully at his old friend. "Any news from Libby?"

"I'm dying not being with her. And the frustration of not even being able to find the Indians. You know what these Indian tactics remind me of?"

"No, what?"

"Mosby. John Singleton Mosby."

"The Grey Ghost."

"Yeah, Mosby's Raiders. He raced all over Virginia harassing our troops. Attacking innocent citizens. Never actually staying for a fight. Just harassing and fleeing. Tying up good cavalry looking for him. Chasing him."

Custer looked back down at the map, and then walked over to the tent opening. Looked out over the camp. At the disgraced sentries still marching in circles.

"The only thing that comes from the way Mosby and the Indians fight, Martinez, is the death of innocent civilians. And a lot of dead horses."

He stood in the tent entrance and looked out over the vastness of what appeared to be the empty Kansas prairie. Knowing that they were out there. Out there by the thousands.

And Libby was on her way here.

34

July 5, 1867

Seven weeks later, Custer had been marching his forces west for ten hours. Forty-five miles. Into the Colorado Territory. His orders were to reinforce Fort Sedgwick. Then to bring the Sioux and Northern Cheyenne who were terrorizing the trains, the settlers, and the stage coaches along the South Platte in for a negotiated treaty. Or at least convince them to go back north to the Dakota Territory where they were supposed to be living. Going on three years since Chivington had tried to settle matters at Sand Creek, and the Indians were still wreaking unspeakable havoc on Colorado.

One of his Whitewashed Reb's now trotted up to him.

"General?"

"Yes, Private?"

"I've been asked to see when you're planning to make camp, sir?"

"I intend to make camp along the banks of the South Platte, soldier. Only another twenty miles. By eleven maybe? Maybe five more hours?"

"Many of the dogs have dropped dead on today's march, General."

"I'm sorry. You be sure to run back up here if we lose any of the horses. Or any of the men."

"Yes, sir."

The two rode on in silence.

"Is there something else, Private?"

"Yes, sir. I've been trying to work up the courage for the past three days to congratulate you."

"For what?"

"Four years ago. At Gettysburg when you stopped J.E.B. Stuart's charge."

"Four years, two days ago, actually. Were you there?"

"Yes, sir. I'm proud to say I fought with J.E.B. Stuart's cavalry. We believed if it weren't for you, our support of Pickett would've carried the day. Some of us still believe that if it weren't for your Michiganders, Lee would've realized our dream of winning the war."

"Your dream, son?"

"Yes, sir. Our passionate dream."

"Are you from Virginia?"

"Yes, sir. Annandale."

"Did we meet at Gettysburg?"

"Yes, sir. You shot me. At close quarters. With your pistol."

Custer looked over at him. Looked more closely.

"I suppose," Custer said, "I'd be more likely to remember who shot me than somebody I shot. Was it bad?"

"A flesh wound. Enough to knock me off my horse, though. I was able to kill two of your Michiganders before I fell unconscious from the bleeding. A doctor patched me up and I got back to Virginia with my unit."

Another mile of silence.

"Thanks for congratulating me, Private. You got your answer. Maybe only fifteen more miles now to go before the river. Hope some of the dogs make it."

The Virginian saluted, turned his horse, and started back.

Custer stopped. Looked back. "I hope someday, son, you'll be proud to say you fought with George Custer's Seventh Cavalry."

"Me too, sir."

Crook had sent a company to the Malheur River in response to several ranchers' complaints of recent attacks and thefts.

Today, they joined the nearby ranchers and defeated two Paiute villages. Taking captured Indian women and children to the fort, and returning the stolen horses to their former owners.

Custer reached the South Platte at his expected 11:00 pm arrival time. A sixty-five mile forced march in fifteen hours. He was about thirty miles southeast of Fort Sedgwick.

He had outrun his command. His small, exhausted force fell asleep where they dismounted on the east bank of the South Platte.

35

July 6, 1867

Custer and his men awoke at dawn to find they were still alone. They had been so tired that they had slept through the night's rain storm. Everyone was soaked. Custer sent scouts up and down the river, and back the way they had come to find the rest of his command. They ultimately found them camped about three miles downriver.

As they finished setting up the combined camp, two men rode in. They rode up to Custer and dismounted.

"You the commanding officer here?" the younger man asked.

"Yes. Colonel George Custer, Seventh Cavalry. You?"

"I'm John Iliff. This here's Holon Godfrey. We own ranches about thirty miles upriver." He pointed vaguely to the southwest.

"What can I do for you gentlemen?" Custer asked.

Iliff looked genuinely surprised by the question.

"While you and your men slept here last night, Colonel, the Indians attacked Dennison's station about a mile west of here. And then they tried to burn out a ranch about a fifteen minute walk from here. Due east. You all sleep through that?"

"I'm as surprised as you, Iliff. We were dog tired from a fifteen hour march. Where are the Indians now?"

"We figure they're holed up in a canyon about thirty miles from here. Easy targets for a force this size."

"Mr. Iliff, we've been sent here to make treaties, not war. We'll get to rounding up your Indians as soon as I get my orders. Is there a telegraph station near here?"

The two ranchers looked shocked.

"You mean we can't expect any protection from your men?"

"I'll let you know when I get my orders, gentlemen."

"Riverside Station is near here," Godfrey said. "Or used to be anyway. Unless the Sioux got to it last night. I can take you there."

"Martinez. Take a dozen men to the station with Godfrey here and try to get our latest orders from Fort Sedgwick. I'll stay back here with Iliff and see what he can teach me over breakfast about fighting Indians and protecting ranchers."

Martinez returned just before dusk, just as Custer's scouts returned with Iliff from an expedition to several neighboring ranches.

"What'd you find, Iliff?" Custer asked.

"Pretty much what we already knew. The ranchers and stations are holding out day to day. But without some relief from the Army, the Sioux and Cheyenne will eventually turn the South Platte into nothing but a run of prairie dog villages. It's getting so even the miners are reluctant to come through. Something's got to be done."

Custer looked to his scouts for affirmation and got it from their body language.

"Martinez. Did you get through to Fort Sedgwick? Tell them of these people's situation down here?"

"I did."

"And?"

"They telegraphed back that they knew the situation and were sending cavalry and infantry units down here tomorrow."

"And our orders?"

"We have a problem on that score, General."

He waited for Custer to signal him to continue. Custer nodded.

"They wanted to know what we were doing here. It seems they sent a dozen men with our orders over a week ago and those men haven't been heard from since. Under the command of a newly minted West Point lieutenant."

"They certainly never reached us. What were our orders?"

"Same as they are now, General. We were expected to reinforce Fort Wallace several days ago." He looked over at Iliff. "The Indian problems here are a picnic compared to the slaughter going on in western Kansas."

Custer thought about the missing lieutenant.

Then about Libby.

"Benteen. Martinez. Prepare the men for a dawn departure. We have our orders. And a dozen soldiers' lives may be at stake."

As Custer set out to lead the Seventh on a forced march to the southeast the next morning, to retrace the just concluded ride, Martinez came up riding hard.

"General."

Custer turned in the saddle. "Yes, Major? What is it?"

"Thirty-seven of the men deserted during the night."

Custer looked back out over his gathering cavalry.

"No senior officers are missing, sir. All of the Whitewashed Rebs are still here. I think this was too near the gold fields for some of the men to pass up. That, and the prospect of a hundred seventy-five mile march back into Indian country."

"This is war," Custer said. "Deserters should be shot. But we're more than a week behind our orders already and we may be needed to rescue a dozen more deserving men."

And Libby was waiting for him at Fort Riley, or worse, on her way to him through Indian country.

"Let's move out Major."

Barely over four hours, and a mere fifteen miles, later, Martinez again came racing up the ranks.

"More deserters, General."

Custer halted the column. "How many? Where'd they go?"

"It looks like fifteen. Some on foot. They lagged further and further behind and suddenly were gone. Almost certainly they headed southwest. Toward Denver City."

"Take thirty of your best soldiers, Major. Chase them and shoot them down."

"You can't do that, Colonel," Benteen said.

"I certainly can, Captain. Desertion in time of war is a capital offense and you know it."

"Not without a court martial, George. You can't just shoot down your own men."

"I can and I will. Desertion from the Seventh Cavalry stops now."

"Major. You have your orders."

Martinez led his men at a full gallop southwest. Custer ordered Benteen to set up camp for the night.

It had been a miserable beginning to an urgent mission.

Martinez returned at dusk with five wounded soldiers.

"Those on horseback had too long a head start on us, General. These were on foot."

"Put them under guard," Custer said. He looked over at Benteen. "They are under arrest. We'll deal with them if they make it to Fort Wallace."

"What about their wounds?" Martinez said.

"These prisoners are to receive no medical attention," Custer said. "None at all. Those medical supplies are for innocent citizens and members of the Seventh Cavalry who come by their wounds honestly."

Benteen started to say something, caught Custer's look, and clamped his jaw shut instead.

The Seventh rode eighty miles over the next two days back to their original encampment at the Republican River. Two days and about forty miles later, they came upon a dead horse. U.S. cavalry. No equipment left on it.

"It fall from exhaustion?" Custer asked.

"A bullet to the head," the scout said. "Could be he gave out and they shot him. Could be Indians caught them from behind and this is just the first of what we're going to find. They were riding faster here, but not at a full gallop."

"We'll know soon enough," Custer said, pointing to a large group of circling vultures a couple of miles ahead.

They rode slowly now, partly out of fear of what they were going to find, partly out of caution so as to not miss any important signs.

"They were galloping here," the scout said. "A dead run now. No formation or organization. Indian ponies mixed in here."

Every one of the officers knew what this meant. Ten organized soldiers taking up defensive positions could hold off an army of hundreds of Sioux and Cheyenne for days if need be.

But a retreating line of racing U.S. cavalry against a dozen well-armed Indians would live only as long as the Indians wanted them to. Most likely, a long, painful time.

"You say this was a new West Pointer?" the scout said. "No question what's up ahead then. These sorry men never had a chance out here."

An hour later they spooked the vultures, dozens rising from a field a hundred yards ahead and to their left.

"You smell it?" Martinez said.

"Not yet," Custer said. Then, "Yes. Oh sweet lord."

They halted at the next dead horse. Stripped of all equipment. Fifty yards ahead was the form of what had been a man. He had crawled away from the horse. The blood stained path of a man on all fours leading up to what was left of his corpse.

Then, scattered in a rough semicircle, they found the rest of the dead soldiers.

Ten soldiers and an Indian scout. All scalped. All naked. All but the Indian scout had their heads beaten in and mutilated beyond recognition. The Indian's scalp was left by his head, a sure sign that it had been his own tribe who had done this. They would not take the scalp of one of their own away from the body.

Each mutilated corpse bristled with arrows. It was as if the Indians had planted a field in which hundreds of arrows had now sprouted and were climbing to the sky.

The flies were horrendous and the stench unbearable.

"If we brought the mothers of these ten men here, none would be able to identify their own boy," Martinez said. "No way to tell which one's the lieutenant."

The men of the Seventh Cavalry just stared. Each knew this could have been them. Each knew that it still might come to pass.

Custer thought of Libby. Where was she? She must not leave Fort Riley. Or had she already?

After burying the party in a mass grave, Custer led his Seventh Cavalry the next day on another all day forced march.

The unit bore little resemblance to the force that had left the Republican River a week earlier.

Four days later, having discovered that Libby was still at Fort Riley preparing to travel to him, a thoroughly discouraged and worried George Armstrong Custer invented an excuse to take a part of his command on a three day, one hundred fifty mile, fifty-five hour march east to Fort Hays.

After a brief rest he then drove them the sixty miles to Fort Harker in twelve hours, arriving at 2:00 am.

There, he awakened the commanding officer and convinced him to let him jump on the next train for the ninety mile trip to Fort Riley.

And, finally, to a reunion with Libby on the 20th.

36

July 21, 1867

The previous day, Crook had led two hundred of his soldiers and scouts in what he intended to be a major thrust to attempt to force the Snakes into a final dead run away from the Oregon settlers.

Marching at night, Crook headed toward the Nevada border.

This would be a change in the type of war he was waging. They would surprise every village and every Snake party they could find. The scouts out ahead of the night marches, leading them to daylight surprise attacks.

He had told the men this would be a long week of marches and fighting, but that he expected it to be decisive.

Custer and Libby had reunited the night before. The two relieved and delighted to be together again.

They were finishing breakfast when the three officers arrived at Libby's Fort Riley quarters.

Colonel Custer answered the knock and opened the door.

"Yes," he said.

"Colonel George Armstrong Custer?" said the senior officer.

"Yes?"

"You are under arrest for the desertion of your command of the Seventh Cavalry and for being absent without leave from your duties."

George Armstrong Custer's tour of duty as an Indian fighter on the American plains had come to an end.

With no fanfare and no victories.

37

July 27, 1867

Crook had marched his forces for seven straight nights and fought pitched battles with the Paiutes wherever he could find them for seven straight days.

The Indians, outmanned and outgunned, were no match for the relentless Crook. He had chased the Indians initially down to Nevada and now back up again to Fort Warner.

Crook returned in triumph after a week of devastating attacks against the Snakes.

Lily and Nick had traveled to the nearest stage station, partly to purchase some fencing materials Lincoln had asked for, but mostly to catch up on news.

"Crook's been driving the Snakes clean out of the state," the station master was saying, "or so we're told."

"Anybody near us here have any troubles?" Lily asked.

"Not that we hear. You?"

"Not since winter. Most of the troubles are now west and south of here. Toward California."

"Some soldiers were through here a few weeks ago saying that the railroad's finally headed this way from back East."

That caught Lily's attention. Just as John Arnold had mentioned.

"Railroad?" she said. "Where?"

"Dakota Territory. They're laying a railroad from Nebraska just north of Colorado, then down to here. Pretty much following the Oregon trail."

"Where north of Colorado?"

"They said they had already laid out a town a couple hundred miles due north of Denver City earlier this month. Two thousand people showed up practically overnight. They're calling the town Cheyenne."

"They say how far this Cheyenne is from Fort Laramie?"

"Maybe a hundred miles southwest."

My valley, she thought to herself. John Arnold had been right. And Iliff had beaten her to it.

"Why do you ask, Lily?"

"Just curious. If Crook can clean up the Snakes, there's gonna be plenty more folks comin' this way. Shouldn't be long now."

Nick looked at her. Laughed.

"That's not why you asked, Lily."

"Hush Nick. It's nobody's business. Go load up the wagon."

He laughed again as he headed out the door.

She knew that Nick and Lincoln suspected she was considering selling the ranch and moving on to Dakota, but there was no need for anybody outside the family to know.

Yet.

38

August 15, 1867

After months of unrelenting attacks by both Crook and Arnold on Paiute villages and their roving bands of warriors, Arnold marched his forces and the horses he had procured from California back into Colonel Crook's Oregon camp that afternoon.

The strategy of splitting their forces had succeeded in scattering the Indian bands all over the territory. Constantly finding themselves on the defensive, the Snakes had been on the run, with much less opportunity to harass the settlers.

That night, the two commanding officers settled in for their first dinner together in over six months.

"How much longer can they hold on?" Arnold asked.

"They'll surrender next spring or summer. They'll have no choice. Their few current advantages will have been exhausted and they'll realize they have no advantages in the future."

"It's sad in a way, George."

"How's that, Arnold?"

"Wherever we go, the Indians try to accommodate the early settlers…"

"Some do. Not all."

"Okay, some try to accommodate. But as more and more settlers arrive, the Indians' source of food is driven away. And their attempts to stay and eat the new game the settlers bring with them are met with understandable resistance. More settlers arrive, and the Indians are pushed back. Out of their homes and out of their cultures."

Crook looked for a while into the fire. Then looked searchingly at his second in command.

"We're paid to make this land safe for the settlers, Arnold. And that involves killing Indians more likely than not. If you didn't want this job, you shouldn't have stayed in the Army after the war."

"No, General. Of course I know all that. I didn't say it wasn't necessary. I merely said it was sad. In a way."

"I can't disagree with you. But the hundreds of thousands of boys killed in the war were sad in every way, John. It's just the way of the world we live in and work in. It's the nature of our job."

The two men resumed eating and looking into the fire. They both knew all the issues. There wasn't much to be gained for Arnold by continuing on the subject.

"General," Arnold said. "I've been looking to meet one of your scouts. His name's Gus Smoot. Is he here in camp with us?"

"You never met Smoot?"

"No. Apparently he got to you about the time we split our forces in January."

"Gus Smoot was the best of the volunteer scouts I've seen out here. Good at tracking and an even better interpreter. And, irrelevantly, according to the soldiers, a damn good poker player."

"Was?" Arnold said.

"Yes, he was wounded very badly at the end of January. In a battle they're calling the Battle of Tearass Plain."

"He live?"

"Maybe. I think so. We had to leave him at a camp. There was a decent enough doctor there. I heard that he would likely survive. But his scouting days could be over. He said he fought with you at Valverde, but that you wouldn't know him."

"I know his wife. Knew her in New Mexico during the war. Despite his professed doubts, I think he and I might have known each other."

Lily came into the foyer of the house to find Gus wrestling on the floor with two-year old John and almost one-year old Antelope.

"I guess your recuperation is officially complete?" she said.

Gus, lying on his back, held each child up in the air with one hand. Each flailing at the other through their laughter.

"I think I'm going to be fine now, Lil. I could've been up and around weeks ago. You know I've always been quick to heal."

He dropped a giggling Antelope onto his stomach and rolled John into a somersault toward the couch.

"Lincoln tells me it's only a matter of time until I can be as good again as Nick around the ranch. It'd take more than a couple of Paiute arrows to slow me down for long."

"You're never going to be as good as Nick around the ranch," she said, laughing. "And it's got nothing to do with strength or ability." He sat up, tossed Antelope into the air, and caught her again with his stomach. Her favorite game.

"As long as I can pull chips into my pile and ride a horse, I'll be fine Lil." And he ducked as John dove at him.

"Nevertheless," she said. "We'd all feel better if you'd leave your Indian fighting days behind you."

"Tell that to the Indians," he said, as John knocked him over diving from the couch.

The Indians are one thing, she said to herself, but how are you planning to deal with John Arnold? She had told him about Arnold's visit and had pleaded with him to stay away from the Army.

But he had laughed it off. "All that's in the past, Lil," he had said. "Nobody's going to care about all that any more."

Custer met with his lawyer and Martinez at Fort Leavenworth.

"The charges are ridiculous," Custer said. "This court martial is baseless. I did not desert my command. I received orders and permission all along the route."

Martinez and the lawyer exchanged glances.

Custer let out an exasperated sigh. "We had completed our assignment. I had returned my command to Fort Wallace. Despite the desertions I faced and the massacre of the very party bringing me my orders."

"George," Martinez said. "Each of your superiors is prepared to say that you had no permission to leave Fort Wallace. And that our mission to bring the Indians to treaties was, at best, yet to be completed."

"Furthermore," the lawyer said, "The commanding officers at Forts Wallace, Hays, and Harker are prepared to say that you misrepresented your intentions and received their permission only under false pretenses. In addition, Benteen has come forward with accusations of your inhumane treatment of your men. That the desertions and breakdown of morale were a direct result of your incompetent command and illegal orders."

"Including," Martinez said, "that you ordered the punishment and execution of deserters without following procedure."

Custer stood and looked out the window, hands in his pockets. Turned back to the two men.

"What do you say, Dennis?"

"I say Benteen has a vendetta against you, General. Always has. Several of the other men and I will testify that your actions were justified under the conditions."

"What extenuating conditions?" the lawyer asked.

"We're cavalry officers, sir." Martinez said. "General Custer chased the Indians with a relentlessness no other officer has equaled. Our inability to actually engage Indians was accordingly more frustrating to the General and his officers than to the other units."

"And the deserters?"

"Most of them had only joined the Army as a vehicle to get to the gold mines. When we got to Colorado without ever engaging any of the Sioux or Cheyenne, it was too much of a temptation for many of them."

"And the state of the General's mind?"

"I'm perfectly fine," Custer said.

"We were all frustrated by the periodic evidence of murders and mutilations by the very savages that we couldn't ever find," Martinez said. "With his wife so near and rumored to be traveling through the Indians, and with us unable to even find the Indians…" He looked at Custer. "General, what does Libby say? Is she still supportive of your military career?"

"I'm a cavalry officer, Major. West Point trained. I risked my life and that of my men to help hold the Union together. This is my career. Libby knows that and supports that. She is as baffled by these charges as I am."

"So," the lawyer said. "You want us to fight to save your career?"

"Yes, sir. That is what my wife and I would like."

"Thank you, General. We will do our best."

And the lawyer shook each man's hand in turn and left the quarters, heading out on to the parade grounds.

"Martinez?"

"Yes, General."

"Do you still believe in me?"

"Yes, of course I do, George, or I wouldn't be here. We can beat the Benteen charges. And your explanation of the trip to Fort Riley is your word against theirs, sir."

"I certainly hope so. I never in my life would consider leaving my post and my men."

"Yes, sir."

Custer looked out the window at the parade grounds for several minutes.

"Dennis, did you know Auggy Damours during the war in New Mexico?"

"Yes sir. What does Auggy have to do with this?"

"You know he's been accused of stealing hundreds of thousands from the Army, the New Mexico Territory, and the Church, right? And of going AWOL."

"I heard about it."

"You think he did it?"

"I don't know what to think, General. He was very likeable. General Canby thought the world of him back in New Mexico, sir."

"And Canby thought the world of him in Washington as well."

Custer stood and went back to the window. Stared out for several minutes. He turned to face his friend and comrade.

"On the day Lincoln removed McClellan as commander of the Army, I ran into Damours on my way into Canby's office. The war going to hell, and Canby was very worried about Damours. Apparently he had bronchitis and Canby had sent him to see a New York doctor. He told me of his concern for Auggy even before he got around to telling me of McClellan's new assignment and that he was reassigning me to the cavalry. Canby sent Damours to New York, yet he was later convicted of being AWOL."

Martinez frowned.

"It's just ironic is all," Custer said. "Now, five years later here I stand. After faithfully doing my duty, falsely accused of being AWOL."

"Do you think Auggy was falsely accused, General?"

"I have no idea. He was never heard from again. He could have died of bronchitis in a Maryland or Pennsylvania hospital for all anybody knows. But I do know that he had nobody to support him. To listen to his case or his side of the story."

"And you do, George."

"I certainly do. I have the support of my wife and of my friends. And of my men."

"General, you asked me earlier if I believed in you."

"And you said you did."

"I did. But more importantly, do you still believe in yourself?"

Custer didn't hesitate.

"Absolutely, Dennis. I will survive this unfortunate start to my Indian fighting assignment. I will survive this to lead the Seventh Cavalry again, Major. You can count on it."

39

September 24, 1867

John Arnold gazed across the campground at the scouts sitting in front of their fire. He and Crook's combined force had been marching by night for two weeks, south and west into California. Despite the increasing desertions due to the hardships of the night marches, their goal continued to be to rout the Snakes and Pit River Indians that had fled from the Oregon battles.

Arnold could clearly see Gus Smoot sitting by the fire, talking to one of the Modocs. It had been nearly six weeks since he had initially asked Crook about Smoot, and now, today, Smoot and several ranchers had caught up with the Army. Smoot claiming to be fully recovered from his wounds.

The full beard and the passage of five years could not disguise from Arnold that this was indeed Augustyn P. Damours, late lieutenant of the U.S. Army, and the former aide de camp to General Canby. AWOL going on five years now. Embezzler of hundreds of thousands of dollars. A wanted man.

And husband of a friend.

Arnold walked over to the campfire.

"Hello Auggy," Arnold said.

All the scouts except Smoot looked up.

"Lieutenant Damours?"

Still Smoot didn't look up.

"Smoot."

Gus stood. "Hi John. I hear you visited my wife."

At this point there was a commotion at Crook's tent. Crook was calling out to Arnold. The Major looked over, and, without a word, spun around and headed over to Crook.

"Yes, sir."

"This idiot," and Crook pointed to one of the scouts that everyone knew he mistrusted. "No, you tell him yourself."

"The Paiutes discovered our fire just up ahead," the terrified scout said.

"Ridiculous," Crook said, furious. "He built a fire about ten miles ahead of our position. Near where we knew their major encampments were."

"They see it?" Arnold asked.

"See it?" Crook said. "You can see their signal fires all around us. Two weeks of stealth marches and we won't see an Indian now for weeks. If at all."

"I'm sorry," the scout said.

"You are dismissed from your service. Leave immediately."

Crook stalked wordlessly into the woods fifty yards to the west.

Nobody knew what to say. The humiliated scout walked to his horse, looked around at his former colleagues, and rode north alone into the darkness.

Arnold found Smoot at the northeast edge of the camp, looking out after the disappearing scout.

"So, Auggy, how have you been?"

"The name's Gus Smoot, Major, and I've been fine."

The two looked into the darkness, side by side.

"Are you going to stick with this fiction about Gus Smoot, Auggy?"

"Let's suppose I knew what you were talking about, John. If I did, then it would be best if I remained Gus Smoot. If I didn't, then I am Gus Smoot. Either way it's all the same to me."

"I met your children. Saw Lily."

"I know. I doubt she told you she had any knowledge of Auggy Damours, right?"

"Right."

"Issue's dead then, John."

"If you say so."

Smoot held out his hand. They shook.

Arnold released Smoot's hand. "Gus," he said.

Then they heard the yelling in the woods to the north. They grabbed their horses and galloped toward the noise.

They came to a clearing and found the humiliated scout bound, with a rope around his neck.

"Release that man," Arnold said.

"He betrayed us all, Major."

"Release him," Smoot said. His revolver pointed back and forth at the two soldiers next to the scout.

"A whole lot of us going to die thanks to him," a voice said behind Arnold.

"Maybe so," Arnold said. "But we don't execute anyone without following procedure. Not in this Army."

"Cut him free, Private," Smoot said.

Arnold and Smoot side by side, facing ten angry soldiers.

They cut him loose and rode back to camp.

Arnold signaled wordlessly to the scout to ride on.

"Sorry, Major," the scout said.

Arnold and Smoot remained silent until the scout had ridden out of sight.

"What happened to Cummings back in that arroyo?" Arnold said.

"I heard Kit Carson said a lone Indian shot him."

"I asked what happened, Gus. Not what Carson said happened."

Smoot shrugged.

"What happened to the money?" Arnold said.

"How would I know?"

"Are the charges still out against you?"

"You mean against this Damours fellow you keep yammering about?"

"Yeah, Gus. Are the charges still out against Auggy."

"You got me. Last I heard, Damours had bronchitis, Canby sent him to New York to see a doctor, and he was cleared of all the charges when he returned."

"Good luck to Auggy with that story. Last I heard there's a bounty hunter dressed all in black searching the West for Damours. He seems to think the charges still stand and that Damours is alive and well. And is his ticket to riches."

"Well, Major, if he actually exists and shows up, maybe you and I can set him straight."

40

September 26, 1867

Contrary to their expectations, when Crook's discouraged force set out to try to find the Snakes two days later, they found them.

And they were spoiling for a fight.

After a five mile southeast march, Smoot and the Modoc scouts came galloping down from the high bluffs to their right.

"There's a large force of Indians up there in those rocks," Smoot said.

"Which way are they heading?" Crook asked.

"They aren't running, General. They took a couple of shots at us from a hidden ravine up above the rocks."

"Arnold," Crook said. "Place fifty men to the south and fifty men to the north of those rocks. Smoot, get the scouts up above and let us know what we're up against."

"Yes, sir," from both men.

"And Smoot? What is this place called?"

"Infernal Caverns, sir. Sorry I didn't see this coming. The Indians believe this area is impossible to overrun."

"That's okay Gus. We all thought they'd left. You couldn't have expected them to stand against us. Get up there and let me know how to make them wrong."

Gus and the scouts raced to a spot above the caverns. From there, they could clearly see over a hundred well entrenched Pit River Indians and Paiutes. Smoot called over one of the volunteer scouts.

"Tell Crook that there over a hundred Indians and they have built a fortress of barricades by moving in hundreds of lava boulders all the way up the bluffs and against the lava walls. There are several stone forts that were not there before."

And down two of the scouts went to Crook with the news.

Crook rode over to Arnold with his conclusion. "Major," he said. "We're going to have to advance straight up those bluffs toward that lava wall."

"There's no way to see where the shots are coming from, General."

"That may be Major, but best we get is a stalemate if we sit here letting them pick us off."

Arnold rode off to direct the soldiers on a mission to surround the Indians and start climbing toward them.

Both sides kept up a barrage of rifle fire all day and into the dark, with little effect. Ricocheting bullets were the biggest risk to all. Friendly fire was as dangerous as hostile.

And then at dark, a lightning storm struck.

As the rain pelted down and the lightning lit up the eerie lava caverns and boulders, both sides dug in for the battle against the elements that night and against each other the next day.

The scouts stayed above, seeking shelter where they could find it. Each lightning bolt lit up the area below like a stage. The scouts could get strobe-like views of both the Indians and Crook's soldiers. The Indians would not be able to move without the scouts seeing their intentions.

Occasionally, a scout would get off a shot in the pelting rain when a sudden stream of light revealed a vulnerable Indian. But it was hard to hold a rifle steady in the surprise jolt of light, and there was never evidence of any damage revealed by the next bolt of light.

With each flash of light, Gus could see Crook and Arnold's hiding place. He leveled his rifle and aimed at where he'd last seen Arnold.

The next lightning bolt startled Gus and his rifle jerked upwards, but Arnold had clearly been in his sights. Then the crash of thunder. The lightning was close.

He leveled his rifle against the stone in front of him. Steadied in anticipation of the next lightning flash. Flash. Thunder. He held steady through it.

He leaned forward, wondering if he really could do this thing. Flash. Thunder. He thought of Lily. The love of his life. The mother of his children. Back home at her dream ranch. Her dream, not his. He knew about her friendship with Arnold. He'd let it go when she named their son John. Had wondered if Arnold wasn't really the man in black. Really looking for Lily and not Damours.

Flash. Thunder.

Steady. Wait.

Flash. Thunder.
Steady. Wait.
Flash. Thunder. Pull.

Arnold and Crook leaned against the lava boulder as protection against the wind and the sheets of rain. They both winced when the night lit up like day from a lightning bolt, illuminating the rain like ice sheets plummeting downward. Then came the immediate crash of thunder.

"They're getting closer," Crook said.

They heard a crack sound two feet above Crook's head, then the sound of a whining ricochet, and then the crack sound again in the rocks just below.

"A bullet?" Crook asked.

"You'd have to be damn lucky to hit anything intentionally in this mess," Arnold said.

"Just the same, let's move over there for better concealment. Lucky or not, friend or hostile, you'd be just as dead either way."

They duck walked through the rivulets of water to a less dry but better concealed spot.

"What'd Smoot call this place?" Arnold said.

"Infernal Caverns."

"That what the Indians call it?"

"So he said."

"No need to improve on their name for it. Heck of a place to die, though."

"The Indians don't mind."

Us or them, Arnold pondered.

Lily looked up at Lincoln, Nick, and Elly standing on the other side of the table.

"Elly, the dishes can wait. I have something I need to tell you."

The three sat back down.

"I've decided we're leaving the Owyhee. We're going to sell the ranch and move on," Lily said.

"You don't mind my asking," Lincoln said. "Does Gus know about this, or is he staying on to help the new rancher and the Army finish settling Oregon?"

"Gus and I decided this together, Lincoln. It's his ranch as much as it is mine. We figure to get through the winter, then sell. Crook can finish the Snakes off without Gus."

"We headed to Dakota then?" Lincoln asked. "Lame White Man will be happy to find out that Gus, the great Indian killer, is coming back."

"You coming if we do?"

"I get to decide?"

"Of course. Our ranch will always be as much yours as it is mine, Lincoln."

"Seems like we got a whole lot of owners on this ranch, and only one person doing all the deciding and announcing."

"Then it's agreed, you'll come?"

"Most likely," Lincoln said. "We can talk about it later."

"Nick? Elly?"

"Can I buy the ranch, Lily?" Nick said. "It's what my father dreamed of."

Everybody except Nick laughed. Lily reached out and took Nick's hand. "Honey…"

He recoiled.

"Lincoln," she said. "How long until you think Nick can have his own ranch?"

Lincoln looked amused. Then switched to all serious when he saw the look on the boy's face.

"Ten years, Lily. At least. No fourteen year old boy is going to be able to run a ranch. The cowhands and rustlers'll steal him blind." He turned to Nick. "Son, I've only got three years' experience and I've got a long ways to go before I could even think of it. Lily and I talked about me earning my own ranch, but no way before another five years or so. It'll take that long to earn the cowboys' respect you gotta have to run a ranch."

"Can I stay here then?" Nick asked. "In Oregon, like my Dad wanted?"

"If that's what you want, Nick," she said. "Any number of the ranchers out here'll be happy to take you on. Up to you."

"The Indians are even worse out in the Dakotas, Lily. That's what my Dad said. You sure you want to do this?"

"Look outside, Nick. Whaddya see?"

"I don't need to look. I know it's raining, Lily."

"It's always raining in Oregon, Nick. That is, when it's not snowing. I've had it with the rain. Now that the trains and towns are already in Dakota, I'm already late." She looked at Lincoln shaking his head. "Maybe too late."

"Things never moving fast enough for you, Lily," Lincoln said. "That Cheyenne town's not even three months old and the railroad won't be there for another two or three months. You're not too late."

"I want my ranch in those plains we saw southwest of Fort Laramie. The Army'll take care of the Sioux and the Cheyenne."

"And Gus?"

"And Gus what, Lincoln?"

"He'll want to be taking on the Sioux and Cheyenne, too. You want that Lily?"

Lily glared at Lincoln. Turned to Elly.

"You want to come with us or stay, Elly?"

"I want to be with John and Antelope Thunder. I really do. But I need to check with my mother, right Lily? I can't just up and travel hundreds of miles and take all her money, can I?"

"We'll have to go through Fort Boise on our way, Elly. You can decide then. You can see what your mom wants when we get there and then decide. John and Antelope will want you to come with us."

Lily looked at each in turn. Laughed.

"I had thought we all shared the same dream. But I guess it's my dream. Yours may be the same or not. We'll find out. I'll have to be content with know-ing that Gus and the kids and Auggy the bear and I will be going to the Dakotas next spring or summer some time."

"Auggy the bear's going?" Lincoln said in mock surprise. "Well that settles it for me. Count me in, then."

Nick and Elly laughed.

"And," Lily said, "I'm counting on you to recruit the cowhands we need to stay with us all the way to the Dakotas to help us set up. And then help us build the ranch."

"You remember Lame White Man's prophecy from Sitting Bull about him and Gus, right Lily?" Lincoln said.

"And you remember Gus's response, right?"

"I do. But being told you're going to die of something and actually causing it to happen are different things."

"A prophecy is either right or wrong, Lincoln. No point in dwelling on it. It'll happen or it won't."

"Sure, but there's no reason for a moth to circle a flame if there are better alternatives. That's all I'm saying, Lily."

41

September 27, 1867

Crook launched a two prong attack against the forces dug into the Infernal Caverns in the morning that lasted all day.

They prepared to attack again the next morning only to discover that the Indians had fled through the labyrinth of tunnels during the night.

It was over.

"What are the casualties, Major?"

"Eight dead, eleven wounded," Arnold said. "The most in the Snake War, by far."

Crook looked out over the Infernal Caverns. "It was worth it. We won this battle and we'll win this war. Only a matter of time now. They have no place else to go."

42

October 11, 1867

"Ten hut."

All rose in the Fort Leavenworth court room as the officers entered at the front of the court.

"At ease."

Everyone sat.

"Colonel Custer."

George and Libby Custer rose alongside Custer's lawyer.

"Yes, sirs."

"This Court finds you guilty on all counts. You are guilty of absence from your command without leave. You are guilty of desertion. And you are guilty of inhumane treatment of prisoners."

"Yes, sir."

"You will be remanded to your quarters here at Fort Leavenworth until your sentence shall be determined and executed next month."

"Yes, sir."

"Do you have any questions, Colonel Custer?"

"No, sir."

"This Court is hereby adjourned. You are dismissed until called before us for sentencing."

"Yes, sir."

Benteen and Martinez left the court room without a word to each other or to their now disgraced commander.

43

November 20, 1867

"Ten hut."

The three people in the Fort Leavenworth court room rose as the officers entered at the front of the court.

"At ease."

The three sat.

"Colonel Custer."

George and Libby Custer rose alongside Custer's lawyer.

"Yes, sirs."

"You are hereby sentenced to one year suspension of rank, and one year suspension of pay."

"Yes, sir."

"Do you have any questions, Mister Custer?"

"No, sir."

"Then this Court is adjourned and you are dismissed."

"Yes, sir."

Libby Custer and her husband, George Armstrong Custer, West Pointer, hero of Gettysburg, American war hero, failed Plains Indian fighter, and now civilian, headed home to Michigan and an uncertain future.

Libby's faith in her husband was unfazed.

The former General's confidence in his lifetime plan of a heroic and decorated military and political career was now in some doubt.

44

March 20, 1868

Lily and Gus watched as the two men rode under the Fort O'Reilly sign and out the gate. The new owners of the L Bar S Ranch.

"You okay, Lil?" Gus asked.

"Sure, honey. Why?"

"This was your dream. Your ranch in the Washington Territory. And we just sold it for much less than you wanted for it."

"The money doesn't matter, Gus. Auggy the bear's medicine is all we need. Only the dream matters."

They both looked back at the bear on the front porch, Lincoln standing next to it, watching them.

"And the dream now's a ranch in the Dakota Territory?" Gus asked.

"As we agreed. In that valley we saw on the way here. South of the trail from Fort Laramie."

"As we agreed," he said.

Lincoln walked over. "It's done?"

"Yes, Lincoln. It's done."

"You sold everything?"

"All but the wagons, the furniture, and the livestock you wanted us to take. The horses, the oxen, and, of course, your four pet cows."

Lincoln chuckled. "You'll be happy you kept them four, Lily. You get what you wanted for everything?"

"No. They know we wanted out. Everybody knows it was the worst winter ever out here. We weren't in any position to bargain. They're probably buying out anybody who's had enough."

"Forty for the cows?"

"No. Thirty-three a head for the fifty of them. Best we could do, Lincoln."

"Can't do better than your best, Lily," Lincoln said. "When do they want to take over?"

"They wanted it now," Gus said. "But I'm headed out with Crook next week, so they agreed to let us stay until July. We should pretty much be done with the Snakes by then."

"That's for the best, anyway," Lincoln said. "It'll take a while for us to pack things up. Sort out which of the cowboys are gonna come with us, and which are gonna stay. Those gentlemen'll probably offer more to your cowhands to stay than you're gonna offer to go with us."

"I guess not everybody shares Lily's Dakota dream," Gus said.

"No," Lincoln said. "Some of the boys prefer it here. Maybe even Nick and Elly. We'll see."

"Lincoln, you tell us who you want for the Dakota ranch. I'll persuade them to come, okay?"

"You persuade those new owners of anything I need to know about Lily?" Lincoln asked.

Lily laughed.

"Yeah, they wanted the Fort O'Reilly sign and Auggy the bear. But I told them they weren't for sale."

45

May 31, 1868

The lieutenant and his sixty troops and scouts followed Smoot up the canyon to Castle Rock where he had seen the ten-pole Paiute camp the day before.

"I'm pretty sure this is the heart of the major band we've been chasing and fighting for months," Gus said.

When they arrived, they joined a large force of white settlers already engaged in a gun battle with the Snakes.

When the shooting stopped, one Indian lay wounded on the ground and the rest had their hands high in the air.

Gus recognized one as the chief of the band, one of two key chiefs left at large. He pointed his rifle at the chief's chest.

"You want to fight some more, or you want to talk now?" Gus asked, signaling to the lieutenant to ride over.

"We talk now," the Paiute chief replied.

With his hands still raised, he walked away from Gus, toward one of the lodges.

The sound of cocking rifles and pistols could be heard throughout the canyon.

The chief sat on the ground in front of his lodge. The lieutenant and Gus joined him.

"I only have sixty braves and their families left. They are starving. You give us no time to even hunt for food. You promise us a meeting with General Crook. Then I promise I will return with my band tomorrow and with the answer from the other chiefs."

Gus looked at the lieutenant.

"Do you believe him?" the lieutenant asked.

"Can we speak for Crook?" from Gus.

"I think he'll travel down from Portland if we tell him it means the cessation of the war."

"To tell you the truth, Lieutenant, I believe the chief more than I believe you."

Gus turned back to the chief before the angry lieutenant could respond.

"We promise you General Crook if you stand by your word tomorrow."

"Then you will see me tomorrow," the chief said.

He stood, walked over to his pony, mounted up, and rode alone up the canyon.

At dawn the next morning, he and his people stood among the lodges as promised. Unarmed. And with word that the rest of the Snakes would meet with General Crook to end the Snake wars.

46

June 24, 1868

"Are you going to have everything ready to leave a week from today?" Lily asked Lincoln.

"Everything will be ready," he replied. "But there's still no word from Gus. Are you planning on leaving without Gus?"

"Gus knows the plan. We agreed to leave the first of July. He said to go on without him if he wasn't here. He'll catch up to our wagons quickly enough if he can't be here on the morning of the first. How many of the cowhands are coming with us?"

"The three I wanted. They'd rather be in the Dakota Territory than here, which is why I hired them. The rest are near to worthless and agreed to stay here with the new ranch, just like we were counting on."

"Is Jimmy one of 'em coming with us?"

"Yeah. Jimmy doesn't fancy being the only Negro on the ranch when we leave."

"How's Nick feel about going to Dakota?" Lily asked.

"He said he'd talk to you about it. Seems to want more comfort than I can give him."

"He'll come. He's devoted to John and Antelope, and there'll be nothing here for him when we leave."

"Lily?"

"Yes, Lincoln?"

"I get my own place ten years after we arrive in the Dakotas, right? Like we agreed?"

"Yes. But something else is bothering you, Lincoln. What is it?"

"I'm worried about Gus. I know you think he'll catch up with us."

"Or show up before we leave."

"I just hope your right's all. Dakota's not going to be any place for a woman ranching alone. Not in the early days, anyway."

"I got you and Jimmy and Nick. At least for ten years. It's going to be fine, Lincoln. Don't worry it. Gus'll be along."

She walked over and hugged him as John and Antelope Thunder came clamoring out of the house and down the steps.

47

June 29, 1868

Crook and Gus rode at the head of the line of soldiers up the canyon along Rattlesnake Creek. There were wickiups all along the creek for more than a mile as they approached Camp Harney. Indians watched them in silence all along the last half hour of the route.

Crook had returned from Portland almost four weeks earlier when the reports of the surrendering Snakes at Castle Rock had reached his headquarters.

"You believe they're done, General?" Gus asked.

"All the reports say so, Smoot. The skirmishes over the past month have been tapering off. The Indians have been coming in steadily now this week. They seem to have lost their will to keep on fighting. But, we'll know soon enough. Tomorrow."

"Then I'm heading home, sir. My work for you is done. We sold the ranch. I told you I'd promised my wife I'd join her for our ride to Dakota on the first. Day after tomorrow. I can just make it if I leave now," he lied.

Crook looked at the scout as they rode.

"You'll do no such thing, Gus. I need you tomorrow if it goes badly. We both know you can't make it in two days. She'll either wait for you for a few days, or you'll catch up with them as they head north. Which is what you were planning anyway. Either way, you can keep your commitment to both of us."

The two rode on in silence, looking at the sad assortment of Snakes gathered and watching along the path.

"I have more confidence in your regard for my translating skills, General, than I do in your insights about women."

Crook laughed. "Smoot, tomorrow you'll wish she was here with you. This will be a sight. A true, Grand Council."

48

June 30, 1868

Lily rode toward the house.

She had just left the cowhands to check on the wagons for the next day's start of the trip to Dakota. They were down river, rounding up the oxen and the horses they were taking on the trip, separating them from those they had sold with the ranch.

Lincoln and Elly had stayed at the house packing up last minute belongings with the kids.

As she rode around toward the front porch, she had an uneasy sense that it was too quiet. There had been no gunfire or sounds of trouble, so until this, probably silly, alarming feeling there had been no cause for concern.

As she rounded the corner, she saw a man sitting on the porch next to Auggy the bear. Something about him looked familiar, but she couldn't place it.

Her curiosity disappeared when she noticed that he was dressed completely in black.

Crook had elected to place his wife and the other civilians next to him on the Camp Harney parade ground. Between his troops and the assembled Indians.

"This is taking a terrible risk, General," one of the sergeants said.

"I seriously doubt that, Sergeant. The four Paiute chiefs sitting over there on their ponies didn't bring their families and all their people here so that they could all be massacred when they provoked us by attacking a few civilians in plain sight."

"All it would take is one crazy savage to mess up your plans, General."

"There are no women or whites with me here against their will. This assures that there will be no Indian unsure of my intentions, Sergeant. Or of our confidence."

"I hope you're right, General."

"I always hope I'm right, Sergeant," Crook said as he threw his right arm over Gus's shoulder and led him over to the waiting chiefs.

The chiefs looked down at the two men.

"We are here to end a great war," Crook said, Smoot interpreting. "You must all dismount and drop your weapons. Then we will talk."

He gestured toward the spot where his troops sat waiting.

One mounted warrior broke from the assembled Indians toward Crook, gestured a clear unwillingness to comply, and whirled his pony in a circle in defiance.

A general, unruly noise broke out among the Indians behind the chiefs.

The man in black looked up at Lily as she approached on horseback. A rifle leaning against Auggy the bear and a holstered pistol on each of his hips.

There was a black horse tied to the porch railing on the other side of the stairs.

"Can I help you?" Lily asked.

"You'd be Lily Smoot, right?"

"And you'd be Johnson, right?"

He nodded in appreciation. Tipped his black Stetson in acknowledgement.

"So we can spare the introductions, then?"

There was a meanness to his voice and his mannerisms that Lily was unaccustomed to, even from the worst of the men at The Brickhouse in Virginia City.

"Where's Lincoln?" Finding that she had to fight now to keep her voice under control.

"Would Lincoln be your nigger cowboy?"

She didn't answer. Decided to let him take this where he wanted for now. At his pace. He was playing with her and there'd be nothing gained by pushing back.

Not yet, anyway.

"You wouldn't happen to know where Augustyn P. Damours was, would you Lily?" he said.

"I have no idea. Where are my children, Johnson?"

"Oh, them. On that note, your nigger left me little choice but to kill him."

Lily felt coldness. Fear.

"I gave him an out, though," he said. "Nice guy that I am, I told him that I wouldn't kill the girl and the two little children if he'd get everybody quieted down in the back room over there in the bunkhouse."

Lily looked over to where he was pointing.

"After he tied them up and gagged them, I rapped him upside the head. Knocked him out. He'll live. At least until you and I are done with our business here."

"I have no business with you, Johnson."

She climbed off her horse, tied it to the railing, and walked past Johnson into the house.

The hostile warrior had managed to get many of the Paiutes into a state of near-hysteria. One of the Paiute chiefs confronted the defiant warrior, and the two rode back toward the assembled Indians.

"Why are they here if they're not all willing to surrender?" Gus asked.

"I don't think they thought we would disarm them before the council,"

Crook said. "They expected to be able to disarm themselves. Not to be helpless during the negotiation."

"Should we at least get your wife and the civilians off the grounds?"

"No, Gus. This is precisely the time for us to stand our ground in confidence. The chiefs got them here. They'll restore order."

The chief rode among the now-threatening warriors, calming one group, then another.

One brave raised his rifle at Gus's chest and approached at a deliberate pace.

Gus held his ground. He and Crook looked as though they were supervising a routine parade at the camp.

Johnson followed Lily through the front door into the foyer of the ranch house.

She satisfied herself nobody else was in the house. They must be in the bunkhouse, as Johnson had claimed, she thought. However this played out, at least she wasn't going to be distracted by the children's presence.

She came back into the parlor, calmer now.

Johnson was sitting in a chair by the door. Blocking her access to the front porch.

"Where's Damours, Lily?"

"I already told you I didn't know." She sat down across the room from him.

"When's the last time you saw him?"

"It'll be six years in September, Johnson. I saw him just before he and General Canby headed to Washington."

"There's a greaser in Santa Fe says you and Marshal Cummings tracked Damours down and found him."

"Yeah, that'd be Chacon. If you push him he'll tell you Cummings told *him* he killed Damours in Cuba. C'mon, Johnson, if you believed anything Chacon told you, you'd believe that Cummings killed Damours, and you wouldn't be here. Fact is, Cummings and I never found him," she lied.

"Cummings isn't available for questioning, Lily." He followed her eyes to her right boot. "And you are."

"What's your deal, Johnson? Damours has been missing for over five years. Nobody's seen him since he walked out of the War Department in November of sixty-two. He could be anywhere. I certainly have no idea where."

"Fifteen thousand dollars is my deal, Mrs. Smoot. I find him and bring him back, I get fifteen thousand dollars. Damours, dead or alive. Think of it as my career. I'll never have to work again once I bring him in."

"You're wasting your time here, Johnson. The sooner you leave us alone, the sooner you might get your hands on that money. Nobody here has ever seen him except me, and I haven't seen him going on six years."

"If you don't stop looking at your right boot, Lily, I'm going to guess there's a derringer in there. That would make shooting you an act of self-defense."

Lily stood, stepped behind the couch, and put her hands on the back of the couch in plain sight.

"If you're looking for Damours, Johnson, it's time for you to move on. What I don't understand is you threatening us. Threatening innocent children and hired hands and ranchers is illegal, Johnson, even if you're an officer of the court looking for a fugitive."

"Your word against mine," he shrugged.

"My word and Lincoln's and Elly's against yours. I'd like you to leave my ranch Mr. Johnson. Now."

He looked at his watch.

"From what I hear, it's only going to be your ranch for another eight hours or so. I could hold you here till then and you'd be the one trespassing."

One by one, the Indians rode over, dismounted in front of Crook, and laid their weapons at his feet.

At last only two remained on horseback, engaging in an angry exchange. As one headed sullenly toward Crook, the other turned his pony, fired into the air and raced into the willows out of sight.

Crook signaled for all to remain standing. Nobody returned the shot or pursued the lone Indian.

The last Paiute dismounted. Unlike all the others, he passed his rifle, arrows, and bow directly into Crook's hands.

Crook bowed, and handed him his bow. Bowed again.

The last Indian walked over to the Paiute semi-circle as Crook and Smoot sat down with the other officers between the Indian semi-circle and the now-seated soldiers.

The four chiefs walked over across from Crook and his officers. The tallest offered his hand.

Crook kept his hands in his lap, refusing to rise or to take the hand.

"Gus, tell him I have come to hear what they have to say, not touch the hands of those Snakes who have killed our people."

The murmuring among the Indians resumed. But they were signaled to quiet by their chiefs.

"We are tired of fighting, General Crook. We Paiutes cannot live like this any more. The white soldiers and white ranchers have driven away our game and won't share their food with us. We had thought we could find a way to live within our traditions and let you whites find a way to live with us. But you won't."

"Do you all want peace?"

"All but a very few."

"That is good about the very few, because I do not want peace."

Gus stopped translating to let the murmuring die down. Crook looked at him curiously, indicated for him to go on.

"You do the talking, General," Gus said. "Leave the acting to me."

Gus turned back to the chiefs. "I am not like you chiefs," he said for Crook. "I am a soldier. I am paid to fight. I do not have responsibility for my family's and my tribe's way of life. I do not see my warriors falling in number. I have an unlimited supply of warriors from the Great White Father in Washington."

Crook looked at his soldiers, then at the Indians, and finally back at the chiefs.

"You," Gus pointed at the chiefs. "You see a hundred soldiers killed, and a hundred soldiers arriving to replace them. You see one warrior die, and you know it will be twenty years before that baby can replace him." Gus pointed to a little papoose cradled in its mother's arms, and she cringed and wailed out.

"Year after year, your numbers fall and your people can't eat, while our numbers grow and the ranchers prosper." And he paused as he thought of Lily and John and Antelope preparing to ride to Dakota.

Again Crook looked at him, waited for him to finish what he had said.

"I hope you decide to keep fighting. Then I will win a Great War against the Snakes until you can fight no more."

The four chiefs talked amongst themselves.

"So you are not asking us for peace, General Crook?"

"No. I am paid to fight the warring Indians until they disappoint me by coming and asking me to stop."

The four leaned together for several minutes in animated conversation. Finally, they each stood and walked back to their warriors. Some conversations were moderate, some heated, but eventually the four returned and sat on the ground.

"We are then sorry to disappoint you, General Crook," one of them said to the nods of the other three. "It is my duty to report to you that the Paiutes are gathered here today to ask you to stop fighting and killing our people. Your war with the Paiutes is over."

Crook stood and extended his hand to the chief whose hand he had refused. Then to the other three.

"We will agree to the precise terms as time permits. In the meantime, please lend me ten of your best braves as scouts for our war in California against the Pit River Indians."

Even Crook was amazed at how quickly and how enthusiastically ten warriors rode over, dismounted, and began donning the cavalry uniforms provided for the occasion.

For his part, Gus Smoot said his goodbyes to Crook and the other scouts and headed northeast to intercept his family. His last glimpse of the camp grounds was of ten mounted Indians in full military uniform, rifles and bows held over their heads, circling the celebratory crowd of Indians and soldiers.

Something about that image haunted him. Mounted Indians in blue cavalry uniforms, circling. He shuddered, turned and headed to catch up with his family.

"Johnson, you're becoming tiresome," Lily said. "The rest of my ranch hands will be bringing in the livestock in less than two hours. The number of witnesses to your growing number of crimes will be increasing by the hour. It's going to be your word against a dozen witnesses soon enough."

"Where you moving to, Lily?" Johnson asked. "Where's your next ranch going to be?"

"That's really none of your business. I'm sure whoever told you we were selling certainly told you we're headed further northwest in Washington Territory."

He nodded. "Just checkin' to see if you're telling the truth. Where's your husband?"

"More business that doesn't concern you."

"I'm told Gus Smoot is out chasing Indians and is due back before you head out, in," he looked at his watch again. "In going on seven hours."

"Gus is doing his duty for the people of Oregon. He'll return when he can. Again, none of your business."

"Isn't Gus a commonly used nickname for Augustyn?"

Her heart skipped a beat. Damn. She hadn't figured on anybody having the opportunity to put those two names together. How stupid.

She laughed. "Johnson, I married Gus years after I had last seen Damours. I had never given Damours another thought after Cummings and I couldn't find him. He was gone. Out of all our lives."

She crossed her arms across her chest in feigned anger.

"Gus'd never even heard of Damours until your efforts brought him to our attention. The similarity of the names never occurred to me. Why would it? Damours was a poker player I knew in Santa Fe. Gus is a man I fell in love with years later. I've never thought of the two of them together. Maybe you think too much, Johnson. Maybe more than you can put together and make sense of."

He tipped the black Stetson toward her again as he stood up.

"I don't really care whether or not you approve of my methods, Mrs. Smoot. Or my abilities, for that matter. Trying to earn fifteen thousand dollars is turning out to be hard work. Whether you get it by delivering on the wanted poster or by getting somebody to buy you off the chase."

And there it was. As bold an offer of blackmail as you could ever expect to hear. Lily could only hope her face didn't betray her fury.

"Either way, it's the same fifteen thousand dollars. Right, Lily?"

"No matter how you look at it, Johnson, neither Damours nor fifteen thousand dollars is going to drop from the sky here on my ranch. You're wasting your time."

"So you say."

He headed for the door. Opened it. Then turned back.

"I'll head out from here and find your Gus Smoot, Lily. The Army'll know which Snakes he's chasing where. We'll see how it plays from there."

She didn't say anything.

"Does he know you were a common whore in Nevada, Lily? And a pretty good one at that?"

Again, she remained silent. Glared at him.

"I do find it odd, though, Lily, that you say you married Gus Smoot some-time in the last six years. But your name in Nevada ten years ago was already Lily Smoot. I need to see what your husband knows about that."

He pushed the door open, looked back, and said, "Say goodbye to your nigger for me. Tell him I look forward to the next time we meet."

He closed the door. She could hear him walk across the porch, mount his horse, and ride off to the west.

So that's where I knew him from, she thought. Ten years ago. Now she remembered. The sunovabitch was as mean as a snake even back then. He treated all the girls at The Brickyard with equal disdain.

She hoped Gus had the sense to shoot Johnson on sight. Either that or she was sure she hadn't seen the last of the man in black.

49

July 5, 1868

They had just forded the Snake River in Idaho Territory, about a day's ride from Fort Boise, when Lincoln looked toward the horizon on a far hill. There, sitting next to his horse and waving his hat, was a familiar figure.

"Hey Lily," he said. "I think somebody's waiting for you." He nodded his head forward.

Lily looked up, at first worried it might be Johnson. Then hoping it could be John Arnold.

But there, with his crazy grin visible through his jet black beard was Gus Smoot. Waving his hat like crazy.

"Is that Papa?" John said, jumping up and down next to Lincoln.

"Sure is," Lincoln said, flicking his whip over the oxen's ears. "Let's head up there. Save him the trouble of doubling back down here to us."

And Lincoln urged the lead wagon toward Gus as Lily raced her horse up on ahead. The other three wagons with the four cowboys followed, with Elly and Antelope Thunder in the last wagon. Auggy the bear riding watch on the back of the wagon.

Lily reined her horse in from a full gallop, dismounted, and ran into Gus's arms.

"How long you been waitin' cowboy?"

He lifted her and they kissed hard. He put her down, and slapped her bottom with his right hand.

"About three, four hours. I busted my butt to get here, knowin' this'd be where you'd head east. The ferry operator said no party matching your description had come through."

"Lincoln was expecting you to show up at the ranch, but I knew better. How's Crook going to do without you?"

"That's where I was. Crook beat the Snakes. The war's over. We had a Grand Council at Camp Harney and they all asked for peace."

"Honey, really? You really think the war with the Snakes is over."

"No question. Crook even got Paiute warriors to volunteer to go with him to California to try to end it down there."

She looked at the approaching wagons, seeing the excitement of the kids.

"The man in black came by the ranch looking for you," she said. "Johnson. He threatened the kids and he beat up Lincoln."

"He know my true identity?"

"Suspects it. Went looking for you after he left us."

It was Gus's turn to look at the oncoming wagons.

"That must have been who I saw a couple of days out of Camp Harney. I saw Arnold's Company of cavalry on a ridge to the west of me. I thought about riding over to them to give them the news from Crook, but I was in too big a hurry to intercept you."

"Johnson was riding with the cavalry?"

"He was riding up front with Arnold. Heading to Camp Harney to hook up with Crook."

"Johnson was with Arnold?"

"Either that or John Arnold was riding with another cowboy on a jet black horse dressed all in black."

Damn, she thought. And Arnold knows what Johnson wants to know, and worse, he knows where we're going.

"One other thing before the kids drive up, Lil."

"Yes, Gus?" she looked up into his face.

"Kit Carson died five, six weeks ago."

"Indians?"

"No. Died in his bed in Taos. Just after his wife died."

"That's so sad."

"I know. I knew you'd want to know."

She hugged him. "Sorry, Gus. He was a great man."

"Papa," John said, as Lincoln dropped him one-handed off the side of the wagon.

"Papa," Antelope Thunder shrieked, forcing Elly to drop her and let her chase off after her brother on her stubby, churning legs.

Gus swooped each up in turn, holding one in each arm and kissing them over and over again on their proffered cheeks.

Nick rode over, leaned down to the three kissing Smoots, and slapped Gus on the back.

"Good to see you, Gus," he said. "I made a bet with Lincoln that you'd catch up with us before Fort Boise."

"Aw, don't listen to that boy, Gus," Lincoln said. "He hasn't learned to listen any better than he's learned anything else. I told him Gus'd be in Dakota waiting for us with the ranch already built. That boy's got a ways to go before I'm done with his training."

Lily just shook her head. "Gus, it's nice to have you home. These boys are impossible when you're not around."

PART III
WYOMING TERRITORY

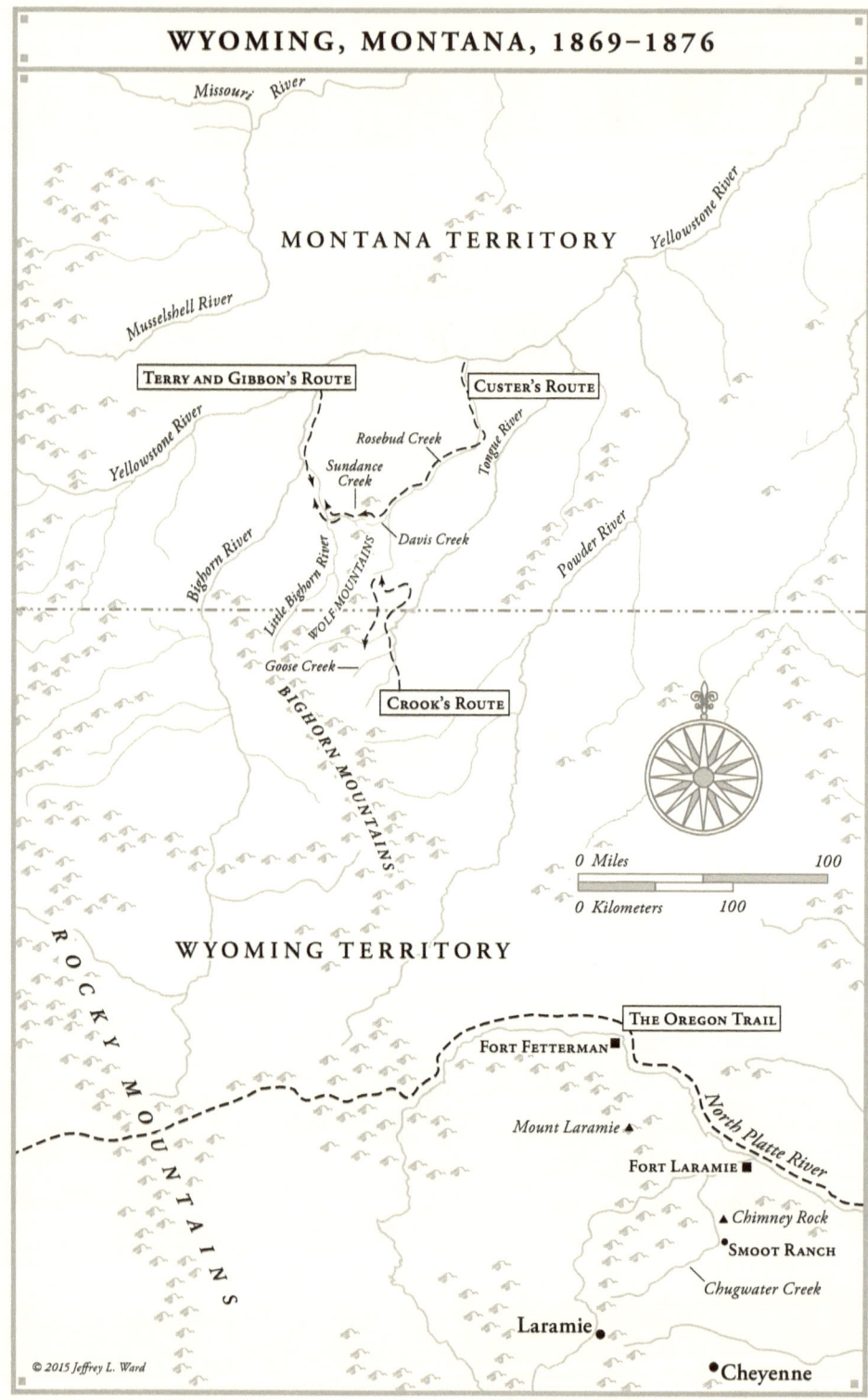

WYOMING, MONTANA, 1869–1876

Missouri River

MONTANA TERRITORY

Yellowstone River

Musselshell River

Yellowstone River

TERRY AND GIBBON'S ROUTE

CUSTER'S ROUTE

Rosebud Creek

Sundance Creek

Tongue River

Bighorn River

Little Bighorn River

Davis Creek

WOLF MOUNTAINS

Powder River

Goose Creek

CROOK'S ROUTE

B I G H O R N   M O U N T A I N S

WYOMING TERRITORY

0 Miles 100

0 Kilometers 100

R O C K Y

THE OREGON TRAIL

FORT FETTERMAN ■

North Platte River

Mount Laramie ▲

FORT LARAMIE ■

M O U N T A I N S

▲ *Chimney Rock*

● **SMOOT RANCH**

Chugwater Creek

Laramie ●

© 2015 Jeffrey L. Ward

● **Cheyenne**

50

August 31, 1868

The Smoots had joined a wagon train heading east from Fort Boise. The winter of '67-'68 had been more than enough for a large number of Oregon settlers. Some were headed back East, some to Colorado.

The train had retraced the Oregon Trail without incident, crossing into the newly anointed Wyoming Territory three weeks after it achieved its official status. They had then arrived within twenty miles of Fort Laramie three days before, August 28.

There, at precisely the spot where Lily had looked south down Chugwater Valley and seen Lame White Man in June 1865, there was now a trading post. It looked for all the world like a structure from Fort Wicked or Fort O'Reilly, with several gun ports in each wall of the post.

There, they had readily agreed to let a platoon of cavalry from the fort escort them south to Cheyenne.

Lily rode out in front of the four wagons. Mostly riding alone. She was content to memorize the landscape, looking for a spot for her dream ranch. They rode south along the large buttes on the eastern edge of the Chugwater Valley. Occasionally she'd see small groups of cattle, hardly large enough to justify being called herds. Occasionally Gus, Lincoln, or Nick would ride with her, but she was in no mood for talking. None of them knew what she needed to find out, so they mostly let her ride on up ahead.

"Lieutenant?" she said, calling back to the platoon leader.

He trotted up. This was the first time she'd addressed him in the two days they'd been traveling. "Yes, ma'am."

"What's that structure up ahead?"

"Chimney Rock, ma'am."

They rode on together, side by side, in silence until, as they were passing the giant rock structure on their left, she saw a building on the south side of the rock.

"What's that?" she said.

"That's the Clay homestead. Charles Clay and his baby and Indian wife, Fingernail Woman, live there."

"He have a cattle ranch?"

"No. He has a small trading post and they do some farming. Sell some buffalo meat to the whites."

"She a Cheyenne?"

"Lakota. Sioux. The Indians leave ol' Charles Clay alone because of his wife and kid being Sioux. She still goes off with the Indians on buffalo hunts."

Lily looked thoughtfully at the homestead as they rode past.

"When I came through here more than three years ago, the Sioux and Cheyenne wouldn't let any of the whites settle here. What changed, Lieutenant?"

"The Union Pacific, ma'am. The railroads brought the towns, the townspeople attracted the cattle ranchers, and the ranchers and the towns of Cheyenne and Laramie needed the Army for protection. Just like everywhere else, the railroad, the settlers, and the Army are pushing the buffalo and the Indians further and further north."

Lily looked back over her left shoulder at the rock and the homestead.

"How many ranchers are out here now?"

"Just a few. The Sioux and Cheyenne still see this as their rightful territory by the fifty-one Fort Laramie Treaty. Even with us out here, the ranchers are taking a big risk. The railroads are killing the buffalo and pushing them out of the Indians' traditional hunting areas. Now the cattle ranchers are doing the same."

"But it's possible to succeed?"

He looked at her but didn't respond. They rode for a couple more miles, picking up Chugwater Creek on their right, the high mesas a few hundred yards on their left. "Hi Kelly's place is right up ahead. This side of the creek. We can stop at his place and you can ask him yourself."

A couple of miles later they came to a ranch house. Several men were building a larger, brick house behind it. As they rode up, a woman came out on the porch, leaned against the railing and watched them approach.

The men stopped working and took off their hats.

"Afternoon, Lieutenant," one of them said.

"Afternoon, Hi. This here's Lily Smoot. Her husband Gus and their family are in those wagons behind us. Lily, this is Hi Kelly."

"Afternoon ma'am. This is my wife Elizabeth."

The two women nodded to each other.

"How long you been out here, Hi?" Lily asked.

"Going on four years now," Kelly replied. "I found this spot for us in sixty-four, and Elizabeth and I got married at Fort Fetterman later that year."

"We came through here in sixty-five and didn't see any sign of you. Late May, early June."

Kelly shrugged. "Wasn't anything built here that soon, right Elizabeth?"

Elizabeth laughed. "Hi had me living in a tent that none of my mother's family would even enter that first year. It was tiny. Nobody could even see it among those trees along the creek."

Kelly nodded. "Mostly that spring the two of us were negotiating down south for cattle with Illif. I didn't put these walls up until later that summer."

"How's John?" Lily asked.

Kelly looked more closely up at her. "Who are you, again?"

"My husband, Gus, and I," and she gestured back toward the four wagons. "Are looking to start a ranch somewhere here in this valley. We worked for John back in sixty-four in Colorado for a year on our way to Oregon. We were told that the Sioux and Cheyenne were inclined to look with disfavor on a ranch back then, so we went out to ranch in Oregon. But we hear that things have improved since."

"Elizabeth's mother is a full blooded Sioux and her father a French trapper. The Sioux made an exception for us and Ol' Clay up at Chimney Rock back then."

"And the Cheyenne?"

Kelly looked at his wife. She shrugged.

"It seems to be working out now," he said. "And with the railroad and Cheyenne and Laramie and the soldiers, they mostly stay up north and west where the buffalo have moved to."

"So a ranch is possible?"

"If you've got the money to buy the cattle, the gumption to build your ranch, the willingness to deal with the sort who are willing to be ranch hands, and the ability to live through these winters it is." He looked over at his wife. "I leave anything out?"

"Luck. You'll also need some luck, Mrs. Smoot. It's all a gamble. A big gamble. Year after year."

Lily looked west across Chugwater Creek at the massive rock buttes towering over the Kellys and their home. Thought about the rolling ranch land she'd glimpsed just on the other side of those rock formations.

"Mr. Kelly, thank you for the information and for your time. I think you and Elizabeth just got yourselves a new neighbor."

She doffed her cap to Elizabeth and spurred her horse toward the south. Toward Cheyenne.

The lieutenant caught up with her after a mile, and they rode on in silence, leaving Chugwater Creek behind. They led their wagons through miles of grama grass and buffalo grass, as far as they could see in every direction.

"Iliff was right about this land," she said. "It's perfect for cattle ranching. And he's already started proving it."

"Ma'am," he said. "With due respect, some ranchers're gonna succeed out here and some are gonna get killed trying. The Indians are being respectful to their own with Kelly and Clay. There's no guarantee that will continue if more and more ranchers start showing up. The Indians know that they were guaranteed these lands forever. If you find a way to get along with them, maybe you'll get rich teaching everybody else how to do it. But if I were you, I'd either give up on the idea, or make sure you build a fortress and hire an army of cowboys who don't mind Indian fighting."

She nodded to the officer. Looked over the miles and miles of grassland, and thought to herself, there's nothing like this land anywhere. He's a soldier and sees danger, and I'm going to be a great rancher who sees opportunity.

The army of Indian fighting cowboys was a good idea, though. She begrudgingly gave him credit for that, even though she'd been ahead of him on the fortress idea. And she knew just the man to find and hire those cowboys. And just where he'd find them.

51

September 4, 1868

"This is far as we go, Lily," the lieutenant said. "Cheyenne's a half mile over this hill. You won't be needing us any more."

He saluted. "God speed and good luck with your ranch."

Then he turned his reluctant platoon around for their return ride back north and east to Fort Laramie.

Lily, Gus, Lincoln, and Nick left the four wagons with the three cowboys, Elly, and the kids, and rode up to the crest of the hill for a look.

They looked at the city along the railroad tracks down below.

"How could Cheyenne be this big?" Gus asked.

"I thought the railroad wasn't even here a year ago. I didn't expect to find a city here already."

"This is bigger than I remember Denver City," Gus said. "No wonder the lieutenant didn't want his men down there. I don't see anything but saloons and gambling halls from up here."

"Must be five thousand people," Lincoln said. "How could this have happened in less than a year?"

"One thing for sure," Lily said. "I'm not taking Elly and the kids down there 'til we see if there's anything civilized." She looked back at the wagons. "I feel about you six cowboys the way the lieutenant felt about his men. I'm not letting any of you out of my sight."

52

September 24, 1868

George and Libby Custer entered the home of friends in Monroe, Michigan, on the west shore of Lake Erie. As usual, Custer's customary military punctuality had resulted in the Custers being the first to arrive.

No sooner had the rest of the guests arrived and sat down at the table, than there was a knock at the door.

Their host came back with a sergeant carrying a telegram.

Everybody stood.

"General Custer," the sergeant said.

"Yes, Sergeant?"

"I have a telegram for you, General."

Custer walked over. Opened it. Read it and turned to Libby.

"It seems the Indians are refusing to stay on their reservations in Indian Territory and have been continuing to kill Kansas settlers. I've been asked to return to Fort Hays. I have one week to retake my command against the hostile plains Indians."

He nodded to his host. Then turned to the sergeant. Saluted.

"Please tell General Sheridan that I will be on the next westward train."

And the Custers took a hurried leave, not waiting for dinner.

Eleven days later, Custer led a detachment from Fort Dodge, Kansas thirty miles southeast to Bluff Creek.

Upon his arrival, he walked up behind Major Martinez in the mess tent. Several of the officers started to rise as he clapped a hand on his friend's shoulder.

"At ease, gentlemen," Custer said as Martinez whirled around in his seat. "I must admit to being a little surprised that neither the Cheyenne nor the Major here cared enough to hold a suitable welcoming ceremony."

Martinez stood and turned toward Custer. He grinned and started to salute just as gunfire erupted on the edge of camp.

All the officers grabbed their weapons and headed toward the sound of the shots.

Several Cheyenne were riding just within range on the west edge of camp, alternately lying almost invisibly on the far side of their ponies and rising and firing into the camp. Galloping back and forth at full speed.

The soldiers spread out over a two hundred yard skirmish line and began returning fire to no effect.

The Indians would come racing out from behind a hill in single file, either coming in close enough to fire into the soldiers on a dead run or taunting them from safely out of range. One pony went down, struck by a bullet in the neck. It's rider never missed a beat, rolling off his pony and running as if nothing had happened, then leaping behind one of his comrades onto his pony on a dead run.

"I'd almost forgotten what magnificent horsemen they are," Custer said. "This the first encounter, Major?"

"No, General," Martinez said. "They practice this every day."

"They just waiting out there hoping you'll try to chase them?"

"Yes," Benteen said. "All those ravines out there. At least one of them is full of Indians waiting for us to come after those three. Chasing them is what they want. Indian tactics haven't changed in the past fifteen months, General."

Custer hadn't seen Benteen until now. He turned and returned his captain's salute.

"It's nice to be back, Captain," Custer said.

"Yes, sir," Benteen said, and turned back to futilely shooting at the Indians racing by.

Martinez caught Custer's eye and neither man said anything further.

"Hold fire," Benteen commanded.

More than a hundred Cheyenne now came out of a ravine to their left and from behind the hill on their right. Out of range. Riding and taunting the soldiers. Raising lances and bows, whooping and shouting, as their ponies raised a dust cloud over them.

"It's good to be back, Dennis," Custer said that night by the fire.

"You have no idea how great it is to have you back, George," Martinez said.

"Anything I need to know?"

"Frankly, General?"

"Yes. Of course frankly, Dennis. The Army's not going to give me a third chance."

"You have to treat the men better. There are some new men since you've been gone. Some more of the unhappy ones are gone. The new soldiers are good, mostly Irish and Germans just off the boats. They speak enough English to get by and they'll give you the benefit of the doubt. You're the Gettysburg hero to them. They don't believe what some of the men say about your ill treatment. They'll be loyal if you treat them well."

"I have every intention of doing precisely that, Major. You have no idea how many times I've gone over last year in my head. I'm going to make these boys proud to have served in the Seventh Cavalry. This is going to be a glorious campaign."

They both looked into the fire, Martinez sipping a whiskey.

"What about Benteen?" Custer asked.

"He hates you," Martinez replied. "And that's not going to change. He'll fight hard and he'll follow orders. But he'll never forgive you. Just his nature."

Custer looked into the fire. No general ever had the unquestioning approval of all his officers, he thought to himself. Well, maybe Lee. But nobody else he could think of.

53

October 6, 1868

Lily and Gus walked into the 17th Street entrance of the cattle company building which was across from the Masonic Hall and the newspaper. Down the street from the two best hotels in Cheyenne.

They waited patiently as the man at the desk looked through some papers.

He looked up. An astonished look came across his face, then he burst out laughing.

He stood. "They told me that a woman wanted to meet with me but wouldn't give her name. Who else could it have been but Lily Smoot? I should have known."

He reached across and shook both their hands, unable to take his eyes off their beaming faces.

"Hello John Iliff," Lily said. "I thought we had a deal that you'd let me know when I could come back this way to start my ranch."

He shrugged, smiling. "Well first of all, I had no idea where you were. And secondly, I'm not in the habit of creating my own competition. I thought I'd taught you that down in Colorado."

"How have you been, John? How are Holon and Matilda?"

"Fine. We're all fine. Same old complaints. Too much rain, too little rain, too cold, too hot. The ranching business recovered well after the Indians settled down some to the southeast of us and Denver started to grow again."

"Denver?" Lily asked. "When did Denver City become just Denver?"

"Last year. Everybody thought they'd become civilized. But now the Indians are becoming a problem down there again. Then the railroad arrived here in Cheyenne ten months ago, I got the contract to supply beef to the workers, and everything exploded. Holon actually built the road from Denver to here. There are six thousand people living here now."

"All this in a year," Gus said. "It's hard to believe, even with seeing it in person."

"Less than a year. First permanent structures weren't until this past May, Gus. Five months ago. Everything was run out of tents for the first twelve months."

"Even the saloons and parlor houses?" Gus asked.

Iliff laughed. "Yes, Gus. Them, too. And even the law once we got some here. Vigilantes kept some semblance of peace for almost the entire first year. Same thing's now happening over in Laramie, except they're six months behind us. And how about you, Gus? You ever take to ranching any? Or are you leaving all that to Lily?"

"Some."

"Lincoln still with you?"

"Yes. And he's still better at it than I am. But I guess you already guessed that. I help out some. I'm daddy to our two kids and the third one on the way." He took Lily's hand and she gave him what passed for an understanding smile.

"Turns out that I'm a pretty good Indian scout for the Army, so I did some of that for Crook in Oregon. And I still practice poker enough so that my contributions to the family don't go unnoticed."

Lily took her hand out of his, looked to see if he was finished, then said, "How's your wife, John? Any family yet?"

"No, Lily. I've been lucky in ranching, but not so lucky in life. In December of sixty-five, less than a year after we were married, she died from delivering our son, William."

"Oh, we didn't know. I'm so sorry John. I'm so sorry."

"Thank you. Cattle and my bank here in Cheyenne, are pretty much my life."

"And that's pretty much why we're here, John. We had a nice starting ranch in Oregon. We learned a little beyond what you taught us, then came here as soon as we heard the railroad was coming through. We're starting our own ranch here."

"Where?"

"North of here, in Chugwater Valley. A couple of ranchers beat us there, including, I hear, you. But there's plenty of space for other ranchers for open range ranching. We've staked a claim on several acres on Chugwater Creek and have started looking for help."

"What help do you already have?"

"The two of us. Then Lincoln, a girl to help out with the kids and meals, and two cowboys we can trust. One other we brought with us promptly quit when we got here and got work with the railroad."

"What more do you need?"

"I figure we'll need at least five to six more cowhands for the next year. To help us start the ranch with our initial herd and build the ranch houses before spring."

"And?"

"I want two girls who prefer working with a family than in one of the cribs. Girls I can trust because they've experienced the alternative."

"And because you'll be a better boss. And pay them better."

"There's that."

"You're probably better off looking for the girls in Laramie than here in Cheyenne. If you're going to make enemies by poaching girls, better for you if they're not your neighbors' girls. You'll have no trouble hiring cowboys or cowhands here. It's an open market and they're arriving by the trainload."

"What else did you teach me that I'm forgetting, John?"

"How are you fixed for cattle, Lily?"

"That's why I'm here. You have cattle, and, more importantly, experience in knowing which thousand breeding cows we should start with."

"Some'll come with yearlings, Lily. And you'll need at least forty bulls."

"You taught me all that, John. Now I'm looking for you to provide the right herd."

"True, but that'll cost you."

Lily laughed. "We didn't come here looking for a handout, John Iliff. Cash is the only thing we have more of than we need right now. Oregon ranching was good to us. We'll pay you more than the railroad does for the cattle you have that are good enough for us right now, and you can deliver the rest in the spring."

"No haggling, Lily? It'll run you going on thirty-three thousand."

"It's an open market, John, so I know the going price. But I owe you and we trust you. We'll be doing business together now for as long as that holds. Draw up a bill and plan on dinner at our ranch the night you deliver the rest of the herd to us."

They stood and shook hands.

"Thank you, Lily. And welcome to Wyoming, the only place in the country where you can vote."

"It wasn't why we came, John, but it can't hurt."

Gus took Lily's arm and they headed to the door.

"Oh, one other thing, Lily. You still have that grizzly bear or'd you leave it in Oregon?"

54

October 28, 1868

Lincoln and Nick had ridden from the ranch to Laramie in a day and a half. Now, after only two hours in town, they were leaving their third failed set of parlor house negotiations.

"Sorry kid," Lincoln said. "Lily and I should have known this was no job for a fifteen year old kid. Not even a tough one."

"I'm okay, Lincoln. It's fun."

"I didn't mean that it wasn't fun for you. It just might not be good for talking the girls into coming with us."

"We'll see. I'm much less intimidating than you, Lincoln. It might well work out. You find the right girl, and let's see if I can convince her to come back to the ranch with us."

"It's just that this is much worse than we thought. We knew that four thousand men have arrived here since the rails got here six months ago. And that seven hundred girls arrived right after them, all working in the saloons and cribs. What we didn't know is that there's clearly no law here able to protect anyone. Let alone a working girl in town."

"There any truth to that woman's claim that the girls are afraid of you, their employers, and the three half-brothers who run the town at the end of their rifles?"

"She seemed sincere enough. Not much point in lying to us as we walked out the door."

The two stepped out of the mis-named Gilded Lily and came face to face with a man wearing a badge.

"You two looking for anything in particular?" the badge asked.

Lincoln looked him over. The badge said sheriff, but the man's appearance said deputy. He was small in stature and even smaller in presence.

"Who's asking?" Lincoln asked.

"I'm the sheriff here in Laramie. People are saying you two boys don't fit the mold of the usual customers we've been getting at the cribs. It raised my curiosity. Some other folks, too."

"Fair enough, Sheriff," Lincoln said. Nick, bigger than the sheriff, had moved off to the side, naturally deferring to Lincoln. "The two of us are ranch hands from a ranch being built north of Cheyenne. The ranchers asked us to come to Laramie looking for people to join up with us."

"Whores?"

"Well cow hands mostly. But yes, sir, whores too. My boss is of the opinion that some of the girls take to whoring less than others and don't view it as a lifetime career."

The sheriff looked over at Nick, and then back up at Lincoln. "I've pretty much discovered the same thing about deputies here in Laramie. What'd you say your name was?"

"Lincoln. Joe Lincoln. I'm the ranch foreman. This here's Nick O'Reilly."

"I'm guessing Nick here has had more experience gathering cows than whores."

"Me too, if you want to push me on it," Lincoln said.

The sheriff let that sit in the air, while he appeared to appraise Nick.

"Here's my problem, Lincoln," he said. "I've been having what you might call a control problem with some of the local elements in town. Most of my deputies decided it would be a better career, as you call it, working with thieves and murderers who control the saloons and cribs than working with me. Most of the people coming here had hoped to be able to make an honest living providing food and drink to the railroad workers and soldiers. But it's not working out that way."

"And you wanted to see whose side we were likely to be on? Two guys who just rode into town?"

"The two of you aren't what normally rides into Laramie. You called attention to yourselves with the nature of your questions. Your negotiations in the parlor houses were, well, they were unusual."

"And, as I said, you wanted to see which side we were on?"

"Likely to be on is more like it."

"We're not likely to be here long enough to take sides, Sheriff."

"As luck would have it, you have to decide now."

"And why is that?"

"Because a group of vigilantes have had enough. They've decided to take matters into their own hands tonight. This was a bad day for you to just wander in, Mr. Lincoln."

"You suggesting we just ride on back to Cheyenne before we've had a chance to finish our business?" Nick asked.

Lincoln and the sheriff looked over at him.

The sheriff ignored him and turned back to Lincoln. "I'm guessing you have a pretty good feel for fairness and justice, right Lincoln?"

"We both do, Sheriff," Nick said before Lincoln could respond. "What's your point?"

Now both men looked at Nick, amused at the boy's impatience.

"My point is, Mr. O'Reilly, that on any other day, anybody could just ride into Laramie and buy or rent anything they darn well pleased. Most likely they could finish their business and keep on riding. But even on normal days, a few aren't so lucky. They wind up staying against their will, buried outside of town."

"And today?" Lincoln asked.

"Today, everybody's either hiding or taking one of three sides. And each of the three are going to see you two as a possible threat or a possible help. I've already had four people coming running to me about you."

"This is some town, Sheriff," Lincoln said. "We've been here all of two hours and have already had four people recommending us for jobs to the sheriff."

"Three." He looked back and forth between the two men. "One nominated you for target practice."

Two hours later, as the sun began to set into the purple mountains looming over the small town, the three were sitting in the sheriff's office.

"Only thing I don't understand Sheriff," Nick said. "Is why you just don't approach the vigilantes yourself? Enlist them as deputies?"

"I can answer that for him, Nick," Lincoln said. "Because then his deputies have to arrest them and hold them in that jail back there until a trial. The problem is back again when they break out or are freed by a judge or a jury."

"Or freed by their friends," the sheriff said.

"I thought you pegged us as caring about justice?" Lincoln said. "If you're right, we wouldn't be the vigilante kind."

"I did. And I still do. I just have more confidence that justice'll be best served if the two of you are here with the vigilantes tonight than if you were riding back to Cheyenne."

"Or buried outside of town," Lincoln said.

That night, by prearrangement, Nick and Lincoln were at a side table in the Bucket of Blood Saloon, each sipping their second whiskey. One of the half-brothers had been tending bar when they arrived. There were eleven other men drinking at the other tables.

Now, the other two brothers walked in with three girls. Lincoln recognized two of them from the Gilded Lily, both staring at Nick. The third girl said something to the taller of the two brothers, looking at Lincoln. All five looked over. Lincoln tipped his cap to the girl.

The two brothers walked over.

"You looking for girls?" the taller one asked.

"No," Lincoln said. "I was. But it was a bad idea. Didn't work out."

"Who sent you?" It was the other brother. The bartender was leaning on the bar, watching them. As was practically everyone in the bar.

"The rancher I work for. Over near Cheyenne."

"What do you need girls for?" the second one again. "Not enough in Cheyenne?"

"I said it was a bad idea. We need girls and we need cowboys to work the ranch."

"Cows too, I'd bet," said the taller one.

"No. Plenty of cows to buy in Cheyenne. More coming up from Texas through Colorado. Why do you ask? You three looking for work?"

They both ignored the question. "Who's this young fellow with you?" the taller one asked, either trying to be the meaner of the two, or actually maybe he was. "He the ranch foreman? Does he talk?"

"Nick? He usually answers direct questions. You got something to ask him, I'm sure he'll answer you."

"Hey, Nick. When are you and your nigger, here, planning on leaving Laramie?"

The saloon had become quiet.

Nick looked at his drink. Looked over at the bartending brother.

"Well," he said. "As Mr. Lincoln has explained to you, our plan failed. Our boss will want to hear soon as we get back. We were pretty much thinking of riding back in the morning. But now I think after our next drink will be a good time to leave instead. Unless your brother doesn't want to sell us any more whiskey."

The bartender held up an empty whiskey bottle. "I think my brothers are suggesting that the time for you two to move on has arrived."

At that moment, four men walked into the saloon. They nodded to the brothers, then the girls, and walked over to the bar.

The two brothers left Lincoln and Nick's table and approached the four men.

"What do you want Jim?" the taller brother asked. "You know you're not welcome here at the Bucket of Blood. All four of you get out. Now."

The two brothers drew their Remington revolvers.

"You going to shoot us down in cold blood right here in your saloon? That can't be good for business. Word'll get back all through the Territory."

At that moment, three more men walked in the swinging door carrying shotguns. The girls retreated behind the bar. The bartender pulled out a shotgun and placed it on the bar. It was pointed at Lincoln.

"I'm giving you fair warning," the taller brother said to the man he had called Jim, ignoring the three newcomers. "You get out of here now and take your six friends with you. We'll forget this ever happened the minute the doors slaps your butt."

"It's you three who are leaving" Jim said. "Put your guns down there. On the table."

"You don't leave right now, I'll shoot you right where you stand. Self-defense. Creating a public disturbance. Threatening us. I assumed you were armed like your friends." He shrugged. Said, "Your choice."

"Actually," Lincoln said, "The choice is yours, friend."

The bartender reached for the shotgun. Nick waved him a warning gesture with his left palm as he aimed his gun at the bartender's chest.

The other two brothers looked over their shoulders at Lincoln.

"You going to shoot both of us, nigger?"

"Like I said, and I just *hate* to have to repeat myself, it's your choice. If one of the three of you pulls a trigger or even turns around, then the next three shots will kill you all. I *know* you're armed, I don't have to assume."

The bartender stepped away from the bar. The other two brothers holstered their pistols. The man with the shotgun nearest the door motioned the girls and the other eleven patrons out of the bar. The two girls looked expectantly at Nick as they backed out the door.

"What now?" the taller brother asked after everyone had left.

Under the cover of the three shotguns, the four men who had entered first disarmed the three brothers and handcuffed them behind their backs.

"Now we're going to kill you."

Lincoln and Nick had accompanied the men with the three captives to a cabin less than a block away. The cabin was unoccupied and hadn't been completely built. There were six other vigilantes there, with three other handcuffed men.

"Where's Scotty?" one of the shotguns asked.

"He ran, so we shot him down. Left him lying on Front Street."

"Dead?"

"Yes. No point in dragging him over here."

"And the three deputies?"

"They were out cold. Drunk in their cabin. We just shot them and left them there."

"You are dead men." It was the bartender brother. "All of you. We'll be back."

"We're not sending you anywhere you can come back from. Only chance this town has is with you ten gone. Permanently gone."

"Where's the sheriff?" the taller brother asked.

"Sleeping the sleep of the innocent in his bed at the hotel. I don't think he'll be asking after you."

One by one, they gagged the six men, and then lynched them from the cross beam and dragged the six bodies out and left them on the street.

The one the brothers had called Jim turned to Lincoln and Nick.

"We never got your names," he said.

"That was the way we agreed. We never want yours either. We're headed out of town. No need for names now."

"You're both welcome to stay in Laramie."

"Thanks, but there's nothing for us here. We found that out our first two hours here."

"If you change your mind, I think I could arrange to make you half owners of a saloon down the block. It's looking for new management."

As Lincoln and Nick rode by the Bucket of Blood, two horses emerged from the alley on the other side of the street.

Both men drew their pistols. Saw four hands up in the air and four terrified wide eyes.

"Can we please go with you?"

It was the two girls who had eyed Nick.

"We arrived in town five days ago," the one on the left said. "The three brothers killed our brother and forced us to work at their crib, the Gilded Lily. Just before you left, the woman who runs it threatened to carve us up if we talked to you again."

"We'd be happy to give your ranch a try," the second girl said. "If you'll still have us. I'm Lizzie. She's Mary. You can always drop us off in Cheyenne if you change your mind."

The two men holstered their pistols, rode over to the two terrified girls.

"No, you can come with us to meet our boss," Lincoln said. "Then you can decide on your own what you want to do."

"You'll like our boss," Nick said. "Her name's Lily, but she's not gilded."

55

November 12, 1868

Custer, at the head of his Seventh Cavalry, began the march south into hostile Indian country.

After their failed foray to Medicine Lodge looking for hostile Indians the month before, they had marched back west to establish Camp Sandy Forsyth ten miles south of Fort Dodge on the north bank of the Arkansas River. There, they had spent three weeks organizing, training, and forming the cavalry. And selecting and training the forty best sharpshooters in one unit, the corps d'elite. And selecting thirteen Osage scouts, led by one of their chiefs, Little Beaver.

They had trained and organized the horses into companies by color. The companies of blacks. The bays. The browns. The chestnuts. And the greys.

The Seventh Cavalry now marched south to the strains of their band playing "Garryowen," Custer, Benteen, and Martinez at their head. Behind the three officers came three companies of cavalry. Then four hundred wagons of supplies in four parallel, hundred wagon lines; three companies of cavalry in three lines on both the left and the right of the wagons; with the final three companies of cavalry and the infantry trailing the wagons.

Little Beaver and his twelve Osage scouts were already disappearing ahead of the regiment into the distant Kansas plains.

"So, Colonel," Benteen said, "You going to tell us where we're going?"

"Following those Osage scouts for now," Custer said.

"How you planning on telling the peaceful from the warring Indians, George?" Martinez said.

"Any Indians camped within twenty miles of Fort Cobb are protected, subject to Army rations and presumed to be at peace. Most of the Kiowas, Comanches, Plains Apaches I'm told. But not all."

"Then who are we after?" Benteen asked.

"Most, but not all, of the Arapaho and Cheyenne. Their Dog Soldiers have refused to come in. They have committed most of the raids and murders the Kansans have been claiming. The governor is coming right behind us with a thousand Kansas Volunteers. They want to rescue two Kansas girls they claim the Cheyenne took after killing their parents."

"We going to wait for the Kansans?" Benteen asked.

Custer snorted. "I'm not mixing this regiment with any rabble of vigilantes. We'll give 'em their girls if they ever arrive." He looked back at Benteen. "Little Beaver knows we're headed a hundred miles due south to set up a base camp."

The three rode on in silence for two miles, listening to the fading strands of the band behind them.

"Little Beaver knows that any warriors we run into this far from Fort Cobb are ours. And, above all, he knows that the days of chasing and not finding Indians are over."

56

November 15, 1868

Black Kettle sat in his lodge with a few family members, including Medicine Woman and some of their children. Twenty-one year old Antelope and twelve year old Thunder Bull were there as well. Their village of fifty lodges was the westernmost of a string of Indian villages along the Lodgepole River, the Washita River, in Indian Territory. Most of the other villages along the river, largely Cheyenne and Arapaho, were still at war with the whites.

The senior Arapaho and other Cheyenne still at peace with the whites arrived at Black Kettle's request.

"No, you may stay," he said to his family and the children at the arrival of the men. "There is no need to leave the warmth of the lodge."

After the initial greetings and the passing of the pipe, the newcomers settled themselves on the buffalo and deer skin rugs and turned their attention to their host.

"Our new father at Fort Cobb has asked us to come," Black Kettle said. "He wants to hear if we remain at peace."

"What more can they ask?" the oldest of the Arapahos said. "What have we not done? We have signed their treaties. We have moved our villages here, to where they tell us. We have stopped our young men from joining in the war parties against the white settlers?"

"The Dog Soldiers tell us this is a trap," said a Cheyenne chief. "They tell us that the soldiers at Fort Cobb plan to kill all the Cheyenne and Arapaho. They will kill those foolish enough to travel from the safety of our villages here."

"Yes," Medicine Woman said. "The Cheyenne, Arapaho, Kiowas, Comanches, and Kiowa-Apaches here along the Lodgepole River are too many for them to attack. We have more than a thousand lodges here. I do not trust the new father at Fort Cobb. I only trust our thousand braves."

"Our village is at peace," Black Kettle said, signaling to include the others. "Most of our neighbors here are not. Against our wishes, some of our young men do join the warring Cheyenne and Arapahos. We know that many would rather die in battle than be killed in their lodges."

"If we cannot control our young men," the Arapaho said. "And if we live among those at war, our father at Fort Cobb cannot protect us."

All were quiet as they thought about this old, old story. Antelope looked as if she wanted to say something, but Black Kettle signaled her to remain quiet.

"You cannot continue to quiet our young braves and women, Black Kettle," Medicine Woman said. "You are traveling the path again that brought us to Sand Creek. All know this. Our young people do not feel safe living where the white soldiers tell us."

Black Kettle looked at his wife and then at each of the Cheyenne youngsters.

"Somebody coming," Benteen said to Custer. "In a big hurry."

Custer galloped over and looked where his officers were pointing.

"Indians," Custer said. "Can anybody tell if they're our scouts or something else?"

"If it's not our scouts," Martinez said, "it's some pretty foolish Indians. There's only five of them. You've got to like these odds."

Custer halted the Seventh and waited as the small party raced up Beaver Creek. In time, it was indeed five of their Osage scouts that came into clear view.

"A war party," Little Beaver said, reining in his pony from a full gallop to a full stop in a matter of a few yards. "Between a hundred and two hundred."

"How far away?" Custer asked.

"Less than a day's ride."

"Slow down, Little Beaver," Benteen said. "Did you see them or just their tracks?"

"Tracks. A big party of warriors. They were headed that way." He pointed to the northeast, toward the Kansas settlements. "Yesterday."

Custer looked to the southwest. Where they had come from.

"Cheyenne?" he asked.

"Yes. A Dog Soldier war party."

"So, if we take the Seventh back where they came from, we can take their village," Custer said.

"What about our wagons?" Martinez said.

"The infantry should be sufficient to guard the supplies while we go do our job on the village. This might be the best chance we get to put an early end to this war."

"And if it's a trap?" Benteen asked.

They all looked at Little Beaver.

"This war party is only a small part of the Cheyenne," the scout said. "There are thousands wintering south of here. Cheyenne and Arapaho."

Custer looked again to the southwest. Turned back to the scout. "Do they know we are here?"

"They know you are coming, General. Small parties travel constantly between their lodges and Fort Larned in Kansas."

"But do they know we are here? Now?"

"If they did, they would not send such a war party across your path."

"Would they use such a large party as a decoy?"

"No. If they wanted to be chased there would be fewer and they would come closer."

"Or," Benteen said, "They could have left those tracks yesterday, and then circled back to their villages. Their full force could be waiting for us back wherever those tracks start from."

The commanders of the sharpshooters and the infantry rode up. Custer briefed them on the situation.

"I want to take the initiative with the Seventh Cavalry. Follow those tracks to where they came from. No more waiting to find Indians. We need to attack."

"I don't like it," the head of the infantry said. "Maybe we could hold off all the hostiles from taking the four hundred wagons and maybe we couldn't. You might come back here after a wild goose chase, General, to find all your supplies burned and gone. And us with them."

"Or," Benteen said, "find the Seventh outnumbered and trapped in a battlefield of the Indians' choosing."

"What do you think, Martinez?" Custer asked.

"I'd feel much better if we had some idea of what we were up against. I'm all in favor of surprising a superior force at a time and place of our choosing. But Captain Benteen's right. Unless the scouts know what's up ahead, I think we should set up the camp south of here like we planned. Then join the other brigades and plan an attack under known circumstances."

"Little Beaver?" Custer asked, now frustrated.

"I would rather I knew what was out there. Where you were having this fight, General. You will win this war, but the Cheyenne and Arapaho will win the fights that they choose."

Custer again looked southwest. "They're out there, and they're mine. This is an opportunity lost, gentlemen. Mark my words."

Little Beaver and Benteen exchanged glances as Custer gave the order to continue riding south. Straight through the tracks of the war party.

"Yes, my wife," Black Kettle said. "What you say about our path four years ago is true. And many of our young women and braves do not feel safe near the white soldiers. Or where the white soldiers tell us to live. All know we are here. And at peace. We are not hiding." He looked at Antelope. "What do you want to say to us, Antelope?"

She shook her head and looked down at the ground.

"Tell them, Antelope," Medicine Woman said.

Antelope looked over at Thunder Bull.

"Do you trust any white man, grandfather?" Thunder Bull asked.

Black Kettle looked at the other men. "I have long known that we cannot defeat the white man, Thunder Bull. More keep coming. We keep getting fewer. They take our land. They chase away the buffalo and the deer. They do not understand or honor our place on the prairies. The white men do not know or accept their place in these lands. They are not a part of the spirit of the prairies."

He looked at the young people. "Thunder Bull, no, I do not trust the white man. There is no white man I trust. Many lie. Some soldiers *do* tell the truth. But those soldiers do not control other soldiers. It is the same as a lie to us. We all know that Sweet Medicine warned us about the white man. That they would keep coming. That the people should resist becoming like them. That must be our path now."

"Then why should we travel to our father at Fort Cobb?" Antelope asked.

"She is right, Black Kettle," said the Arapaho chief. "Maybe it is a trap. If not a trap, then maybe a waste of our time."

"Time is something we have much of," Black Kettle said. "The white man cannot kill us all. If it is a trap, then they will kill only those of us who go there. But, as Medicine Woman says, our people here will have the safety of being here at the Lodgepole River with the other tribes. If it is not a trap, then our father will tell us where we may be safe. It is of no use for us to anger our father."

"Do you believe going there will make our father happy?" the Cheyenne chief asked.

"I do not know what makes white men happy," Black Kettle said. "As I told Thunder Bull, I do not trust any white man. But our father is there to help us on our path of peace. He does not control the other soldiers, but he may know where it is safest for us to be."

"The last time you pursued this path, grandfather," Antelope said. "The soldiers came and killed my family. They shot Medicine Woman twenty times that day."

There was silence for a very long time.

"Yes," the Cheyenne chief said. "As we all know, that is why the Dog Soldiers and other clans will not agree to peace. Why they still attack the white settlers."

"Killing settlers will not avenge the murders of our people," Black Kettle said.

"No," the Arapaho chief said. "But our young men do not see why they should sit and wait. Only to be killed in their lodges like old women. Just because you believe what they tell you."

"I do not believe what the white soldiers tell me, old friend. But I believe we cannot win by fighting them. The white man's greed knows no limit. Even *everything* is not enough for them. I think we must do as Sweet Medicine warned us. I believe the right path is to live as near our homes and as close to our ways as we can. At peace."

He stood as if to go. "We all know we will die someday. My responsibility is to seek the path that gives us the best chance to live the path of the people. Those of us who seek the path of peace will go visit with our father at Fort Cobb. To see where he thinks we should live. To let the soldiers know we are not at war. So that we can be on that path."

"And," Medicine Woman said. "You old men should know that this old woman will choose not be killed *like an old woman* in her lodge. Shot again by white soldiers."

"Then," Black Kettle said, "this old man will go to our father. He will work hard to see that you do not." He looked up and raised his arms. "I turn my eyes, my ears, and all my senses to Maheo. I pray to him for guidance for the people. I send all my senses with the smoke up through the smoke hole into the sky. I pray Maheo will show us the path."

57

November 20, 1868

Black Kettle and the small party of Cheyenne and Arapahos arrived at Fort Cobb after the five day, hundred mile ride across the snow covered plains. Their agent immediately ushered them into a meeting with Fort Cobb's commanding officer.

Characteristically, the officer began the meeting with no time offered for even the barest of politeness or amenities, dismissing the agent as his first act of business.

"Your agent informs me that you come in peace, Black Kettle," he said.

"Yes, Colonel. We do. We have been invited here in peace." He answered quickly, like the whites did. The other chiefs were visibly uncomfortable at his failure to take his time before answering.

"Where are the rest of your people?" Looking at each Indian separately. "I see no women accompanying you. Only a few young men and several children."

"They are back at our villages on the Lodgepole River," Black Kettle said. Taking more time before answering. "The young people who came with us wanted to see the fort."

"Why do you peaceful Cheyenne and Arapaho live at the Washita near those who are not peaceful?"

"We traveled north of the Arkansas River," said the eldest of the Arapaho chiefs. "Our father at Fort Larned asked us to come there for our supplies and provisions. There is always trouble and fighting for us north of the Arkansas. So we came to our Indian Territory here."

"Four years ago," Black Kettle said, "My people were attacked by Colorado soldiers and many were killed. So we came here to Indian Territory to live in peace. As required by the Medicine Lodge Treaty we signed."

"You chiefs signed the Treaty, but not your braves."

The chiefs were silent at this.

"Father," Black Kettle said. "We have come to ask you where you want us to live. Our villages are in Indian Territory. We wish to live in peace. Now we are told it is not safe for our people to live so close to those clans that do not wish to live in peace."

"You are correct to worry, Black Kettle. A great war chief is being sent against the Cheyenne and Arapahos who are at war with the Great White Father. The Cheyenne cannot continue killing settlers and stealing women and children and expect to be safe by retreating to Indian Territory. I cannot protect you from those war soldiers."

Custer stepped out of his tent into a blinding snowstorm. They had set up Camp Supply on the Canadian River two days earlier and were now awaiting the arrival of General Sheridan.

"Have the scouts located Sheridan's forces?" Custer asked.

"Little Beaver just rode in," Martinez replied, stamping his feet and thumping his arms across his chest in the bitter cold. "Sheridan will be here tomorrow morning. Three of the Osage scouts stayed with him to show him the way."

"Any news on the Kansans?"

"They're a week behind. Little Beaver said the soldiers say that the Volunteers' horses are faltering. They didn't bring enough food for their horses. They can't keep up."

"The weather is perfect for us, Dennis. The Indians will sit in their lodges and the civilians aren't prepared to fight in this. Let it snow. The more the better."

"Can we march in this?" Benteen said.

"Yes we can. And yes we will. The hostiles are sitting by their fires not imagining we can attack in this. Nobody would expect us to ride eighty to ninety miles in this and then mount an attack."

He looked south, but couldn't see more than ten yards in the driving blizzard.

"Only we can imagine it, because only we can do it."

Lily looked out the window of the makeshift kitchen. She could see the two new sixteen year old girls from Laramie playing with Antelope Thunder and John.

"Why did you bring in them two new girls?" Elly asked.

"To help you and me with the kids and the ranch houses."

"We woulda been fine Lily. Even with the new baby."

"As Gus and I told you when they arrived here, Elly, this is going to be a big ranch. There will be more babies. And at least a dozen cowboys before you know it. There will be plenty of work for all three of you soon enough. Don't worry. Now go out there and ask Lizzie to come in and help with the dinner."

She didn't like Elly's body language as she walked toward the four figures out near the creek. Maybe Elly should've stayed back in Boise, she said to herself. Maybe managing girls was going to be tougher than raising cattle.

Lincoln walked in, stamping the snow off his boots and almost sticking both hands into the fire. "I'm sure not in South Carolina any more, Lily."

"It ever snow there?"

"Three times in my memory. Every other year a little bit, but three times it was enough to even get the white folks excited. Everybody stopped working and went out and played in it together. I don't have many good memories. But those are some of them."

"The branding done?"

Lincoln had hired six new men in Cheyenne two weeks before and had brought Iliff's cattle up without a hitch. Twelve cowboys, counting Gus and herself. Eight hundred cattle, getting their new L Bar S brands. It had been gratifying to see how well the branding went under Lincoln and Nick's direction. Even in all the snow.

"Yes, ma'am. We just got in. Everybody's over at the barn cleaning up the horses."

"Even Gus?"

He laughed. "Yes, Lily, even Gus."

"We all set for the winter then?"

"The men will go out in pairs every two weeks or so, just to make sure there's no trouble. It's our first year, so we'll worry more than the other ranchers. They all told me, 'leave 'em be, they'll all be there in the spring'. But this first time, I want to be more careful. It's why I hired the extra boys. In the future, we won't need so many in the winter. Nothing to do but hunt in the winter."

"And when do you go hunting?"

"Gus is taking three of the boys day after tomorrow. Up over that mesa to the east. I'm headed out with Nick and the two from Oregon the next day. Up north toward Mount Laramie. That'll leave the three best at carpentering to try to finish up on the house during the week we'll be gone."

"I figured you'd take Jimmy with you."

Lincoln looked at Lily for what seemed to her to be longer than necessary. "Just 'cause Jimmy and I are both escaped slaves, both Negros, doesn't mean we're gonna be friends, Lily."

"Sorry. It's just…"

"I like working with Nick better. Anything else, Lily?"

"No. Thanks, Lincoln. See you at dinner."

She watched Lincoln walk out toward the barn and what passed for a bunkhouse. She saw Elly and Lizzie arguing about something in front of the kids, and couldn't help but smile to herself.

Something to build on, she thought. A beginning herd. A beginning family. Her ranch.

"Colonel," Black Kettle said, "We have no desire to deal with this war chief you say is coming. We are here at peace…"

"Not all your young braves are at peace, Black Kettle," the colonel said, interrupting. "Some are not in your control and join the war parties with the other clans. They then come sleep in your village and claim they are part of the peaceful clans."

The chiefs were silent a great long while in the face of the colonel's rudeness.

"What you say is true," Black Kettle said after checking with the other chiefs. "Unlike the whites, we cannot completely control our young men. They have grown up listening to the war stories of their elders. Some hear the cries for vengeance by the Dog Soldiers. If you wish, we can solve this by bringing our villages here. Away from the temptation. Away from talk of war."

"Yes," said the elder Cheyenne chief. "We will then bring our people here to Fort Cobb. Under your authority, father."

"I am not authorized to make peace with the Cheyenne and Arapaho people. Only the new war chief can do that. You must make peace with him. Again, I cannot protect you from him. If you move here and bring him here, you put my Kiowas and Comanches in danger."

There was a long silence.

Finally, the chiefs rose as one.

"We understand, father," Black Kettle said. "It is not our wish to make your responsibilities more difficult. We will ride back to our people with your answer. Then we will decide where our people will live. This Indian Territory designated by our treaty is our home. We have no desire to live elsewhere. All our needs are met here in our lands. At peace with the white man."

The next morning, freshly provisioned by their agent, Black Kettle started his small band on the hundred mile ride through the blizzards back to their village on the Washita.

58

November 23, 1868

"Your compass working, General?" Martinez asked, looking southward into the driving snow.

Custer smiled at his friend. "Have you lost faith in your scouts, Major?"

Martinez just stamped his feet in the hole his boots had created and turned his back to the wind.

Eight hundred and fifty men, twenty companies, stood waiting for their orders in the one to two feet of snow that had been dropped by four days of blizzards. Many hoping Custer would wait until they could see where they were going.

The five hundred men of the Seventh Cavalry stood in groups, near their horses. They knew better. This was the weather Custer had hoped for.

Wagons filled with provisions for a month stood ready, teamsters with their coats up to their chins, horses shaking the snow off their coats.

The order carried down through the ranks, "Boots and saddles."

When all were ready, "To horse."

Then, "Prepare to mount."

"Little Beaver," Custer said. "Head out. Each scout within sight of the scouts immediately in front of him, and have the trailing scouts make sure we can see them."

He turned his attention to the waiting soldiers.

When all was silence and readiness, he ordered, "Mount."

Custer made sure that the last two Osage scouts were still within sight, saluted General Sheridan, and then ordered, "Advance."

And the band started up "The Girl I Left Behind Me" as they marched south.

They hadn't traveled an hour when Benteen saw Little Beaver on his horse slogging his way back toward the soldiers. The Osage scouts trailing him as a group.

Custer, Martinez, and Benteen trotted out as fast as they could to meet them.

"We can't see anything," Little Beaver replied.

"How far do you think we have come?" Custer said, turning the scouts around and riding with them back the way they had come. The soldiers and wagons continued along behind them.

"Maybe two miles," Martinez translated for Little Beaver.

"Ride just a little ahead of us, then. We'll continue to march due south with our compasses to guide us. You just guide us around any obstacles."

"Or alert us to any hostiles in our path," Benteen said.

Little Beaver just looked over at him without comment. Then turned to Custer.

"There is no reason to hurry through this storm, General. The Cheyenne are not going anywhere in this storm. They will wait for you in their villages."

"And there is no reason *not* to hurry, Little Beaver. Will the Cheyenne expect us to be traveling in this weather?"

"No."

"Will they be expecting an attack?"

"No."

"Won't the storm cover our tracks?"

"Yes."

"Then we ride. Maybe ten miles more. You and my compass will keep us on track." He looked back at the Seventh and his band. "We ride."

59

November 24, 1868

Reveille played out over the camp at four in the morning.

The soldiers came out of their tents and looked up at the cloudless sky. The Milky Way was luminous overhead. The combination of starlight and the blanket of reflecting snow enabled them to see the camp and the landscape as clear as if it were broad daylight. They could see their shadows from the stars on the moonless night.

Breakfast and preparations for departure were completed in the crisp winter air, just as dawn made its first appearance in the sky to their left. The combined condensed breath of the soldiers and the horses raised a cloud over the force as the call to "Advance" rang out.

One of the white scouts looked over at Custer and said, "Traveling is good overhead, General."

He rode off toward the Osage scouts to the sound of the officers' laughter behind him.

Black Kettle's small band of Cheyenne and Arapaho were halfway on their journey from Fort Cobb. Another three day's ride back to their villages.

Antelope and Thunder Bull were riding well ahead, practicing chasing each other on their ponies.

"Where do our children get so much energy?" one of the Arapaho chiefs asked.

"Maybe worrying slows us old men down," Black Kettle replied.

"Perhaps. Or maybe the Great Spirit just gives each a limited amount for our time here. Maybe as children we use it up?"

"If this were true," Black Kettle said, "Then the quieter children would make the best warriors. And maybe the best chiefs."

They both watched Antelope's pony skirt a large snowdrift and dash through a copse of trees as she counted coup on Thunder Bull.

"Some girls make good warriors," the Arapaho chief said.

"Antelope said something to me by the fire last night," Black Kettle said. "She told me that the white man's greed is hard for her to understand."

"It is hard for all the people."

"Yes. She asked me what will happen when they have everything. What will they want then?"

"After a time she said, 'Then they will be free.'"

"Did she tell you what she meant?"

"Yes, Antelope said then, 'No matter how long the people live here with the white man, the whites will always want more. Until they have everything. We should make them think they have everything. Or else they will never be free from their greed. They will never let the people live in peace until then.'"

"She's just a young woman," the elder Cheyenne said.

"Yes," Black Kettle said. "But what more wisdom do any of us have about the white man? What have we, or any of the animals on the plains, learned of the white man different from Antelope's view?"

The men rode in silence, watching the two young Cheyenne ahead of them chasing each other through the endless snow drifts. Behaving as if they were as free as the two eagles floating above them in the bright blue, cloudless, sky.

60

November 26, 1868

Custer and Martinez sat on their horses on the Antelope Hills looking out over snow in every direction. They had traveled sixty miles from Camp Supply in three days.

At dawn, Custer had sent the companies of greys and half the Osage scouts due west to start looking for the hostile Cheyenne and Arapaho. The rest of his command was crossing the Canadian River just below him. The last of the wagons was just reaching the south bank and the rest of the cavalry were preparing to cross, when Custer saw a lone horseman galloping down the river toward them.

He pointed at the figure and looked through his field glass.

"Indian?" Martinez asked.

"Yes. One of the scouts."

They both headed down the hill as they saw the scout cross the river and ride up to Benteen. He was pointing needlessly back up the river. The two then rode toward Custer.

"What is it?" Custer asked as they converged.

"They came across a trail of a war party," Benteen replied. "About a hundred and fifty, headed south."

"How far from here?" Custer asked.

"About twelve miles," the scout replied. "Due west."

"Are the cavalry following them?"

"Yes. But they asked me to ask you to hurry. The greys will not be enough. It is a big war party."

"Benteen, get him a fresh pony."

"Yes, sir."

"Take this message," Custer said. "Tell them to pursue the hostiles until eight tonight. Tell them to wait for our arrival at that point. Go. Now."

"Yes, General." He tied his pony to the fresh pony, jumped on the new pony, and headed back up river.

"Benteen, Martinez."

"Yes, sir."

"Put together an eighty man detachment to guard the wagons. Everybody else is to form up to ride out now. Each man is only to take what he can carry on his horse. Everything else stays in the wagons. The wagons should follow behind at their own pace."

"Sir?"

"Yes, Benteen?"

"It will be below freezing tonight and there won't be food enough for either the men or the horses until the wagons catch up."

"Correct, Captain. We were sent here against the hostile Indians. We have found our Indians. These are the conditions most favorable to us and least favorable to them. This is war. Now, form up your companies as ordered and prepare to do your job."

Custer turned his horse back down the hill.

"We ride to war."

Twenty minutes later, led by their Osage scouts fanned out before them looking for any signs of either the Indians or the greys, the Seventh Cavalry rode through the now-melting snow from mid-morning to an hour before sunset without stopping. Slogging through foot high snow, slush, and then ice was tough going, but the horses were kept as fresh as possible by switching out as they tired.

Twenty miles, an hour before sunset, one of the scouts signaled success from the southwest.

Custer got to him first, followed by the other officers.

He dismounted and joined the scout standing over the tracks, looking south.

"It is a war party," the scout said. "At least a hundred and fifty Cheyenne and Arapaho ponies."

"And the greys?" Custer said.

"Following them. The greys are traveling faster."

"Will they catch up with them in two more hours?"

The scout walked down the trail. He joined two of his Osage tribesmen and they conferred. Then the three trotted through the snow back to Custer.

"We think not. The Cheyenne were at this spot before the sun was highest in the sky. Your greys maybe only an hour or two ago. They will not catch them unless the Indians stop to camp for the night. Or if they see your troops coming and turn to attack them."

Custer couldn't contain a smile. "Let's push on, Major. They're stopping in two hours. With any luck we should be with them and ready to stop at nine o'clock."

Antelope and Thunder Bull raced each other through the snow into camp, Thunder Bull the first to arrive by a horse length.

The rest of the Cheyenne party, led by Black Kettle, arrived ten minutes later. The Arapaho chiefs had stopped to rejoin their camp five miles down the Lodgepole.

Black Kettle dismounted, entered his lodge, and went to where Medicine Woman was by the fire with the children. After the children told their father all about the storms and the problems with their ponies while he was gone, their parents grew silent.

"What did our father have to say?" Medicine Woman said after the children ran out to take advantage of the last hour of daylight.

Black Kettle told then what they had learned.

"If our father cannot protect us here and he cannot protect us there," Medicine Woman said. "We must move the village."

"Unless there is a better way. I will call the people to a council tonight."

Little Beaver and two of the scouts who had traveled all day with the greys, came up the path and greeted Custer and his scouts in a heavily wooded area along a deep stream running in the direction they were headed.

Custer had reached the greys close to his nine o'clock estimate. Seventeen hours since their last break at reveille.

"Benteen," Custer said. "Re-form all the companies into one brigade. We will rest for one hour. Coffee and hard tack for the men, oats for the horses."

"Yes, sir."

Custer and Martinez sat with the scouts and the captain of the greys over their coffee and meager meal.

"How are your men faring, Captain?" Custer asked.

"Probably better than yours, General. We'll get a two hour rest to your one."

"Any idea how far we are from the Cheyenne village?"

"We think we are very close," Martinez translated for Little Beaver. "The war party was following this stream for many hours. They continued well past where we are camped now. I think they are down there," pointing south. "Probably where this stream runs into the Lodgepole River."

"The Washita?" Custer said.

"Yes," Little Beaver said. "The Cheyenne call it the Lodgepole River because the trees on the banks make the best lodge poles. The war party was starting to move faster about a mile back upstream. I think they knew the stream and were following it to their village."

"Are we close enough for them to hear us approaching?"

"It is possible, but I do not think so. Maybe five miles. Probably a little farther."

"Then we should ride quietly to the village," Custer said. "And attack at dawn. They will not be expecting us or ready for an attack."

The scouts discussed this among themselves.

"We do not know how big the village is. We do not know where it is," Little Beaver said.

"I don't know, George," Martinez said. "They have a point. We are what, seven hundred and fifty?"

"Seven eighty," Custer asked. "And with the element of surprise."

"It may be better," the captain said. "To get close and then use the scouts to find out where and how large the village is. It can't hurt to have that intelligence before we attack."

"And move on them with a rested brigade," Martinez said.

"Let's move out, gentlemen," Custer said. "We're here to punish these Indians. A surprise attack at dawn will be the start of the end of this war."

He stood up and threw his coffee into the modest fire on the stream bank.

"Prepare the men to ride through the night if necessary. Orders are to be as quiet as possible. Nothing above a whisper. Little Beaver, lead us to the village. Major, prepare the Seventh to advance."

"Yes, General."

Black Kettle sat in his lodge in council with the older men of the village and some of the wives.

He led off by summarizing what they had learned at Fort Cobb. This was followed, characteristically, by a long silence, as each Cheyenne collected his thoughts.

"Did our father tell us to go to this war chief?" one of the men said. "To tell him we are at peace. To ask him where he would like us to move our village?"

"He said he could not protect us from him," Black Kettle said. "That we must make our peace with the great war chief."

"What direction is he coming from?" Medicine Woman asked.

"From the north. From Fort Larned and Fort Dodge."

"Then we have time," one of the chiefs said. "That is one hundred days ride away. The white soldiers cannot travel that far in this weather."

Several of the men in the back of the lodge were talking among themselves.

"Yes?" Black Kettle said.

"A Kiowa raiding party returned today. One of them said he had seen tracks of a very large party. The tracks are a long day's ride northeast of here."

"That must have been the returning Cheyenne war party. They also returned today," Black Kettle said.

"We laughed at him. That's what we told him. As we all know, young Kiowas are not very good trackers."

"If they are right, though, we must move our village now," Medicine Woman said. "If the war chief is coming this way, he could be here tonight. Or tomorrow."

"Our village is the first one they will come to if they are arriving from that direction," the eldest Cheyenne said. "We are the northernmost of all the villages."

"Also," one of the wives said. "One of our young men returned with the Cheyenne and Arapaho war party. His pony tired. When he went back to get him, he thought he saw white soldiers on the ridges to the north."

"Why do our young men not stay at peace here in the village?" Black Kettle said. "That is the problem our father has with us."

All became quiet in the face of Black Kettle's expressed frustration.

"Our choices are few," the eldest Cheyenne said.

"Yes," Black Kettle said. "We must either move our village in the morning. Or we must send a delegation to meet with the war chief."

"Or leave now," Medicine Woman said. "Now. Do we want the white soldiers to slaughter our people again? At dawn?"

For an hour, they discussed whether to leave or to approach the war chief. The eventual consensus was to move their village south and west, away from the neighboring villages along the Lodgepole River. They would leave in the morning after they had time to inform the entire village and gather their ponies.

Black Kettle listened thoughtfully to his wife as she had the last word. "We must leave now. Tonight. Our people and our neighboring tribes are telling us they have seen the white soldiers. That they are coming now. We must leave tonight."

But the council had spoken. They would leave in the morning.

"I think the village is maybe a mile from here, maybe a little more," Little Beaver said.

"Move the men very quietly," Custer said. "Not a sound. The Osage scouts will take you to the spot where we dare go no further."

He turned to Little Beaver and his two senior officers. "Martinez, Benteen come with us. Let's go see if Little Beaver can show us the village."

The three officers walked behind five of the scouts who were fanned out in front of them in the near-pitch darkness. They came to a ridge, lay on their stomachs, and looked down through their condensed breath.

Into empty blackness.

"Nothing," Custer said.

Little Beaver remained quiet.

"It's a village," he said. "A very large Indian village."

Custer stared. "I see what looks like a herd of buffalo or deer by the river, some moving slowly in the dark, but most are absolutely still."

"That is a herd of ponies. Maybe a thousand. Very large village."

"How do you know?"

"I heard a dog bark. Just one, but it was a dog. Not a coyote or wolf. An Indian dog."

They continued to stare down into the area across the river.

"Yes, I heard a dog bark just then," Custer said.

And then Custer heard a bell tinkling. Buffalo and deer did not wear bells. But the lead ponies of some Indian pony herds did.

And then he heard a baby cry. One lone papoose. One small cry.

Custer had found his Indians.

61

November 27, 1868

"We attack at dawn," Custer told his assembled officers just past midnight. "We will surround them tonight. Not a sound. Leave sabres behind the lines. All heavy overcoats, too. Each company assign a soldier to stay back to guard our belongings."

"Do we know the size of the village yet?" Benteen asked.

"Not precisely. It is a very large village. Little Beaver?"

"It is a very large village," Little Beaver replied. "Many Indians. It is too risky to get any closer. It is too dark to know for sure. I think maybe sixty lodges. Maybe three hundred Cheyenne. There may also be other villages down river. The war party we followed were not all from this one village. Too many warriors, not enough lodges. We can scout tomorrow in daylight."

"So, we have no reconnaissance?" Benteen asked. "No idea of what we're really up against?"

"We know," Custer replied. "That even if the entire war party is in that village, we have them outnumbered five to one."

"Surprised and trapped, the women and young men will also fight," Little Beaver said.

"Any other comments or questions?" Custer asked, ignoring his scout and Benteen.

Each man was left with his own thoughts in the ensuing silence.

"Divide into four equal groups. One hundred eighty to a hundred and ninety each. Three groups move into position from three different directions. The rest of us, including the corps d'elite and the band, will remain here with Martinez and me. We will attack into the dawn sun. All should be ready to attack at dawn when I give the order. The band will play "Garryowen" at the sound of that order."

Custer looked over at the moon. It was low on the western horizon and looked like it would leave all in complete darkness for the final two hours before dawn.

"Move out now. There should be no sound except horse hooves on snow. The men are not to stamp their feet for warmth and there are to be no fires. Warmth will be best sought next to the horses and the company of other soldiers."

"God speed and may He be with us in this exercise of our duties."

Antelope awoke. It was her first night with her adoptive family in their lodge in almost two weeks. She had kept waking from a dream where she and Thunder Bull were chasing white soldiers in the snow. The soldiers were chasing and slaughtering a herd of buffalo. There were many soldiers. They covered the meadows into the trees. She and Thunder Bull kept counting coup on the soldiers, but the soldiers ignored the two of them and kept killing the buffalo, all of whom were stumbling and having trouble running in the deep snow. In fact all were riding and running in slow motion in the deep snow.

Then the buffalo were all dead and the soldiers had turned and started chasing Thunder Bull and Antelope. They were riding through the snow banks, firing their rifles.

She sat up. She heard ponies walking on the snow and ice. Crunching near her lodge.

She got up and walked out of the lodge to her pony. He was tethered where she'd left him. She reached up and scratched his ear. And he nuzzled her chest in return. A dog barked. She looked in the direction of the barking and saw Medicine Woman standing outside her lodge. Medicine Woman was looking into the woods where the dog was, not noticing Antelope.

There it was again. The sound of ponies walking on snow. Antelope walked slowly over to the main pony herd. They were gathered on the northeast end of the camp. This was unusual. They were usually on the other side. Many of the ponies were walking nervously rather than sleeping. Ponies walking on snow and ice.

She decided to return to her lodge and not bother anyone with the petty fears of a young woman.

Martinez woke Custer two hours before dawn, just as the moon set, plunging all into darkness.

The two moved among the officers and the white scouts, listening with satisfaction to the general air of optimism.

"We've caught them napping," Custer said.

"Any word from those who headed out last night?" Martinez asked.

"No. There would have been gunfire. Any news would be bad, Major."

"The men are clearly ready. They are impatient with chasing and not finding Indians."

"Me too, Dennis. Me too. Where are the Osage scouts?"

"Behind us. Over there, all huddled under the low branches of that huge fir tree."

They walked over to the scouts, who were now completely dressed in their battle clothing and ferocious war paint. Little Beaver was almost unrecognizable.

"Little Beaver," Martinez translated for Custer. "Are your scouts ready? It is time to advance."

"Yes, General."

"We go now."

Little Beaver and Custer led the remaining two hundred men the three hundred yards down toward the village. As close as they dared until the order to attack at dawn less than two hours away. They stopped at the nearest ridge. Peered down.

"At the initial attack, Dennis, I want you to take a detachment straight through the village to secure their ponies. I want to totally destroy this village and its ability to wage war."

"Yes, sir."

"It is totally quiet," Custer said. "Is it possible they discovered us and have abandoned the village?"

He and Martinez turned around, expecting an answer from Little Beaver. But Little Beaver and his Osage scouts had disappeared. To somewhere behind the cavalry lines.

It was dawn. Thunder Bull could hear a dog barking furiously in the woods at the Lodgepole River. And he thought he heard the ponies prancing nervously on the east side of the village. He was sure he and the other watchers had left them on the west side, away from the river.

He stepped out of his family's lodge. There were one or two braves holding their Henry rifles and staring into the timber stand to the east.

The dog started barking again. Thunder Bull couldn't see the dog, but he noticed one of the young Cheyenne raise his rifle and fire it in the direction of the sound.

And then time stood still.

Custer, on the verge of ordering his soldiers to mount up, heard the shot.

"Attack," he ordered, firing his pistol into the air.

"Martinez, mount up. Capture their ponies. Now."

The band struck up the first few notes of "Garryowen" as the Seventh Cavalry attacked from four directions. The only sounds were the bugles signaling charge, shouting men, the hooves of the horses furiously striking frozen snow and ice, and a fusillade of gunfire aimed at those few visible braves and into the lodges.

But there were no rollicking notes of "Garryowen." The band's instruments had frozen as saliva hit freezing air and frozen instruments.

Black Kettle and Medicine Woman, along with hundreds of waking Cheyenne, came rushing as one out of their lodges. The gunfire and thunder of hooves was deafening. All around them was confusion. Men, women, and children ran out of lodges, some trying to mount their ponies.

Mounted soldiers were crashing through the village, shooting in every direction. At men, women, children, dogs. Into the lodges.

Dozens of braves with rifles and bows and arrows ran into the timber along the river banks to set up defensive positions. They were able to cover many Cheyenne fleeing down river to the east and north.

In the village, all was pandemonium. Black Kettle and Medicine Woman managed to join a group of Indians mounting terrified ponies to try and race south and eastward through the village to escape around the pony herd to the other villages. Several were cut down as they rushed to the pony herd.

Having found and mounted his pony, Thunder Bull reached down to Medicine Woman's arms as she was being pushed onto a pony by Black Kettle.

"Run," Black Kettle said as Thunder Bull turned to lead her away from the onrushing cavalry. "Save yourself. I will find this war general and tell him we are at peace."

"Run yourself, old man" she said over her shoulder. "They don't care. They will kill you and all the people who stay. They are not here shooting the people to make peace."

A young brave next to them was hit and knocked off his pony by the force of the shot.

Thunder Bull grabbed Black Kettle by his shirt and pulled him on to a pony.

"Run. You are no good for the people here. Run to the Arapaho village."

The three Cheyenne, along with a dozen braves and women, galloped south along the eastern edge of the village and turned left around the pony herd, toward the river.

The company of greys galloped up the bank of the river, half of them attacking the braves in the defensive position to their west, and half taking off in pursuit of the fleeing Cheyenne.

Martinez and his hundred men had raced through the village and surrounded the terrified pony herd. Ten soldiers followed the trail of the ponies that had fled, and, presently, returned with them and reassembled the entire herd. In the meantime, several of his soldiers found themselves engaged in fire fights with isolated braves along the edge of the village.

"Sergeant. Tighten up the men around the ponies. Take the rest later. Don't let them have open shots at your men."

Martinez heard the captain of the greys off to his left yell, "Here's for a brevet or a coffin," as he led his troops after the fleeing Indians. Martinez held his hand up to block the glare from the rising sun, watching them race to the east. Maybe twenty soldiers with him. Maybe less.

He looked around to see if he could afford to send men after them. Looked over at the remaining greys descending on a group of Indians firing bows and arrows. He decided he couldn't risk letting the ponies escape. He turned his attention back to the village. Saw Custer shooting his way into the village, saw Benteen shoot a young boy on foot who was firing at him.

Martinez grabbed several men on foot, signaled to Custer, and headed north. Toward the Cheyenne braves at the river embankment covering the retreating Indians.

"Black Kettle," Thunder Bull said. "Turn. The soldiers coming behind us will cut us off. Run to the timber on the other side of the river. Under the rising sun."

As he turned to point, he saw Black Kettle go down. Shot in the back. And then Medicine Woman went down, she too dead from a shot in the back.

Several other surviving braves and women now rode with him away from the oncoming grey company. It was now to be a race, just like with Antelope, yesterday. Was that just yesterday, he thought? I was just a boy then.

On the Indians ran, through snow and ice. Twenty grey horses following them. The soldiers shooting at the Indians, not realizing they were riding straight toward the much larger Cheyenne camp five miles to the east.

With the entire brigade now converged on the village, the shooting intensified. Custer, Martinez, and Benteen organized the foot soldiers to eliminate the clusters of fighting braves on the river banks. Individual braves were cut down as they emerged from their tipis.

"Don't shoot into the lodges," Custer said. "I want the women and children captured, not killed. I want hostages."

Martinez had ridden to the eastern edge of the captured pony herd. He thought he heard gunfire to the east, but couldn't see anything between him and the horizon. In any case there was now gunfire all around him. He looked back to the river to where the remaining soldiers of the grey company had dismounted and had joined the sharpshooters shooting at the Indians dug in on the river bank. He joined the rest of his men going from lodge to lodge looking for captives.

Thunder Bull and the fleeing Cheyenne had gained a hundred yards on the greys. He looked ahead and saw a hundred Cheyenne in full battle dress and paint galloping toward them. He drove his pony into a full circle so that he came in parallel to the lead braves now running straight toward the white soldiers.

"Hello little man," said the leader.

"White soldiers attacked our village. They killed Black Kettle. They killed many women and children."

The charging Cheyenne slowed as they saw the captain of the greys pull up ahead of them and organize his twenty cavalry into a defensive circle in the snow. Protected by the snow banks and their own horses that they had shot to use as bulwarks.

"Send these white soldiers to their gods," one of the warriors said to Thunder Bull. "Then we will go back to Black Kettle's village and rescue the rest of the people."

The first brave tossed Thunder Bull a hatchet. The second gave him a Remington revolver.

"Avenge Black Kettle, little man," he said.

The hundred Cheyenne circled the twenty soldiers. Riding out of gunshot range to draw their fire, just as back at Bluff Creek, but with one difference. This was no attempt to draw the soldiers out to fight a superior force concealed and waiting for them. The superior force was circling right in front of them.

Once the perimeter of the firing range of the soldiers was established, the Cheyenne began sending in sorties of ten to twelve braves shooting invisibly from the sides of their ponies.

"Choose your shots carefully," the captain of the greys said. "Custer will send reinforcements shortly. Conserve ammunition until then."

"Where did these Indians come from?" asked a sergeant.

"Doesn't matter to us, Sergeant. Wherever they came from just send them to their gods now."

"It might have been nice to know they were out here." He then added, almost as an afterthought, "Save your last bullet for yourself."

The situation for the soldiers was desperate. They could shoot at the galloping Indians in front of them, but the Indians had unobstructed views of the backs of the men on the other side of the circle.

One by one, they began to be shot from behind.

No sign of Custer.

One of the braves broke from the circling Indians and dashed straight toward the soldiers at a spot where the shooting had stopped. He leaped over the dead soldiers, leaned down as his pony passed over the far soldiers and tapped a startled soldier on the back of his shoulder with his lance.

He raced back to his colleagues to the thundering sound of tremolos and derision for the increasingly helpless soldiers.

Thunder Bull broke from the circle and raced straight at the captain of the greys. For the second time that morning, time stood still as his pony galloped straight ahead throwing snow and slush to the sides and behind, like some great snow spirit in a dream.

The captain of the greys saw him coming. A young boy. No war bonnet. No paint. Nothing but a breech cloth. He took aim. Fired. Missed.

Thunder Bull's pony leaped over the captain as Thunder Bull leaned down and tapped the captain's shoulder with the harmless back of the hatchet. And then he was gone. Through the circle of soldiers and out into the snowy plains.

The captain rose to get another shot at Thunder Bull's receding back, and three of the circling Indians shot at him. One bullet caught him in the shoulder, spinning him around. A second bullet caught him full in the chest, and he went down.

Counting coup on the leader of the soldiers and then watching him shot down. All in slow motion for Thunder Bull.

Time resumed flowing normally as the soldiers were killed one by one. Until all was quiet.

And the whooping Cheyenne descended upon the bodies of the very members of the Seventh Cavalry who had first come upon the Indian trail twenty-four hours earlier. The trail that had led them to die at this spot on the snow-covered plains.

It was just after ten o'clock. The shooting had stopped. The soldiers were going from lodge to lodge, gathering the women and children who had not escaped or been killed by the gunfire in the village, bringing them to the large center lodge.

"General," Benteen said, pointing up to a ridge more than a mile downriver.

"Yes, I saw them earlier, Captain. They're the Indians that got away during the fighting."

"That many?"

Custer had not looked at the Indians for over half an hour, not worrying about a handful of escaped braves. He grabbed his glasses and now looked more carefully. There were now more than a hundred. In full war paint, with brightly colored feathered bonnets and lances with pendants floating in the wind. More were joining them from the east and north. Those Indians were not from this village.

"Martinez, Little Beaver, let's go talk to the captives. Find out what we've got here."

Benteen looked up at the gathering Indians, turned to Custer and started to say something. But he thought better of it and headed to the lodge with the other officers.

The party entered the lodge containing the fifty-three captive women and children.

One of the older Cheyenne women approached Martinez and indicated she'd like to talk. After assuring all the assembled women and children that they would be treated well and taken to join other Cheyenne on the reservation, Custer indicated for her to speak. Little Beaver and Martinez translated as best they could as she alternately talked to her fellow Cheyenne captives and Custer. Antelope sat in the back, near her adoptive sister and aunt. She looked to the back of the lodge to see if she could escape. But there were soldiers guarding all sides. Two of them looking at her.

After a long speech characterizing both the lack of leadership and the bravery of the fallen warriors, she approached Custer and offered him the hand of one of the young women.

"She wishes to cement the bond between the great war chief Long Hair and the people," Martinez said as Custer held the hand of the maiden.

Custer ushered the young woman back to the group. "Please explain that I accept the friendship of the people and of the beautiful young woman, but that I am long spoken for by Libby back home. After you smooth that over, ask who the warriors are up on the ridge to the southeast."

"Actually, General" Benteen said, returning from a walk outside the lodge, "They are now on all the ridges surrounding the village."

"How many, Captain?"

"Several hundred."

Custer started to walk outside, but turned his attention instead to the Cheyenne woman who was now listening to Martinez. She pointedly ignored Little Beaver. After Martinez asked her his questions, she walked out of the lodge to look for herself. She returned and began speaking.

"She says this is a small village on the edge of a large number of villages. Fifty lodges here, as we know. More than two hundred Cheyenne. Less than three hundred. She says we outnumbered the warriors five to one here. That this is Black Kettle's village and he was at peace with the other generals. But not with Long Hair."

"What does she say about the other villages?"

"She says that they are at war with all the generals, not only Long Hair. She says there are four or five more villages down the Washita. They call it the Lodgepole. The farthest village is more than a half day's ride from this spot. More Cheyenne. Also Arapaho, Kiowa, Comanche, and Kiowa-Apaches."

There was a great murmuring among the captives. Antelope again looked to the rear of the lodge, at an unsecured flap along the bottom. Again caught the gaze of the two soldiers.

Martinez paused. Asked the woman something.

"How many, Major?"

"She says over a thousand lodges, General. That'd make it six thousand or so Indians, General. She asked me to tell Long Hair that she thinks the Indian warriors coming to surround the village outnumber his soldiers five to one."

Benteen exchanged glances with Little Beaver.

Custer turned to Little Beaver and Martinez. "Do you believe her?"

"Little Beaver," Martinez said, "says his scouts discovered the villages during the fighting this morning. This was a small village among many. The other prisoners were murmuring in agreement. He thinks she does not exaggerate. Little Beaver says you have found your Indians, General."

A half hour later, the officers assembled.

"We've lost one and over a dozen wounded," Benteen said. "And the captain and nineteen men of the greys are missing."

"They chased some of the escaping Indians to the east," Martinez said.

"We have to go find them," Benteen said. "Now. They could still be under attack."

"No," Custer said. "Twenty men will be all right. We have to first organize the Seventh. Then deal with the greys."

"We can't leave twenty men out there to fend for themselves against a thousand Indians, General."

"What were the Indian casualties, Martinez?" Custer said, ignoring Benteen.

"Over a hundred dead at last count, General. Including women and children."

"Couldn't be helped. Given all the resistance. How are we on ammunition?"

"In need of our wagons, General. We're low."

All the officers followed Custer's gaze to the surrounding ridges and growing number of Indians.

They were interrupted by a clattering of wagons and horses at the north end of the village. It was the ammunition wagons arriving, accompanied by the men who had stayed behind with the overcoats and sabers.

"We were attacked by Indians, General," the sergeant in charge of the detail said. "We had to abandon all the belongings. By chance, the ammunition wagons arrived while the Indians were stealing everything and before they could attack our positions, sir."

"The men's overcoats?" Custer asked.

"All gone."

The officers looked out over their men, who were awaiting orders and oblivious to the fact that they were now surrounded by two enemies. Several thousand Indians and the bitter cold temperatures to come that night.

"Martinez." Custer said. "Round up a hundred of the ponies so we can bring the prisoners with us."

"The ponies are terrified of the soldiers. They won't let us near them."

"Then go get the women and children. Have them each find and bring in a pony. Try to get them to also bring in twenty or thirty extra."

"And the rest?"

"Only three options, Major. Taking them with us slows us down and makes us an easy target. Releasing them means we'll be fighting Indians on them some time again soon."

"And the third option?"

"Kill them, Major. Get the captives out here to select their ponies. Then kill the rest. Then I want this village burned to the ground. Let the prisoners carry their own belongings, but I want everything else burned. Lodges, belongings, everything. Tell the men no souvenirs. We are going to have to travel light. And let's get started. The Indians on the ridges don't seem to be leaving."

Martinez and several soldiers went back to the lodge to gather all the prisoners and send them after the ponies and their belongings.

"And Benteen?"

"Yes, General."

"Organize groups of cavalry to go out and chase the Indians off those ridges. And send one group to the east seeing if they can locate the greys. Let's keep the Indians guessing and on the move. They don't need any more time to figure this out."

"Yes, sir."

Antelope and her younger cousin, twenty year old Spring Grass, went back to her lodge with the two soldiers assigned to them. They ducked in as one of the soldiers followed. Antelope turned and pushed him out. She tried to look threatening, and he laughed.

"Where are your parents?" Antelope asked Spring Grass.

"The soldiers killed both of them. Over by the river." Spring Grass pointed through the entrance to the east.

"Oh, Spring Grass. I am so sorry." They hugged each other by the fire.

Antelope looked closely at her cousin, then they gathered up some of their things. Antelope, slipping a knife into a shawl, looked around, and then gave the soldier half her things to carry. She tied the shawl around her waist, the knife tucked safely against her stomach

The two young women disdainfully pushed by the soldier and stepped outside the lodge. Antelope thrust the rest of her things into the other soldier's arms causing him to drop his rifle.

"My pony is on the other side," Spring Grass said, and hurried off before Antelope could stop her.

Antelope joined a small group of women and children walking among the unsettled ponies. She glanced back at her two soldiers, standing there holding her things, no longer looking at her.

She worked her way through the ponies, staying low, now out of sight of all the soldiers. She could not see Spring Grass anywhere.

She waited, hidden in the herd, until stillness had returned. All the other prisoners with their selected ponies were now away from the herd, holding and calming what looked like a hundred ponies.

Some of the soldiers were now moving the captured women and children and their ponies toward the north edge of the village, away from the herd. She saw one of her two soldiers looking among the prisoners for her.

She sensed the ponies around her becoming nervous even before she saw the soldiers starting to maneuver into a circle around them. She nuzzled the nearest mare to calm her and received a soft head butt in return. Two captives seeking solace in companionship.

She looked around for some possible hard ground in all the snow, and, for the first time, realized she was still barefoot. She saw the soldiers moving directly behind and to the east of the herd at the same time she heard a fusillade of rifle fire from just west of the herd. Then she heard the screaming of the ponies and felt the momentum of the terrified ponies all pushing themselves toward her and her now-terrified mare.

No choices now, she leaped on to her mare, leaning down on the side away from the soldiers so they wouldn't see her coming. She drove the mare out of the herd directly at two startled soldiers. They were waving blankets to try to prevent their escape and it was working with the herd, as the ponies on the edge were frantically trying to avoid the soldiers.

But Antelope's mare galloped straight at them with Antelope hidden along its right side, knife held in her left hand above the neck of the mare.

She made the mare veer to the left and knock the left-most soldier to the ground just as she struck out and cut the other soldier's arm as she rode past. She never looked back. She could hear, among the fusillades on the other side of the herd and the screaming pones, individual shots. Closer. No doubt coming from the soldiers pursuing her.

She could hear the individual shots, decreasing in number, until she was well out of range and could only hear the pounding of her mare's hooves crunching on the snow and ice.

It was now late afternoon, and Custer and Martinez watched as the men finished slitting the throats of the remaining ponies and burning the lodges and all the village's belongings. Even in broad daylight, great leaping bonfires illuminated the bloody snow around and amidst the seven hundred dead ponies.

The women and children captives watched in shock as their village went up in smoke. They each had their pony and the things on their backs. All else was gone. All their men. Their brothers and fathers and uncles and cousins. And many of their mothers and sisters and aunts, lying dead around them. Black Kettle's village was no longer at peace with the white man. Black Kettle's village was no more.

"What do you recommend we do with them?" Custer asked, pointing up at the still-gathering warriors. "Does the presence of the women and children prisoners guarantee they won't attack us on our return to Camp Supply?"

Little Beaver looked up at the surrounding ridges covered with a growing number of painted warriors. Hundreds, maybe thousands of braves from the many tribes, all fully decorated for war in bonnets, lances and colored ribbons.

Martinez translated for Little Beaver. "Each of those braves has spent his life since early childhood preparing for hunting, skirmishes, and battles. And for the opportunity to engage in a great war, General. But they have never witnessed anything like what you have done to the Cheyenne here today. Ponies are stolen in wars, not entire herds killed. You strike at the people's ability to live. To hunt. To live here on the plains. All of them up there knew that Black Kettle was at peace with the white man. And they have witnessed the destruction of his people."

"The question, Little Beaver, was what will they do if we leave?"

"Each of them feels that he has waited his whole life for this chance to either kill you or be killed by you. But as a group, having seen this, they will want their chiefs to decide what to do. This is not a skirmish to be answered with a skirmish. This is not only about them. This threatens all their sense of the people, not just each brave."

Benteen rode up with a dozen men.

"General," he said. "There's no sign of the greys to the east, and the Indians don't seem inclined to run off when a handful of us race toward their ridges."

"Thank you, Captain." He turned back to Little Beaver, nodded for him to continue.

"This morning, Black Kettle's village was a group of Cheyenne lodges. It was vulnerable to your attack with a larger force of eight hundred men. Now, it is a village of white soldiers. The lodges are gone and it is even more vulnerable to an attack by a superior force. You are outnumbered, General."

"General," Benteen said. "We cannot have the Seventh Cavalry abandon twenty men to those Indians."

Martinez and Custer ignored him, as Martinez continued translating Little Beaver's message, "If you start your troops and prisoners back west to your camp, they will chase you down, continuously cutting you down from behind."

"Martinez, Benteen," Custer said. "We can't stay here and we can't retreat."

There was no response.

"So we will attack. Form the Seventh and the prisoners for a march directly at the Indians."

Custer mounted his horse, and turned toward the east end of the smoldering ruins of the village. "Signal when ready and I'll order the Advance," he said as he galloped to the front ranks, toward the ridges covered with Indians.

Just before sunset, the bugles sounded the charge as the Seventh Cavalry, slowed by their prisoners and the hundred Indian ponies, rode southeast. Directly at the largest group of watching Indians.

Several groups of Cheyenne and Kiowa braves looked down at the advancing soldiers from a ridge a mile to the east. All had watched the burning of the village and the murder of the pony herd.

Antelope and Thunder Bull had now joined them.

From their perch, they could see other groups of Indians, painted, with shields and lances at their sides, watching the soldiers from the surrounding ridges.

Each of the braves knew in his heart that he had trained from boyhood for this moment. To fight the soldiers. To kill, to count coup, and maybe to even be killed by them.

But the presence of the Cheyenne women and children in the soldiers' midst was something they had not been trained to deal with. And they had never seen entire villages burned. Women and children killed in cold blood. An entire herd of ponies slaughtered.

And there was nobody on the ridges empowered to decide to carry out an all-out war against the white soldiers. No way to assemble the various chiefs to decide whether or not to attack eight hundred armed soldiers. With fifty Cheyenne women and children and a hundred Cheyenne ponies.

There would need to be preparations. Councils. Dances. Each brave would need his best medicine and his finest war clothing and weapons. War would have to be celebrated and prepared for.

One by one, the groups of braves turned and headed back to their individual villages down the Lodgepole. To consult with their chiefs. There would be time to attack the soldiers if that was to be the decision of the chiefs.

Antelope and Thunder Bull rode east with the Cheyenne warriors to their camp. Antelope, having lost her second family. Thunder Bull, having become, in all senses, today a Cheyenne man.

They rode solemnly by the twenty greys and the slaughtered, now-mutilated, white soldiers, many with ten to twenty arrows sticking out of their bodies. Some with their heads crushed and partially severed from their bodies.

When it was clear the Indians were departing, the surviving members of the Seventh Cavalry rode due north back toward Camp Supply.

Custer in the lead. Benteen, Martinez, and Little Beaver together behind him. The rest of the Seventh followed with the captured Indians and ponies.

"He should be relieved of his command," Benteen said.

"For abandoning the greys?" Martinez asked. "You were sent after them and couldn't find them."

"No commander leaves his men behind to be slaughtered by Indians."

"And endanger the entire Seventh Cavalry?"

"He *did* endanger the entire Seventh Cavalry," Benteen said. He looked over at Little Beaver, riding silently alongside. "He ignored the scouts' warnings. You didn't notice, but Little Beaver and his Osage were all dressed and decorated with their death paint. Not their war paint. Custer overruled the scouts and ordered no reconnaissance. It was completely reckless. It turned out we were completely outnumbered. We're lucky that any of us survived today, Dennis."

They rode on in silence for a half mile. The only sound was the snow crunching under thousands of hooves.

"So," Martinez finally said. "You give him no credit for successfully destroying the hostile village and then advancing on the Indians and chasing them off?"

"It was reckless and you know it, Martinez. We could have been slaughtered had the Indians chosen to attack us from above."

"I were you, Benteen, I'd let it go. Maybe he was just lucky. Or maybe he knows the Indians better than you do. But the generals aren't going to relieve their only successful Indian fighter of his command. Not when he's just been the first to defeat the Cheyenne."

"It was just pure dumb luck and you know it Martinez. We attacked a superior force with no support and, as it turned out, no winter coats."

"Best to let it go, Major. It's not new. During the war, the papers back east called it Custer Luck."

Benteen snorted in derision, and, before he could say anything, Martinez said, "I don't think they'll ever be talking about Benteen Luck, Captain."

And he kicked his horse into a trot to join Custer at the head of the troops.

62

December 10, 1868

Nearly two weeks later, Custer gazed down at the frozen remains of the company of greys. Still in the circle of their fallen horses, all perfectly preserved, frozen in their mutilation. The Seventh Cavalry and reinforcements had marched, now fifteen hundred strong, from Camp Supply three days earlier.

Custer looked over at Martinez, but refused to make eye contact with Benteen.

"Take the bodies back to camp for burial, Major."

And the party, carrying their fallen comrades, rode somberly back to their camp at the former site of Black Kettle's village on the banks of the Washita.

"We will ride to Fort Cobb in the morning," Custer said. He was surrounded by his officers around a large bonfire in the center of the camp. On one side of him was Little Beaver, on the other Spring Grass. "Our orders are to bring the Kiowas, Arapahos, and Cheyenne into the reservation at Fort Cobb. Given our numbers, surprise is impossible. We will see no Indians who don't want to be seen."

"Then," Martinez said. "To ask the obvious, how do we bring them in?"

"We have their captives. We will trade and negotiate. Our captive Cheyenne women assure us that the Indians will have no more desire to fight after what happened to Black Kettle."

"Do you believe them?"

"We will see."

As the meeting broke up, several of the officers retired to their tents with the Indian women captives they had brought with them from Camp Supply.

Custer said good night to his officers and walked with Spring Grass into their tent.

63

March 27, 1869

Lily sat in the living room with Gus and Lincoln in their newly finished ranch house. Almost surrounded now by their nearly completed fortress.

"It's time to start rounding up the cows," Gus said. "Branding the new calves."

"Any idea yet how many we lost during the winter?" Lily asked.

"We'll know that after the roundup," Lincoln replied. "Probably not till sometime in May."

"Just in time for the new baby," Gus said. "Then I gotta go. I'm here for the roundups until after the baby, Lil. Then, as we discussed, I've promised to help scout for the Army down on the Platte. The Cheyenne again."

Lily frowned as she put both her hands on her protruding stomach. "No, we discussed needing you here, Gus. We're not just ranching temporarily on a small spread in Oregon any more. Sitting around practicing and waiting for the chance to come here. This is permanent. This is our home. This is our ranch."

"It's your ranch, Lil. I can help out. I can help the carpenters some. Help with the roundup. But I'm the thirteenth best cowhand we've got."

"We only have twelve," she said.

"Precisely." He paused, but when neither Lincoln nor Lily said anything, he went on. "I spent the winter hunting antelope and buffalo. I'm good at that. We have enough food to last you and the cowboys and the girls and the kids until next winter."

"I need you here, Gus."

"I'll head out and see how the preparations are going," Lincoln said, getting up.

"No, Lincoln," she said. "The three of us need to figure this out."

He sat back down. Didn't look happy.

Gus just looked amused at Lily.

"Lily. I'm good at poker. And I'm good at tracking and hunting. Both animals and Indians. And, as you always told me, I'm great at earning people's confidence."

"And you're great with me and the kids. And at producing kids." She touched his shoulder. "We need you here, Gus."

"And I'm terrible with any kind of building implement. And I'm terrible at earning any cow's confidence."

This time Lincoln laughed.

"Lil, you got your ranch. And you got your man. I'm that man and I helped you get your ranch."

"And it's the nicest ranch in Wyoming Territory."

"And I'm going to be a part of the nicest ranch in Wyoming for as long as I'm alive."

"An important part," she said.

"Yes, an important part. And so's he," pointing at Lincoln.

"But I'm gonna go crazy sitting around for six, seven months at a time, playing with kids and babysitting cows. Poker'll keep you in finery Lil, and scouting for the Army as long as they need me will keep me from going crazy. I'm good at it, and they need me."

"It's not a sharing arrangement I'm happy about, Gus. Please promise me you'll do both as little as you can?"

"As little as I can, Lily. You have my word."

"And that you're not going to get killed by some gambler or some Indian?"

Gus grinned back at the two of them.

"With my charm? No chance."

"What's your plan, General?" Martinez asked.

"Same one that worked with the Kiowas and the Arapahos two months ago at Fort Cobb," Custer replied. Both officers looked across the firelight at the dozen senior Cheyenne. There had been hundreds of Indians at the start of this dinner near their village at the tributary of the Red River. Little by little the Indians had been wandering back to their lodges as they finished eating.

"But with them we actually had captured their chiefs and held them hostage until the tribes came in and surrendered at Fort Cobb. Here, we're sitting across from all of them. Having a peace parlay."

"And we know they are all planning to leave with the entire Cheyenne tribe while we sleep," Custer said, not taking his eyes off the chiefs.

During the dinner, several Cheyenne men had been invited to sing to the assembly. Spring Grass told Custer, and his interpreters confirmed it for him, that she had never seen this done before. She confided she had no idea why the chiefs had brought in the singers.

"The wailing covering up the sounds of the Indians leaving?" Martinez asked.

"That's what I think," Custer replied.

An hour later, four Cheyenne chiefs and only forty young men and braves remained behind.

Custer stood and signaled the officers who he had ordered to remain to stand with him. They completely surrounded the remaining Cheyenne. They all had cocked pistols at their sides and their right hands held up in peace.

The chiefs stood, one with a cocked pistol, the others threading arrows in bows held in front of them.

"I have something important to tell you," Custer said, with Martinez interpreting. They both threw their pistols to the ground in front of the chiefs.

"I do not want any fight. I do not want any shooting. I came to the Kiowas in peace. I came to the Arapahos in peace. They are now at the reservation. We do not want any more killing of Cheyenne. It is my job to have you go to the reservation in peace."

"And if we want to live in peace on the plains?" the oldest chief asked.

"Then you must fight us. And more of your people will be killed. You will lose your lodges. Your belongings. Your people. You are too few now to stand up to my soldiers."

One of the chiefs calmly threaded arrow after arrow on his bow, thumbed the sharp points, and looked down the length of the arrows at one, then another officer. Several of the young Indians jumped on their ponies in the circle of soldiers. The chief had now selected a number of arrows and held them at his side.

Custer pointed to the four chiefs as a signal to the assembled officers.

"You must help us help your people. We do not want to hurt even one of the Cheyenne people."

Several of the young braves raced through the soldiers, several on horseback.

"Don't shoot," Custer ordered in English, and Martinez shouted irrelevantly in Cheyenne.

In the ensuing melee, all but the four chiefs were allowed to escape back to the village.

"If you will disarm," Custer said. "I will free one of you to go to the village with a message."

Martinez had to repeat this three times through in the tension created by the silence from the impassive four chiefs.

"Should I get our Cheyenne women to help convince them?" Martinez asked.

"No. Let them think. I don't trust all our captives."

Several of the officers behind Custer smirked at that, but he didn't see it.

"If you do not give up your arms, I will force you to. You have deceived us this night. Eaten our provisions, promising peace, while you have sent your people to leave the village behind our backs." He turned to the officers. "Bring another fifty men."

When the other soldiers arrived in front of them, the four placed their arms on the ground in front of Custer and held a conference among themselves.

"I am selected to take your message, Long Hair," the oldest chief said. It was the first word uttered by any of the chiefs since they had been challenged. A sense of relief swept over the soldiers as the tension passed.

"I promise you safe passage," Custer said. "Both to take my message to your people and to return with your answer."

The old chief just stared back.

"I want the two white girls you have stolen from Kansas and that I know are in your village."

No response.

"I want the Cheyenne people to proceed from here to their reservation at Camp Supply. To finally and forever live in peace with the white soldiers."

"I want," and here he reached back and gestured toward his tent, "I want you to please take Spring Grass with you." She came out of the tent at the gesture and mention of her name.

"She will assure you and all the Cheyenne people of my good intentions."

The four Cheyenne discussed this among themselves as Spring Grass stood next to Custer.

"I will come back with our answer, Long Hair."

And he and Spring Grass strode out of the firelight toward the Cheyenne village by the river.

64

March 31, 1869

"We are going to the old reservation," Thunder Bull said.

"At Fort Cobb, with the Arapaho?" Antelope asked.

"No. Two days above the Lodgepole River. Near the soldiers' camp. Between Fort Dodge and where Long Hair's soldiers killed Black Kettle."

"Why there?"

"It is where the white soldiers say they can protect us," Spring Grass replied.

"The chiefs have all agreed?" Antelope asked.

"Yes," Thunder Bull replied.

"Will you go with us, Spring Grass?"

"No, Antelope. I will go with my husband, Long Hair. I will go and live with him at Camp Supply."

"But the other women say he has a wife in one of the white man's towns. That he will not take you away with him."

"I am carrying his baby. He will take me with him."

"And if he does not?"

"I think he will. But if not, then I will come back to my family at the agency. With Long Hair's and my baby."

The three friends were sitting on the bank of the Red River.

The Cheyenne villages were all in excitement. Some because they were returning to the plains near the Canadian River. Their old territory. Some because they believed they would be at peace with the whites at last. And some because they were breaking camp and headed for the first great buffalo hunt of the spring.

"What about the Northern Cheyenne?" Antelope asked. "They live near the Sioux on the plains as they please. Hunt the buffalo still as they please."

"Long Hair says the Sioux and the Northern Cheyenne will someday also have to join us."

"I see Long Hair with you around the camps, Spring Grass," Antelope said. "He has very beautiful hair. And very beautiful blue eyes. Is he a good man? And the other soldiers? How is it living with the white soldiers?"

Thunder Bull grunted and walked up the river bank, leaving the two cousins alone to compare notes about men.

"In many ways the white soldiers are like our braves. They want to fight and hunt. And they drink too much. Long Hair is very nice to me. Some of the soldiers are very mean to the other women and to each other. But some are very good. They are men. But they don't work together like Cheyenne men. They don't help each other."

"I miss my husband," Antelope said. "I sometimes wonder if there will be another."

The two young women chatted a while and then got up and caught up with Thunder Bull.

"Thunder Bull," Antelope said. "What are you going to do?"

"Many of the braves and their families want to join the Northern Cheyenne after the buffalo hunt. They are saying they will go to Camp Supply, and then leave."

"Will Long Hair try to stop them?" Antelope asked, turning to Spring Grass.

"He says he expects many Cheyenne to join their families up north. He says they will come back some day. The railroads and the soldiers are going there next. The buffalo will leave the land of the Northern Cheyenne next. It will become too difficult for the people to live there in the winter."

"I will go the reservation," Thunder Bull said. "But then I will go north. I promised Lame White Man I would join him when I became a Cheyenne brave."

"Will you join the Dog Soldiers?" Spring Grass asked.

"If they will have me. We will see what Lame White Man says."

"I will go with you Thunder Bull," Antelope said. "There is nothing for me here. My second family is now killed by Long Hair. I will go back with you to the land where I was born."

65

May 27, 1869

Two months later, Lily and Lizzie were working in the kitchen when they saw Jimmy riding hard.

"Indians," Jimmy said, galloping up to the house.

Lily came out on to the porch. Stood next to Auggy the bear and looked where he was pointing up at the top of the mesa to the east. There were several Indians, maybe a dozen, sitting on their ponies just under the rising sun. Her hand covering the sun enabled her to see them clearly, but not make out their intent.

"How many hands we got, Jimmy?"

"Lincoln took most of the boys out yesterday looking into reports of rustlers down the valley. I think there's four of us still here. Where's Gus?"

"In Cheyenne," she replied. "Get the four of you up and armed, then. I'll get the three girls and the kids organized in the main house, then come join you."

She looked up again.

"Maybe they're not hostile," she said without any confidence.

"Maybe they're just heading north to join the main tribes," Jimmy said, then turned his horse and rode back to the bunkhouse. Eyes on the mesa.

There were fifteen Indians. They'd ridden down the mesa and were now in a line along the willows at the top of the western bank of Chugwater Creek. A couple hundred yards away from the porch at that point. Fifteen Cheyenne warriors, counting what looked like four women. None were in war paint or war dress. All had their right arms raised to the sky, no visible weapons.

"What do you think Lily?" Jimmy asked.

"I think they see eight fully armed ranchers and mean us no harm."

"Then what do they want?"

"I have no idea. Food? Information? They don't seem to be in much of a hurry."

"You want me to shoot over their heads?"

"No, let's not give them a reason to mean us any harm."

One of the Indians pulled back and rode behind the others to talk to a large man in the middle of the line. Another rode over to join them and the three talked something over.

Lily watched closely as the one that had pulled out of line, got off his pony and started walking toward the house, leading the pony behind him.

"No," Lily said out loud. Then said to herself, got off *her* pony. It had been four and half years, but she knew Antelope when she saw her.

Lily began running across the field toward Antelope, as Antelope began running as well.

"No," Jimmy said. "Lily. No." Jumping on his horse, rifle raised.

"It's good, Jimmy," Lily said back over her shoulder. "Stay back. They're friends."

Then she stopped. Yelled back at the house, "Lizzie! Bring Antelope Thunder out here to me. Now."

Then turned and ran as fast as she could toward her friend.

Lily walked with Antelope back toward the house. The four cowboys were now up on their horses, off to the right between the ranch house and the bunkhouse, looking down at the two approaching women. Four year old John stood on the porch hiding behind Mary's skirts, while Elly held the three-week old Sam Smoot in her arms next to them.

At the bottom of the stairs, three year old Antelope Thunder Smoot stood looking up at the twenty-two year old Indian woman walking toward her. She leaned back against Lizzie, whose hands were on her shoulders.

"Antelope Thunder," Lily said. "Do you know who this is?"

"The Indian girl you named me after?" Antelope Thunder said.

Antelope looked at Lily, and Lily loosely translated for her.

Antelope got on her knees and held out her arms. Antelope Thunder said, "Hi Antelope," and ran over to her. The two held each other until Antelope stood and held the little girl on her hip.

"Thank you, Lily. I am glad you kept your promise. She is a beautiful little girl."

She turned and signaled to the other Indians. One pulled on his pony's reins and kicked him to a gallop toward the house. Jimmy pulled his rifle out of its scabbard and Lily signaled him no with a shake of her head.

The young man galloped to Antelope, came to a full stop, and dismounted next to her, creating a billowing dust cloud over the group.

Lily looked at him and gasped. "This young man can't be Thunder Bull?"

Both Antelope and the nearly thirteen year old Thunder Bull nodded yes.

"Thunder Bull became a man this year," Antelope said.

"How?" Lily said looking up at him.

Antelope looked back and forth between the two. "Old Cheyenne custom." Then looked away, up at the group on the porch.

"Will you ask your other friends to come to our house?" Lily said.

"No," Thunder Bull said. "They do not trust white people."

A general silence fell over the group.

Finally, Lily said, "Elly and Mary, please bring Sam and John down here and get some food and water. Lizzie, please get some blankets in the living room for our guests. Antelope and Thunder Bull, please come in our house."

"No," Thunder Bull said.

"The porch then?"

"Yes," Antelope said. "We will be happy to join you next to your famous bear."

"Famous?"

"Yes, Lily. How do you think we found you?"

Lily sat on the porch with her two guests and her three children, Antelope holding Sam while Antelope Thunder had been edging closer and closer to where Thunder Bull was sitting. It had been a surprise to both the little girl and to Thunder Bull that she had also been named for him.

She was happy. He was impassive.

They told Lily about the massacre of Black Kettle's village by Custer.

"I thought Black Kettle was at peace," Lily said.

"Black Kettle's Southern Cheyenne were at peace both times," Thunder Bull said. "At the Lodgepole and against Chivington."

"Why did Custer attack then?"

"Why do the whites always attack the people at peace in their villages?" Thunder Bull replied.

After an uncomfortable silence, Antelope said, "Black Kettle's village was the first in a group of villages. Some of the other villages were not at peace with the whites. My cousin told me that is what Long Hair told her. Also Long Hair says some of Black Kettle's young braves were sneaking off to attack white ranchers."

"How does your cousin know Custer?"

"She left the village with him as a hostage. She says she is now his wife. She now carries his child."

While Lily thought about what to make of that, Thunder Bull reached out and took Antelope Thunder's hand. She stared at the huge brown hand that had swallowed her tiny fingers, and giggled.

"Was Lame White Man killed, Antelope?" Lily asked.

"No. He survived the attack. He has now joined the Dog Soldiers and is attacking the ranchers and soldiers in the south. In Kansas and Colorado."

Gus, she thought. Gus was going to be scouting for the Army against the Cheyenne in Colorado next month. Lame White Man is there. She shuddered.

"I am sorry to hear Lame White Man is fighting the ranchers. He was so nice to us at your village. He also met us on our way to Washington Territory, and told us of the Chivington massacre. He gave us a gift for John."

She looked out at John playing in the yard.

"John," she said.

"Yes, Mommy?"

"You know your Indian pony? Cheyenne?"

"Yes?"

"It was a gift to you from Antelope when you were a very little boy."

John looked up at the two Indians on the porch, then at his mother.

"Thank you Antelope," he said, and resumed playing.

Even Thunder Bull laughed at that. He picked Antelope Thunder up, carried her down the stairs, got down on all fours, and put her up on his back. He crawled toward John, and, when John backed up, he crawled toward him quickly with Antelope Thunder giggling on his back.

"Horsey," she said.

Then John figured out the game and Thunder Bull chased him around the yard, both children shrieking with delight.

The women watched from the porch.

"Are Gus and Lincoln here, Lily?" Antelope asked.

"No. They are both away today. They will both be sorry they missed you. They will not believe how beautiful you have become, Antelope. And what a man Thunder Bull has become."

"Or maybe a bull," Antelope said, watching him chase the little white boy around on all fours.

"Lame White Man also told us that Sitting Bull had a vision that he and Gus would both die on the same day. In a great battle."

"Yes, he told me of this."

"Do all of Sitting Bull's visions come true, Antelope?"

"The Lakota say so." She looked in her lap, then out toward her friends under the trees. "We must go, Lily."

"Where are you going?"

"To join the people. The Northern Cheyenne are gathering for the summer hunts north of here. Many days journey. We have decided to not live where the white man tells us to live far to the south. Many Southern Cheyenne have decided to stay there. But we will join the people in the north."

"Will we see you again?"

"I do not know. I am not Sitting Bull."

And they both laughed easily together.

"If you want to visit our village again someday, here take this."

She handed Lily one of the buffalo-skin parfleches she had brought down from her pony. She stood and reached her hand up to Auggy the bear.

"Does the bear still have the eagle feather I gave him?"

"Yes," Lily said.

"There is a twin for it in there. I will spread the word that if a beautiful white woman with my beaded parfleche comes with a bear with twin eagle feathers, she has safe passage to and from our village. All Indians will respect this medicine."

She hugged Lily, walked down the steps to her pony, and she and Thunder Bull rode back to the group of Cheyenne waiting at the creek.

66

July 11, 1869

"Why are the dogs barking?" Lame White Man asked.

"Our wolves say the white soldiers are not near here," the chief of the Dog Soldiers said. "Let's go see."

The two trotted east out of the village, the surging South Platte River on their left, and up the protecting hill. A low lying fog covered the valley and the two warriors could see nothing beyond a hundred yards.

A half mile to the east, Gus Smoot and Buffalo Bill Cody crept forward with over a hundred Pawnee scouts. They, and the Fifth Cavalry behind them, had been chasing the Dog Soldiers across Kansas and Colorado for over a year.

"You think the Pawnees are right, Gus?" Cody asked. "They're over there by the river?"

"Eighty lodges are pretty hard to misinterpret, Bill. The scouts say that's what's over there after following a pretty big trail. I don't think the Platte is fordable anywhere near here under these conditions. So it's probably them."

"This finally it for the Dog Soldiers?"

"Be my guess. They'll stand and fight to let their families get away. They're the best at attacking settlements and disappearing. They got at least two Kansas women in that village. But standing and fighting against a force this size, with their backs to their women and children? Probably won't work out well for them today."

"Be my guess, too."

The two Cheyenne chiefs trotted back to the village. It was midafternoon. The women were skinning hides and preparing food. The children and dogs were running around amusing each other and the women, but annoying the Dog Soldiers. The other warriors, nearly a hundred, had gone southwest at dawn looking for buffalo and would not be back until nightfall, if at all.

Lame White Man went into his lodge to get his rifle. He then made his rounds to make sure the braves were all prepared in case the wolves were wrong and the dogs right.

He emerged from the last lodge to see the pony herd running into the village. They were being driven by the fifteen year old boy who had been watching them.

He could hear the "pop, pop, pop" of gunfire and saw that the boy was weaving his pony back and forth and ducking from the gunfire as he drove the herd.

The old chief yelled to the women and children to abandon the village. South and west.

Lame White Man sent half the Dog Soldiers into a ravine east of the village and south of the South Platte. The other half followed the two chiefs back up the hill to the east, toward the sound of the gunfire. They looked over the hill's summit.

A shot killed the head chief of the Dog Soldiers instantly.

Before he ducked back down, Lame White Man saw the hundred Pawnee and the eight companies of the Fifth Cavalry behind them.

He also saw Gus Smoot in the midst of the Pawnee. As he clambered back down the hill to set up defensive positions on the edge of the village, he remembered Sitting Bull's prophecy.

If this was going to be Sitting Bull's predicted great battle, it was going to be a good day to die.

A chill went down Gus's spine. He had seen Lame White Man at the moment their eyes met.

Half the Pawnees headed to the right and surrounded the Cheyenne warriors in the ravine. The Dog Soldiers in the ravine, caught by surprise, only had their bows and arrows. The Pawnees took their time shooting at them with Army issue pistols and rifles. There was no hurry. When the Cheyenne arrows were gone, the Pawnee would move in and finish off this half of the Dog Soldier defenders.

The rest of the Pawnee, accompanied by Gus, Buffalo Bill, and the cavalry, attacked the other half from the south.

The Cheyenne warriors fought a courageous rear guard action from lodge to lodge. Their job was to give their families time to get away. They could duck into lodges to get new pistols, rifles, and ammunition, and use the lodges as shields. They held off the attackers. But they could hear the shooting and the cries of the victorious Pawnee ahead and to their left.

Gus saw Lame White Man dodge from lodge to lodge. He kept one eye on him, while he shot at anything that moved. Two Pawnee slipped to Lame White Man's right, and Gus watched as the Cheyenne chief slipped around the lodge and headed for the river.

"Why are you so intent on that Indian?" Cody asked, as they both took a shot at a Cheyenne on their right.

Before he could answer, they heard the whooping of the Pawnee as they began slaughtering the Dog Soldiers in the ravine off to their right. The Cheyenne's arrows had been exhausted.

Gus looked up and saw Lame White Man drive three ponies into the South Platte and jump in after them. The fleeing Indian grabbed the tail of the frightened pony in front of him and submerged himself to avoid the ensuing gunfire.

The Dog Soldiers were now being routed. It was each man for himself as they backed through the village toward the river, trying to avoid total annihilation.

As the few surviving Dog Soldiers grabbed ponies and headed southwest or into the river, Gus stood and watched Lame White Man ride north on the other side of the South Platte. Out of range of the rifles.

"Who is he?" Cody asked.

"His name is Lame White Man. We've met in battle before. Oddly, he's personal friends with my wife."

Cody looked curiously at him. "That's a new one on me. Sounds more like a Kit Carson story than something I'd expect to hear from you, Gus."

Gus laughed. "Well, I have some of those Kit Carson stories, too, Bill. Maybe for a later day."

"Kit was the greatest American I ever knew."

"Me, too," Gus said. "As for Lame White Man, Sitting Bull had a vision that he and I would both die on the same day. In a great battle."

"I guess today wasn't Sitting Bull's great battle."

"Guess not." He looked at the horizon and the disappearing figure of the Cheyenne chief. "Lily will be pleased."

67

August 26, 1869

"You think Iliff will deliver those cattle to us next spring, like he's promising?" Lincoln asked.

The three of them had just left Iliff's Cheyenne office and were walking along Eddy Street, heading back to the Union Pacific Hotel.

"I have no reason to doubt him," Lily said. "He offered us a fair price for our two year olds. Why would he jeopardize the relationship?"

"And he even offered up a couple of his men to show us how to best separate the calves from their mothers in open range," Gus said. "Guess he's worried we didn't get enough practice in Oregon."

"I'm sure the price next spring will be different then he offered us today," she said. "But we'll be fine when the time comes for John to deliver."

The street was crowded with new arrivals from the train that had just arrived from Omaha.

"I need to check on something here in the bank," Lincoln said. "It's Thursday, and they asked me come by before Friday to pick up your paper work."

"I'll be over at the Bar None," Gus said.

"I'll wait here for Lincoln," Lily said, clearly not wanting any part of Gus's poker hangout.

"Suit yourself," Gus said. "I'll only be a minute."

A half hour later, Gus stepped out of the saloon and looked down the block.

He saw Lincoln and Lily come out of the bank and start heading his way.

He noticed a confrontation developing outside the sleazy saloon on the other side of the bank. He knew that no self-respecting woman would be caught dead in that place. Yet there were two well dressed women and a man in a derby hat in a heated exchange with someone at the door. The three of them must have just stepped off the train. Gus knew the man arguing with them at the door, a bartender at the saloon. In fact he had almost had a fight with him the night before over a disputed bet.

"Hey, Lily," he said, trying to get them to move more quickly before it got worse.

Lily looked up at him, but so did the three strangers at the door of the saloon. One of the women looked directly at him, then at Lily.

Taking the distraction as an opportunity, the bartender slugged the man in the derby hat, knocking him to the ground. He then grabbed the two women and pulled them, kicking, biting, and swinging pocketbooks vainly at their attacker, into the saloon.

Lincoln and Lily reached Gus.

"Should we go look into it?" Lincoln asked.

"Get the sheriff," Lily said. "He should deal with it."

"He won't," Gus said. "That's the place we got run out of last winter looking for cowboys and one more girl back when you were unhappy with Elly. It's a thinly veiled slave trade, Lil. The owner keeps the girls against their will and the sheriff hasn't found a way to stop them."

"Let's at least go give the two women a hand," Lincoln said.

Gus held out his arm to block him.

"Look," he said. "Let's give it a moment yet. The only thing I'd like better than plugging that bartender is having somebody else do it for me."

"You know that man, Gus? I wish you'd stop coming into town for poker. I really do."

"Later, Lily," he said walking toward the scene.

They watched as a tall thin cowboy walked across the street toward the saloon. He stopped, looked at the unconscious man who's derby had rolled into some horse dung in the street, picked him up, and dunked him in the horse trough.

The two exchanged some words. Then the cowboy retrieved the hat, dunked it in the trough, shook it off, handed it back to its owner, drew his Colt, and walked into the saloon.

Gus and Lincoln were now at the back of the sizeable crowd that had gathered. They could hear loud voices inside the saloon. But no shots.

Presently, the two women hustled out of the saloon, arms around each other's' waists, followed by the cowboy backing out. Now two Colts pointed into the saloon.

As he passed Lincoln, he said, "Which is the fastest way back to the Laramie-bound train?"

Lincoln pointed at the alley across the street.

The man grabbed one of the women's arms and hustled them toward the street.

"Your name, Lily?" Gus said.

The woman nearest the cowboy turned and looked at him curiously.

"Thought so. Hers, too," pointing at Lily walking toward them.

They watched the trio hustle through the ally.

"Nice spot you come to play in," Lily Smoot said. "Nice to see all your friends."

And she walked toward the Union Pacific without the two men.

68

April 5, 1870

"Looks like my Army scouting days may be over, Lil." Gus said.

She looked over at him and didn't respond.

They were sitting in the house, waiting for Lincoln to come in from the stables with his report on the roundup. The kids were running in and out, driving Elly and Mary and Lizzie crazy as they all tried to take advantage outdoors of the first really warm day of the spring.

Lincoln walked into the dining room.

"The herd looks like it survived very well," he said. "Too soon to tell, of course. Everybody out there sorting through whose cows are whose still. But almost all of our cows are accounted for, at least ninety percent. And we've just started rounding them up."

"Calves?" Lily asked.

"It looks like pretty near every cow is pregnant. A few have already dropped their calves. Gus, you going to be helping us out with the branding?"

"Yes. I was just telling Lily when you walked in that the Army won't be needing me any more."

"Somebody declare peace with the Indians and I missed it?" Lincoln asked.

"Around here, apparently. With the Dog Soldiers finished off and new treaties being negotiated with both the Cheyenne and the Sioux, the Army's expecting things to calm down. Maybe even forever."

John came hurtling into the room and jumped on Gus. The two wrestled for a few minutes before Lily shooed all the kids back outdoors.

"Elly. Gather these kids up and you girls take them down to the creek."

"Not everybody's as lucky as we are, though," Gus said, catching his breath. "I'm told that Crook arrived in Arizona last month. The Apaches simply won't stay on their reservations, so they've sent Crook to try to repeat his Oregon success."

John Arnold, Lily thought to herself. Back in Arizona fighting Apaches.

"Cochise?"

"I assume so. But it's not only him. It's all of them down there."

"You gonna go down there and help, Gus?" Lincoln asked.

"No. They'd have to arrest me and tie me to my horse and drag me down there before I'd ever go back to those godforsaken deserts again."

Lily looked up at his unfortunate choice of words, but it appeared that Gus hadn't even thought about it, so she let it go. Had to in front of Lincoln anyway. There was no point in the Chief of Thieves ever returning to the scene of the crime, and she was relieved to see that he knew it.

"We going to sell all the two year olds in the fall, Lincoln?" she asked.

"Yes. There are about two hundred. We should be able to get well over the thirty a head Iliff sold 'em to us for."

"And what about this year? How many more cattle can you handle, Lincoln?"

He looked thoughtfully out the window. Thinking.

"Hey, Lincoln, I learned the darndest thing from some of the officers in Cheyenne last night. They're paying guys to play base ball now back east."

"Really?"

"Yeah. Somebody in Cincinnati hired some ballplayers. Paid 'em to barnstorm around the country playing local teams. The Cincinnati Red Stockings."

"Anybody beat them?"

"Not according to the officers. They won all sixty-five games they played. Imagine that. Paying guys to play base ball."

"The world's changing," Lincoln said. "That's for sure."

He shook his head, turned back to Lily. "I'd say the boys and I can handle another five hundred head, Lily. With all the calves, that'll more than double the herd. If you have the money, the boys and the range could handle even more than that."

She looked at Gus. "You still winning at poker, honey?"

He grinned. "It's easier than tracking a herd of buffalo in the snow. We're going to be fine, Lil."

Especially, she thought to herself, with the Bank of Auggy the Bear out there on the porch.

"Lincoln," she said. "Tell Iliff we'll take five hundred more."

69

November 3, 1870

"Everybody ready?" Lily asked, her horse wheeling around in a full circle as the two cowboys came riding out of the stables.

"Yes," Jimmy replied. "Lincoln and the other three are with the other ranchers about five miles down the valley. They said they'd hold off on any confrontations until you got there."

"Lizzie. You and the other two girls get yourselves armed. Rifles and pistols. Make sure to lock, bolt, and barricade all three doors. And keep the kids away from the windows. You three girls stay away from the windows except to peek out from corners."

"Yes, ma'am."

"Gus'll be back tomorrow morning. You don't open that door for anyone but Lincoln, Gus, Jimmy, or me."

"Yes, ma'am." She ran into the house, grabbing Elly's pistol out of Auggy the bear's holster.

"Where's Gus?" Jimmy asked.

She gave him a withering look. "Cheyenne. How many rustlers Lincoln thinks he's got out there?"

"He was guessing five. But said there's no way to know until we get there and confront them."

"Then let's go."

She kicked her horse's flanks and the three galloped forward trailing flying slush and ice behind them.

An hour later, they arrived at Lincoln's campsite, just as it was getting dark.

"About time, Lily," Lincoln said, teeth gleaming in the early moonlight.

"Doin' the best I can, boss." She dismounted, slapped him on the back. "What've we got?"

"Somewhere between five and ten rustlers. Those three cowboys over there by the fire from the new ranch up the valley spotted them this afternoon. Branding some cows and a bull about three miles down the valley. Due north."

"Any chance they're on the level and not rustlers?"

"We'll be sure and ask them tomorrow morning when we wake them. But no rancher out here has any business branding cattle on the open range in November, Lily, and you know that."

She stared at Lincoln in a way that left no misunderstanding even in the dark.

"I don't want to be party to killing any innocent men," she said. "You either, Lincoln. How reliable are those three cowboys?"

"We know them. We'd never hire them for the L Bar S, but they're honest men, Lily."

"There are ten of us. We're not going to be overwhelming them, so let's pretend we're Custer and they're a sleeping Indian village. Surprise attack at dawn. I don't want a fair fight."

"Jimmy," Lincoln said. "Two alternating sentries all night. Nick and I'll take first watch. You take last watch, and wake us all at three."

Jimmy walked off to let everyone know their orders, including the three cowboys at the other fire.

"Lily," Lincoln said.

"Yes, Lincoln?"

"No offense meant, Lily."

"Lincoln, you know better than to apologize to me. Seven years together and you have yet to make a wrong step. We're equal partners."

He nodded, his face lit up by the fire.

"Now, since you have first watch, shouldn't you be facing out of our camp-site rather in here at me?"

Lincoln chuckled as he walked out into the darkness shaking his head.

Jimmy, twenty-nine, and Nick, now seventeen, had spotted the rustler's horses before they saw their campsite. Crept in closer to be sure, then walked their horses back to the others.

"They're maybe two hundred yards down the creek," Jimmy said. "I counted seven horses and seven bags. You, Nick."

"Yes. Seven."

"Recognize any of the horses, Jimmy?" Lincoln asked.

"Not enough light for that yet."

"How do you want to do this? You're the Buffalo Soldier. We've had expe-rience pinning down rustlers, but you're the military man. You take over."

"Never got above sergeant and you know it, Lincoln."

"Excellent chance for you to prove you shoulda been an officer, then."

Jimmy shook his head and frowned good naturedly.

"Okay then, men. Oh sorry, and Lily."

"'Men's' fine, Jimmy. Get on with it."

"You five stay right here. The five of us will walk our horses a hundred yards to the west and then get directly behind them. No riding. Only walking from here on and keep your horses silent.

"In twenty minutes, you five fan out to form a semicircle from the creek to here and to the west. Try to stay fifty yards from them."

"How far apart do you want us to be?" asked one of the cowboys from the other ranch.

"Do the best you can. You'll figure it out. Once in place in the full circle, we just sit."

"Lincoln, Lily? You want to shoot the first one that wakes up?"

"No," Lily said. "The first one of us sees one of them wake up, shoot in the air. Everybody follow with one shot in the air. Then everybody walk in on them rifles aimed squarely at any you see getting up."

"I'll order them to stand down," Lincoln said. "But any that fire a gun you're free to shoot."

"But aim low," Jimmy said. "Remember, you've got a partner in your line of fire just on the other side of the rustlers. We're moving out now. Twenty minutes."

It took an hour, but finally one of the rustlers sat up. Stretched his arms out in the dim dawn light.

Three simultaneous shots rang out. Then immediately seven more, one slamming into a heavy branch of a tree at the creek.

"Nobody moves," boomed Lincoln's voice. "Any of you so much as flinch and you'll have half a dozen bullets in your hide before your friends know what hit you."

Six more heads popped up. Lincoln fired into the embers of their camp fire and sparks shot into the air, ricocheting among the rustlers.

"I want to see fourteen hands straight up in the air," Jimmy said from the other side of the men.

Twelve complied.

"Friend," Lily said. "You there with your hands in your bag. I'm not even going to give you a chance. Your hands don't go up right now, they're going to be clutching a bullet wound somewhere in your sleeping bag as appropriate punishment for indecision."

No hands.

Two shots rang out and the man yelled in pain and writhed in his bag in the snow and ice. Continued yelling.

The ten walked into the camp as one, leading their horses, rifles pointed at the six men with their hands up.

"We have it on good authority that you men have been rustling cattle just west of here."

Nobody said a word.

"This gang got a leader?" Jimmy asked.

Silence.

"How about a spokesman then? Who are you? Who do you work for? What are you doing here?"

Lincoln walked over to one of the men. His hands were in the air, but his head was hanging down on his chest.

"Well what have we here?" he said. "Lily come on over. If I'm not mistaken, this here's Sam. Used to work for us."

Lily walked over.

"Hi Sam. Who you working for now?"

Sam shook his head.

Nick shot his six shooter into the snow at Sam's feet.

"Sam, you don't answer Lily, I'll shoot you down where you sit."

Sam pointed at the man still writhing silently in pain in the blood soaked sleeping bag.

"Gentlemen," Lincoln said. "The penalty in this county for cattle rustling is death by hanging."

He looked over at the trees along the creek bed.

"Unless someone produces some evidence of an alternate profession or some evidence that you are all mute, it's going to turn out very convenient for us that you camped by those big poplars along the creek."

"Hey Lincoln," Nick said. "There are a set of branding irons by the fire."

Two hours later, Lily and Lincoln and the three cowboys from the other ranch returned to the camp with the two men they had taken to the site of the rustling.

"Any trouble while we were gone?" Lincoln asked.

"None." Nick replied. "They started saying their boss and twenty men were on their way this morning."

"They say who that was or what they do for him?"

"No. Sam's been crying some. Says Elly put him up to this. She's waiting for him to come back with some money so they can go on to Laramie to live."

"Sam, that true?" Lily asked. "You and Elly?"

"Yes, ma'am. She wanted me to make more money so we could move out on our own."

He wiped his nose on his sleeve. Looked at the ground.

"How's the wounded gangleader?" Lincoln asked.

"Gutshot," Jimmy replied. "He's not going to make it."

"He admit to anything?"

"He's in no condition to explain anything, Lincoln."

"We found rebranded cattle just like the boys said we would. Ours and theirs. It's a clear cut case of rustling. They were rebranding to a brand none of us has heard of."

"Any of you willing to say who hired you?" Lily asked. "At least to save your own skin for when we confront him?"

"The only one who knew our boss's name is the man you shot," Sam said. "For all we know, he's the one hired us."

"Anybody else? The only thing that'll save you is a name."

Silence.

"Untie them, then tie their hands behind their backs," Lincoln said. "Get them up on their horses. Get the branding irons in the fire and we'll brand each of them. At least whoever their boss is will know what happened to them."

As he and Lily walked away, there was a sudden commotion.

Shots rang out. They both dove into the snow and looked back, guns drawn.

Two of the rustlers were brandishing pistols. They had somehow worked their arms free while the cowboys from the other ranch were untying them and had grabbed their guns.

The two were now working their way back toward their horses, firing the pistols as they ran in the slush.

All eight cowboys were now sprawled in the snow, shooting at them as they ran.

One of the rustlers went down.

The other had reached a horse and grabbed another pistol out of a saddle-bag and started shooting back. As he rode by the camp, he shot into the cowboys. One went down, then the rustler was shot out of his saddle, going down hard in the snow.

Lincoln and Lily ran back into the camp. The two rustlers were dead. Another had been wounded in the leg.

Lincoln went to the fallen cowboy. It was one of the men from the other ranch. He was dead.

"Last chance," Lily said. She looked at the two dead rustlers already hanging from the tree. "If we have no name, then you hang."

"I have a name," said the disconsolate Sam.

All eyes turned to Sam.

"Yes?" Lily said.

He whispered something unintelligible.

"Not going to do you any good, if we can't hear it, Sam," Lincoln said.

He looked straight at Lily.

"Elly."

"What?" Lincoln said. "Elly hired you all to rustle cattle? That's ridiculous. String him up next, Nick."

"No," Sam said. "Wait. Elly knows the name of our boss. She's the one who sent me to him." Pointing at the wounded man. "To him over there. She knew him and his boss. Take me to her. I'll show you. She'll tell you."

"Lily?" Lincoln asked.

"We'll take Sam back with us. See what Elly has to say."

"Hang the rest," Lincoln said. "Now. Hang their wounded boss last. Maybe he can hear it all happening. Maybe he can't. But hang him last."

Four hours later, they were done interrogating the couple in the living room.

"Elly, you can go join Lizzie and Mary and the kids," Gus said. "Nick, Jimmy, take Sam back to the barn. We'll meet you out there in a few minutes."

"But…"

"You've said enough, Sam. I don't want them to have to hogtie you. Go."

Lily, Gus, and Lincoln moved into the kitchen after everybody left.

"What do you two think?" Lily said.

"I think Sam was telling the truth about Elly being sweet on him," Gus said. "She was lying about that."

"But why?" Lily said. "Why not admit she liked the kid?"

"She's afraid you'll fire her," Lincoln said. "Have you ever talked to the girls about staying away from the cowhands?"

"Yes. But just for their own protection. I never told them they couldn't take up with one, just warned them they might get hurt."

"Thanks, Lily."

She shot him a glance, saw he was kidding and let it go.

"What do you think the girls actually think about that, Lily?" Lincoln said. "Do they think you'll fire them if they take up with one of the boys?"

"You may have a point. I suppose being hauled in here like this, she could have been afraid of us. More importantly, is she lying about not knowing about the rustling?"

"No," Gus replied. "I don't think so. She was too shocked by that. She lied about liking Sam, but she had no idea what he was up to. Lincoln?"

"I agree. There's a lot of playing back and forth between your girls and my cowboys. She's probably sweet on most of them, off and on. Mary too, for that."

"Not Lizzie?"

"Not so much. Lizzie's pretty standoffish, except now and again with Nick."

"Nick is such a dear." She smiled off in the distance. "I'm not so sure Elly didn't fool you guys. You don't know girls like I do. If she liked Sam and didn't want to admit it, she could have set him up with something. It'd be a reason she denied even liking him. If she got him the job, Sam takes the risk. She doesn't lose anything if Sam's out there hanging from a poplar tree tonight. If it works out, she runs off with him and gets the benefits."

Both men scratched the backs of their heads while they thought about it. Looking alike, like two brothers, she thought.

"Let's say you fire her and hang him out there by the creek, Lil," Gus said. "And she had nothing to do with it. And everybody but you thinks she's innocent. What does that do to our family? Our ranch? Won't that change everything? For everybody?"

"And let's say we let Sam go and Elly off the hook, and she *did* do it? What then?"

"I can tell you," Lincoln said. "You put Sam on his horse and tell him he better never be seen east of Laramie again, he'll be in California before Gus gets back to Cheyenne. Innocent or guilty, that's the last you'll ever see or hear of Sam."

"I agree," Gus said.

"And Elly?"

"Elly's on notice, Lil. Whether or not she did what Sam said, she knows there'll be no third chance. She'll know you'll never give her any slack. And you never will."

"Men are so stupid about women. We'll do it your way. But I don't want one word out of either one of you if we have bigger problems with that girl down the road."

"I'll go give the news to Sam," Gus said. "You have whatever talk you want with Elly. We agree, she's yours from now on. Us men'll just have to agree that we don't get it about girls, right Lincoln?"

But Lincoln was already half way out the door, on his way to the barn.

70

June 12, 1871

"A lone rider coming this way, Lily." Lincoln said. "Riding from the south. Trailing a packhorse."

She was in the stable with Nick, looking over the horses. They were all getting ready for tomorrow's two week roundup and branding down the valley.

"Gus?"

"No. It's the man in black. It's Johnson. Definitely."

"After three years? You sure?"

"It's him. And this time, he has four riding about a half mile behind him."

"All in black?"

"I don't think there's anything funny about this guy, Lily."

"Well, he doesn't give up. I'll give him that."

She rubbed her hands on her thighs and walked out into the bright sunlight.

"Nick, go find Jimmy and the others. All hands, as they say."

She looked up the creek. Didn't see anyone.

"How long till they get here, Lincoln?"

"Half hour. A little more if they stop to look around first."

She sighed. Couldn't decide if it was a good thing or a bad thing that Gus was never here when this guy showed up. Probably a good thing, all thing's considered.

"How many of the boys are here?"

"Fifteen counting you and me. Although, come to think of it, three are over at Clay's buying some provisions. So make it an even dozen."

"I'll be right back. I'll get the girls and the kids set in the house. Can you please get my horse? This time, let's surprise him. It's our turn."

A half hour later, she, Lincoln, Jimmy, and three of the cowboys sat on their horses in front of the porch of the ranch house. Auggy the bear looming over them.

Nick and the other five cowboys sat on their horses in the barn, awaiting the signal to move either to the back of the house or down to the creek.

Johnson rode up on the top of the small hill to the southeast of them, between them and the creek. Looked over at them. No sign of the other four men. Or Johnson's packhorse.

They all watched him come the last hundred yards. Jimmy and the two cowboys on the left moved out from the porch so that the six of them formed a rough line that he was riding into.

He stopped twenty yards in front of them.

"Morning Lily. Lincoln."

He tipped his hat into total silence.

"You expecting trouble?"

"No," Lily said.

"I see you still have that bear."

The six stared at him wordlessly.

"How's the ranching business in Wyoming compared to Oregon? Looks like you got yourself quite a spread. Staff's growing, too I see."

"If you have no business here, move on," Lily said. "If you do, state it."

"And *then* move on," Lincoln said.

The man in black looked deliberately at each of the six of them, then up at the bear.

"I'm looking for Auggy Damours."

"Never heard of him," Jimmy said.

"Hadn't really expected you to, but Lily has," never taking his eyes off Lily.

"Same answer as last time. I last saw Auggy going on eight years ago now. In Santa Fe. Then he went to Washington and disappeared."

"Then how about the man you call Gus Smoot? He here?"

"Let me make this really clear, friend," Lincoln said. "First of all, you're no friend. Second of all, you're either hiding a badge or you're trespassing. Third of all, I owe you a beating. If you don't start treating Lily like a lady, I'll get around to it sooner rather than later."

All seven sat up straighter in their saddles, causing all seven horses to fidget around, prancing in place.

The four other riders and the packhorse now emerged up out of the creek bed and started riding slowly toward Johnson's back.

Nobody else moved.

"One of the odd parts of your behavior, sir," Lily said, "is that you ride around the territory like some sort of obsessed fool. Year after year. Asking the same questions of the same people. Expecting the answers to change. Like some sort of evangelistic preacher without a congregation who's just spitting in the wind."

"I hold a wanted poster for Lieutenant Damours. I'm..."

"But not for Gus Smoot."

"No, Miss Smoot, not for Gus Smoot. But everywhere I go, he was just there and now he isn't. That must strike even you as odd."

"Maybe you're just unlucky," Jimmy said.

Two of the four riders moved out to Johnson's left and two moved to his right, trailing the packhorse.

"What's your point, mister?" Lily asked.

"How do you think this is going to end?" Lincoln said. "You so tired of failing to find your man, that you now want to see your own face on a wanted poster for killing eighteen innocent ranchers?"

"I only see six," Johnson said.

"Well, if Jimmy is right about you being unlucky, you'll get to see the rest," Lincoln said. "'Course, that'll probably be the last thing you see."

Johnson leaned back in the saddle. Sighed.

"Tell us what you want or leave," Lily said.

"I want to talk to Gus Smoot."

"Then you can move on, because he's not here."

"Unlucky *and* deaf," Jimmy said, shaking his head.

"When's he due back?"

"I don't know," Lily lied.

"You don't seem to spend much time with your husband, Miss Smoot. I know personally that you were Lily Smoot when you were whoring in Nevada."

Lincoln clutched hard at his saddle.

"And I have it on good authority that you were Lily Smoot when you were dealing poker in Santa Fe and working with Augustyn P. Damours to embezzle money from the Army, the Church, the Territory, and countless citizens. And I now happen to know that Augustyn "Gus" Smoot is the very same person as Augustyn "Auggy" Damours."

"Time for you to leave," Lily said. "And it's *Mrs.* Smoot."

"Even before Lincoln's beating, Miss Smoot?"

"Move on. While you still can of your own will."

"Actually, we brought enough provisions for the five of us to wait two weeks. We'll just camp out if you don't mind until Mr. Augustyn, or Mr. Gus, Smoot arrives."

"Actually, you won't," Lincoln said. "You're trespassing now. You've assaulted us in the past. And you've insulted Lily and Gus for the last time."

He drew his pistol and pointed it at Johnson's chest before anyone could move.

"All five of you will now drop your weapons on the ground. Very slowly. Then you will dismount. Also very slowly."

Lily, Jimmy, and the three cowboys drew their pistols and aimed them at the five men.

"You gonna gun us down in cold blood, Lincoln? I'd love to hear what your story's gonna be."

"I'm happy to tell you. Trespassing. Threatening assault. Past actual assaults. Refusal to leave the premises. There'll be more before you die. General rudeness to a lady in front of her family. Threatening her and them. Where I come from, repeatedly wearing out my patience and being boring is a capital crime."

He let out two distinct shrill whistles.

Nick led the other five cowboys on a dead gallop out of the barn and into position behind the five men. Between them and the creek.

"Look, mister, ma'am?" one of the four men said. "We didn't come here looking for trouble. Like the man said, we just wanted to talk to Mr. Smoot is all."

"Then," said Lincoln. "You should've hired out with somebody who's better at inducing conversation."

"Drop the guns," Nick said from behind the five men.

Three of the men jerked their heads and the heads of their horses around to look back at Nick, just as Johnson drew his gun and shot at Lincoln.

Everybody started shooting at once. Johnson went down, shot by both Lily and Lincoln.

The cowboy next to Jimmy went down. Then Nick and Johnson's four riders were shot off their horses all at once.

One of the four riders scrambled up and started to run. Jimmy ran him down and shot him in the back.

It was all over in less than thirty seconds.

The man in black and his four riders were dead. The cowboy next to Jimmy had a flesh wound in his upper arm.

"Nick!" yelled Lily racing toward the fallen boy on foot.

But Nick, a month from his eighteenth birthday, and only seven years out of Ireland, was dead.

Lily fell on top of him, crying.

Lincoln reached out for her, then stopped. Everybody just stood there. Nobody had any idea what to do. What to say.

Lily had been the one to talk Nick into leaving Oregon.

He now lay dead on the Wyoming ground.

71

January 11, 1872

Gus Smoot rode up behind Buffalo Bill Cody and reined in his horse. Cody was sitting on the ground with a group of Sioux.

"Hey Bill," Gus said, looking down from his perch in his saddle.

"Gus?" Cody said, peering up, one hand sheltering his eyes from the sun.

"Been a while, friend." Gus had just ridden to Fort McPherson, Nebraska from Omaha, where he'd arrived after the five hundred mile train trip from Cheyenne the day before.

"What are you doing here?" Cody asked.

"Just passing through," he replied in passable Sioux.

Buffalo Bill and the Indians stood up, all laughing at that. Cody looked around. "Seems unlikely, Gus. Not much out here to find, either accidentally or on purpose." He peered up at Gus, still sitting up on his horse. "I thought you had a ranch out by Cheyenne somewhere. What are you really up to?"

"Heard there were some Nebraska ranchers looking to get out of the ranching business. Willing to sell some or all of their herd."

Cody looked at him. Then at his Indians.

"And you heard what we were up to and decided to see for yourself," Cody said. Gus didn't say anything, so Cody went on. "You tired of ranching? Want a real job?"

"No. Still got the wife, the kids, and the ranch, Bill."

"And occasional Indian scouting."

"And that."

"I'm out of the scouting business," Cody said.

"So I heard. Killing buffalo for sport and entertaining folks with Indian stories and real wild Indians is less risky."

"And pays better. You want to join, Gus?"

"I don't think Lily would approve."

"I bet she'd rather you pretended fighting these Sioux here than actually fighting Cheyenne and Sitting Bull at that big battle he predicted for you."

"She might at that, Bill. If it didn't involve me being away all the time."

"Have it her way, then."

Gus dismounted and shook Cody's hand. "Thanks for the offer, though."

"Let me know if you change your mind. You want to help General Custer and us with a big buffalo hunt over the next two days as a show for the Grand Duke Alexei Alexandrovich of Russia?"

Gus smiled. "I'd heard about that in Omaha. Where you going to get the buffalo?"

"These Sioux parked them out that way." He pointed vaguely west. "With the rest of their tribe. The Grand Duke promised them a great reward in return for a great hunt."

72

January 13, 1872

Custer, Buffalo Bill, and their guests watched the assembled Sioux put on the orchestrated battle the Duke had requested, complete with preliminary dueling war dances. It was a great treat, even for the veteran American soldiers and scouts. The Sioux were expecting great things from the Grand Duke and were prepared to exceed his expectations, both this day and at next day's buffalo hunt.

At the invitation of President Grant, this was the midpoint of the Grand Duke's two month tour of America. Custer and the Duke's party had spent the day traveling by train from Omaha to the fort. And then Buffalo Bill, Gus Smoot, and the Sioux had led them fifty miles by wagon train to the spot chosen by the Sioux for the Grand Duke's twenty-second birthday buffalo hunt.

After the war dances and mock battle, the Sioux entertained everyone with breathtaking displays of horsemanship, lance throwing, and bow and arrow shooting from horseback. Cody and Custer joined them in target shooting from galloping horses, and, to their surprise, it was the Sioux who were entertained, as no brave could equal the horsemanship and accuracy of Custer's shooting with two drawn pistols.

The Sioux ended the day by hosting a great firelight buffalo feast under a spectacular star-studded sky.

When the occasion presented itself after the dinner, Gus walked over to Custer.

"It's nice to see you again, General," he said. "I'm looking forward to seeing you as Grand Marshal of the hunt tomorrow."

"Do I know you?" Custer cocked his head, golden hair down to his shoulders glowing in the light of the fire.

"It's been over nine years, General. You were running up the steps of the War Department to see Canby, and I was headed to New York to see a doctor."

Custer stepped over so he could see Gus more in the light, shook his head, "Auggy?"

"Gus now, General."

"I never would have recognized you, Auggy. The beard. What are you doing out here?"

"Some ranching. Raising kids and cattle with my wife. Some scouting for the Army against the Cheyenne. A few years with Crook in Oregon against the Snakes. Turns out I can understand their languages pretty quick."

Custer looked at him curiously. "And here?"

"Oh, Buffalo Bill and I did some scouting together over in Kansas and Colorado. I was in Omaha the last couple of days looking at some cattle, and heard you were both going to be up here, so I came for the show. Bill offered to let me help tomorrow."

"What about that problem with Canby, Auggy? There was a lot of talk that you were AWOL and were wanted for embezzlement. That Carleton wanted to hang you personally."

Gus laughed. "All a misunderstanding. It was a major by the name of Cummings took the money. After he was murdered in New Mexico Territory, Kit Carson found the money in his saddlebags."

Custer looked unconvinced. "I wonder if anybody ever told Canby. He was down in charge of South Carolina after the war. He mentioned to me in Charleston that he was still shocked, and awful disappointed in you."

"That all got cleared up. The Army dropped it after Cummings' death."

Custer looked thoughtful.

Guess Lily was right, Gus thought to himself. This might have been pretty dumb after all. She'll enjoy reminding me.

"Where's Canby now, General?"

"Well, that's the devil of it, Auggy. He's headed to Oregon to finish off the Modoc's while Crook has gone down to Arizona against the Apaches."

"Oregon," Gus said. "We were ranching there until eight years or so ago, when we came to Wyoming. I'm sorry I missed him."

"Maybe you can help him out while you're explaining that you aren't AWOL, Auggy. Help him clear it with both you and the Indians all at once."

Might do that, Gus thought. Just might.

"Auggy," Custer said, interrupting his thoughts.

"Yes, General."

"Do you remember Dennis Martinez? From New Mexico?"

"Of course."

"He remembers you, too. He's my right hand man in the Seventh."

"How is Dennis doing? He was a terrific soldier in the Volunteers."

"Fine. He told me he thought you were innocent. None of us knew you'd been cleared, though. Odd nobody knows."

Gus knew why that was, but decided there was no benefit in discussing it any further with Custer. The two shook hands and headed to their respective tents to prepare for the grand buffalo hunt the next day.

73

August 11, 1872

Lizzie brought the six month old Pepper Smoot in for Lily to hold.

"I think she's the prettiest of our bunch, Lil," Gus said. "I'm no judge, but she's a beauty. We should stop now that we have the winner."

"They're all perfect, Gus. But I'm thinking you're right. Four's enough. You being thirty-six and all. Probably too old for any more anyway."

"Not too old for making them. But we need you running around the ranch. We don't need you having any more babies." She stuck out her tongue at him. "Any more news on your Association?" he said.

"The Wyoming Stock Growers Association?"

"There's another one?"

"May have to be. Not much has happened since we formed it in April."

"You still the only woman?"

"Yes. Pressure from Iliff made that happen. They know we have a successful ranch, but don't seem to be as enthusiastic about women ranchers as they are about women voters. To answer your question, I don't think the Association is going to last too long. It's too soon. Nobody knows what they want. All these men know how to do is to compete with each other. They're not so good at figuring out how to work together. That'll take a good deal more time."

"Stick with it, Lil. Iliff knows how good you are. When the time's right, you'll be able to help those old guys figure it out."

They both looked out the door at the sounds of horses approaching.

"What's all the noise outside?" Lily said. "What's going on? Elly, come take Pepper."

She grabbed Gus's hand and the two walked out on to the porch.

John, now seven and a half, came running up the stairs. "Lincoln's driving up. He just got back from Denver. Who are all those people with Lincoln Mommy?"

"No idea honey. Let's wait and let him tell us himself."

John and Antelope Thunder jumped off the porch and started running toward the oncoming wagon and the half dozen riders.

Lily looked up at the grinning Lincoln.

"Afternoon Lily."

Lily decided to say nothing, just nodded. Looked at the pretty Negro woman sitting on Lincoln's right. Then at the six riders behind the wagon. One of them looked familiar, but Lily couldn't place him. This was Lincoln's show and she was happy to see how it played out.

"You gonna invite us in Lily?"

"You don't need an invitation, Lincoln. This is your home."

"Who's the pretty lady, Lincoln?" Antelope Thunder said, jumping up and down, unable to control herself.

"Well, Miss Antelope Thunder, this is Rachel Lincoln," then added, too quickly, "And those scruffy looking boys back there are your new cowboys. Well, all accept for one of them, anyway."

He climbed down from the wagon, held his arms out for the lady and helped her down from the wagon.

"Lily, Gus, I'd like you to meet my wife. Rachel Lincoln."

"Your wife?" Gus said, stammering. "I thought you were going to tell us you'd found a long, lost baby sister in Denver."

"Thanks for the compliment," Rachel said. "Lincoln's much younger than he looks. Only fifty-two. And parts of him are younger than others." She held out her hand. "You must be Gus. My husband isn't too good at introductions."

"Yes, I'm Gus."

"And you must be Lily?" holding out her hand.

"Yes, Rachel, I'm Lily." In truth Lily found herself to be speechless. Lincoln? Married? Without telling them?

"I hope someday that Lincoln thinks as highly of me as he does you, Lily."

Lily looked at Lincoln. Wiped away a tear.

"Please come in, Rachel. When did you and Lincoln get married?"

"A year ago July."

Lily stopped dead in her tracks on her way toward the porch. Turned around.

"A year ago?" She turned on Lincoln. "You've been leaving this girl all alone in Denver for over a year?" She stopped to think. "All those trips to Denver for the past two years? You said you were looking for better cowboys."

"It started out like that, Lily. But once I started attending the Zion Baptist Church down there, well, I found something even better than good cowboys."

"Why didn't you tell us about Rachel? Tell us you were married? This isn't like you."

"He couldn't bring himself to tell you that I wanted him to come live in Denver," Rachel said.

Gus and Lily looked at Lincoln, but he was looking at the ground, hat in his hands, not wanting to meet their eyes.

"There's nothing about Wyoming, ranching, killing rustlers and Indians that attracts me to this place, Lily."

"Then why are you here now?" Gus said.

"Because Lincoln talked me into it. It took the big guy two years to do it, but he did it."

John and Antelope ran over and each hugged one of Lincoln's legs.

"I'm concerned about one thing," Lily said.

"What's that?" Rachel said.

"What did that big guy promise you that changed your mind?" Looking at Lincoln, now grinning again.

Rachel laughed. "He promised me four things. First, that I would love the Smoots. Second, that he and Gus would build me the second nicest house in Wyoming. Third, that you would give him a big raise for having a family. And fourth, that I could name our new baby this December whatever I wanted."

"Getting three out of four right's not too bad, Lincoln," Lily said. "And, Rachel, I promise you. You don't want Gus anywhere near the building of your new house. Keep him well away."

She took Rachel's hand and headed toward the porch. "Come on in the house now. It's time you met everybody else. Lincoln, you bring those new cowboys into the kitchen and let's celebrate."

Rachel stopped on the second step and looked up.

"And you," she said. "Must be Auggy the bear. I thought you'd look much friendlier." She looked more closely. "Much friendlier. Lincoln's not too good at descriptions either."

Everybody was in the kitchen. Mary had given everybody steak sandwiches and tea. And the new cowboys were introduced around by Lincoln. One was actually from Cheyenne, not Denver as it turned out. And two of them were Negroes. One had served with Jimmy in the Buffalo Soldiers and one had known Rachel at the Baptist church.

"Where are you from, Rachel?" Gus said.

"Alabama. My family left for Colorado after the war. All the people at the church came from the south after the war."

"Even me," Lincoln said.

"Lincoln, there were six cowboys rode in with you," Lily said. "But you only brought five in here for us to meet."

Lincoln looked at Rachel.

"The other one's not a cowboy, Lily" Lincoln said. "He wanted to clean up before seeing you."

"What is he, then? A carpenter? We've got plenty of help already."

"Actually, Lily, turns out he's a cook. And turns out he's the best cook in Denver."

"Well, we don't need a cook either."

Just then Lily turned around and saw an overweight man with a withered left hand standing in the doorway. Hat in hand.

"Hi, Lily. Hi, Gus. I see you did find your ranch in Washington Territory."

Lily looked from Lincoln to the man and back again, a quizzical look on her face. This was the cowboy who had looked familiar. But she still couldn't place him.

"I'll be damned," Gus said.

Lily looked even more confused now. She'd never heard Gus curse before. Not even back when he was Auggy.

"It's Jack Madson," Gus said. "Li'l Jack. It's Li'l Jack Madson."

He shook his hand. Slapped him on the back. "You lived Li'l Jack."

"I did. But I'm afraid I'm not so little any more." And he laughed as he put both his hands and his hat over his belly.

Lily overcame her shock. Walked over and hugged him. Hard. For a very long time.

"Do you mind if I still call you Li'l Jack?"

"I insist, Lily. I insist."

The introductions were once more made around the kitchen, and Li'l Jack was, apologetically, fed what was described by Mary as "not a restaurant quality steak sandwich."

"I couldn't help but overhear that you won't be needing a cook, Lily," Li'l Jack said through a mouthful of sandwich. "And this sandwich confirms it."

Mary blushed.

"So," he said. "I'll go on and take a look around Cheyenne, and maybe Laramie. If there's nothing there, I'll just head back to Denver on my own."

"Don't be ridiculous," Rachel said. "Once Lincoln discovers that I can't cook at all, you'll be welcomed with open arms at the Lincoln ranch house."

"I think," Lily said, "that us five women will benefit greatly from a good cook. I'm sure that the girls won't mind the help or the guidance." She looked around the room and got the affirmation she expected.

"Li'l Jack, you're hired," Lily and Rachel said simultaneously to a roomful of laughter.

"Good job, Lincoln," Gus said. "Before you drove up, we had one boss here at the L Bar S Ranch. Now we have two."

74

February 23, 1873

"Are you serious about this, Gus?" Lily asked.

"Yes, Lily. I told you a year ago that Canby had been sent to replace Crook in Oregon."

"And General Custer felt that General Canby can't beat the Modocs without you, right?"

"I owe Ed and you know it, Lil. And after my days with Crook, who knows? I may be of some help with the Modocs."

"One of these days, your recklessness is going to get you killed, Gus. I don't want you to go."

"Lily…"

"Just because Custer bought your story about having been cleared doesn't mean that Canby will. Just because Johnson is gone, doesn't mean there aren't other bounty hunters still looking for you. And just because you survived your Indian wounds in the past doesn't mean that some Indian isn't going to kill you one of these days."

"Don't be silly. Scouts don't get killed. And there are no bounty hunters out here still looking for a ten year old Civil War officer's disappearance back East."

"And Canby?"

"Ed's going to be so consumed with getting Captain Jack back on the reservation, that he'll be more than willing to believe I've been cleared of all those embezzlements. If I have any skill at all its in getting people to believe what they want to believe. You, of all people know that, Lil."

"Why can't you just stay here with us, Gus? The ranch is doing better than we ever hoped. We're over four thousand head now. Your kids adore you and never understand why you go away like you do. I'm lonely and I miss you when you're gone."

He stepped toward her, but she pushed him back.

"You are becoming unnecessarily reckless, Gus. It's one thing to play poker with gamblers instead of working for your ranch and for your family. It's quite another to voluntarily expose yourself to being murdered by Indians or arrested by some unlucky run-in."

"Lily…"

"Why can't you just stay here with us? Continuing to build what we've started?"

"I'll be careful, Lil. I'll only be gone two months. We're done with all the hunting we need this winter. The boys will still go out for some more antelope, but we don't really need it. And I'll be back for the spring roundups. I promise."

"You don't know that, Gus. You could be gone for years. You could be gone forever."

"Lil…"

"Just go, Gus. Just go. I love you. Your kids love you. We need you here. Come back as soon as you can. And for God's sake, be careful. Come back, Gus. Just please come back."

75

April 10, 1873

"I'm here to see General Canby," Gus said.

"What's your name?" the sentry asked.

"Tell him that I served as a scout under General Crook here five years ago," Gus said. "And that General Custer suggested I might be of service to him. Tell him that I served under him in New Mexico, but he won't remember my name."

"Wait here."

Gus looked around while he waited. It was if he'd never left. Wet Oregon spring, ragged soldiers, green as far as you could see in every direction.

"The general says come on in," the sentry said as he walked up to Gus.

He led Gus to Canby's tent.

Canby looked up as he entered.

"Hi, General. It's Auggy Damours."

Canby looked up. Peered at him.

"I never would have recognized you, Auggy. The beard. And you've put on a little weight these past, what has it been, ten years?"

"About six months more than that, General."

"How was your visit to that New York doctor I authorized? The treatment take you a little longer than you expected, Auggy? Through the end of the war?"

"No, sir. General, I'm here both to apologize to you and to offer you my services."

"Frankly, you have a lot of nerve, Auggy. You made a fool out of me and the Army. You're a felon and then a deserter. Tell me why I shouldn't have you arrested and shot on the spot."

"If I were guilty, would I have traveled over a thousand miles by train and horseback, then the past two weeks or so slogging all over Oregon through these unrelenting rains, looking for you?"

"Auggy, I'm in the middle of very intensive negotiations with Captain Jack and his Modocs. I'm meeting with them personally tomorrow. I don't have time right now to conduct a private court martial of my former aide de camp. If you're here to tell me you weren't guilty of stealing all that money and that you've been cleared by the Army..."

"I am, sir."

"I can check that out, Auggy. And I will. And while you're in my custody. But even so, you went AWOL under my command. *That* you did, without question."

"Cummings stole the money, sir. When he confronted me in New York..."

"He said he never found you."

"Cummings was a thief and a liar, sir," finally finding an opportunity to say something truthful. "He tried to kill me and pin the thefts on me. I escaped to Canada. It would have been foolish for me to contact the Army under the circumstances."

Canby looked up from what he had started writing while they talked. "I always liked you Damours. I hope you are right about being cleared. It's going to take a lifetime for me to get over my disappointment at your performance."

"Yes, sir." Lily had been right. He was an idiot to have come to see Canby. Arrested now. And Canby would find out the truth from the Army that he was still a wanted fugitive. Idiot, indeed.

"Before I call the guards, Auggy, how do you think you can you help me with the Modocs?"

"I helped Crook fighting down here. You can't let them down into the Infernal Caverns unless you're willing to create a long siege and starve them out."

"I suspected that. The Peace Commission and I are trying to prevent that. I think I can personally convince Captain Jack tomorrow that further resistance is futile."

"You have a problem there, General."

Canby looked back up at him. "What is it, Auggy?"

"I spent the last two weeks searching for you. You'd be surprised how hard it is to find the commanding general of an Army."

"What is my problem, Auggy?"

"In asking for you, I met several local Modocs and Snakes and half breeds. They are unanimous in believing that you've backed Captain Jack into a corner. He believes that a number of his tribe will kill him if he agrees to any terms you ask. He believes his only hope is to escape from the negotiations."

"And how could he do that?"

"Either by negotiating in bad faith and escaping to the Infernal Caverns, or by killing the Peace Commission. He has no other way out of being murdered by his own people."

"Thank you, but I think I know Captain Jack better than you do, Auggy. Now, if you'll excuse me, you must be tired after your long trip."

He stepped to the front of the tent, opened the flap.

"Sergeant?"

"Yes, sir."

"Mr. Damours is under arrest. Please assign two guards to him at all times, disarm him, take his horse away, and send this telegram to the Secretary of the Army."

He handed him the piece of paper he had been working on during the conversation.

"Yes, sir. Shall we put him in chains, sir?"

"No. Mr. Damours has come here to help us. He will not be trying to escape."

"Yes, sir."

76

April 11, 1873

Canby opened the council meeting with a long speech about the inevitability of losing any fight with the white man. A speech that all the Indians had heard from Crook and Canby many times before.

Captain Jack was accompanied by six other Modocs. All seven were dressed like white men. Captain Jack was wrapped in a blanket.

Canby was accompanied by three Peace Commissioners and two interpreters, one of whom was Auggy Damours.

By agreement, the meeting was held outside the peace tent. All participants had agreed to come unarmed.

Two Modocs lay hidden behind some trees one hundred yards away. They were armed with rifles.

After Canby's opening plea for peace, he looked directly at Captain Jack.

"Your laws are crooked, General Canby," Captain Jack said. "Your agreements are crooked. A few weeks ago, we both agreed to stop fighting. We Modocs have done nothing since then, right"

"You have not," Canby said.

"Yet here you are with your entire army. You have stolen our ponies and threatened our people. You have backed us up to the Lava Beds. Yet we have done nothing."

He looked at Canby, who remained silent. Nodded for him to continue.

"Do not talk to me any more about beautiful places to live far away. Tell me today that we can live in our home. That we do not have to live somewhere else. That the soldiers will go away and leave us in peace. Your word is not worth much to me now. But if you promise this, I will accept it here today."

In the ensuing silence, one of the Modocs stood, walked over to one of the Peace Commissioner's horse, took the coat off the saddle, and put it on.

Auggy watched him warily.

"Now I am a soldier and a Peace Commissioner," the Modoc said.

"Here, take my hat, too" the commissioner said. "Then you will be complete."

"I will have the hat soon enough. I do not need it now."

He went back to his place and sat down.

Auggy looked at Canby. Tried to signal him a warning, but Canby was looking at Captain Jack.

"General Canby, will you agree to take the soldiers away? To let us live in our home?"

The Peace Commissioner who had lost his coat but still had his hat said, "General Canby, just say yes."

Captain Jack stood up, walked by Auggy and then behind one of the horses.

One of the other Modocs said to the other Peace Commissioner, "You promise us this. You can do this."

"I promise that we will ask the Great White father in Washington. We will ask him to promise you this."

Captain Jack walked back and sat in front of Canby. Said, "All ready then. Let's do it." He reached into his blanket.

Auggy scrambled to his feet as Canby looked to the other interpreter, waiting for a translation.

Captain Jack fired point blank into Canby's face.

Misfire.

Fired again. The bullet tore into Canby's head and knocked him backwards. He jumped up and ran away from Captain Jack. One of the other Modocs tripped him and slit his throat with a knife.

The two hidden Modocs ran to the rest from the trees, handing out rifles.

One of the commissioners was shot in the heart. The one who had lost his jacket was shot seven times. Auggy ran over to Canby to check on him. He was dead.

All the other whites ran for the soldiers' camp. Some to sound the alarm, all to save their lives.

As Auggy looked back, he could see the Modocs stripping the three whites of their clothes and preparing to return to their camp.

Auggy ran straight to the back of the soldiers' tents, found his belongings and raced to find his horse in the herd.

His two guards were nowhere to be seen.

The horse guards stopped him. "What are you doing?"

"The Modocs are coming," he said, pointing back where he'd come from. "They killed General Canby and the other Peace Commissioners. They're attacking the camp."

The two guards raced toward the commotion at the opposite end of the camp.

Auggy looked for his horse. It wasn't in the herd. They must have hidden it so I couldn't escape, he thought to himself crazily.

He opened the gate and grabbed the biggest and healthiest horse he could find, led it out, closed the gate, mounted up, pulled his saddlebags up behind him, and pushed the horse to the fastest it could gallop away from the camps.

"Now I'm a horse thief, too," he said out loud, kicking his heels into the horse's flanks. "Well, they can only execute me once."

77

November 30, 1873

Lily hated pay day. It created a tension that she hated. Lincoln and Gus had long ago, back in Oregon in fact, ducked out of paying the help. Having to pay the hands eliminated, at least for one moment, the illusion of partnership. So they'd stuck her with the chore.

Most of the cowboys, and Lizzie and Mary, were pretty good about it.

Nick had always been great. Only asking for a raise now and then. God, how she missed Nick.

She shook her head to clear it. But some of the help would harangue her for hours about needing more money. And always for some different reason.

She walked out to Auggy the bear, checked to make sure nobody could possibly see her, fiddled with the hidden catch, and reached in for the pay packet.

Nothing.

Her heart stopped. Auggy the bear was empty. She walked into the house to think.

When had she last checked? This morning. Two hours ago. She had started to get the pay packet after breakfast, felt it, and then stopped when she heard voices out by the barn. She had sat on the porch until she was sure they had not seen her, then went back into the house.

Only she and Gus knew Auggy the bear's secret.

Could Lincoln have figured it out? So what. Lincoln was her partner. He didn't have a crooked bone in his body. Rachel would shoot him if she discovered he did such a thing. And they both felt they were getting too much already.

She walked back out on the porch. Nobody anywhere to be seen.

She reached all the way down into each compartment. Finally felt some of the bottom bags way down there. Whoever had done this had either been discovered, run out of time, or had shorter arms than Lily.

That immediately generated five suspects. Li'l Jack, the three girls, and Rachel.

Not Rachel. Four suspects.

And it had to be someone who had left in the last hour or so, or still had the money on the ranch.

She headed up the stairs to tell Gus.

Think, Lily, think.

"Lincoln?" she said, knocking on the door. She smiled when she heard the crying baby inside. Little one year old, darling Sarah. "Lincoln," she said, louder.

He came to the door. Saw the look on their faces. Stepped out on to the porch.

"Lincoln, Gus and I may have to do a very terrible thing. So bad that not even Rachel can ever know."

"What is it?" Concern spread over his big, black face.

"First we need to know if you can help us do something so bad that it will have to be a total secret from everyone," Gus said.

"Can someone else besides me do it?"

"Yes. It has to be either you or Jimmy. We don't trust anybody else."

He frowned. "Which one of us do you want?"

"You, Lincoln," Lily said. "You're our partner. But you may be too good a person to do this. So you have to decide if you want to do this without knowing what it's going to be."

"And you can't tell me first?"

"No."

"How long will it take?"

"It could take two, three days."

"I guess it should be me."

"Dress warm, then," Gus said. "We're going hunting."

"Okay, Lily," Lincoln said, walking beside her towards the bunkhouse. "Tell me what's happened."

"I can't tell you everything, Lincoln. I can't *ever* tell you everything, but we've had a theft. It has to be some of the hired hands. Our first job is to find out who's missing while Gus gets our provisions for the hunt."

"And our second job?"

"Let's find out who's missing, then decide together."

"What do you want me to do?"

"I already checked the house. Mary and Elly are not around. They left all four kids with Lizzie."

"Lizzie know where they are?"

"She said no."

"You want me to check the barn and stables?"

"Gus already did that. Nobody's there."

"You want me to check through the bunkhouse?"

"We'll do that together. This isn't going to be much fun for anybody."

"There are only six cowboys here this winter besides you, me, and Gus."

"Anybody out hunting?"

He laughed. "On payday? At lunchtime? Not today. Not ever."

They entered the bunkhouse, looked in each room with an open door. Nobody.

Lincoln knocked on the first closed door. "Jimmy?"

The door opened.

Lily breathed a sigh of relief.

"Jimmy," she said. "Please go out to the stables and the pasture and get me an inventory of missing horses. I need to know if anybody's horse is missing. And how many others."

Jimmy's eyes widened. "Lincoln coming with me?"

"It's a one man job," Lincoln said. "And she needs it quick."

Jimmy threw on his coat and ran out of the bunkhouse.

They moved down the rows of closed doors. There had been nineteen more cowboys up until the fall sale of the two year olds in Cheyenne. Most of the rooms were vacant. Some still had the belongings of those who had been assured a job in April.

Lincoln knocked on another closed door.

"Yes?"

"You in there, Li'l Jack?" Lincoln said.

"Open up Li'l Jack, this is Lily." The relief evident in her voice.

The door opened, and Mary shyly peered out. Li'l Jack standing behind her, embarrassed.

"Cooking lessons?" Lincoln said, suppressing a grin.

"No," Li'l Jack said. "Well, yes. I guess so. In a way."

"Lily," Mary said. "I'm so sorry. Please don't fire me."

Lincoln looked at Lily. Raised his eyebrows.

"Mary," Lily said. "You're fine. Lincoln and I were both twenty-one once. This isn't a convent. You're fine. Just not on payday any more, okay?" And she walked down the hall.

"Does she mean that, Lincoln?" Mary said.

"No. She was joking. But it's never a bad idea to behave better than expected on payday. And the day before, too."

He closed the door on their faces and followed Lily down toward the other closed doors.

In quick succession, each closed door revealed a sleeping cowboy. Four in all.

They knocked on the only door left.

No answer.

"Slim?"

No answer.

"Slim?" Lily said.

"Yeah that's what we all call him. He's the one you never liked."

He knocked again. Opened the door.

Empty.

"That's odd," Lincoln said. "His gear and clothes are gone, too. I'm sure he was here at breakfast."

"No more doors. That means there's also one other missing person," Lily said.

"Who?" Lincoln said.

"Elly." She turned and headed outside. "Let's go see how Jimmy's doing?"

They found Jimmy heading for them, head down to keep the freezing wind out of his face.

"Any horses missing," Lincoln said.

"Four packhorses."

"Any others?" Lily said.

Jimmy made a pained face. "Yeah. Slim's horse is gone. Elly's too. I couldn't find a trace of either one."

Lincoln, Gus, and Lily had been riding for two hours into the wind. The trail of the six horses was easy to follow in the snow, and the three of them rode at a gait that Gus said was faster than was indicated by the six horses ahead of them.

"You gonna tell me what this is all about?" Lincoln asked.

"No," Lily said. "I told you before you decided to help that Gus and I need to handle this as best we can. Without you knowing what was going on. We need your help however it goes."

"I almost fired Slim two summers ago. In seventy-two. He was complaining about you. Talking about the accusations from the man in black. Saying you two were thieves."

"Why didn't you?"

"He's one of the best cowboys we've ever had. Tough. A good shot. We talked and he agreed to let it go." He stopped riding. Looked around. "One of them split off here. Elly. She went over there. Around that hill toward the trees. Slim went on straight ahead with the packhorses."

"She probably wanted some privacy over in the woods," Lily said. "Does it look like he slowed down his pace?"

"Yes. Probably to let her catch back up."

"You two follow him. I'll follow her," Lily said. In case she stashed some of the money to hide it from Slim.

A half hour later, Lily caught back up with them.

"I was right," she said. "I'm sure you saw her tracks rejoin back there. They headed to Laramie you think?"

"Looks like it. They're going to have to stop for the night, though. With the packhorses it's at least a two day ride."

He caught up to Gus.

"You're being awful quiet, Gus," Lincoln said.

"I've got nothing to say. This is going to be bad business, Lincoln. Lily should have stayed back at the ranch. Should have let us do this without her."

"I haven't had much success talking Lily out of things."

"Like I said, I've got nothing to say."

They rode on another hour.

"I been thinking," Lincoln said. "Slim's a helluva shot. If they think we'd follow them, it'd be easy for him to have Elly keep going, while he circled back around and picked us off."

"You think Slim's a killer?" Lily asked.

"Since I have no idea what this is all about, and I got lots of time to think, I'm picking at every possibility."

"Keep your eyes open then. If it's any comfort, I doubt they'll worry about being followed. And I doubt Elly would want to take the chance of being hung for murder."

The three of them rode on in the darkness, lost in their own thoughts.

"There's enough light to still follow their tracks," Lincoln said. "If I lose the tracks in the dark we'll have to stop. I'm hoping we'll spot their campfire up ahead eventually. I'll watch the ground, you look for the fire."

They rode on in silence.

"If we don't see their fire soon, I'll have to stop," Lily said. "Much longer and they'll be well rested and we'll be tired and hungry when we meet. That's not going to work."

"You're the boss."

They rode on. The horse's hooves made no sound in the snow.

"And there it is," Lincoln said. "You can just make out the fire flickering in and out among those trees. Maybe a mile up and to the right."

"Yeah, I see it," Gus said. "Let's hope it's them."

Lily peered at the tent. Flap down. Looked over at the six horses, Gus and Lincoln standing in front of them.

"What's in all the bags?" Lincoln said.

"Sugar," Gus said. "Flour."

Gus headed over to Lily by the tent.

The sounds of sex were clear coming from inside the tent. Elly's moans in the night air. There wasn't likely to be a better time.

Gus pulled open the flap, shot his pistol twice through the top of the tent, then pointed both pistols at the two startled lovers.

"Do not move," he said. "Either one of you."

They both propped up on their elbows. Elly whimpering. Slim cursing.

"Don't even think about it, Slim. Lily's right by your head outside the tent with her rifle and a pistol. I have absolutely no hesitation about killing you both right where you lie. The wolves can have you."

"But..."

"Not one word from either of you. Elly, crawl out the front of the tent."

"But I'm naked."

"And if you don't get out right now, you'll be naked *and* dead."

She crawled out slowly, her butt waving in the moonlight. Then a gasp when she saw Lincoln.

"Now you, Slim. Slow. I'll shoot you if I even get nervous."

He stepped out. Lincoln clubbed him in the back of the head, and he went down hard in the snow like the dead weight he had suddenly become.

Gus threw out all the clothes he could find and crawled out of the tent.

"Elly, get yourself dressed. Then dress your boyfriend. We don't want either of you freezing to death."

"Is he dead?"

"No. Now get dressed before I change my mind."

While Elly did as she was told, Lily walked Lincoln over to the horses and told him how they were going to play this. All but the ending.

"Okay, Gus," Elly said. "Now what?"

Lincoln tied Slim to a tree by the horses. Then rode out into the darkness beyond the trees.

"How did you know where the money was, Elly?" Lily said.

"What? What are you talking about?"

The sound of the slap was so loud that all eight horses jumped.

Elly was too stunned to cry. She looked at the blood in the snow in the moonlight. The brightest red she'd ever seen. She wiped her mouth with her coat sleeve. Blood dripped to the ground.

She got up and Gus slapped her by the eye with his pistol.

Elly fell back into the snow. She was crying now. And bleeding profusely.

"How could you steal money from John and Antelope Thunder and Sam and little Pepper?" Lily said, standing over her. "How could you do that?"

Gus pulled Lily away from the cringing girl.

"Go stand over there, Lil. You shouldn't be a part of this."

"I don't trust you and Lincoln to get the information we need, Gus. She fooled you with Sam. I'm not leaving her until we know who else knows."

"How could you do this Elly?" Gus said, towering over her, pistol aimed at her head.

Through her sobs, Elly said, "Slim always told us that it wasn't your money. That you killed a man who came here and explained that you two stole all this money. And anyways, you still have the ranch and all the cattle."

"How did you know where it was, Elly?"

She sat up. Crying. Bleeding.

"Unless you tell me everything," Gus said. "How you knew? Who else knows? Slim? Sam? Jimmy? Unless you tell me everything, the wolves'll be eating your stomach and heart by morning."

"And if I do tell you?" Elly said through her sobs.

"Everything?"

"Yes, everything."

"Then you'll be in Laramie looking for a train or a job tomorrow night," he lied.

"And Slim?"

"Depends on what the facts are."

"Jimmy found the money and told me 'n Slim to take it to Laramie. Said he'd cover for us and meet us there."

"Where'd he find the money?"

"He didn't tell me…"

Slap.

Gus fired a shot in the air, and Lincoln came riding in.

A look of horror came over his face at the sight of the bloodied girl.

"Get up," Gus said.

Elly got to her knees. Fell back to a sitting position, sobbing.

"Elly, here's what's going to happen," Gus said. "It's your choice. You're either going to tell me the truth, or Lincoln's going to finish what I started. I'd as soon kill you both, but Lincoln has considerably more experience with getting information from people. Don't you Lincoln?"

"Yes, I do."

Elly shook with terror.

"You see, Elly," Lincoln said. "The people in South Carolina where I was a slave knew how to mistreat people. It was their nature. They whipped my wife, Sarah, to death in front of all of us. They got big bucks, bigger 'n tougher than me, to babble anything they wanted to hear. Until they heard the truth come out of their bloodied mouths."

He walked over to the sobbing girl. "There are hundreds of bones in your body, Elly. They can each be broken, one at a time, without coming close to killing you. I've been forced to watch it done. Big, strong men faint. The snow in your face will wake you up for more."

"Now, Elly," Gus said. "You want to talk to Lily and me, or should we leave you alone here with Lincoln?"

"You…ou… ou, Lily. You. Please." Through her sobs.

Lincoln got on his horse and rode back out through the trees.

"Elly?" Gus said.

"Yes," she sobbed.

"Where was the money?"

"It was in Auggy the bear."

"Who told you?"

"Nobody. I saw Lily look in one morning. So I looked in. I recognized the packets from paydays."

"What did Jimmy say?"

"I made that up. Only Slim and me knew."

Gus put his pistol in her face.

"It's the truth."

"Sam?"

"Who?"

"Your rustler friend. Sam. From three years ago."

"Oh, Sam. No. Back then Sam and me were going to run away and live together off the rustling money. He was going to come back for me. But I haven't seen him or heard about him since that day you ran him off. Honest."

"Did you introduce Sam to the rustlers?"

"No. I encouraged him to join them. But I told you the truth that day about the rustlers. He found them himself. I lied about Sam and me liking each other. But the rest was the truth."

Gus held the pistol up in the air. "One last try before I call Lincoln back here, Elly. Who besides you and Slim know about Auggy the bear."

Elly sobbed. "Nobody. Lily, please make him stop. Just us two. I didn't tell Slim until this morning. I promise. I didn't want to split the money with anybody else but Slim."

"What else do we need to know?" Lily said. "Who else is a problem at the ranch?"

"I don't know of any problems, Lily. Slim thinks you and Gus are crooks. But that's all. All the ranch hands adore you and," she shuddered, "and Lincoln." She looked pleadingly into Lily's face. "And I do too."

Good to know, Lily thought to herself.

"Can and I go on now? We'll never tell anyone. I promise. Just give us today's pay and we'll go. We'll go to California. We won't tell anyone."

"I know you won't, Elly," Lily said. "I know you won't."

Gus helped Elly stand.

"Now go over there and untie Slim," he said. "I'll bring your horses over to you."

Lily pulled herself up on to her horse and rode into the woods where Lincoln had gone.

Gus followed the girl over to Slim tied to his tree, watched her kneel over him. Hands fumbling at the rope.

Two shots rang out in rapid succession. Then a third. Then a fourth.

Lily and Lincoln galloped in, guns drawn, saw Gus walking toward the four packhorses. Saw the boy and girl slumped against the tree.

Lily dismounted, walked over to the tree, cut Slim's ropes and let both bodies fall into the snow.

She and Lincoln looked over at Gus.

"They met with an unfortunate accident," Gus said. "Leave their stuff here. Let's go home."

78

September 6, 1874

"To what do we owe this pleasure John Iliff?" Lily said.

Gus and Lily had come out on the front porch when Lizzie said they had a visitor. Iliff was just riding up.

"Hi, Lily. Gus."

He dismounted and looked up. Shook his head.

"You two and that bear," he said. "I'm surprised you don't get cowboys using it for target practice. Kids, too."

They both laughed. "Everybody out here knows better than that," Gus said. "Lily'd give me up in an instant if somebody kidnapped Auggy the bear and asked for me as ransom."

"Horse thieves, we've forgiven, John," Lily said. "Attacks on Auggy the bear? We would not."

Iliff walked up and they walked into the parlor.

"Where's Lincoln?" he asked.

"We've been having trouble with wolves going after the cattle," Gus said.

"Don't I know it? The wolves aren't only picking on you, you know?"

"Lincoln took our boys out with some of the other ranchers for an old fashioned wolf hunt a week ago," Gus said.

"And you missed out?"

"Not my idea of a good time. Hanging out with a bunch of predators, shooting at other predators. Besides Lily has informed me that she prefers me here with the kids, rather than out having fun hunting wolves and Indians."

"Is the Cattlemen Association coming back?" Lily asked. "Is that why you're here?"

"Sure and you'll be a part of it when it does. We need you. But that's still a ways off before the others discover they really need it. But that's not why I swung by."

He reached for his tea. Looked out the window.

"Gus, you mentioned hunting Indians. I heard you had been doing some scouting for the Army."

"Yes. Against the Dog Soldiers five years ago, and then I was in Oregon when Canby got killed by the Modocs last year. But Lily wants me to stop. Wants me to finally settle down and be her assistant rancher."

"You heard they hung Captain Jack last October, right?"

"No. I heard that the Modocs finally surrendered, but I hadn't heard about Captain Jack. Served him right. Canby was pure cold blooded murder."

"So you weren't scouting up north last summer in the fights against the Sioux on the Yellowstone? With Custer?"

"No. Lily asked me not to go. And, besides, the President had promised the Sioux that country for them. He promised we wouldn't build the railroads up there. I wanted no part of that."

"I had been planning a trip up there to visit some friends in a Cheyenne camp," Lily said. "But I decided not to go when I heard about the Custer expedition. It wasn't any threat to us down here, so I didn't see any point in Gus getting involved."

"And that's precisely why I'm here, Lily," Iliff said. "I came up from Denver to meet with my brother-in-law to discuss how to protect our ranching interests up here. I think the peaceful days with the Sioux and the Cheyenne up here are about to be over. I think our ranch up here may be in danger. Yours, too. Everybody's, actually."

"Why? What's happened?" Gus asked.

"Custer and the Seventh Cavalry returned last week from a two month exploration into the Black Hills. Gold has been discovered. It's going to be crazy up there now."

"But," Gus said, "That land is sacred to the Sioux. President Grant promised it to them forever."

"Forever is apparently a short time in our promises to the Indians," Lily said.

"I agree with you, John," Gus said. "Sitting Bull and Crazy Horse are not going to stay at peace after this. This threatens all of us in Wyoming. Certainly in this valley."

"There's no way the politicians in Washington and the Army didn't know what the consequences were going to be. Rumors have it that both General Sheridan and General Terry were already reinforcing all the forts north of here, and that Crook will be headed here from Arizona soon enough."

"So it's true, then," Lily said. "That Crook finally defeated the Apaches?"

"Yes, the Apache wars are over."

Thoughts competed with themselves in Lily's head. How would this affect the Cheyenne? Antelope? Thunder Bull? How am I going to stop Gus from getting involved? And finally, the one she'd been pushing away for so long. John Arnold. He was with Crook.

79

January 25, 1875

Lily was in the kitchen with Mary when she saw Jimmy and two of the cowboys ride out of the stables and head south toward the back of the ranch house. Snow, ice, slush, and mud flying up in the air from their horses' hooves as they galloped by the Lincolns' house.

She heard Jimmy yell something, but couldn't make it out. Lincoln came out on to his front porch and looked after them.

"Gus," she said up the stairs. "Something's going on. Somebody may be coming from Cheyenne."

She grabbed a towel, drying her hands before grabbing a coat and walking out on to the porch. John and Antelope Thunder were coming up the porch stairs.

"Looks like soldiers, Mom," John said. "Probably a platoon headed up to Fort Laramie."

"Does it look like they were with the stage to Deadwood?"

"No, Lincoln said he saw the stage go by about an hour ago, right on schedule."

Gus came out and joined them on the porch. The four of them looked out at the approaching soldiers. Saw their three cowboys meet them. They could see the soldiers talking and then saw Jimmy pointing at the house. Lincoln came around the house and walked up the stairs to join them.

"This is going to be about the Indians," Lincoln said. "Nothing else going on."

"We'll know soon enough," Gus said.

Jimmy and the soldiers crossed the creek, disappeared behind the hill. And then came back into view as they crested the hill and started on the down side.

Lily licked her lips, put her hands on her hips, and pushed her hat up. John Arnold, she said slowly to herself, watching the men riding toward her. He'd reacquired his Arizona sunburned face. It was definitely John Arnold.

Jimmy pulled out ahead and galloped to the house.

"The major says he knows you. Says he's looking for the Smoot ranch. I hope it was okay to show him the way."

"He'd a found it without you," Gus said. "If that's Major John Arnold, he'd a found it with or without your help."

The platoon rode up, Arnold at the head. Stopped about ten yards in front of the porch.

"You and that bear," Arnold said. "That's got to be the most traveled bear in the country by now. As I suspected, it makes you easier to find."

"Hello to you, too, John Arnold," Lily said.

He tipped his cap. "Hello Gus. Lily. It's Lincoln, right?"

"Yes, Major. Good to see you again. What's it been, eight years?"

"Just about to the day, actually. Just about eight years to the day."

He looked at Lily.

"What can we do for you today, John?" Gus said.

"I'm in the area for a couple of months. Today's purely a social visit. We have to be back in Cheyenne night after next. Can we camp here for the night?"

"Is there room in the bunkhouse, Lincoln?" Lily said.

She ignored Gus's annoyed look.

"In the winter, we got room for two platoons in that bunkhouse."

"Tell Li'l Jack that he gets to cook that feast he's been looking forward to. Tell him we've got twenty-five guests for dinner."

"Not very surprising," Arnold said. "But John and Antelope Thunder grew up a little between my visits. How old are they now?

"John will soon be ten and Antelope Thunder nine," Lily said.

"And those two I saw looking down the stairs?"

"Sam is going on six and Pepper three."

"Any others?"

"No," Gus said. "I think cattle are going to be the only new arrivals at the L Bar S ranch from now on."

"Did that girl come back with you? Elly something. Burgess, maybe?"

"Things didn't work out for Elly," Lily said.

"And how about Nick, the kid from the wagon train who was working with Lincoln?"

A general silence descended over the room.

Arnold looked puzzled.

"Remember the man in black you warned me about?" Gus said.

"Yes."

"He came here looking for Damours one day when I was playing poker in Cheyenne."

Gus looked at Lily. Arnold followed his look.

"It was about three and a half years ago now," Lily said. "There was a brief discussion. The man in black killed Nick."

"What happened to the man in black?" Arnold said.

"He seems to have disappeared," Lincoln said.

"I'm pretty sure," Gus said, "We won't be having to be warned about him any more."

Breaking the resulting silence, Arnold said, "How's the ranching business?"

"Great," Lincoln said. "We're near five thousand head. One of the biggest ranches in the Chugwater Valley. We've gone from learning, to leading the ranching business."

"So you did find your dream, Lily."

"I did. You?"

"Still looking."

Pepper came running down the stairs. Looked at the four adults like she was shopping for one. Chose Arnold and climbed into his lap.

"Didn't you have a girlfriend in Santa Fe named Pepper, Lily?"

"Yes."

"She was killed in a bank robbery, right?"

"Long time ago, John."

"For all of us."

"Which," Gus said, "brings us to today. Why are you here, Arnold?"

"Here in Wyoming, or here at your ranch?"

"Both."

"General Crook said he didn't need me mopping up the Apaches as much as he needed me scouting out our next assignment. He's the next Commander of the Department of the Platte. He expects to be heading out in late March and wants us to be waiting for him in Omaha when he arrives in April."

"John Arnold, speaking of mopping up Apaches, how is Cochise?" Lily asked.

"He died last June."

"Killed by Crook?"

"No, he died of old age. At his stronghold."

"That's sad. I'm sorry. I met him the same day I met you, remember?"

"I do."

"And Red Cloud?"

"I have no idea."

"What is the Army expecting from the Sioux?" Gus asked.

He looked carefully at Gus while he thought. "Of course, nobody knows for sure, but let's just say that we expect Crazy Horse and Sitting Bull and even some of the Northern Cheyenne to break their word and start living and hunting wherever they please."

"Didn't the Army break the treaty first, John?" Lily said.

"I'm just a little ol' Major in the service of my country, Lily. I'm not a politician. But if we're ordered to protect citizens and towns..." He looked up, "...and ranchers. From marauding Indians, that's what we'll have to do."

"And here at our ranch?" Gus said. "Why did you come here? To us, John?"

Arnold looked at each in turn, then at Pepper who was still watching his every word.

"Shucks, Lieutenant, I wouldn't think riding forty miles to catch up with old friends for old times' sake would seem that unusual."

At the use of "Lieutenant," Lily noted that Lincoln frowned, started to say something. Thought better of it. Gus looked annoyed.

"If that answer doesn't work for any of you," and he winked at Pepper, "I'm here to officially tell you that General Crook specifically asked me to ask if Gus Smoot would consider scouting for us next year."

"John, I don't want Gus to do this."

They were sitting in front of the fire in the kitchen alone. The kids were all asleep, the Lincolns were in their cabin, and Gus was out in the bunkhouse playing in what promised to be an all-night poker game.

"To do what, Lil?"

"Don't start teasing me, John Arnold. You know exactly what I mean."

"Crook and I need Gus against the Sioux, Lily. He's been hunting up there for over six years now. Crook has more confidence in him than in any white man he knows in Wyoming or the Dakotas."

"We have friends among the Northern Cheyenne, John. It's taken me eleven years to get Gus interested in the ranch and the children. I don't want him on another Indian hunt. You know he was with Canby when he was killed, right?"

"No, I didn't know. He went back to Oregon?"

"Yes, he went to help Canby."

"And how did the General react to the reappearance of his former aide de camp?"

"I have no idea what you're talking about."

Arnold got up without a word. Walked outside. He came back with some wood for the fire. He wrestled with a new log and rearranged the fire.

"Lily."

"Yes, John Arnold?"

"Let's talk about us."

"Us? There is no us, John. What are you talking about? I haven't even seen you but once in the past eleven years."

She stood up, walked over to the fire. Hugged herself. Walked around the kitchen.

"I have a family, a ranch more successful than I'd ever dreamed, a staff that adores me, and five thousand cattle to care for."

"And a husband who'd rather be anywhere but here."

"John *Arnold*! Don't you say that. You don't know that. And it isn't even true."

"It is true and you know it, Lil. And Lincoln knows it. If you don't know it, then you're the only one at the L Bar S ranch who doesn't."

She sat down. Glared at him.

"That's better, Lil. You didn't make eye contact with me once during your lecture. That's much better."

She looked away.

"At the very least, we owe each other honesty after all these years. For now, that's all I ask."

"For now?"

"Okay then, maybe that's all I'll ask of you forever."

She laughed. "No John Arnold, that's not all I ever want you to ask of me."

"Let's start over, Miss Smoot. How did Canby react to Auggy showing up at his camp?"

"Gus told me that Canby believed him that he'd been cleared of all charges."

"Do you believe him?"

"Of course."

"Lily. You're really out of practice. Don't avoid eye contact when you're lying."

She laughed. "No, I didn't believe him for a minute."

"That's my Lil."

"Please don't ask Gus to scout for Crook, John."

"First of all, I already have. Secondly, if you and the kids can't stop him, I certainly can't. And thirdly, General Crook is planning to come to Cheyenne himself in July. Unless you can arrange for Gus to be playing poker somewhere, Crook will no doubt ask him himself."

They went for a walk down to Chugwater Creek. It was freezing, but it was one of those crystal clear, moonless Wyoming winter nights. A million stars so bright they could hurt your eyes. Arnold and Lily could see their shadows on the snow from the starlight alone. Their breath crystallized immediately in the air.

"So, John Arnold. How old are you?"

"Fifty-something," he said through his laugh.

"Fifty-ten?"

He laughed again. "You drive a tough bargain, lady. Fifty-eight."

They walked along the creek bank.

"I figure you for thirty-seven," he said.

"Close enough," turning around and walking backwards in front of him.

"I guess we're done arguing," he said. "Now we're a couple of teenagers headed into town?"

She laughed, turned back around, walking. "Eight years ago as you rode away from me, you said you were still trying to figure out your dream."

"True. I did say that. And it was true." Making eye contact.

She laughed. "Found it yet?"

"Yes, I have, Lil. Yes I have."

"Willing to share?"

"Maybe someday, Lil. Maybe someday. If the time is ever right."

80

July 28, 1875

Arnold walked into the gambling hall. It was Cheyenne' biggest, and, at times, its most reputable. He had been told that Gus Smoot was playing in a high stakes poker game that had been going on for three days.

"I'm looking for a poker game," he said to a young woman who had approached him the minute he entered. "The one that Gus Smoot is in."

"Back right," she said, pointing. "Want to buy me a drink instead? Or at least first?"

"No thanks. Maybe later. Thanks for the help."

He tipped his hat and headed to the back.

Sure enough, Gus Smoot, bottle of whiskey on his right and a pile of money on his left was at the right end of the table, staring at five cards in his hand. Oblivious to anything going on around him, except for the play of the hand.

"You haven't got a thing, sir," Gus said.

"You'll have to wager a bet to find out, Smoot."

"That's exactly what I intend to do." He laid his cards face down in front of him, between the bottle and the money. "I'll raise you ten dollars."

Arnold, who had never acquired a taste for poker, watched the proceedings, waiting for an opportunity to catch Gus's attention.

One by one, the three men still playing threw their cards into the pot.

Gus smiled and pulled the money into his pile. Tossed his cards in with the others.

The girl who had approached Arnold now appeared at Gus's side. Leaned down, whispered something in his ear.

Gus looked up, grinned. "Major Arnold. To what do we owe this honor? I've never seen you at a poker table before. Care to join us?"

"May I speak with you privately, Gus?" Arnold said.

"Sure, John." He stood up, gave the girl some bills. "Hold my spot please, Kitty."

The two walked to the bar at the far end of the saloon.

"What can I do for you, John?" Gus said. "You here about that job we discussed last winter?"

"Yes, Gus. But first, this town is bursting. Is Cheyenne always like this now?"

"It's all about the Black Hills. People say this is worse than California in forty-nine. Worse than Colorado's gold rush. The trains are bringing people to Cheyenne by the hundreds. The town is overcapacity. The road past our ranch on the way to Fort Laramie, then on to Deadwood, is filled with wagons, and horses. People are even walking. It reminds me of roads between cities back East. Lincoln says the cattle are unsettled. Everything is about the Black Hills these days."

"General Crook is at the Union Pacific Hotel and asked me to find you. He wants to talk to you personally about scouting for us. I told him you were a successful rancher up Chugwater Creek and were reluctant to leave your business."

"Why'd you say that, Arnold? I'm looking forward to it."

Arnold shrugged. "Lily doesn't want you to do this. Crook wants you badly. I handed you bargaining power both ways. I also told him you were going to want him to see your ranch."

Smoot looked puzzled.

"Gus. We're marching north in two days. We'll be riding right by your ranch on our way to Fort Laramie. Then on to Fort Fetterman. There are two other ranchers on the Chugwater he wants to personally thank for their help with his officers over the past year. I set this up for you so that Lily won't be able to say no. Not to you, Crook, and me."

"Lily manipulates men, Arnold, not the other way around."

Gus grinned at Arnold.

"Think about it, Gus, this is the best way. You can suit yourself, though. If you'd rather, I'll take you to Crook at the hotel right now."

Gus looked over at Kitty standing by his seat, looking at him. He looked back at Arnold.

"No, you're right. Tell Crook you just missed me but you heard I'm at the ranch. I want this scouting assignment. I always liked working with Crook, and the lack of anything to do at the ranch is driving me crazy. Lily's actually trying to talk me into starting a little farm down by the creek now."

81

August 1, 1875

"It's a pleasure to meet you, General Crook," Lily said. "Gus and Major Arnold have said such nice things about you. Gus was very impressed working for you back in Oregon."

"Thank you, Mrs. Smoot. This is a beautiful spot you picked for a ranch.

Major Arnold tells me you run more than five thousand head of cattle up here now."

"Gus and me, General. And Lincoln." She gestured to Lincoln sitting with them in the parlor.

Crook nodded at the three of them in turn.

"Both your husband and Major Arnold tell me you were friends with Cochise."

Lily blushed.

"They exaggerate, General. I met him and his family in Apache Pass. At a stage station. It was friendly, but I don't think I'd say we became friends."

"Let me be frank with you, Mrs. Smoot. I'm not here to admire your cattle. I wouldn't know the front end of a cow from the back end. Unless it was on a dinner plate. I admire your courage, I certainly do. Fighting sub-zero temperatures, rustlers, all manner of predators, and Indians. Mine's a tough way to make a living, but I couldn't do what you people do. I thank you and I admire you."

"Thank you, General."

"We're headed north to Fort Fetterman. We are expecting Indian trouble."

"What have the Indians done, General?"

"We've asked them to move away from all the white settlers going into the Black Hills. We've offered to renegotiate their reservations. They are stalling. All but refusing. Even Sitting Bull, who is nothing more than a medicine man, is refusing to cooperate. And Crazy Horse is starting to be impossible. Refusing the most reasonable requests."

"But they haven't done anything hostile yet, have they General?"

"Ma'am, with all due respect, you know your business, and I know mine. There are three kinds of war acceptable to this nation. Defensive, offensive in response to provocation, and offensive in anticipation of provocation. We will be asking the Lakota to move from lands that they, rightly, view as their traditional homes. And that they, rightly, believe President Grant has promised them. We expect them to say no or to say nothing. Do you understand?"

"Yes, General. I do."

"That will leave us the choice of waiting to be attacked, waiting until nice people like you and Mr. and Mrs. Lincoln here, and all your children are dead so that we have to attack. Or the third option, which is what we intend to do if they behave as we expect, attacking to prevent future provocation."

Silence filled the room.

"Thank you, General," Lily said. "I see. And what would you like from us?"

"I want to borrow Gus, Mrs. Smoot. I fully understand that if he's half as good a rancher as he is an Indian scout and interpreter, that he will be greatly missed here at the L Bar S ranch. But I promise you that I will do everything in my power to compensate you for his time. Handsomely."

"And how long will this loan last, General?"

Crook laughed.

"I'm having second thoughts, Mrs. Smoot. I'm thinking I've got my eyes on the wrong Smoot. I'm thinking President Grant needs you to negotiate with the savages."

Lily nodded, smiling.

"I think the whole mess will take less than two years."

Lily sucked in her breath.

Crook held up his hand.

"Does it work for you, if we leave without Gus for now? And that I send Major Arnold to bring him to us just before next spring?"

Gus frowned. Looked at Lily.

Lily looked at Arnold. John Arnold you old dog, you, she said to herself, suppressing a smile.

"If it's acceptable to Gus, General, then, yes, that would work for me and our children."

All eyes turned to Gus.

"I'd rather leave with you now, General, but yes, that works for me, too."

"If it's any consolation to you, Lily. May I call you Lily?"

"Yes, General."

"If it's any consolation to you, Lily, my wife, Mary." He paused. "I'm from Ohio. She's from Virginia. Mary refused to let me go to the Civil War. Then refused to let me go to Oregon. Then to Arizona. And just six months ago she sent me a letter forbidding me to come here. You've got it much better with Gus than Mary has it with me. Trust me on that."

Everybody laughed good naturedly as they stood. And the soldiers headed to the door.

"One last thing, Mrs. Smoot?"

"Yes?"

"What is the story about that bear standing there on your porch?"

82

March 2, 1876

"Hey, Lily," Arnold said as he walked into the stables unannounced seven months later.

"You startled me, John Arnold. You can get shot coming up behind people like that."

"Sorry. I called out to you at the house. Where is everybody?"

"The men are out hunting antelope one last time before the roundups start. I don't know where the children are."

"What if I'd been a bad guy? Or an Indian?"

"If you'd been an Indian, you woulda been a friend. If youlda been a bad guy, either Lizzie or I would have made you a former bad guy."

"Fair enough, Lil. Is Gus out on the hunt?"

"No." She made a face. "In Cheyenne."

He walked over. Hugged her.

"You want some breakfast?" she asked.

They sat in the kitchen by the fire.

"How do your cattle survive these winters out here, Lil?"

"This is the worst one ever. I don't ever remember two or more feet of snow all winter long ever before. It's still out there." She shuddered. "John Iliff says it was discovered by accident that they survive it. Somebody once abandoned the cattle he couldn't sell to anybody out here fifteen or twenty years ago. And in the spring, they just wandered back in, fatter than ever. Of course, it stands to reason. The grass is the best in the world, and the buffalo do just fine out there. Shouldn't have been a surprise to anyone. We don't lose more than two, three percent of the herd each winter."

"You still follow Iliff's rule of letting the Indians take what they need?"

"Like I said out there in the stables, John, if youda been an Indian youda been a friend."

He stood up. Got himself some more coffee. Poured her some.

"How's it going up there with *your* Indians, John?"

"Pretty much as we expected. A few incidents here and there. But not many. They're refusing to move to where we want them to. Sitting Bull and Crazy Horse are just ignoring us. Sitting in their winter camps. Frankly, I don't know how *they* get through these winters. The plan is to move on them this spring. Make them go to the reservations. They might go willingly. Might not."

"You here for Gus?"

"I'm here just when Crook told you I would be, Lily."

"And you had nothing to do with it, John Arnold?"

He looked at her. Smiled.

"Orders are orders, Lily. Just a poor soldier doing his duty."

She slapped his shoulder.

"Well, poor, poor Major Arnold. You're just going to have to find something to do with yourself for two days until Gus returns from his poker game."

She held out her hand.

He took it.

They looked out at the trees by the creek. It had started snowing.

Hard.

"Maybe three days," she said, looking directly into his eyes. Showing him she wasn't lying.

83

March 5, 1876

"We need to get going, Gus," Arnold said. "It's over two hundred miles and Crook isn't going to be happy if you're not there before he wants his information on Crazy Horse's village."

"Hold the horses, Major. I'll be right there. I'll help Mary get the kids. I need to say goodbye to the kids. I'll be right there."

Lily walked over to Arnold. Took his hand, the horses between them and the house.

"This is hard, John Arnold."

"I'm going to miss you, but we have to go. We're going to be late as it is."

"Please don't let Gus be too reckless."

"He's got the safe job, Lil."

She laughed. "I'm never going to worry about you, John Arnold. God isn't going to let anything happen to you that would keep you from popping in and out of my life. Not until you find your dream. Or at least until you tell me what it is."

He squeezed her hand. Looked down at her.

"This is hard, Lil. You take care. I'll see you when I can."

Gus, Mary, Rachel and all the kids came out on to the porch.

Gus hugged everybody goodbye and walked down to Lily.

"You take care of the ranch, Lil. Don't worry, I'll be back sooner'n you expect. I promise."

He kissed her as Arnold swung up and into his saddle.

Gus pulled himself on to his horse.

They both turned, waved to everyone on the porch, and headed north.

"Take care," Lily said to their backs. "Please say hello to Antelope for me if you see her. And to Thunder Bull."

PART IV
CHIEFS OF THIEVES

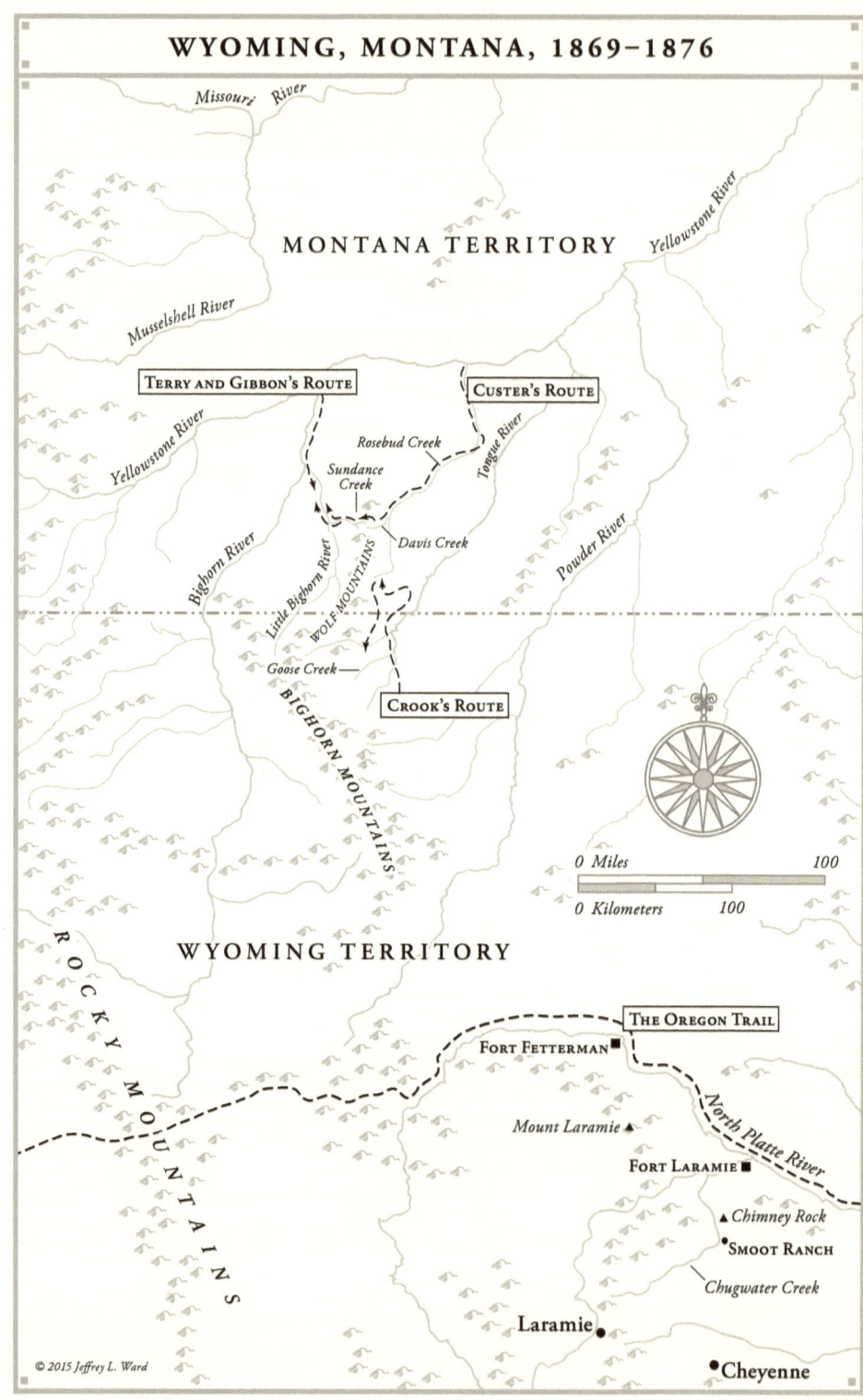

WYOMING, MONTANA, 1869–1876

Missouri River

MONTANA TERRITORY

Yellowstone River

Musselshell River

TERRY AND GIBBON'S ROUTE

CUSTER'S ROUTE

Yellowstone River

Rosebud Creek

Tongue River

Sundance Creek

Bighorn River

Little Bighorn River

Davis Creek

Powder River

WOLF MOUNTAINS

Goose Creek

CROOK'S ROUTE

BIGHORN MOUNTAINS

0 Miles 100

0 Kilometers 100

WYOMING TERRITORY

R O C K Y

THE OREGON TRAIL

FORT FETTERMAN ■

North Platte River

Mount Laramie ▲

M O U N T A I N S

FORT LARAMIE ■

▲ *Chimney Rock*

● **SMOOT RANCH**

Chugwater Creek

Laramie ●

© 2015 Jeffrey L. Ward

● **Cheyenne**

84

March 16, 1876

Arnold and Gus caught up with Crook near the Tongue River at dawn.

"I was beginning to think something had happened to you two," Crook said.

"Sorry, General. I wasn't just sitting at the ranch. Major Arnold had to find me."

"Welcome, Gus."

"Thank you, sir. What do you need?"

"As we knew, there are thousands of Cheyenne, Sioux, and Arapaho somewhere north of here. They're off the reservation. And more are leaving the reservations and joining them. The Army has sent three armies after them to convince them to come in. Colonel Gibbon was ordered to come east with his Montana Column and General Terry west with the Dakota Column, meeting on the Yellowstone and eventually south to the Bighorn River. My Wyoming Column is ordered to complete the encirclement, heading north from down here."

"If Terry and Gibbon have met, they're more than one hundred miles north of here, then, General. Lot of country between here and there to look through."

"There are several thousand Indians, Gus, and they aren't hiding. The trails are pretty easy to follow. They're somewhere between here and there. Our Crow and Shoshone scouts think Crazy Horse's village may be just up ahead at the Powder."

"No Sioux scouts, General?" Arnold said. "I thought that was the plan."

"I approached them last month on the reservation while you were away, and they refused to participate. They warned me that the Lakota and Northern Cheyenne were planning to fight. They want no part of it. Our Crow and Shoshone scouts will be fine, Arnold."

He stood and looked to the north, past the camp.

"Gus, can you ride ahead with the Indian scouts? See if Crazy Horse's village is where I think it is?"

"Yes, sir."

Late that afternoon, Gus rode back to meet the advancing Crook.

"There's a Cheyenne village just ahead," Gus said. "Just at the Powder where you thought."

"Is it Crazy Horse?" Crook asked.

"No, it's a sizeable Cheyenne village. There's a large pony herd, but no Lakota."

"We attack at dawn, anyway. Let's stop here. I don't want their scouts to have any advance warning."

85

March 17, 1876

Crook had crept with his advanced troops to a point overlooking the village.

"Forty Cheyenne lodges down there," Gus said. "We're thinking that Crazy Horse and Sitting Bull's Sioux must be further down the Powder. They will be in much larger villages."

"We don't have the supplies to continue tramping east," Crook said. "Attack this village now. Cut out their ponies. Take them back with us."

Antelope, now twenty-nine, was preparing breakfast over the fire just after dawn when she heard the old man on the hill cry, "The soldiers are here. They are coming."

She rushed into her lodge and grabbed whatever she could find and ran from the tipi through the melted, flowing slush and snow. Children were crying. Women were running with her, some carrying their children, some dragging them through the snow.

She could hear the guns popping behind her as some of the warriors resisted, but the soldiers had raced between the pony herd and the village and had cut them off. All was pandemonium as the Cheyenne tried to reach the river.

The soldiers did not follow the fleeing Indians.

"Burn the village," General Crook said. "Destroy their belongings. Everything."

The soldiers rounded up the pony herd and set to burning the lodges.

"Take the ponies back to Fort Fetterman. We will replenish and come back when it is time."

From the river bank the Indians could see the flames and smoke as their village was destroyed. The nineteen year old Thunder Bull organized the younger braves who had been able to retrieve their ponies and joined the more seasoned braves headed back toward the village.

"Do we go to attack the soldiers?" he asked the chief.

"No, Thunder Bull. We chase them back. Away from the people. They did not follow up their attack. So they do not want to fight us. We will make them pay for that. Chase them. We will then take our ponies back tonight while they sleep."

"But they destroyed all we had. We should attack them."

"They did not destroy our warriors, Thunder Bull. They did not kill our ponies. They let the people go free. There are too many soldiers for us to attack now."

"Then where do we go now?"

"We will first get our ponies. Then we will take our people east to Crazy Horse and Sitting Bull. We will wait to fight the soldiers until they give us no choice, Thunder Bull. Or when our chiefs decide it is time."

The two rode after the soldiers, directing the braves to follow the soldiers from a distance.

"I think that time is not far away, Thunder Bull. You will soon be able to fight the white soldiers."

86

May 16, 1876

"Colonel Custer, what are you doing here?" said the startled Fort Lincoln commander. "I was told you were forced to stay in Washington under orders from President Grant. That General Terry was to take the Seventh from here."

"Politics. I left when the President refused to see me for the third time, even though I was under orders to meet with him. Then he ordered me arrested when I arrived in Minnesota, but Sheridan and Terry had him reinstate me."

"Why did President Grant do all this?"

"Politics. I testified against his crooked brother and his Secretary of War. I guess he took it personally."

The commander started to ask a question, appeared to think better of it. Then said, "What are your orders now?"

"To lead the Seventh Cavalry to rejoin the Dakota Column against the Cheyenne and the Sioux. We leave Fort Lincoln in the morning."

87

June 16, 1876

The Cheyenne scouts had ridden into the village near the Greasy Grass River at dawn, alerting all with their wolf cries. The white soldiers were near and were riding toward the Rosebud from the south.

Thirty-seven year old Lame White Man and Thunder Bull joined the group now consulting with Crazy Horse and Sitting Bull.

"We must wait here," Sitting Bull said. "I think we should not ride the six or seven hours to the Rosebud to attack them there. They might not even find us this far from them."

"Our scouts say they are looking for us," Crazy Horse said. "Our trail is too big. Their Crows will lead them here."

"We have discussed my vision. It showed soldiers falling into camp. Falling on their heads. And they come from the east, not the south."

"These may not be the white soldiers in your vision."

"Do we know who they are?" Lame White Man asked.

"Yes, our Cheyenne scouts say it is Three Stars," Crazy Horse said. "They say he has many soldiers. The valley was black with his soldiers."

"Here in this village," Sitting Bull said, "we are too many for Three Stars to attack. If we travel to him, he will be able to choose his ground."

"No," Crazy Horse said. "We never attack the soldiers. So they are only experienced at chasing us."

"Or," Lame White Man said, "at surprising our women and children in our lodges."

"This time we will surprise them. We will attack them as if we are many and they are few. We will attack and punish them repeatedly. Then we will pull back and they will not follow. They will think it is a trap. I think this is the only way we will defeat the white soldiers. They have no experience defending against our attacks."

"I think it is better to stay here," Sitting Bull said. "Here we are many and they are few."

"Many of the young braves have left already," Thunder Bull said. "They have been taking their medicine and riding to the Rosebud."

"Yes," Lame White Man said. "Many of the Cheyenne and Lakota braves are already dressed and painted for war. Many have left."

"Let us help Three Stars find his Indians," Crazy Horse said. "He will then lose interest in finding our village."

88

June 17, 1876

Crook ordered a halt just short of the Rosebud. His scouts were up ahead, on and below the bluffs looking over the river.

"This whole war is just a repetition of looking for and failing to find Indians," he said.

"Except when they want to be found," Arnold said. "Or when we can surprise a village like the one in March."

"We'll head down the Rosebud today. We'll either find their village, or they'll come out to stop us."

"It's never happened before, General. They've never attacked a force of this size."

"Then we'll keep destroying their villages until they can't survive."

Crazy Horse and Sitting Bull had rested their warriors after the all night ride.

"Our scouts tell us they are at the river," Crazy Horse said. "Just ahead."

"Take two hundred braves," he said to Lame White Man. "Experienced warriors. Do not let the young men attack too soon. Surprise them."

Lame White Man selected as instructed and headed out quietly toward the Rosebud.

Gus and a handful of the Crows had crossed the river.

"The general thinks there is a village downriver," he said, pointing to the east.

"There is no village," one of them said. "The Sioux and Cheyenne left there many sleeps ago. They are in the other direction." He pointed to the northwest. "Thousands are headed to the Little Bighorn, the Greasy Grass River."

Gus looked where he was pointing and his heart stopped. There were three Indians, painted and armed. The one in the middle was Lame White Man.

Lame White Man looked down on the Crows and saw Gus.

He sat still on his pony and motioned those behind to stop. It is a good day to die, he thought to himself as he stared at Gus.

Crook grabbed another cup of coffee from the fire in front of Arnold's tent and heard gunfire to the north.

"The Crows find some buffalo?" Arnold asked.

"That's one possibility, John."

The gunfire continued and became scattered across a wider range. More intense.

"We're about to find out, General," Arnold said. "Either we've found our Indians or some mighty aggressive buffalo."

They both stood as three of the Crow scouts raced toward them. They could hear the gunfire increasing from the other side of the bluffs. And then they saw their scouts appearing on the bluffs, their backs toward them, and shooting back down toward the river.

"War party," the lead scout said. "Lakota and Cheyenne."

"How many?" Crook asked.

"More than a hundred. Maybe two hundred."

"Not just a hunting party?"

"No, Three Stars. They're dressed and painted for war. They were looking for us and began attacking when we shot at them."

"Where's Gus?"

"He's organizing the scouts to defend the bluffs."

"Are all hundred fifty scouts there and standing strong?" Arnold asked.

"Yes, Major. We will need the soldiers' help if there are more coming."

"Not too likely," Crook said. They'll be defending the village down the Rosebud. "Arnold."

"Yes, sir."

"Take three hundred cavalry down the river to look for the village."

"Yes, sir."

"General," the Crow scout said. "There is no village down the Rosebud."

Crook, ignoring him, sent the scouts back and watched as Arnold and his men headed to the right for the Rosebud. Sat down to finish his coffee.

Gus and the Crow and Shoshone scouts fought their attackers hand to hand. Arrows and rifle fire from the single-shot Springfields blazed down from the bluff. They were able to keep the bulk of the Cheyenne and Sioux on the other side of the river by keeping up fire whenever they tried to cross, but were forced back toward and then up the bluffs by the superior numbers and their superior horsemanship.

"Tell Crook we need his cavalry," Gus said to the chief Shoshone scout. He could now see Arnold to his right leading the three hundred soldiers down river. Away from them.

He saw Lame White Man crossing the river, but couldn't get a shot off. All he could see was a leg over and an arm with a Spencer repeater under the pony's body.

Then it occurred to him that he had a stake in keeping Lame White Man alive. If Sitting Bull's vision had been correct, anyway.

And then he saw what looked like a thousand Indians charging to his left around the bluffs and toward Crook.

Crook saw them come around the bluff to his left. Crazy Horse and a thousand horsemen heading to cut off his flank.

"This is not how Indians fight," he said to the colonel on his left. "Who's leading these Indians? George Custer?"

"I've never seen this," the colonel said. "They must be crazy."

They scrambled four companies to their horses. Four hundred galloped out to meet their attackers. Crook sent the rest of the men up the bluff to reinforce the scouts, who were starting to retreat back down the bluff.

This was not a skirmish against the Snakes or the Apaches, Crook thought. This was desperate all-out war. Nothing like what the army had experienced out west before this. In the Civil War, yes. But not against Indians.

Crazy Horse had his warriors attack the soldiers across a three mile front. The tremolos of a thousand braves terrified the soldiers' horses. The defenders were in disarray.

The Indians would attack, then retreat. Attack in a different spot. Then retreat.

"Those are the greatest horsemen I've ever seen," Crook said to the colonel. "I had no idea. I'd heard about the Cheyenne, but they are better than we were told. Their whooping is terrifying the horses and the men alike."

"Can they hold that line, General? They're badly outnumbered."

"Maybe. They're taking casualties greater than they can sustain. Send someone after Arnold. Bring those three companies back. Village or no village, the battle is here."

Major Marcus Reno, Seventh Cavalry, peered up the Rosebud. He and his three hundred soldiers could see their scouts riding back toward them.

He had been under orders from Custer to confirm that the Indians were not to the east of the Tongue River. But, dragging his mules and Gatling gun behind him, he had disobeyed orders and, at his scouts' direction, ridden west, past the Tongue, here to the Rosebud. There, he again had violated orders and headed up river in the search for the Indians. He had stopped at this point in the river this morning to let his scouts follow the two day old trail south and determine where the Indians had gone.

The scouts had ridden twenty miles up the Rosebud, unknowingly to within thirty miles of the then-raging battle between Crook and Crazy Horse.

"Did you find the village?" Reno asked.

"It is a two day ride further to the south."

Reno looked back at his rested men. At the Gatling gun.

"It is a trail of a large number of Indians. Can we reach them in two or three days and defeat them at the village."

"If you and these Sioux and Cheyenne meet, Major, there will be a battle. They will not surrender. They will not let you attack their village. We will all die. It will be a very short fight."

It's one thing to disobey orders and be a hero, he thought to himself. Quite another to cause the massacre of his entire force.

"Let's ride down the river to the Yellowstone, then. Back to rejoin Custer and the rest of the Dakota Column."

Thunder Bull and a hundred Cheyenne under Crazy Horse's urging hurled themselves across Crook's right flank. A hundred ponies galloping back and forth, their riders leaning behind their ponies all but invisible but for the arrows hurtling toward the soldiers, and the smoke from their Spencer rifle fire.

Thunder Bull led a dozen braves straight at the soldiers, now on the ground with the holders behind them holding the terrified horses. They each tried to count coup over the cowering soldiers. Then wheeled around shooting and charging through them again.

After several hours of continuous fighting, the cavalry line broke in places, and the Indians now were circling the disoriented force. Attacking, then retreating. Then attacking again.

Arnold and his three hundred men arrived to reinforce the beleaguered cavalry.

They rushed from the Rosebud at Crook's direction and pushed the Indians back toward the river.

At one point a young Cheyenne had his pony shot out from under him and he was surrounded by soldiers.

Thunder Bull and three Cheyenne drove their ponies toward him, shooting at the soldiers. From behind them raced a lone Indian, swept by them, through the soldiers, reached down and lifted the young brave behind her onto her pony as it galloped through the soldiers to safety.

Thunder Bull led the other three braves back toward the river to cover her retreat. They knew she had saved her brother from a certain death.

"Did you see that?" Crook said.

"I did, General," Arnold said. "I think I've seen it all now."

"Are they retreating toward that valley?" Crook asked. They watched as the soldiers regrouped and followed into the arroyo at the head of the valley.

"Standard ploy, General," Gus said. "They attack, then pretend to retreat and draw you to their waiting forces."

"How many can there be Gus? There must have been a thousand that attacked us, maybe fifteen hundred."

"The Crows say don't follow, sir."

"You averted a disaster bringing me back, General," Arnold said. "Now bring those troops back. There's time to pursue the Indians later."

Crook ordered the Crows to ride and bring the cavalry back. "I agree, John. It's not a chance worth taking."

The exultant Indians, led by Crazy Horse and Sitting Bull, celebrated on the ride back to their village.

They had recovered the bodies of their fallen comrades and were carrying them back toward the Greasy Grass River.

Sitting Bull honored Crazy Horse by letting him lead the ride back.

"You have defeated Three Stars as you said you would," he said. "You were right. The white soldiers can be driven from our land. We learned that here today. At The Battle Where the Girl Saved Her Brother."

Crook met with his senior officers and chief scouts that evening.

"We only brought provisions for four days," he said. "And only one hundred rounds of ammunition per man."

"The Crows tell us that this was not all of Crazy Horse's warriors," Arnold said. "They think many more were left back at their camp yesterday."

"You believe them?"

"Yes, I do. And they say many more agency Indians have been joining them."

"Joining them where?"

"They say the only place they can go with a pony herd of that size will be down the Little Bighorn," Gus said. "I agree with them. They will need to keep moving downriver to graze their herd and hunt for buffalo. Moving north toward the Bighorn and then the Yellowstone, their Elk River."

"What are the chances of successfully attacking a village of that size?" Crook asked.

Gus discussed this with the Crows.

"Ask them, Gus, if we could even get close to a village of that size in order to attack," Arnold said.

"They say there are too many Lakota." Gus said. "Too many Cheyenne. They will have scouts looking for the soldiers from here to the Yellowstone. They say that even with your thousand soldiers, Three Stars cannot defeat these Indians or their villages."

"Will the scouts stay with us?"

"Yes, they say you have their word."

"General?" Arnold said.

"Yes, Major."

"Where did the Indians get those Spencer repeaters?"

"I don't know, but it sure changes the odds. As long as we've only got the standard issue single shot Sharps and Springfields it's going to be an even greater challenge to push them back."

He looked out over his officers and scouts.

"Anybody in favor of chasing after those Indians in the morning?"

There was a long silence, the only sound Gus whispering with the Crows.

"If we can resupply and coordinate with Gibbon and Terry," the colonel said. "I say we then trap them between us. The original plan."

"We have no idea where the others are," Crook said. "Or even if they know that these Indians are not running from even a thousand cavalry. These Indians intend to fight." He looked among his officers. "Anybody for advancing in the morning?"

"Makes no sense, General," Arnold said. "Not knowing what we know now. Better to rearm and regroup."

"Then let's head out in the morning gentlemen. Back to Goose Creek."

89

June 22, 1876

"George?" Colonel Gibbon said.

"Yes, sir," Custer said.

"Your orders, George, are to travel south from here on the Yellowstone, up the entire length of the Rosebud and only then to head west to the Little Bighorn. We believe Reno's scouts that Sitting Bull's village is somewhere between the Bighorn and the Rosebud. You are to cut off any southern escape route for the Indians. You may be able to join up with Crook coming from the south at that point."

"Yes, sir."

"Sitting Bull and Crazy Horse's villages will be trapped between us. You advancing down the Little Bighorn as we ride up the Bighorn from the Yellowstone."

"Understood, sir."

At noon, Custer, refusing the Gatling gun on Reno's advice that it would slow them down, led the Seventh Cavalry south from the camp on the Yellowstone River. He was dressed in his white buckskin suit, his famous long blonde hair cut short. Martinez, Reno, and Benteen followed directly behind him in a row. The buglers played "Garryowen" as the Seventh followed its officers, seven hundred strong.

"Don't be greedy, George," Gibbon said. "Remember, wait for us."

"No, I will not," Custer said, as Martinez smiled and both Benteen and Reno scowled behind him.

"General Crook?" Gus said.

"Yes?"

"I'm guessing we're not heading back up from here at Goose Creek to join the other two Columns any time soon?"

"We're awaiting further orders, Gus."

"From my hunting days, I know a way northeast back up to the Yellowstone that the Crows say neither they nor the Cheyenne and Sioux are very familiar with. Between ridges east of the Rosebud before the Tongue. It's too narrow for buffalo, so they don't hunt there."

"Is it too narrow for us to use?"

"Yes, it's too narrow for your entire Column, but I can sneak back up that way with three or four of the Crows and brief Terry and Gibbon on our fight with Crazy Horse."

"What do the Crows say?"

"They think the Lakota and Cheyenne have left that area and moved west. They're willing to try as long as the party is small and experienced."

"I can go with them," Arnold said. "If it works, I can brief them on Crazy Horse's tactics and armaments last week. It'll be faster and more thorough than the telegraphic communications so far between all the different command posts."

"You two know what you're doing? Those aren't the Snakes or Apaches up there."

"Yes, sir," Gus said. He waited for a response. Receiving none, he said, "One question, General. Is the Seventh Cavalry up there with them?"

"Yes. Why do you ask?"

"I owe Custer. Do you know if he's with Terry or Gibbon?"

"Terry, I think." He looked thoughtfully at Gus.

"Good luck gentlemen," Crook said dismissively.

Gus and Arnold and the three Crows gathered up their things, replenished their provisions and ammunition, and set out from Goose Creek, heading north toward the Tongue.

At sunset, after the twelve mile march up the Rosebud, Custer addressed his assembled officers in his tent.

"We have our orders. Our mission is clear, gentlemen. We are told there are on the order of seven hundred hostiles out there somewhere." He pointed vaguely south and west. "We find them. We prevent their escape. Or we defeat them. Or we annihilate their village. It all depends on when and where and how we find them. In short, we find the Indians, we attack the Indians. Any questions?"

There were none.

"The grumbling by my officers stops now. I left the Gatling guns behind because they would slow us down, and I turned down Terry's offer of a Second Cavalry battalion because we won't need it."

"Are you suggesting I haven't been supportive?" Benteen asked. Evenly.

"The saddle belongs to he who it fits."

"What of my comments are you referring to, Colonel?"

Custer looked long and hard at both Reno and Benteen, and said, "None of my comments were aimed at you, Captain."

All eyes turned on the seething Reno.

"Any more questions, gentlemen?"

The tent was silent.

"We leave at dawn then."

After everyone else had left, Martinez appeared back at the tent.

"Yes, Major?"

"May I come in, General?"

"Of course, Dennis. What's troubling you?"

"That's what I came to ask you, sir."

"It's that obvious? I'm still furious at Terry for suggesting that he lead us and the Second Cavalry battalion instead of me. Openly suggesting that I not command the Seventh."

"With all due respect, General, you owe Terry. If it weren't for him, you'd be sitting in a Minnesota or Washington DC jail right now. He's taking a serious risk with President Grant. When we found the Indians, he would have let you lead the Seventh in the field."

"Anything else, Major?"

"The officers left here puzzled why you would bother to explain yourself. You've never done that before."

Custer frowned. "Hadn't thought about it, Dennis. It's a mistake I won't repeat." He looked out through the tent flap at the group of officers still talking in the growing darkness. "I'm still worried that I'm saddled with Benteen and Reno against Sitting Bull and Crazy Horse. Will they hesitate to obey orders if it comes to an all-out fight, Major?"

"No, sir, they won't. Benteen followed you at the Washita, even though he still is angry about it. Yes, they'll follow you. But, General, they both hate you. And that's not going to change."

"No, I suppose not. Not even after we bring Sitting Bull and his entire village in to Terry and Gibbon."

90

June 23, 1876

"How far until we dare approach the Rosebud, Gus?" Arnold asked over breakfast at their camp on the west bank of the Tongue River. They had ridden thirty miles the day before from Goose Creek.

"We should ride through these ridges due north today," Gus said. "It's only a half-day's ride northwest to the Rosebud from here, but the Crows think there's too big a risk of running into Lakota or Cheyenne who have left the agency and are heading for Sitting Bull's village to the west."

"And you agree?"

"Yes. We need to be far enough north that we can find the Dakota Column before we head west."

"Then let's go. Have the Crows move out ahead of us in small groups. If any one group is spotted, it should look harmless to a large party of agency Indians."

"Should we wait for the supply train?" Martinez asked.

Custer had led the Seventh across the Rosebud to the east bank at daybreak. Benteen had been put in charge of the three companies bringing the supply train up from the rear.

"No. If Benteen is as good as he believes he is, they'll be close behind us shortly."

"He's not happy about commanding the supply train, General."

"My orders are to find and attack the Indians Major, not to make Captain Benteen happy."

"Yes, sir."

The two followed their Crow scouts up the Rosebud in silence.

Antelope and Thunder Bull were riding side by side in the midst of the Cheyenne as they headed down the Greasy Grass, the Little Bighorn. The ponies were starting to show their excitement as they could smell the camp ahead.

Lame White Man rode back to them on his excited pony. "What is the biggest gathering you have seen, Antelope?"

"Nineteen years ago, when I was ten. I think it was the last year that all the Cheyenne came to meet for the New Leaves and Berries first buffalo hunt. All the people came from all the Cheyenne winter camps. From all directions. It was the most people I ever saw."

"Yes, I also was there. It was the last time for us all together on the Arkansas. You are right, Antelope, the last great spring buffalo hunt all together. There were almost five hundred lodges, more than seven hundred Cheyenne warriors."

"I have no memory of such a village," Thunder Bull said.

"You were not yet one," Lame White Man said. "I remember your mother carrying you during the ceremonies that spring."

"How big is the village we are headed to below?" Thunder Bull asked.

"We are told it is one of the greatest villages ever assembled. Many have left the agency to come here. Sitting Bull's Hunkpapa are coming behind us. When we and Sitting Bull have arrived, we are told the village will be more than a thousand lodges. Crazy Horse's Oglala are already there. As are other Sioux, Sans Arc, Minneconjou, and Brule."

"And the people," Antelope said.

"Yes," Lame White Man said. "With the people, there will be many more than a thousand warriors."

"And the white soldiers?" Thunder Bull said. "Is Three Stars chasing us here to the Greasy Grass?"

"Crazy Horse's scouts say no. Three Stars did not follow. They say there are soldiers to the north, between here and the Elk River. But Crazy Horse does not yet know where. Or how many."

91

June 24, 1876

The Seventh had marched thirty-five miles up the Rosebud the day before, and had now resumed the march at dawn. They shortly picked up the trail of a large village moving south.

"This is the trail of a huge village," Custer said. "How large?"

"The scouts say there are actually two trails mixed together," Martinez said. "One is from Sitting Bull's very large village, traveling up the Rosebud and then west toward the Little Bighorn a couple of weeks ago."

"And the other?"

"The Indians from the agency who have been leaving and joining the Sioux since then."

They had been following the Indian trail south all day. It was immense and all were excited, scouts and cavalry alike.

"How far ahead do the tracks leave the Rosebud?" Custer asked.

"Both the Crow and the Akira scouts say maybe ten more miles," Martinez said. "They head west at Davis Creek. Toward the Wolf Mountains."

"At the end of the Rosebud?"

"I was afraid you were going to ask that, General. No. As a matter of fact the trail heads west some twenty miles before reaching the end of our ordered march up the Rosebud."

The two remained silent as they rode, both marveling at the size of the trail left by the travois poles and huge Sioux pony herds.

"Major?" Custer said.

"Yes, sir?"

"Tell the scouts I want to be absolutely certain that all these Indians were going west. That none of these tracks are heading back this way. I want no Indians escaping our march. I want them scouring the trails in every direction."

"Yes, sir." He kicked his horse into a gallop.

"And Dennis?"

"Yes?" He turned back toward Custer.

"Tell the men that we march until the trail heads west."

"Yes, sir."

Antelope watched Thunder Bull join the other young men around the fires that night. Excitement was great, as all knew that Sitting Bull's Hunkpapa had now joined the village and had taken their place up the Greasy Grass at the southern-most circle of lodges.

The scouts reported that no soldiers were near or approaching.

The agency Indians, both the Northern and Southern Cheyenne, and five tribes of the Lakota were now all joined together here on the west bank of the Greasy Grass. Spread out over a mile and a half along the river.

"This is a great celebration for the people," Antelope said to Lame White Man sitting next to her.

"Yes. The defeat of Three Stars and the joining of all the tribes here is a great thing. We can hope we will be left alone to hunt now. We are too many, and the white soldiers have no white settlers to defend here."

They watched together as the Cheyenne danced around the fire. As the young Sioux boys and girls came from the south end of their camp to join the Cheyenne at the northern-most circle of lodges. And then when Thunder Bull walked with several of his friends to the Sioux camps where other dancers celebrated around their campfires.

The two Cheyenne then turned their attention to the twenty Sioux and Cheyenne warriors participating in the dying dance. The young men, including her cousin, had chosen this occasion to celebrate their vow that they would fight to the death in the next battle. The twenty "suicide boys."

As she proudly watched her cousin dance around the fire, Antelope saw Crazy Horse standing in the fire light just north of them, looking silently east across the Greasy Grass. Looking into the distance, his back to all the young dancers.

Crazy Horse, alone at the west bank of the river.

Thirty five miles east, directly in Crazy Horse's sight line, the officers of the Seventh Cavalry were turning in, aware that their thirty mile march was likely to be repeated the next day.

Instead, the trumpet signaled them to meet at Custer's tent.

By candlelight under a moonless sky, their commander gave them their orders.

"We march now."

"The rest of the way up the Rosebud?" Reno asked.

"No," Custer said. "We are ordered after the Sioux, and the Sioux trail goes that way," pointing over his shoulder with his thumb. West, behind him.

"Colonel, with respect," Benteen said, ignoring the murmuring around him. "The men and horses are exhausted. And our orders are to proceed all the way up the Rosebud, *then* west to prevent escape. If we head west from here, we could have Indians before us and below us if some went south."

"Thank you for the respect, Captain. My orders are to find, subdue, and bring in the Indians. *Your* orders are to follow my command."

"Yes, sir."

"I owe you no explanation, Captain. But since you seem in need of one, I will remind you that, as at Black Kettle's village on the Washita, where you also urged no action, surprise was the most important element. The scouts tell us that Sitting Bull cannot know we are coming. Riding thirty miles tomorrow in broad daylight means we cannot surprise his village."

"And," Martinez said. "The Crows could not see a village from the divide above the valley in the late afternoon sun. They feel we need to be on the divide at day break to evaluate the situation."

"So, gentlemen," Custer said. "We ride. The Indians are not up the Rose-bud. They are that way." He pointed again to the west. "On the other side of the mountains. That's where we'll find your Indians, Captain. And your men can rest all day tomorrow after tonight's march, while the scouts and I determine how, when, and where to attack them."

92

June 25, 1876

"Yes, Gus. What is it?" Arnold asked, coming out of a deep sleep and looking up in the dark at Gus's barely visible face.

"The Crows just woke me, Major. Turns out we're camped just ten miles east of a large number of soldiers on the Rosebud."

"What time is it, Gus?"

"One."

"Then let's just ride and catch up with them in the morning as they're breaking camp." He turned back over and tucked his head back in his bag.

"No, John. The Crows say the soldiers broke camp instead of camping for the night. They already are headed west along Sitting Bull's trail."

"They have any idea who the soldiers are?"

"No. But they think there may be a thousand soldiers."

As the young Sioux and Cheyenne boys and girls danced around the fires well into the morning, Lame White Man, Antelope at his side, approached Crazy Horse, who was still staring into the eastern sky.

Crazy Horse acknowledged the two Cheyenne.

After a long while, Lame White Man said, "It is a great time for the Lakota."

"Yes, it is good to see so many join us. From both Cheyenne tribes. And many of our friends now coming from the agency."

"It is a time of joy for the young men and women," Antelope said.

"Yes, they are happy to be back together again. In a time of peace. Not running from the enemy."

The three looked back toward the string of fires up the western bank of the Greasy Grass. At the celebration of the young Indians.

"Are you looking for the dawn, Crazy Horse?" Lame White Man asked.

"No. Sitting Bull is sitting out there on the ridge. You know of his Sun Dance vision? Maybe twenty days ago?"

Both Cheyenne shook their heads no.

"He had a vision that many soldiers and horses and some Indians would fall head first into a village like grasshoppers. Soldiers without ears."

"Soldiers without ears?" Antelope asked.

"Yes. Sitting Bull has gone tonight to see if Wakan Tanka will tell him what village. At each dawn he fears that the soldiers will attack us. He hopes Wakan Tanka will tell him where. And when."

"Sitting Bull once had a vision about me," Lame White Man said. "Many, many years ago. He said I would die in a great battle. And that a white man I know would die in that same battle."

"A white soldier?" Crazy Horse said.

"No, a rancher." He looked at Antelope. "His white wife is a friend of Antelope's. Sitting Bull said it would be a great battle."

Antelope thought about Lily. And about Lincoln. And about the little white Antelope Thunder, who would now be thirteen. She wondered if Lily was still happy with her ranch.

"We are told that there are no soldiers near," Lame White Man said when there was no reaction to the telling of Sitting Bull's vision of his own death.

"Yes, the scouts say that Three Stars is not coming. But…" Crazy Horse's voice trailed off.

"But," Lame White Man said. "We know that there were soldiers north of here. At the Elk River."

"Yes," Crazy Horse said. "You are correct. Our scouts and the arriving agency Indians tell us that many soldiers have been sent out along the Elk River. But we do not know where they are."

"Is Long Hair with them?" Antelope asked.

"I do not know. Why do you ask this Antelope?"

"Several moons after Long Hair attacked Black Kettle's village on the Lodgepole River he came back and made peace with the people. He promised never again to attack the Cheyenne. One of the chiefs spilled pipe ash on his boots. He told Long Hair that if he ever attacked the Cheyenne again, it would mean he had no ears. Maybe Sitting Bull's vision is about Long Hair."

"You were at Black Kettle's village that morning? At the Lodgepole?"

"Yes. Thunder Bull and I, and many of the Cheyenne here now, were there that morning. I saw Long Hair many times after that."

"And they tell me your cousin is Long Hair's wife?"

"Yes. My cousin is now the mother of Long Hair's son."

The three thought about that. Looked once more to the east. Toward Sitting Bull out there in the night. Seeking a vision.

"The attack on us at the Lodgepole was the day Thunder Bull counted coup on his first soldier," Antelope said. "The day he became a Cheyenne man."

"Sitting Bull," said Crazy Horse. "Says the days are coming, when those who will call Thunder Bull father and grandfather will become men without fighting our enemies. Our children and children's children will have no enemies. They will need to find other ways to become men."

"That is difficult to understand, Crazy Horse," Lame White Man said.

"For all of us. Even for Sitting Bull." Crazy Horse looked back toward the east. "I would like to meet Long Hair in battle before that time comes."

"Why Long Hair?" Antelope asked.

"As you say, Antelope, Long Hair has no ears. The Great White Father in Washington promised the Black Hills to the Sioux. It was promised to us forever. It was promised no whites would enter the holy land of the Sioux. Two years ago, despite their promises, Long Hair led the miners into our lands to dig for the yellow iron. Long Hair took away our holy land. I would like to meet him some day in battle."

"I told Black Kettle the day before Long Hair killed him that the white man's greed has no limit," Antelope said. "But he would not listen."

The three looked to the east in silence. No sign of Sitting Bull. No sign yet of the coming day's sun.

The only sounds that broke the peace of the waning night over the Greasy Grass Valley were of the Indians behind them celebrating around the fires in the camp circles all along the river.

"The whites all want everything," Crazy Horse said. "They are all thieves. But I want to meet Long Hair. He is the Chief of Thieves."

At 2:30, under orders to halt, the Seventh Cavalry had fallen exhausted as one from their ten mile night ride. They had halted six miles short of the divide, where their Crow and Akira scouts waited at the Crow's Nest.

At dawn, Custer was awakened from a deep sleep. Two of the scouts had come from the Crow's Nest with a message.

Custer had his officers awakened to meet with the scouts.

"There is a very large Sioux village on the west bank of the Little Bighorn, the Greasy Grass," Martinez translated.

"How far from here?" Custer asked.

"They say half day's ride. But I'd guess maybe twenty miles from their estimates."

"They say anything else?"

Martinez smiled. "I don't think they have confidence in you, General."

The officers waited. Some smiled at that. Some appeared to Martinez to be gritting their teeth either out of frustration or exhaustion.

"They say it will be many days of fighting. They say you will not win." Martinez looked up, grinning. "With respect, General."

"Ask the Crows if there's a place to hide the cavalry out of sight of the village, but nearer than here."

"Yes. They say there's a ravine about four miles from here. Maybe a mile this side of the Crow's Nest. Nobody in Sitting Bull's village can see beyond the crest."

"Okay. You, Benteen, and Reno, take the men to the ravine at eight. Have them rest today and through tonight. After the men are settled, have the scouts take the four of us to the summit. Unless things change, the plan is to attack Sitting Bull's village after a day of rest, at dawn tomorrow. Not today, tomorrow."

"And Gibbon and Terry?" Benteen asked.

"You have your orders Captain."

Arnold, Gus, and their Crow scouts pulled within sight of the rear of the

Seventh Cavalry's supply troops at nine. Arnold and Gus spurred their horses to catch up to the last row of troops. Their scouts prudently trailed behind, keeping a wary eye on all sides for Cheyenne, Sioux, or lagging soldiers. Soldiers mistaking them for hostiles was their biggest concern.

As the two men galloped up, a startled sergeant whirled around, rifle raised.

"Whoa, Sergeant," Arnold called out, hands raised.

The sergeant lowered his rifle and waited along with five of his men.

"Who are you?" the sergeant said.

"That's what we want to know about you, Sergeant. I'm Major John Arnold. This is Gus Smoot. He and the Crows behind me are my scouts."

"Where on earth did you come from?"

"Wyoming." Arnold pointed south. "About forty miles due south. We're with General Crook's Wyoming Column."

"Is Crook on his way here then, Major?"

"No. We came on our own. The Wyoming Column was attacked by the Sioux and Cheyenne a week ago. Crook awaits further orders." Arnold said.

"Who are you, Sergeant?" Gus asked. "What brigade is this? Who's your commanding officer?"

"Dakota Column. Seventh Cavalry. General Custer is in command. He's up there," pointing west. "At the head of the brigade."

"Where are the Indians?"

"We've been marching from the Yellowstone for four days. Nobody tells us anything. Maybe Custer knows. Ask him."

Arnold saluted. "Gus, it looks like you found your general. Let's go discover what else you've found for us."

He and Gus and the Crows urged their horses around the supply train and headed toward the front of the Seventh Cavalry.

They reached the front of the Seventh as the seven hundred exhausted soldiers were being organized into the ravine to sleep.

Reno saw Arnold's party approaching from the rear. He signaled Martinez, and the two officers rode out to meet them.

"Major?" Reno said.

"I'm Major John Arnold, Wyoming Column. This is Gus…"

Gus cut him off. "Dennis," he said." "It's Auggy, Auggy Damours. From the New Mexico Volunteers."

"Well, I'll be," Martinez said. "I never would have recognized you with that beard. Custer told me he saw you with Buffalo Bill four years ago."

"Yes, in Nebraska. Entertaining the Grand Duke."

"He tells me they cleared you of Carleton's charges."

"Yes, he's right. They did."

"What are you doing here?"

"I've been doing some scouting for the Wyoming Column when I'm not at my ranch. Major Arnold and our Crow scouts and I have ridden up from Wyoming to let you know of General Crook's experience with the Sioux last week down on the Rosebud."

"And what exactly was that experience, Major?" Martinez asked, turning to Arnold.

Arnold looked uncomfortable. "With all due respect," he lied, "I'm under orders to speak only to General Custer. Or to Terry or Gibbon."

"After we get the men hidden from the Sioux down in that ravine, then Major, we'll take you to General Custer. It's likely to be a couple of hours before we're called up there, though. You may as well dismount and give your horses and your Crows some rest."

"Actually, Major," Auggy said. "The Crows have asked if they can join your Crow scouts."

"They'll find them over there on that summit point. They're trying to determine the size of the Indian village. Can't hurt to have more eyes before we attack tomorrow morning."

Arnold looked at Auggy. "So I guess it's Auggy Damours again, then? Good to know you've been cleared of all charges." He looked at the retreating forms of the two officers. "And it sounds like your general has found his Indians."

The bugler sounded officer's call at noon, and Custer's officers rode out to join him at the summit of the Wolf Mountains. Martinez escorted the two visitors. Custer looked up at the appearance of the two uninvited guests, and was clearly startled to see Auggy.

"What are you doing here, Auggy?"

Custer's familiarity with the scout caught all the officers except Martinez by surprise.

"Major Arnold," and here Auggy gestured to his companion, "and I rode up from the Wyoming Column."

Custer looked south. "Is Crook here then?"

"No," Arnold said. "He gave us permission to come up a back way that Auggy and our Crow scouts knew to bring you some information."

"You may as well join us, then. The scouts tell us there's a very large Sioux village right down there on the Little Bighorn. Maybe twelve miles down that creek. I was just able to verify a large pony herd through some larger binoculars. Come join us."

The two walked toward the crest together. "You heard that Canby was killed in Oregon, right Auggy?"

"Yes, General. Actually I was there."

Custer looked at him curiously.

"After you told me he was there, I took the train out and offered to scout for him. Against the advice of all of us, he brashly agreed to meet with Captain Jack unarmed. The Indian, bold as can be, just up and pulled out a concealed pistol and shot General Canby dead on the spot."

"That made Ed the first General ever killed in the Indian wars."

"It was very tragic. I liked Canby. Always liked serving with him and Kit Carson." He looked back at Martinez, added, "and Dennis."

The two walked up to the summit in silence, followed by Custer's officers and scouts.

"Gentlemen," Custer said, then stopped as he looked back down the mountain. "What are the men doing riding up here? I thought they were sleeping back in the ravine until tomorrow."

All turned and looked back.

"I guess the junior officers thought the bugle call meant we were moving out, General," Reno said. "If there's no longer any need for silence, we all assumed that we would be attacking the village now."

Custer shook his head, but had nothing to say.

"Gentlemen. The scouts inform me that there is a large Sioux village just down this slope. Maybe fifteen, sixteen miles away. I've verified through my field glasses that an immense pony herd is, in fact, on the other side of the Little Bighorn. I also see a smaller village on this side of the river. I'm told that two sets of Indians have spotted us, but we don't know where they are. The Crows think we will now not be able to surprise the Indians tomorrow."

He paused.

"Do we have any idea of the number of Indians down there?" Benteen asked. "Terry and Gibbon were told no more than eight hundred."

Martinez talked to the scouts. "They say more than a thousand lodges."

"That's as many as two thousand warriors then," Reno said.

"We estimated a thousand last week on the Rosebud," Arnold said.

"Actually," Auggy said, "a thousand is a vague number to the Indians. They don't bother to count beyond that."

"So, then maybe *more* than two thousand warriors?" Reno asked.

Nobody said anything as Custer stared with obvious disapproval at Reno.

"When are Gibbon and Terry due here?" Benteen asked.

"We don't need them," Custer said. "If the Seventh can't handle these Indians, then the whole Army can't handle them. The scouts tell me that we will lose this battle. They say that we, and they, will die. That there are so many Sioux that the battle will take many days."

The officers waited for Custer to go on.

"My point is Captain, that I can tell we're all terrified. The rebels at Gettysburg, then the Cheyenne at the Washita, then all the Indians south of the Washita. Now Sitting Bull. Maybe we should just turn and run back to the Rosebud."

Nobody responded to Custer's sarcasm.

"When are Gibbon and Terry due here?" Benteen asked, again. "Weren't we supposed to send scouts down the Bighorn to them when we found the Indians?"

"We were charged with finding the Indians," Custer said. "There are your Indians, Captain," pointing to the west. "We aren't going to sit here for two days watching them disperse to the winds like they always do. Or letting them choose a point of attack to our disadvantage, while we just hope Gibbon and Terry are on time. Waiting was your advice at the Washita, Captain. It was wrong then and it's wrong now."

He looked at each man in turn. "There are your Indians, gentlemen. The plan was to attack them by surprise at dawn tomorrow, counting on Gibbon and Terry arriving from the north. Now we're discovered. The new plan is to attack the village this afternoon. Gibbon and Terry can capture the retreating Indians and congratulate you when they get here."

"The men and the horses are exhausted, General," Benteen said. "The horses haven't eaten normal in four days."

"The Seventh doesn't fail to attack when the opportunity to attack is right there to be taken, Captain."

"General," Arnold said.

"Yes, Major."

"May I tell you of Crook's experience at the Rosebud a week ago?"

"Certainly, Major."

"Do you know if Crazy Horse is here? Any Cheyenne?"

Martinez and Auggy talked to the scouts.

"They say yes," Martinez said, and Auggy nodded in agreement. "They think there may be as many as a hundred or more Cheyenne lodges. And, yes, Crazy Horse's Oglala are here with Sitting Bull."

"Why do you ask, Major?" Custer asked, growing visibly impatient.

"As we both know, General, the Cheyenne are the greatest fighting horsemen any of us have ever seen. One week ago, twenty miles southeast of here on the Rosebud, the Wyoming Column was attacked by Crazy Horse's Sioux, accompanied by a large number of Cheyenne. As I said, we estimated a thousand warriors."

"They attacked you? Crook didn't attack the Indians?"

"No, General, the Indians attacked us."

"I agree that is unusual, Major. Anything else?"

"Many of them had Spencer repeaters."

"Thanks to the Indian agents. Anything else?"

"Yes. Crazy Horse pursued tactics that Crook and I had never seen the Indians use before?"

Custer didn't say anything.

"Crazy Horse had his forces attack in sequences. They would attack at one spot, then pull back. Then attack elsewhere, then pull back. It was a coordinated sequence of attacks all up and down our lines."

"How did it end?"

"Crook said we won."

"What do you say, Major?"

"Crazy Horse is here. And General Crook isn't."

"Just to be clear, Major, they attacked you, right?"

"Yes. We were still more than a half day's ride from where the Crows said their village was."

Custer looked down at the peaceful valley below. Then back at the Seventh, awaiting his orders. Sitting on their horses.

"I'm not going to sit here waiting for Crazy Horse to attack us. And I'm not going to sit here and watch the village disperse to the winds. If we've learned anything out here, it is that on those rare occasions when you actually find the Indians, you attack the Indians. Terry and Gibbon will get here soon enough."

He looked to see if there were any more questions. There were none.

"Organize the Seventh Cavalry for an attack on the village. We attack now.

"As soon as the men are all mounted and ready."

When morning had broken over the village, the twenty suicide boys, surrounded by older warriors shouting their names, paraded into the village from the western hills. Lame White Man led the singing of one of the chief's songs. Antelope watched proudly as her cousin's name was shouted by the warriors, dancing through the Cheyenne camp and, from there, on up river to the Lakota camps.

Later that morning, Antelope was swimming with several Sioux friends, watching the little boys fishing upstream in the Greasy Grass.

"Have any of the hunters returned yet from the buffalo hunt?" one of the Oglala women asked.

"No. A Hunkpapa returned to say the herd had scattered. The hunters will not return before sunset."

"It is a beautiful day for not working," her friend said.

All the women laughed.

"Yes, Maheo has blessed us here with all the buffalo and the antelope," Antelope said.

"And with blinding the white soldiers so that we can stay away from the reservation."

"Antelope, it looks like your lodges are coming down."

They all looked north, down river, toward Antelope's family lodges in the Cheyenne camp circle.

"Yes, I must go. Our forty families are moving downriver. Some this afternoon and some tomorrow. Not working never lasts long."

And the Sioux women laughed again as she headed to her lodge.

She laughed to herself as she walked past Thunder Bull and many young men asleep under the trees along the west bank of the river. She knew they had not come back from the Sioux parties until well after dawn, as she had seen many sprawled outside their tipis during breakfast.

She kicked Thunder Bull's foot, and he looked up.

"Where are you going?" he asked.

"To our lodges. We are going downriver. I have to go and take down our lodge."

"I thought we leave tomorrow."

She laughed. "You have too many Oglala girls on your mind, Thunder Bull." She kicked his foot again. "What have you done today?"

"Sleep. Then we ate. Then we slept. Then went swimming. Then we slept. I still need more sleep. Go away Antelope."

They both laughed as she walked along the river bank toward home.

Lame White Man and the other tribal chiefs left the lodge in the Sioux circle where they had been smoking together. He walked to the Cheyenne circle of lodges. The day before, the council of chiefs had been in his lodge, but today it had been in Sitting Bull's.

He stopped at the southern edge of the Cheyenne circle and watched as the women started taking down the lodges. Several were taking down the tribal medicine tipi containing the sacred Northern Cheyenne Buffalo Head. He nodded approval at the proceedings. All the tribal chiefs had agreed it was time for the Cheyenne to proceed downriver after the antelope herds.

It was a good day. A good day to move their ponies to the next pasture and to the next hunting grounds. He smiled at all the tired young men, lying under the trees and around the tipis. They would need their strength.

Tomorrow would be a good day to hunt antelope. Today a good day to rest and drive the ponies to the new camp.

He headed with a friend toward the sweat lodge by the river. He would also need his strength for the hunt tomorrow. Today was a good day to prepare.

"H Company is ready," Benteen said.

"Take the lead then, Captain," Custer said.

Benteen started the Seventh Cavalry west down the Wolf Mountains, toward the village.

Three miles later, Custer ordered a halt.

"Benteen."

"Yes, General."

"Take three companies to the southwest. I need you to scout the village from the south and I want you to cut off any escaping from the village."

"With respect, sir." Benteen said.

"What is it now, Captain?"

"We may well be outnumbered…"

"…your usual fear, Benteen."

Benteen gritted his teeth. "Your scouts talk of an immense village, General. Does it make sense to send a fifth of your force away from the point of attack?"

"What else, Captain? Let's get it all out here. Now."

"You may well need us at the village, sir. And sending me out with only three companies leaves me vulnerable to attack if Crazy Horse knows you are here and is planning to outflank you from that direction."

"Take B Company also then, Benteen. Those that aren't bringing the pack train can join you. First you recommend I not split my command and then in the next breath that I split it even more."

He mounted his horse and headed back to the rest of the men.

Said over his shoulder, "You have your orders, Captain. We need hostages. Even Crazy Horse won't attack us with his captive women and children and ponies in our midst."

Custer then turned his back on Benteen as he rode.

"Reno."

"Yes, General."

"Take three companies and start down the west side of that creek," Custer said, pointing down the ridge, just to the right of Benteen's disappearing rear. "The rest of us will travel to the village down the east side."

He then turned to organize his remaining five companies of slightly more than two hundred men.

"Major Arnold? Auggy? Are you and your Crows headed back to Wyoming, or are you going down there with us?"

"Count me in, General," Arnold replied.

"I've hunted this valley numerous times, George," Auggy said. "I may be of some use."

"Okay. Major Arnold, go with Reno. Help him however you can. Auggy, you ride with me."

Six miles later, Custer, Martinez, and Auggy, well out ahead of Reno, came across what they had thought was going to be a small village.

"One abandoned tipi," Custer said. "That's all?"

"The fire's still warm inside," Auggy said. "Food too. There's a dead Sioux warrior on a scaffold. They just left, but this was no village."

A scout appeared on a knoll above. He pointed to the northwest. "Big dust cloud, two, three miles ahead. They're running, General."

"Auggy, if they're that close, why can't we see them?"

"This is very deceiving terrain, General. You can stand on a ridge and see for miles. There could be hundreds of Indians invisible to you in any number of coulees and ravines between you and the horizon. Just like you hid the entire Seventh in that ravine this morning."

"And if they're running?"

"Then you'll see them before they see us, General," Martinez said. At that moment, Reno's battalion caught up across the creek. Custer motioned him over.

"The Indians are running for it two and a half miles ahead. Proceed to the south end of the village accordingly and attack when you see them. I'll support you."

"Yes, sir."

"And Reno?"

"Yes, sir."

"We'll need prisoners. Take prisoners when the warriors are chased off."

"Yes, sir." And Reno rode down to his men on the west side of the creek.

"General," Auggy said.

"Yes?"

"Reno's drunk, sir. You can smell it. And I saw his flask."

Custer watched as Reno crossed the creek down below and started his battalion off to the northwest down the creek.

"Auggy," Martinez said. "You could be considerably more helpful to us if you would tell us things we don't already know."

Custer sent Martinez out with the troops down the east side of the creek.

Custer and Auggy rode out in front and to the right, riding to the high ground, trying to find a spot where they could see the still invisible village.

Three miles later, Auggy pointed. "There it is."

All looked, stunned where he pointed as they reached the top of the bluff.

"That's the biggest village I've ever seen," Martinez said.

"I see the pony herd," Custer said. "There to the west against the hills. I see women and children in the river."

"There must be ten to fifteen thousand ponies there," Auggy said. "I've never seen anything like it."

"There's Reno coming in from the south," Martinez said pointing down and due west. "I don't see any warriors anywhere."

"We've caught them napping again," Custer said. "The warriors are either out hunting or asleep in the tipis. Martinez, send for the pack train. We're going to need the ammunition. This is ten to a hundred Washitas. Reno from the south and us straight down those hills into the village from the east."

He looked down at Reno and waived his hat triumphantly in the air.

"Round up the women and children and ponies, boys," Custer said. "When the warriors return from their buffalo hunt, they will surrender and it will all be over."

Custer's five companies rode, cheering, northwest along the hills just above and to the east of the immense village.

Reno's battalion surged into the Little Bighorn and watered their horses.

Arnold pointed ahead. A scout was racing back toward them.

"They're not running, Major Reno. The Indians are arming and advancing in that dust cloud on the other side of those trees."

"Has anyone seen the size of the village?"

"Yes, the Indian scouts, sir. And now several are stealing ponies from the Lakota herd. They shot several Sioux women. That's what alerted the warriors. The scouts say the village is very large."

"Take that message to Custer. He's up in the hills over there," pointing northeast behind him. "He just waved his hat to urge us onward. Arnold, get the battalion across the river. Prepare to attack."

"Yes, sir."

Lame White Man and his friend had just emerged from the sweat lodge when they looked up and saw soldiers riding on the hill to the east.

They ran to a group of Lakota warriors, shouting and pointing at the soldiers. The warriors ran to their families and to the task of putting on paint and war clothes, alerting others as they ran. Calling out to others to bring their ponies.

Lame White Man ran downriver toward the Cheyenne circle camp.

Antelope had left the Cheyenne camp and rejoined her Sioux friends on the river bank.

"What is that?" she said, looking upriver to the south at some boys running toward them shouting.

"Soldiers are coming," the boys were calling out as they ran through the camp.

"But they always attack at dawn," one of the Sioux women said as they scrambled after the boys into some bushes.

Antelope could hear the distinctive pop, pop, pop of the guns coming from the south. Many guns.

Warriors were grabbing ponies and galloping south toward the other end of the Huncpapa camp circle. She could hear them singing their war songs over the thundering of the hooves. Could hear the old men calling the warriors to battle. Could hear the screaming women and children. Could see women looking frantically for their children, the growing pandemonium.

Thunder Bull awoke to screaming and running.

Old men were crying out, "Soldiers are here. Warriors run to them. Fight the soldiers."

He raced to his lodge, grabbed his rope and six-shooter, and headed to the pony herd, joining the others looking for their ponies. He led his pony back to his lodge and grabbed his war clothes. Then his paint. He heard the gunfire to the south and hurried.

Lame White Man, naked from the sweat lodge, rushed to the Cheyenne camp, grabbed what clothing he could, and looked for his mother among the fleeing Indians.

He found her trying to break down their lodge through her tears, crying children all around. He brought her pony to her and convinced her to ride next to him. The two herded the rest of their family onto their ponies, fleeing northwest in a river of fleeing women and children.

Shortly he reined in and turned to his mother and the rest of his family. "The soldiers are everywhere," he said. "You must quickly ride downstream. But I must join my boys. I will fight today. Even without my war clothing. Even without my best medicine."

Lame White Man then shepherded his family away from the village and turned back toward the battle. He looked to the east, but could no longer see any soldiers on the hills. He turned his pony and headed back toward the pop pop popping at the other end of the Huncpapa camp.

All was shrouded in dust as ponies were readied and warriors raced to the south.

Reno's three companies galloped into a thick dust cloud toward the trees between them and the village. It was too dusty to see clearly and the Indians ahead appeared to be running their ponies back and forth to throw up even more dust. With only vague shapes ahead of them, Reno ordered a halt at a prairie dog village at the edge of the trees.

"Halt. Prepare a skirmish line on foot," Reno said. He took a large drink from his flask.

The soldiers leaped off their horses, three soldiers each giving the assigned horse holders their reins.

"No, Major," Arnold said. "Don't stop. Attack. This is perfect cover for pressing into the village. Custer's orders were to attack."

"Have you seen the village yet, Major?" Reno said.

"No. But if we attack they will run. If we stop here, they will attack us."

Reno turned to the right, said, "Commence firing." Then to the left, "Fire at will."

He turned back to Arnold, "Once the scouts find the village, we'll then see what we're up against."

Pop pop pop pop rang out as the soldiers fired their Colt .45s and Springfields over the prairie dog mounds.

Watching from his lodge just north of the trees, Sitting Bull saw that the soldiers weren't attacking out of the rising dust cloud.

"Go," he said to two warriors. "See if the white soldiers want to negotiate."

The two rode off, signaled they came in peace, and were immediately both shot off their ponies. Then, Sitting Bull's favorite pony was shot dead at his side. The soldiers were now unleashing volley after volley. The Indians could hear the bullets pinging off the tops of their lodges. The ping ping ping overhead competed with the pop pop pop coming from out of the dust cloud.

More and more warriors were racing in from all the camp circles. They were riding at and around the soldiers, returning rifle and arrow fire.

Ten Cheyenne galloped by Reno's right flank, arrows hitting several horses and two of the soldiers. Most of the horse holders were dragged about by the panicked horses, driving more and more dust into the air.

Some of Crazy Horse's Oglala warriors arrived and mounted an attack on Reno's left flank.

Crazy Horse rode up. "No," he said, riding to cut off his warriors. He then gathered the Cheyenne warriors to his men. "Let them shoot. They are shooting too high. They can't see through the dust. The prairie dog mounds are forcing their rifles up. Let them shoot."

He circled his braves. "Not now. Wait. The soldiers' guns will heat up. The guns will stop working. Wait. Wait until I give the signal."

Thunder Bull arrived, having braided his hair and painted his whole body red and black, to match the red and black patterns on his family's lodge.

"We want to attack the soldiers now," Thunder Bull said, as the Cheyenne shot arrows up into the air, dropping down through the dust on to the soldiers and their horses.

"Circle them and shoot from a safe place," Crazy Horse said. "We will attack them soon enough young Cheyenne."

"General Custer," Martinez said.

"Yes?" Custer said, riding northwest along the top of the bluff to join the scouts and several officers.

"Look."

They all looked and sucked in their breath. Below them lay the entire village, in full view for the first time.

"It's bigger than we had seen from back there," Auggy said. "Much bigger. More than a thousand lodges."

Then added, more to himself than anyone else, "Maybe two thousand warriors."

"Too late now," Custer said. "If we'd known, we could have kept the Seventh together. Or attacked from the two directions at once."

"Why not ride back to Reno and get Benteen down there now?" Martinez said.

"Too late. Then we get the three day battle that Crazy Horse wants and the scouts predicted. Better to attack from the east while Reno occupies the warriors at the southern end."

"Then we're going to need Benteen up here quickly," Martinez said. "We'll need all the manpower to attack from the east to support Reno."

"Reno isn't attacking," Auggy said, pointing down to the dust cloud.

"And now, gentlemen," Custer said. "There are your warriors."

They all watched in silence as swarms of warriors rode from all the camps south toward Reno.

"Why isn't Reno attacking?" Martinez asked. "He should attack and drive them where we can attack them from up here."

Custer wrote something on a note.

"We're going to also need all the ammunition on the packhorses, General," Martinez said.

Custer added something and handed it to one of the scouts. "Take this as fast you can to Benteen, son."

The private grabbed the note and galloped his horse down the bluff, heading southwest.

"What's it say, General?" Auggy said.

"Benteen, Come on, Big Village, Be Quick, bring packs…"

"Let's ride," Custer said. "Keep north and west until we see a way down. Attack the village from the eastern hills, and hopefully Reno will finally attack from the south."

As Thunder Bull was firing his six shooter at the soldiers' right flank, he heard Crazy Horse's bone eagle whistle from the west. Then the tremolo of hundreds of Lakota, the thunder of their galloping ponies, and "Hokahe, Hokahe, Hokahe" from a hundred throats.

Crazy Horse unleashed fury at Reno's hundred and fifty soldiers' left flank.

"Steady," Arnold said. "Steady. Keep firing as you back toward the timber at the river."

He looked as Reno downed the rest of his flask of whiskey.

"Back men," Arnold said. "To those woods, but walk backwards and keep shooting at them. Slow them down."

Instead, the line broke and the soldiers raced on foot with their horses, backs to the charging Indians, into the stand of timber along the west bank of the Little Bighorn.

"Set up a skirmish line," Arnold said once they reached the woods. Amidst the confusion and rain of bullets and arrows, the battalion set up a defensive perimeter in the woods.

Hundreds of warriors continued to ride in from the camps and surround the woods in the U-shaped bend of the Greasy Grass River.

Thunder Bull joined some Cheyenne who had gathered with the Lakota on the river bank at the northernmost edge of the woods. He could see more Sioux warriors at the southern end. At Crazy Horse's direction, all were shooting sparingly, waiting to pursue the trapped soldiers when they emerged.

"This is like hunting a herd of deer," Thunder Bull said to the Lakota next to him. And the group of them started a tremolo as if they were trying to spook deer out into the open into a trap on the other side.

He could see increasing numbers of warriors crossing to the east side of the river, hoping to shoot the soldiers as they forded the river.

Reno's soldiers had pulled back further into the woods. They were now back up on their horses. Now the Indians began entering the woods, tightening the circle. Pushing the surrounded soldiers toward the river at their backs.

They started fires around the brush at the edge of the woods. The smoke mixing with the swirling dust.

Arrows and bullets and leaves and branches rained down on the soldiers.

The Indians would ride in and attack at one position, then pull back and attack another.

"Just like a week ago," Arnold said.

"What worked against him last week?" Reno asked.

"A mirror strategy. Attack Crazy Horse's flank. Then his other flank. Harass him like he's doing to us."

"That worked?"

"It was a standoff after several hours."

One of the Indian scouts rode over to the two officers, sitting on their horses.

"What now?" Reno said just as a volley exploded from the edge of the timber and the scout's brains and blood spewed all over Reno.

"Dismount," Reno said. Then, "Mount."

His horse panicked and plunged around the clearing, Reno waving his pistol while trying to get the mess off his face.

"Anyone else who wants out can follow me."

And Reno charged out of the woods toward the river.

"Every man for himself," said one of the officers.

"No," Arnold said, firing into the air to try to get the battalion's attention.

But it was to no avail. The battalion headed for the river and the waiting Indians in a dead, undisciplined panic.

Thunder Bull was astonished to see soldiers coming straight at him. He and the other warriors began firing at them. And then they were astonished anew when the soldiers raced by them into the river.

The pop pop popping was now replaced by a new cacophony of cavalry horses' stomachs slapping like cannon volleys as they hit the river in full leaping gallop.

Thunder Bull and hundreds of Indians leapt in after them, using clubs and rifles and pistols and bows to strike the helpless soldiers. Shooting some with both guns and bows and arrows, and pulling some off into the water in hand to hand combat.

Thunder Bull clubbed one soldier off his horse and shot him as he came up for air. Chased another soldier and shot him in the back with his revolver.

Again, he was reminded of a deer hunt. Shooting, clubbing the trapped animals as they panicked and ran.

He rode to and then up the east bank of the river and urged his pony after two soldiers who were running up the hill on foot.

Exhausted soldiers on exhausted horses rode through the water for their lives, the Indians shooting at them as they swam. Once on the other side of the river, the survivors, again under fire from the Indians, clambered up the hill toward the ridge at the top of the bluff.

"Set up a skirmish line," Arnold said.

"Dismount the men," Reno said. "Set up a perimeter."

Arnold looked down at the river. He could see soldiers' bodies floating. Could see Indians, both warriors and women, killing the wounded, mutilating the dead.

The eighty survivors of Reno's battalion watched this, and watched the Indians now begin to climb the hill, starting to encircle them.

Thunder Bull and a hundred warriors were riding around the north side of Reno's hill, when one of them yelled and pointed to the north.

They all looked. They could see hundreds of soldiers above the village, descending to the village from the eastern hills.

As one, they shouted "Hokahe. Hokahe." And started galloping back into the valley toward the threat to the north. Their tremolos alerted warriors still down on the west bank of the Greasy Grass, and, like a tide suddenly going out, hundreds and hundreds of Cheyenne and Lakota warriors headed down river. Toward the soldiers descending from the hills.

The soldiers had surprised them again.

But it was a good day to die, Thunder Bull thought to himself as he raced north toward these new soldiers.

Benteen, in receipt of his written orders from Custer, arrived while some of Reno's troops were still running up the hill.

"For heaven's sake, Captain," Reno said. "Where have you been?"

"What happened here, Reno?"

"The village turned out to be immense. We were attacked by thousands of Indians. I've lost half my men. Down there." He pointed to the smoke coming up from the woods.

"Yes, I saw your retreat as I rode here."

"It was a charge," Reno said, practically shouting. "It wasn't a retreat. It was a charge, Captain."

Benteen looked at the other officers, none of whom would make eye contact with him.

"Where's Custer? I have orders from Custer to hurry to him. And to bring the packhorses." He gestured behind him to the mules approaching in the distance.

"General Custer went that way about an hour ago," Arnold said, pointing to the hills to the northwest.

"And he just left you here Major?"

"I believe his plan was to attack the village from the east while we attacked from the south."

"And now? Now that you're not attacking?"

They all looked at the Indians still coming upon them from three sides of the hill.

"Let's secure our perimeter here," Arnold said. "Then inform the general as to the change in his plans."

"Reno has been chased up into the hills east of the river," Martinez said, looking down to the south.

"Did he ever attack?" Custer asked.

"No," Auggy replied. "The scouts say the Indians routed him before he ever got to the village."

"Losses?"

"It looks bad," Martinez said. "The scouts say it's hard to tell from this far, but many soldiers are dead in the river and on both sides. Maybe half killed, maybe more."

"Any sign of Benteen?"

"Yes, they saw Benteen arrive to reinforce Reno. The pack train is still several miles behind."

"It would have been better if that fool Reno had attacked as ordered, and let us support him with an attack from here. But as soon as Benteen and Reno get here, we'll have force enough to take hostages down there once we ford the river."

They all looked down at the company that Custer had sent down the coulee toward the river to search for a ford. When they had been unable to find an appropriate ford and had seen the Indians racing toward them from the south, they had started back up the ravine and were just now arriving.

"Major Martinez," Custer said. "Take your three companies and set up a perimeter at that ridge we identified on the way here. Wait there for Benteen and Reno until I get back."

"Where are you going?"

"I'm taking the other two companies around to the north. We'll find a ford to cross into the village. Once we're all back together, we'll take that route into the village and finish this off. Until then, I should be able to draw some of the Indians away from Reno." He looked at his scouts. "Auggy."

"Yes, sir."

"Come with me down there. Show me what you learned hunting up here all those years."

Spying the twenty soldiers up the coulee, Lame White Man and five other warriors crossed the Greasy Grass at the ford and started up after them. As they started up the coulee, they could hear the warriors galloping toward them from below, arriving from the battle upriver.

Antelope was running into the Cheyenne camp when she saw the soldiers above them on the hill. She then saw Lame White Man and the other Indians crossing the ford and heard the onrushing warriors.

Fearing that the soldiers were chasing the Indians, she ran to her brother.

"Are the soldiers near?" she asked.

"No," he replied. "The warriors chased them away. Up the bluffs over there." Pointing toward the hills to the southeast.

"I want a pony," she said.

"No, Antelope. There are a thousand soldiers. This will be no place for you. We are all crossing the river to fight the soldiers."

"But I have watched battles before. I have been in the villages when the whites attacked. I will ride near the warriors."

"No, sister. I must go now to put on my paint. I must put on my war dress." He motioned toward their lodge. "Take down our lodge. Run to the hills with the other women and children."

"No, my brother. Your son is one of the suicide boys. The women tell me the suicide boys are going across the river soon. They tell me your son has dressed for me to watch him. I am going on a pony. It would be good if it was your pony."

They both looked up as they could hear the pop pop popping starting up on the hill.

Her brother handed her the reins of his best pony. They both looked to the east and watched as swarms of Indians started up the coulee after the soldiers.

Custer had left one of his two companies on a hill that surveyed both the village and the southern route back to Martinez. He had just now completed his ride with the rest of his troops around the northern bluffs and then west straight down to reach the east bank of the Little Bighorn.

"There it is," Auggy said. "Right where I remember it. We could easily cross with all the men right there and charge into that northernmost circle of lodges that we saw from above." He pointed. "Around the bend there."

"Attack now and take whatever hostages we can?" Custer said to the captain behind him, but looking at Auggy. "Or wait for the full force?"

Both the captain and Auggy looked alarmed. The captain shook his head.

"I'm not the one to ask, General." Auggy said, looking at the forty soldiers behind them. "But there are thousands of warriors up that river. We know they are racing this way. I'd certainly feel more comfortable if you had the whole Seventh Cavalry together before we crossed that river."

Custer laughed. "And here I thought *you* were the reckless one, Auggy."

He turned his horse around. "I agree. We don't have a sufficient force here to attack. But we found the ford. Let's go get Martinez." He started back up the ravine. "And Benteen and Reno."

When they reached the summit, they could see that matters had deteriorated while they'd been down to the river and back.

Martinez's three companies were spread out and taking sporadic rifle and arrow fire from several fronts. There were hundreds of Indians riding and climbing up the coulees and ravines between Custer and Martinez's three companies.

"Captain," Custer said. "Set up a perimeter here. We'll be right back."

Custer, Auggy, and five soldiers raced east, up and around the ravines toward Martinez. They could see even more Indians climbing up from the river toward the troops as they reached the men.

"Martinez, any sign of Benteen and Reno?"

"None, sir."

"Where could they be? Benteen should have been here long before now."

He stood up in his saddle and looked southeast, where he'd last seen them. Then turned back to Martinez.

"We found a ford at the northern edge of the village. With all these warriors up here, we can ford the river and capture the women and children in and around the village. It's perfect for us. We've got them, Major. But we'll still need more than our five companies to successfully take the hostages from the village."

He looked southeast for reinforcements, as if he could will the rest of the men toward them.

"We're fine here for now, General," Martinez said. "The Indians' shooting is largely ineffective. They're shooting on three sides of us, but the skirmish line is holding. The shooting is nothing more than a nuisance."

"Martinez," Custer said. "Once I recombine my two companies, I will keep moving them north to prevent the Indians from cutting us off from the village. You need to stay here to meet Benteen and Reno. In ten minutes, send the Company of greys straight at those Indians coming up from that coulee straight ahead. Attack them directly and they'll fall back."

"Yes, sir."

"I will keep the path down to the village open." He turned and addressed Auggy. "As soon as Benteen and Reno get here, lead them all to me and then take us back to your ford for the attack." He then addressed the company within earshot. "We got lucky after all. The warriors are up here, while their women and children are down there on the other side of the river. This worked better than attacking the village from two directions after all."

And he galloped back to his two companies.

Thunder Bull was among the increasing number of Lakota and Cheyenne warriors climbing up the coulee. Many had tied their ponies to the sage brush on the way up. Some, like Thunder Bull, still led theirs up the hill by hand.

"Our bullets are not hitting any of the soldiers," one Lakota said on his left as they both peered over the ridge at the skirmish line. "We should use arrows instead."

He began shooting his arrows straight up and into the dust cloud above them. The arrows plunged to earth among the soldiers and their horses. From left and right, and from below, arrows now began filling the sky, arcing up and then down onto Martinez's three companies.

Antelope rode north, staying west of the warriors, watching for her cousin. Watching the arrows soaring up and then down into the dust. She could see that the Indians were now starting to slowly encircle the soldiers. Crawling on their stomachs, they were invisible to the soldiers, except for the puffs of smoke from their guns and the arrows rising as if out of the earth and into the sky.

"Auggy, it's been ten minutes," Martinez said. "Will Custer have reached his troops by now?"

"Should have by now. You can't see them from here, and he can't see you."

"Less than a mile away and out of sight?"

"I warned Custer about these ravines and coulees, Martinez. You see nothing in front or around you and there could be thousands of Indians within yards."

"Thanks, Auggy. The arrows are making that clear without your observation."

Auggy shrugged.

Martinez turned to the captain of the greys.

"Captain. Charge to the top of that ridge over there as the general ordered. Straight ahead. Drive the Indians back down that coulee."

"Yes, sir." He turned to his men. "Mount up."

He rose in his saddle. "Straight ahead. Charge."

Auggy watched the greys charge. The shooting and arrows stopped instantly. Martinez could hear the Indians and their ponies scrambling back even from where he was. He could see the dust off to both the left and the right as the Indians beat a hasty retreat back toward the ravines.

"George knows his Indians, Auggy. Always attack. Even when others would call for a retreat."

Yes, Auggy, thought to himself. Attacking feels much better right now than ducking. And being with Custer feels much better than being with Crook. Or, shudder, Reno. He thought of Arnold for the first time in an hour. Subconsciously looked back over his shoulder to the south. Nothing there but empty plains and rising arrows.

"Where on earth is Custer?" Arnold asked, looking to the north. "He certainly saw what happened to us from up there."

"He's abandoned us," Benteen said. "Just like he did the greys at the Washita."

"What?"

"Custer only cares about Custer. And his headlines." He took a slug of water. "He figures us for dead. He'll leave us here to the Indians while he captures some squaws or hooks up with Terry and Gibbon. And leads an attack on the village in a day or two."

"I thought your orders were to hurry to him. To come on, be quick," Reno said.

"And here I am, rescuing your drunken hide instead, Major? As ordered."

The two stood and moved toward each other.

Arnold stepped between them. Then they all heard shooting to the north. An extended volley of shots.

"Request permission," Arnold said, "To take ten men and scouts to those hills where Custer was last seen, Major. Over to that hill. He may need our help. He may be just on the other side of that hill waiting for Benteen."

"We have our hands full here, Major Arnold. In case you've forgotten, we're surrounded by hostile Indians. And we're still awaiting the arrival of the mules. The packs Custer ordered."

They could hear the occasional ineffective shooting from the Indians to the east and to the south down the hill from their position.

"Permission denied. We need all hands here before a thousand Indians come back," Reno said.

"And we're going to need Custer *here*, Major," Benteen said. "Not you *there*."

Antelope watched as the Indians pulled back from the attack of the forty greys. The soldiers had dismounted and formed a skirmish line along the bluff. From there they couldn't see what Antelope was looking at. There were hundreds of Indians just below them in the coulee. And more in the ravines all around.

But now nobody was shooting. Guns or arrows.

There are the suicide boys she said to herself. She could see her cousin halfway up the side of the coulee. He was wearing the war clothing she had chosen for him. She could see the suicide boys and the soldiers. But they couldn't see her. Or each other.

And there was Thunder Bull over to the left. In the middle of a hundred

Cheyenne and Lakota warriors. All had pulled back and were now looking for ways to skirt around to the top. Toward the company of greys, now spread out in their skirmish line.

And then she saw Lame White Man ride into the melee of warriors. Sitting on his pony surrounded by the warriors. He was shouting something, but she couldn't hear him.

She resumed her ride around the quiet battlefield, riding northwest. Trying to get up to the ridges to watch. There was little shooting now, but the Indians were slowly surrounding the soldiers. Like a buffalo hunt.

Lame White Man, still practically naked and with no war paint, had decided it was time for an old man to show the young warriors what to do. Attack the soldiers now, he said to himself.

"Come young men," he said. "Show yourselves to be brave." He turned his pony around full circle as he shouted. "Come. We can kill them all."

And he galloped up the coulee walls to the top of the bluff, charging through the line of greys, shooting one soldier with his Spencer repeater and counting coup on one with his lance.

Thunder Bull, the suicide boys, and hundreds of Lakota and Cheyenne warriors now poured up the hill. Some on horseback, some crawling up the coulee on their bellies.

One of the soldiers was carrying a Seventh Cavalry flagstaff. He attacked a Cheyenne chief next to Thunder Bull by aiming the guidon like a lance right at the Cheyenne's stomach as he charged. The Indian rode by, evaded the thrust, and grabbed the guidon out of the soldier's hands. He then chased the soldier and counted coup on him as he raced back up the hill.

Over the din, Antelope could hear the Oglala chiefs calling out, "Hokahe. Hokahe." Hundreds of warriors let out tremolos as they scaled the hill, surrounded the soldiers, and hit them with a withering rifle, pistol, and arrow barrage.

Thunder Bull rode through the panicking soldiers. He shot one point blank in the face, wrested the Sharps rifle out of the hands of another. Several of the soldiers' horses pulled loose and galloped down the hill to the river.

Antelope saw soldiers jump on their horses, and, failing to get loose of the attacking Indians, shoot themselves in the head with their Colts.

Lame White Man leaped off his pony and took the blue coat off the first soldier he had killed. All around were milling Indians and panicking soldiers. The dust rose up and all around the hand to hand combat, as Indians yelled and jumped around the soldiers, soldiers shot into the air as their terrified horses pulled at their reins, and the wounded horses screamed and thrashed in pain.

The Indians took the wounded and dead soldiers' weapons from them and turned them on the other soldiers.

The grey company scattered. Some on foot, some riding their terrified horses. Some racing uncontrollably toward the river below. Some back up hill toward the rest of the battalion.

The Indians now found the horse holders and the horse herd in the ravine. They fell on the horse holders, killing them and releasing their herd. The thundering of the herd as they galloped in panic toward the river momentarily brought a lull to the fighting. But it was a brief interruption.

Lame White Man put on the blue coat and remounted. He had found his war clothing.

With the suicide boys following, he now chased after the fleeing soldiers.

Toward what remained of Martinez's three companies arrayed in a thinning skirmish line across the hill above.

Crazy Horse looked at the skirmish line from the east. Saw the hole left by the grey company's initial attack at the coulee. Watched the onrushing Lame White Man and the suicide boys. And now watched the disorderly retreat of what was left of those same greys.

"Now," he said. He blew into his eagle bone whistle. "All warriors follow me. Kill all the white soldiers."

He kicked his pony forward toward the rear line of the soldiers.

"Now."

And, with the air ringing with their tremolos and the thunder of their ponies' hooves, the entire force of Lakotas descended on Martinez from the east.

Sitting Bull was sitting outside his lodge. He looked up and saw the soldiers' horses galloping down the coulee toward the river. Saw some of the soldiers being killed as they fled down the hill on the very ridge he had sat on the night before.

Falling into the village.

He commented to the warriors around him on the realization of his vision.

He told them to caution the men and women that they were not to mutilate the dead soldiers.

In the vision, Wakan Tanken had specifically warned Sitting Bull that mutilating the soldiers falling into the village would doom the Indians to ultimate subservience to the whites.

The warriors raced their ponies toward the river and the hills to join the battle.

Martinez ordered ten soldiers into the space that had been vacated by the attacking company of greys, some of whom were now racing back up the hill.

"Stand and fire," he said. "Hold your positions. Horse holders, double up. Eight horses each. Take the horses down into that ravine."

And now, the sky became filled with descending arrows and black smoke from the furiously increased Indian rifle and pistol fire, reinforced by the Sharps and Colts taken off the dead soldiers. Hysterically bucking horses, with arrows slamming into their backs and necks, pulled the soldiers' arms as they tried to fire back.

With Crazy Horse's attack at their backs, they were now facing fire from all directions.

Auggy looked up and saw his Oregon vision. Mounted Indians wearing blue army jackets. Galloping in front of him. But these Indians weren't performing on a parade ground. They were trying to kill him. They were trying to kill all the soldiers. The Seventh Cavalry was no longer attacking. And the defense was disintegrating.

And then he saw, no more than forty yards away, Lame White Man. Lame White Man in soldier's blue firing a soldier's rifle at the soldiers to Auggy's left.

And then time stood still. Their eyes met. Lame White Man changed course to come straight at him. He let out a war whoop and aimed his rifle.

With no warning, Lame White Man lurched to his right and pitched over his pony's shoulder. Bounced twice in the dust and lay dead.

"Auggy," Martinez said. "Behind us. Auggy, Indians behind you."

But Auggy couldn't hear anything. He was sure he had seen Lame White Man look at him and smile in recognition as he flew through the air.

Augustyn P. Damours was looking at his death sentence. It occurred to him that it was his fortieth birthday. Maybe it was, indeed, a good day to die.

Arnold could hear the volleys to the northwest. Could see the rising dust swirl.

"Major Reno," he said. "Orders or no orders, I'm headed for that hill to the north of us. Either Custer is waiting for us on the other side of it, or he needs to know to come relieve us here."

"Custer has abandoned us, Major Arnold," Benteen said. "You're wasting time better spent on positioning our defenses here."

Arnold ignored him, mounted up and galloped with a company the two miles to the hill.

"There they are," Arnold said from the top of the hill. About four miles in the distance they could see riders on horseback milling around in a dust cloud. They were wearing blue.

Some of his soldiers rode down the hill, heading toward the dust-en-shrouded figures.

"Major," a sergeant said. "Take another look," handing him his binoculars.

In the binoculars the figures were growing in number and were headed his way. And they were not soldiers.

The sergeant quickly rode down to the troops and they scrambled back up to the top of the hill. Benteen arrived with another company while Arnold was setting up a skirmish line.

Benteen planted a guidon at the top of the hill. "Maybe this'll get Custer's attention if nothing else will," he said.

The troops began pulling back, alternating defensive skirmish lines against the approaching Indians.

After a mile, Reno's company came galloping up. Thus reinforced, the hundred soldiers galloped back to their original positions on the beleaguered hill above the scene of their earlier battle at the Little Bighorn.

It seemed to Arnold that much more time than two hours must have passed since they had first encountered the Sioux in that battle at the prairie dog village.

It was now clear that the Indians did not intend to leave them up here on this hill in peace.

The drunken Reno was incapacitated. Benteen and Arnold began setting up stronger perimeters against what now appeared to be a much more formidable attack force arriving from the north.

Where was Custer, Arnold thought? Why didn't he come? Could Benteen be right? Had he actually abandoned sixty percent of his own command?

Custer could hear the sound of increased fire coming from the south. Could see the swirling dust darkening and rising into the sky.

The arrival of Benteen and Reno?

He had succeeded in his plan to move what was left of his two companies further and further to the northeast so as to keep the Indians from getting between him and the ford into the village.

"What now, General?" one of his captains asked.

"Stay on the attack. We can go straight into the village any time we want. But if that dust cloud and the increased volleys mean what I think it means, Martinez and Reno and Benteen will be here shortly. Then we charge straight down to the ford and into the village and take the hostages.

"Ready the attack, Captain."

Martinez shouted orders helplessly as his entire command disintegrated before his eyes.

"No," he said. "Stand."

He leaped back on his horse. Rode back and forth. "Hold your positions."

He glanced at the horses racing down toward the river. Some were captured by the waiting Indian men and women. But some had reached their goal and were just standing in the Little Bighorn, all four legs astraddle, drinking.

He now commanded a cavalry battalion essentially without horses.

His line to the left was breaking and most of the soldiers were fleeing toward the river, those few on horses southwest toward the ridges along the hill. Indians were pulling them off their horses and beating them to death. He watched in horror as some soldiers shot themselves in the head on a dead run.

His right line now also began breaking. Some running by him and down the hill insanely into the waiting mob of whooping Indians. Some with their hands raised over their heads. Others working together, some back to back, trying to make a coordinated escape to the north, and, hopefully, to the waiting Custer.

Martinez chose the north.

"Auggy," he said. "Take us to General Custer." He gathered his remaining men, those who could grabbing a random horse, and followed Auggy through a rain of arrows and gunfire to the north.

Where was Reno? Where was Benteen?

Antelope watched proudly as Thunder Bull and hundreds and hundreds of Indians now chased the white soldiers like the herd of buffalo they had become. All their lives the men trained for the ultimate buffalo hunt, and here it was.

She watched as her pony moved among the dead soldiers. She occasionally looked down curiously at the individual dead soldiers as her pony's hooves kicked dirt and dust on them. The dirt the whites would not let the people live on in peace.

And then she saw the war clothes she had chosen lying behind in the dust. Her cousin left behind. On the ground between two dead soldiers.

She galloped over and dismounted. He was still alive. Shot, but still alive. She looked down the hill at the peaceful Cheyenne camp circle below. Then up at the retreating figures of the warriors chasing the soldiers.

She sat by her brother's son's side and held his hand. She heard her own words come back to her after all these years. The white man's greed has no limit.

Maybe Black Kettle had been right not to listen to a young girl so long ago. Maybe he had been right. In the end, it didn't matter. Maybe every day is a good day to die.

Custer looked up as Martinez and his twenty remaining men galloped the last of the two miles to join them on the hill.

All around them, it had all gone suddenly quiet. The shooting had stopped. Not even any arrows falling from the sky.

"Is Reno here then? Benteen?"

"No, General. There's no sign of them."

"Where are the rest of your men, Dennis?"

"This is all that's left, General. There are thousands of Indians out there. They just keep coming."

Custer looked genuinely shocked. "Where are they now?"

Martinez looked at Custer, head cocked. "All around, General. We're surrounded. Completely surrounded."

"Certainly not, Major. We still have the route down to the ford. We still have enough to take the hostages." He turned to Auggy. "Auggy, lead us to the ford."

To his men, "Mount up. Attack the village now."

"I just went out there, General," Auggy said. "I'm afraid that Martinez is right. There are now hundreds of Indians to your north and west. They've outflanked you. There is no avenue of attack to the ford or to the village."

George Armstrong Custer looked disoriented. He lived to attack. Every battle he'd ever entered, he knew only to attack. Chickahominy. Gettysburg. Cedar Creek. Appomattox. On the plains when they couldn't even *find* the Indians. Washita. Attack. Attack. Attack. It's all he knew.

"There *must* be an avenue of attack, Major."

"No, sir." Martinez turned to the men. "Shoot those ten horses around the perimeter. Set them up as breastworks around the hill. We don't have much time before they come for us. Share the ammunition and set up the perimeter. We might still be able to hold out until Reno and Benteen get here."

Thunder Bull joined three Lakota crawling on their stomachs through the grass below the soldiers on the hill.

One would leap up, fire, and fall back. The soldiers would fire back too late. Arrows were now continuously falling from the sky on the soldiers and their horses. Occasionally they could hear a soldier yell in pain. A horse scream from an arrow hitting home.

And then, the thunder of hooves, as the soldiers released their remaining horses.

Thunder Bull and the three warriors rolled out of the way just as the horses galloped by them headed down toward the river.

Three soldiers took off running toward their right. The mounted warriors in that direction could be seen running them down as if they were three buffalo separated from the herd.

Thunder Bull rose up and shot his pistol into the remaining soldiers' position.

"Releasing the horses did not draw them away, General," Martinez said. "The three men who panicked were cut down in fifty yards."

"Just shoot, Major," Custer said. "We keep firing until relief arrives."

And a shot from down below, pop, and Custer fell. Hit in the chest.

Auggy looked over as Martinez eased over to his friend. Watched them talking, their faces close together.

Both the arrows raining down from the sky and the pop pop popping of the Indians' rifle fire now increased.

The remaining soldiers kept shooting at anything they could see through the dust and the smoke.

Fifteen soldiers suddenly bolted. Running straight down the hill.

Auggy watched stunned as what looked like hundreds of Indians chased them down on foot and on horseback and murdered them as they ran down the hill.

He turned. There were now Indians rushing their position from every direction, shooting rifles and pistols.

He turned and ran toward the fallen Custer to see if he needed a hand. As he neared him, he saw Martinez calmly shoot Custer in the temple.

"No," Auggy said. But it came out only as a grunt of exhaled air as he felt something slap him on the back. No pain. Just knocked flat.

Everything went dark for Auggy as he fell onto one of the dead horses.

93

July 4, 1876

Thirteen year old Antelope Thunder came running into the house, breathless from her run from the creek.

"Mommy, Mommy! A man's riding down the bluff. I think it's Daddy."

Lily dried her hands and walked out onto the porch. Stood next to Auggy the bear and looked at the man riding down the hill.

He was dressed all in brown, right up to his brown hat and down to his brown horse. She could see his rifle in its scabbard on the right side of his saddle. A brown scabbard. It wasn't Gus and it wasn't a soldier. She squinted into the distance, trying to glimpse anything familiar. Just watching.

In her experience, good news never came from strange lone riders on horseback.

"Honey, go get Lincoln," she said, continuing to stare at the figure.

"Might be Arnold," Lincoln said.

"I don't think so," Lily said. "Hair's too long. No uniform."

The two of them watched the figure zig zag down the hill. At one point he stopped and looked at them. Didn't wave.

"You're right, Lily. He didn't wave to us."

The two stood there silently, cradling their rifles in their arms, watching the figure work his way down the mesa.

Once he reached the bottom, he disappeared for a long while.

"Can you tell if he headed north, away from us, or is he following the creek bed this way?" Lily asked.

"He's headed this way. I saw the top of the hat bob over there. About a mile out."

"Go get your brothers, Antelope. Take them to the stables. Ask the men to come out here with their rifles."

"Yes, ma'am." She ran around the porch to the back of the house.

"You think you and I can't handle this Lily?"

"I just have a bad feeling about it, is all."

Ten minutes later the man emerged from the trees by the creek and stopped at the sight of the five armed figures on the porch.

He took off the hat and waved it over his head. Whistled.

"It is John Arnold," Lily said. "You were right, Lincoln. Sorry boys. You can tell the kids to come on out. Everybody back to work."

Lincoln rode out and met Arnold half way. The two shook hands and Lincoln's shoulders slumped after a few words from Arnold.

Lily felt weak in the knees and sat down as the two rode toward the house together. When Lincoln turned away from her without making eye contact and headed to the stables rather than ride in with Arnold, she felt even more dread.

She watched Arnold ride the last quarter mile alone in silence.

"Hi, Lily," he said when he reached the porch.

"Hi, John Arnold."

"May I come in?"

"Of course. Where's your uniform, John?"

"Long story," he said as he dismounted and took her in his arms.

The kids came running around the porch and grabbed him excitedly, pulling him away from their mother.

"Where's Daddy?" Antelope Thunder asked.

"Where's Daddy?" the boys echoed.

"Long story, kids. Let me talk to your mom, all right?"

The two of them walked out to the creek.

"Gus was killed wasn't he John?" she said.

"Yes. How'd you know?"

"You never evade the kids, and I saw Lincoln slump from whatever you told him."

She took his arm.

"What happened John?"

"He was scouting for Custer."

"I thought you were with Crook."

"We were, but the Sioux drove us back. Crook decided he'd had enough of Crazy Horse, so Auggy and I offered to take word to the Army up in Montana. We joined Custer and wound up in a pitched battle with the Cheyenne and the Sioux."

"Auggy? When did he become Auggy again, John Arnold? He was still Gus when you left here."

"Yes, Custer and Dennis Martinez both knew him from before. From back in New Mexico and Washington. He became Auggy Damours again when they saw us ride up."

"Before he was killed."

He turned and hugged her. "Yes, Lily. Before he was killed."

"The Indians attacked you?"

"No. Custer attacked them."

"Like at Washita."

"Yes, like at Washita. But with different tactics this time."

He looked over at the ranch house. "Different result."

"How'd he die, John?"

He took her hand and they walked among the trees in silence.

He stopped and leaned back against a tree. Sat down.

She sat down next to him.

"He was with Custer and his two hundred ten soldiers. I was with the rest of the Seventh trapped by the Indians on a hill about seven, eight miles away."

"Stop this, John. Tell me what happened to Auggy."

"The Sioux and Cheyenne massacred Custer's entire force, Lil." He reached out, but she pulled away.

"All of them? Two hundred of them?"

"Yes." He looked down.

"Even Custer?"

"All of them."

She tried, and failed, to stifle a cry.

Arnold held out his arms and she fell into him, crying.

"Was it Antelope and Lame White Man's village?"

"Yes, we're pretty sure it was them. Crazy Horse and Sitting Bull's Sioux, too."

"Was Auggy killed quickly?"

"None of us got there for two days, Lil. Not until Terry and Gibbon arrived. We were surrounded and fighting for our lives ourselves. We didn't even know it had happened. We were under heavy fire for two days. We thought Custer had abandoned us."

She looked into his eyes. "Was Auggy killed quickly, John. Please tell me."

He looked away. "It was impossible to tell, Lil. It was two days later."

She gasped. "Was Auggy tortured? Mutilated by the Indians?"

"No," he lied. "His body was next to Custer's."

She cried softy and wiped her eyes on Arnold's sleeve. Then looking up with wide eyes she asked, "Was Antelope there? Is she dead, too? Lame White Man? Thunder Bull?"

"There is no way to know, Lil. The Indians took their dead and scattered when Terry and Gibbon arrived. Before we got there and saw the bodies."

"Two hundred killed? Custer, too?" She shook her head. "This will be the end for the Indians, won't it?"

He shrugged. "I don't know. Nobody knows."

She looked at his face. "Where's your uniform, John?"

"I left the massacre after we buried the men." He looked away from Lily. "Then I rode back to Crook. That gave me days to think about things. The Indians were minding their own business. Hunting buffalo and antelope. Not bothering anybody. It was us broke the treaty. Why *would* they want to live at the agency?"

"Antelope once told me that the white man would never leave the Indians alone. Never let them live their lives."

He took her hand. "They had agreed to stay out of our country. I told Crook I'd had enough of the Army. I'd had enough of killing Indians. It makes no sense any more. I resigned."

"What'd Crook say?"

"He said he understood, but he doubted that there would be much more time left for killing Indians. He agreed with me it made no sense and would end soon."

The two sat for a long time thinking. Lily working at regaining her composure.

"I worked so hard for this ranch, John. Why couldn't Gus…why couldn't Auggy just have been content to stay here with us?"

"People are who they are, Lil. The things you loved about Auggy had nothing to do with any abilities he had to be a rancher. He was a thief and a good one. And he was reckless. And you needed both."

"But I do love Auggy…Gus."

"He's the father of your children, Lil. And he made your ranch possible."

"But he was no rancher."

"Right, Lil. Auggy was no rancher."

"What now, John? Did you just come by to give me the news? Or will you stay here with us?"

He took her in his arms and held her for a long time.

"I had time to think about that, too, Lil, riding down to Crook. Do you remember the first words you said to me when you got off that stage in Apache Pass fifteen years ago?"

She laughed through her tears, "I asked you what you were in charge of."

"No, that's the second thing you said. The first thing you said was, 'Captain, do you know how long we stay here? And, I guess, can you tell me where exactly we are?'"

He kissed the top of her head.

"I came here to tell you that I think I'm the rancher you've been looking for. I'd like to apply for the job anyway." He squeezed her as they both looked over at the four kids eyeing them, pretending to be playing on the porch.

"And it took me fifteen years, but I can finally answer your two questions, Lil. First, we're staying here forever. And second, I can tell you exactly where we are, Lily Smoot. We're home."

Author's Historical Note

Libby Custer worked tirelessly throughout her lifetime to elevate the memory of her husband and the massacre of his Seventh Cavalry battalion to the level of American mythology. She died on April 4, 1933, four days shy of her 91st birthday. For over a century that myth was reinforced by the American press and entertainment industry.

Too many excellent books have been written on that particular battle for me to even begin to list them all, other than to praise my two favorites, in fact two of the very best. Nathaniel Philbrick's *Last Stand: Custer, Sitting Bull, and the Battle of the Little Bighorn* is a masterpiece, a product of great research and great writing. Gregory F. Michno's *Lakota Noon: The Indian Narrative of Custer's Defeat* is one of a number of books dedicated to disabusing the mythologists of their preposterous point of view that no witnesses survived to tell us what happened. In fact, not only did thousands survive, but many ultimately shared what they had seen and experienced that day at that spot.

Including Antelope.

Chief of Thieves is a work of historical fiction, a novel. Unlike Philbrick's and Michno's books, it is not a work of factual history. It is a fictionalized version of factual, historical events. To the extent possible, I have kept true to the history of those events over the almost fourteen years of this story, including the events of June 25, 1876 at the Little Bighorn. Despite deviating in places from some historians' views, I believe the actions of the battle as portrayed on these pages is what did, in fact, occur. Any errors on my part, changes to scenes to make the narrative more efficient, and interactions between fictionalized and historical figures, should be viewed by scholars of "Cowboys and Indians" as part of the fiction. As an example, the fictional Dennis Martinez is a composite of many of Custer's senior officers, including, of course, his brothers.

In the end, *Chief of Thieves* is Lily's story. And John Arnold's, and Auggy Damours', and Joe Lincoln's, and Antelope's, and Thunder Bull's, only three of whom actually lived, and only two of whom we know with certainty were there that 1876 June day in Montana.

It is quite clear from the vast majority of the Indians' recollections that they did not find out until well after the battle that "Long Hair" was present that day.

The Lakota and Cheyenne warriors and women did not obey Sitting Bull's warning from his vision. They mutilated Custer's soldiers to the point that the by-then naked bodies were largely unrecognizable to Benteen, Reno, Gibbon, and Terry's soldiers when they arrived two days later and began the burial process.

Auggy Damours, while an actual historical figure, disappeared to history on November 5, 1862 as portrayed in the Foreword to this book. He and Custer *were* the aide de camps of General Canby and General McLellan, respectively, so it is likely, but not provable, that they knew each other in Washington. Like Martinez, Auggy was a composite of many scouts over those twelve years. If I may borrow from Black Kettle's philosophy: as good a con man as he was, Augustyn P. Damours died somewhere of something. It could have been at the Battle of the Little Bighorn. Why not?

Lame White Man *did* lead the critical charge and *did* die as portrayed in this book. Some of the Indians who were there believed he was killed by friendly fire. Mistaken in his blue coat for one of Custer's Crow scouts.

After the Little Bighorn, Crazy Horse and his Oglala continued to fight the white soldiers until his surrender in May 1877, nearly a year later. General Crook ordered him arrested several months later as a result of confusion about some of his statements about scouting for the Army. On September 5, 1877, at the age of 36 or 37, he was stabbed by a guard at the stockade and died. It is also possible that he was stabbed by Little Big Man in the fight.

Sitting Bull refused to surrender to the U.S. Army, instead leading his Hunkpapa to Canada in May of 1877. He and nearly two hundred followers returned and surrendered August 26, 1881. He left the reservation to join Buffalo Bill Cody's Buffalo Bill's Wild West in 1885. After touring with Buffalo Bill, he returned to the reservation, and, on December 15, 1890, at the age of 59, he was killed in a fight with Army and Indian police trying to prevent his rumored departure from the reservation.

Speaking of Buffalo Bill Cody, he left the scouting profession and joined the safer, and more lucrative, entertainment profession in 1872. In 1883 he founded Buffalo Bill's Wild West, changing the name in 1893 to Buffalo Bill's Wild West and Congress of Rough Riders of the World. He died at the age of 70 on January 10, 1917 in Denver, Colorado.

John Iliff died at the age of 46 of jaundice on February 9, 1878. The town of Iliff, Colorado is named for him.

Holon Godfrey, 82 years old, died in February, 1899. Matilda, 55 or 56, died in 1879.

Elbridge Gerry, the Paul Revere of Colorado, may or may not have been related to the founding father of the same name who went on to be the inventor of "gerrymandering" and a Vice President of the United States (1813-4 under James Madison). Our Elbridge Gerry married as many as eight Indians and had fourteen children. He died at the age of 56 or 57 in 1875.

Charles Clay, a cousin of Kentucky's Henry Clay, and his Lakota Wife Fingernail Woman ran the trading post at the foot of Chimney Rock in the Chugwater Valley. Clay, then 26 and impoverished after the Civil War, left his native Virginia to go west. He was variously a sutler and merchant. A rumor was that he won Fingernail Woman in a poker game. She left to join Crazy Horses' band after the Little Bighorn, actually surrendering to the Army before her chief. She died at age 47 on July 14, 1902 on the Pine Ridge Indian Reservation. A street was named after Clay in Chugwater, Wyoming (the name of the creek, valley, and town reportedly came from the sound the buffalo made when they hit the ground after the Sioux herded them to their death off of Chimney Rock). Clay later remarried, was elected to the Wyoming Legislature, and served as town marshal in Elma, Washington. He died at age 67 in 1905 in Washington of gangrene as a result of being kicked in the groin by a drunk.

General Edward R. S. Canby was the only U.S. Army General killed by the Indians in all the United States Indian wars.

John M. Chivington, as correctly chronicled on these pages, slaughtered over a hundred and fifty Cheyenne at Sand Creek. Two-thirds were women and children. Several investigations were conducted including two by the military. A captain who had ordered his men to not participate was murdered in Denver City weeks after his testimony to a civilian Committee. Kit Carson testified about the atrocity: "Jis to think of that dog Chivington and his dirty hounds, up thar at Sand Creek. His men shot down squaws, and blew the brains out of little innocent children. You call sich soldiers Christians, do ye? And Indians savages? What der yer 'spose our Heavenly Father, who made both them and us, thinks of these things? I tell you what, I don't like a hostile red skin any more than you do. And when they are hostile, I've fought 'em, hard as any man. But I never yet drew a bead on a squaw or papoose, and I despise the man who would." No charges were brought against Chivington. He died thirty years later of cancer at age 73 on October 4, 1894 in Denver, Colorado, still defending his decision to order the massacre.

George Crook, generally credited with being the most successful General in the Indian wars, was previously a successful Civil War General for the Union. He returned to Arizona (without John Arnold) in 1882 and defeated all the Apaches except Geronimo. "Three Stars" to the Plains Indians was "Grey Wolf" to the admiring Apaches. Red Cloud, Lakota, said of "Three Stars," "At least he never lied to us. His words gave us hope." Crook spent the last half decade of his life speaking out against the mistreatment of the Indians. He died in Chicago in 1890 at age 61, and is buried at Arlington National Cemetery.

Frederick Benteen was as fond of Custer as is portrayed on these pages. After the Little Bighorn, he continued his career with the Army fighting the Indians. He testified at the 1879 Reno inquiry that to have followed Custer's written order to "come quick" would have been suicide for his troops. Critics continue to maintain that he could not have known that at the time, and it might have been suicide for Reno and him to stay atop Reno hill if Gibbon and Terry had not arrived. He was promoted to major in 1882, convicted of drunk and disorderly conduct in 1887, and retired from the Army in 1888. He died at age 63 on June 22, 1898 and is buried at Arlington National Cemetery.

Marcus Reno was suspended from the Army for two years by President Hayes, who overruled a Board of Inquiry's recommendation of dismissal as a result of charges of public indecency and immoral conduct six months after the Little Bighorn Battle. In 1879 Reno demanded a Court of Inquiry to clear himself of charges of drunkenness and cowardice at the battle. Largely viewed as a whitewash with witnesses claiming they were coerced, the Court neither sustained any of the charges against Reno nor praised his conduct. In 1880 he was dismissed from the Army for drinking and conduct unbecoming an officer. He died of tongue cancer in Washington, DC at the age of 54 on March 29, 1889. Libby Custer successfully blocked a memorial to Reno on the battlefield site. A 1967 review board reversed Reno's 1880 dismissal from the Army, and, on September 9, 1967 his remains were, incredibly, reinterred in the Custer National Cemetery on the Little Bighorn battlefield.

According to Cheyenne accounts, Spring Grass, or Monahsetah, was George Custer's wife and did bear him his only son in November or December of 1869. Antelope, among others, spoke of it, and Gail Kelly-Custer, who claims Spring Grass as her great grandmother, has written extensively about her Custer ancestors. Many white historians remain skeptical, claiming that Custer was unable to sire children, most likely as a result of syphilis. The Cheyenne version is that Spring Grass's father was a chief and her mother an Irish immigrant, both killed at Washita. Thus, Yellow Hair, her son by Custer, was only one-quarter Cheyenne. Not surprising that he had yellow hair and a pale complexion. When Spring Grass met Custer at Washita she was six weeks away from delivering her first son. She later married John Isaac and changed her name to Mary Isaac. Yellow Hair changed his name to Josiah Custer, married a Sophia Miller and had a daughter named Sophia Custer, who then bore Gail Kelly/Custer. Spring Grass died in 1921 near the Washita River in either Oklahoma or Texas.

Both Antelope and Thunder Bull were at the Little Bighorn that June day. This novel became Lily's and their story. I am not Native American, but I worked very hard to try to capture what life was like for the roughly 2,500 Cheyenne on the Plains from 1863–1876. Their customs, their day to day lives, their ceremonies, their relationships with each other, with the animals of the Plains, and with the white settlers and soldiers. Their conversational style was gleaned, necessarily, from 19th and 20th Century translations. I, alone, am responsible for any errors, misinterpretations, oversimplifications, exaggerations, and outright mistakes in that attempt.

Antelope was Northern Cheyenne. She was at both the Washita and the Little Bighorn battles. For her accounts, or at least the translations of her accounts, to be accurate she had to be born in 1847. Some white biographers, however, say she was born in 1854. Some say she died in 1959. I believe both dates to be suspect. Her nephew that she called her cousin, the son of her brother White Bull, one of the "suicide boys," died of his wounds that night back in camp. Her reservation name was Kate Bighead. She had a son, William Bighead, who was a Cheyenne policeman in the 1920s.

Thunder Bull was present at the Little Bighorn. Despite the fact that his being there is historically accurate, he's the one historical character whose activities in battles I embellished. In essence he was a composite of many young Cheyenne braves in those battles. He later served in the United States Indian Scouts, later as an Indian soldier, then the Indian Police. He married Big Belly

Woman. He died in 1920. One of Thunder Bull's great grandsons is the founding Director of the National Museum of the American Indian that ironically looks out over the U.S. Capitol Building from the mall in Washington, DC. One of Thunder Bull's great great granddaughters is a Professor of Psychology at the University of Illinois, Chicago. One of his great great grandsons is a screenwriter in Hollywood.

Glossary

Tipi: A portable, conical Indian dwelling made from buffalo hides on a frame of poles. Also referred to as "lodges."

Counting coup: Earning prestige in battle through an act of bravery, often, but not always by using an implement (e.g., a bow, arrow, rifle, lance, hatchet) to touch an opponent during battle.

Sacred arrows ceremony: The Cheyenne ceremony used for blessing and renewing the sacred arrows handed down originally by the supernatural prophet Sweet Medicine to the people. Two were to be carried out to cause buffalos to become confused and vulnerable before a hunt. Two were similarly to be used to make enemies confused and vulnerable.

Two man arrows: the two sacred arrows to be carried out before war to confuse the enemies of the Cheyenne.

Grandfather: what Cheyenne people called old men.

Rancheria: a small group of native American dwellings, usually smaller than what would be called a village.

Wickiup: a native American hut, consisting of a rough frame of saplings or small tree trunks covered with sage, grass, or brushwood. Used as living quarters by many southwestern tribes (e.g., many Apache tribes) and northwestern tribes (e.g., Snakes).

Cousin: a close relative.

Readers Guide

True or false:

1. Pagosa Springs still exists to this day.
2. The number of Cheyenne Indians never reached 3,000 before 1877.
3. Fort Wicked actually existed.
4. If true, it is still standing on the east bank of the South Platte.
5. Libby Custer kept the Appomattox surrender table until her death.
6. The Owyhee River in Oregon was named by early 19th Century Hawaiian explorers.
7. Owyhee is an alternative spelling for Hawaii.
8. Antelope's cousin was the mother of George Armstrong Custer's only son.
9. On the order of twenty-five percent of cowboys were black.

Questions:

1. Antelope, Kate Bighead, talked in 1927 about her Washita and Little Bighorn memories. She was twenty-nine at the latter battle. She makes no mention of a husband in her life before 1876. Why do you think she doesn't mention a husband? What are the possible reasons that a twenty-nine year old Cheyenne woman would have never married? If there was a husband, what are the possible reasons she wouldn't mention him?

2. Picking up on General Crook and Lily's discussion, who *did* have the roughest life in the west? Ranchers? Soldiers? Officers? Cowboys? White women? Native Americans?

3. Given Custer's utter failure his first time on the Plains, why would the Army

in general, and Sheridan in particular, have had the confidence to send him back?

4. What could Black Kettle have done differently to better protect his people?

5. Should Custer have heeded Little Beaver's advice to wait for intelligence on the Washita village before attacking? Was Benteen right that Custer should have been court marshalled for his rashness? Or are results all that matter?

6. Is Lincoln's relationship with the Smoots realistic?

7. Is Lily's relationship with Antelope and Thunder Bull realistic (Note: Antelope and Thunder Bull's relationship *is* realistic, as it was quite common for young Cheyenne boys to develop a close relationship with an older, unrelated, girl)?

8. What choices did law abiding western citizens have (in this story, in Oregon and Laramie) other than to hire/become vigilantes?

9. What other choices, besides lynchings, did ranchers have in dealing with rustlers?

10. The Founding Fathers' solution to the conflict between the Indian tribes and the encroaching 18th Century white settlers in the east was to cede land to the Indians that the whites were required to respect and stay away from. The Army was charged with keeping the whites out of these Indian lands. The solution broke down because the Army refused to repel or evict trespassing white settlers. Some ninety years later, Grant and Custer played this out in the Black Hills. In retrospect, what other solutions might have worked besides the tragedies that occurred? What other results might have occurred other than the consequences we are living with still to this day?

11. Today's male Cheyenne (and Sioux) are descended from men who were trained from birth solely to hunt and raid. Today, these Cheyenne men are only four or five generations removed from the Little Bighorn. What would have been reasonable to expect about their assimilation? To be expected of their patriotism toward the United States of America? How were those expectations realized?

12. Which Wyoming museum do you think is currently holding Auggy the bear? The one in Chugwater? Cheyenne? Laramie?

For those specifically interested in Custer and the Little Bighorn Battle:

True or false:

1. It is totally inappropriate for writers (and readers) to second guess military commanders who must decide, react, and adjust to real time developments in the field.
2. Reno should have attacked the Little Bighorn village as he was ordered to do.
3. Benteen should have followed orders and ridden to reinforce Custer.

Questions:

1. Should Custer have followed orders and traveled all the way up the Rosebud, rather than deviating by pursuing the Indians to the west as he did?
2. Given his experience with the importance of surprise, should Custer have heeded his Crow scouts' (and Benteen's) advice to wait for intelligence on the Little Bighorn village before attacking?
3. In fact, Custer never did receive the benefit of any intelligence from General Crook's experience with Crazy Horse on the Rosebud the week before the Little Bighorn Battle. In *Chief of Thieves,* this information is delivered to Custer by the fictitious Major John Arnold. Some historians have speculated it would have made him more cautious. How would you expect Custer to have reacted to this information? Is it realistic to believe that he would have used it to reinforce or accelerate his sense of urgency and need to attack as portrayed in this book?
4. Custer has traditionally been criticized for splitting his forces at the Little

Bighorn (but not at the Washita). In his experience, you could only defeat Indians by attacking them when you found them, and capturing their women and children (the purpose of sending Benteen to the west) and by surprising them by attacking from more than one direction at once (Reno from the south, his own two companies from the hills in the east, and, importantly, Gibbon and Terry coming from the north). And, of course, Sheridan, himself, had split the entire force into three Columns: Crook from the south, Gibbon (and Custer) from the east, and Terry from the west; then they even split off Custer as a 4th unit. Does this traditional criticism of Custer have any validity?

5. Sitting Bull famously recognized that if Custer had forded the river he could well have won the day. Given that speculative comment from a fairly reputable source, why does the fault lie with Custer? If Reno had attacked as ordered and if Benteen had followed orders to reinforce Custer's troops above the village to join him in fording and attacking and capturing women and children from the northeast, how is the fault not with Reno and Benteen's refusal or failure to follow orders?

6. Is it a fair criticism to level at Custer that when Reno failed to attack and Benteen failed to arrive, he should have either attacked the village with what was left of his two hundred men or ridden back to Benteen and Reno? Put differently, at what point in the battle, then, should Custer have either "given up" or led a perilous and risky charge into the village without his full force?

7. If your answers to 5) and 6) above exonerate Custer for his tactics, then shouldn't the focus be on crediting Lame White Man's courage in attacking the greys, and then leading the charge up the hill, rather than on blaming Custer for the outcome of the battle?

www.ingramcontent.com/pod-product-compliance
Lightning Source LLC
Chambersburg PA
CBHW020418030726
47495CB00006B/1567